"TRUST ME. I TO HELP YO

Dylan stroked Clai

"I'm not one of your birds," she answered. "I have no broken parts."

"None that show," he said softly. "Except in your eyes. I see it when you sing, when you touch a lost or injured bird."

"My songs are just songs," she cautioned him. "It's all part of the act."

Dylan's strong arms enfolded her like gentle wings. He kissed her deeply, longingly, as his hand sought the softness of her breasts. Claire wrapped her arms around him. Her senses responded so totally that her body curved against him instinctively.

"Is this part of the act, too?" he asked.

But Claire didn't need to answer....

SONG OF THE SEABIRD

Christina Crockett

A SuperRomance from
HARLEQUIN
London · Toronto · New York · Sydney

First published in Great Britain in 1985 by
Harlequin, 15–16 Brook's Mews, London W1A 1DR

© Christina Crockett 1985

ISBN 0 373 70146 2

11–0985

Printed and bound in Great Britain by
Cox & Wyman Ltd, Reading

Dedicated to the workers of miracles at the Suncoast Seabird Sanctuary, Indian Shores, Florida— especially Ralph Heath, Jr. and Dianna King, who live the dream daily and share it so graciously.

CHAPTER ONE

CLAIRE PARNELL TUGGED THE SUN VISOR lower over her eyes to shield them from the bright glare of the sun reflecting off the white sand. Striding purposefully across the broad, unoccupied beach, she picked out a spot facing the shimmering water of the Gulf of Mexico to deposit her canvas bag and set up the collapsible chair. Finally settling into the low-slung macrame beach chair, Claire listened to the soft sweep of the waves as they swished over the half-hidden rocks at the end of the jetty. It was good to be home again.

Claire had spent her school years in the small community of Palm Shores, a tropical resort island off Florida's west coast. Returning to the island community after six years, she had been stunned to see the transformation it was undergoing. The village atmosphere had changed.

Many of the familiar clusters of one-story cottages were gone, replaced by towering monoliths of glass and concrete. The remaining quaint, weather-worn cottages, with their screened porches and sun decks, were rapidly being displaced by numerous exclusive multistory condominiums and time-sharing complexes. And there were the expensive beach houses of natural wood, poised on pilings above the white sand.

Cadillacs and Porsches parked where station wagons and bicycles once were. Palm Shores had a new affluence that occasionally contrasted with the few businesses and residences of old-timers who refused to yield to the pressure of eager resort developers.

But even with the obvious commercialization, Palm Shores still enchanted Claire. Her return to the island months ago had been a solemn reunion. "I guess we've both grown up," she had admitted pensively as she strolled along the boardwalk at Frenchman's Pass, window-shopping as the fishing boats unloaded their daily catch. Yet, just a few hundred yards from the shops of Frenchman's Pass, Claire had found her favorite beach relatively unchanged and essentially overlooked, since a towering condo blocked it from view of the casual passerby. It was this sandy crescent of beach by the jetty that welcomed her home.

Like her two brothers who had benefited from the multiple musical talents of their parents, Claire Parnell had become a professional musician, joining a band and going on the road. Like her brothers, she had eventually been disillusioned and had come home again. For her brothers the reason was financial. Life as a road musician was tough and the money was erratic. Pete and Robby Parnell had come home to a place where they could settle down. The lounges and clubs on the beaches and in the city of St. Petersburg provided steady work, the faces were friendly and life became reassuringly sane once more.

Claire had been the youngest and the last Parnell to follow the Pied Piper. At eighteen she had fallen in love with a dark-eyed guitarist whose voice was as rough as sandpaper and whose songs touched her heart with unexpected passion. Poetic, temperamental and ambitious, Wes Raines had been irresistible. When Wes asked Claire to join his group as keyboard player and backup vocalist, he made one concession that none of the other band members enjoyed. He dropped the rule that wives or girlfriends did not work or travel with the group, and then he asked Claire to marry him. At the time the match seemed to be perfect. It wasn't.

Now, as Claire slowly spread tanning lotion over her long legs and smiled at the arrogant sea gull standing just beyond her shadow, she noticed she no longer had the beach and the jetty to herself. Stepping from one rock to another, a broad-shouldered fisherman with a straw hat made his way past her toward the farthest end of the rocky projection.

On one flat-surfaced slab of cement, which jutted horizontally over the water, the man placed his fishing rod and tackle box. He dropped his hat casually beside them, then peeled off his T-shirt. Still clasping the shirt in his hand, he stood with his back to her, staring out over the Gulf of Mexico as if he were looking for something particular. Exchanging his shirt for the straw hat, he shielded his eyes as he stared into the sky, standing like a sentinel on the outcrop of irregular rocks rimming the north side of Frenchman's Pass.

Nice body.

The thought formed in Claire's mind with surprising frankness as she assessed her jetty companion. The wide, muscular shoulders of the silent sentinel were already tanned a deep golden bronze, eloquently testi-

fying to countless hours spent outdoors. Even his
thick mat of tousled sandy-brown hair was streaked
with light gold, as if the sun had capriciously highlighted certain errant strands. Clad only in faded
khaki shorts, the Golden One strode back down the
jetty toward the shore, while Claire watched him from
beneath her lowered visor.

Something about the grace and ease with which he
moved intrigued her, and she had to fight the urge to
turn around so that she could continue to watch him as
he stepped out of view. He would be back. His fishing
gear and shirt were still on the flat jetty rock. But as
she waited, Claire found herself growing impatient to
see his lean silhouette against the brilliant sun. There
was a natural quality about him, a sense of belonging
in this setting of sea and sand, that appealed to her.
Man stripped to the bare essentials of survival. Claire
smiled at the thought.

Observing him had reminded her how much she belonged to this place. How special it had always been,
particularly back in the golden years of her childhood,
when she had sunned and surfed along the extent of
these beaches. They had been years of joy and music
and laughter, when the natural beauty and abundance
of the Gulf Coast had filled her with rapture. Then she
had not realized how essential these things had been to
her. While she was traveling with the band, the
memories of Palm Shores had always beckoned. Now
she had returned to heal, to let Palm Shores revive her.
To start again.

"How about a cold beer?"

The words came from slightly behind her as a tawny

hand thrust a dripping can of chilled Budweiser into view. "I went to get one for myself. Then I saw you sitting here baking in the sun. Since we're sharing the jetty and the beach, I thought it would be neighborly to share a beer, as well."

Being neighborly was an attitude Claire had assumed was also missing from this more sophisticated Palm Shores community. The man in the straw hat moved around to face her.

"It's a little early for me." Claire tilted her visor up so she could see the face that accompanied the extended hand. The wide, slightly lopsided grin that greeted her gave a slightly boyish quality to an otherwise rugged, quite handsome face. The intense blue-green eyes that regarded her with friendly amusement disarmed her. Claire had been prepared to respond with a firm but polite rebuff. She had not come to the beach to be picked up by a stranger offering a Budweiser. But this was not the face of a stranger. It was the face of a friend whom she simply had not met before.

"I do appreciate the thoughtfulness," she added hastily, softening her refusal. "Actually, I'm not much of a drinker." It was a quirk in her metabolism. Even a glass of wine made her very sleepy, and a beer in the hot sun would make her drowsy all day.

"Then how about a soft drink?" The tanned body shifted to a crouch as the man landed the small ice chest in the sand next to her. He opened the lid, digging through the ice. "Ginger ale?"

"That sounds more like it." Claire accepted the green-and-white can. The sun was beating down, glistening off the scented suntan lotion she'd spread over her body. Already she could feel the rays penetrating, radiating through her limbs. "I was so disorganized today I forgot to pack cold drinks."

"I see that you managed to bring a good-sized shovel." Her companion stretched out in the sand next to her. "Obviously you came prepared to do something. Are you hunting for buried treasure?" He grinned as he picked up the square-nosed metal sand shovel protruding from her beach bag. Red and slightly rusty, with a well-worn wooden handle, the shovel was a priceless relic from her childhood. That shovel and Claire Parnell had seen a lot of beaches together.

"I like to build sand castles," Claire said shyly, realizing the idea might sound a bit foolish coming from a twenty-four-year-old woman. "It's a throwback to my youth." She joked in an attempt to hide her self-consciousness. But the bronzed man, who appeared to be in his thirties, apparently didn't think she was childish at all. He was already sitting up, holding his cold beer in one hand and the shovel in the other while he dug, stacking one shovelful of sand on top of the next. The slight smile on his face indicated an acceptance that put Claire at ease. When the clear sea-blue eyes met hers, she saw that he was as delighted as she was.

"People should never stop building sand castles," he said softly. "Folks who come to the beach with loud radios and lounge chairs never sit on the sand or hear the waves. And they think they are communing with nature. This is nature," he added as he let the sand trickle off the shovel. "Castlebuilders are a rare breed these days," he said with genuine regret. "We have so many destroyers and so few creators." He looked at her steadily for a moment, absorbing every detail of her appearance, from her ash-blond hair to her well-oiled legs. His look was both curious and gentle.

Abruptly he deposited his beer can in the sand and offered her his hand. "Dylan. Dylan Jamison," he said, introducing himself. "Beach aficionado and sun devotee—much like you," he teased.

"I'm Claire. Claire Parnell. Castlebuilder." The name he had given her—castlebuilder—pleased her.

"Do you live near here?" Dylan-with-the-sea-blue-eyes asked while he added another scoop of sand to the pile he had started. Claire knew he wasn't pressing for details. His straightforward manner was only friendly interest.

"Right now I'm living in St. Pete," Claire replied. "I work downtown by the bay, but the beach still feels like home. Whenever I can afford it, I'll be looking for a place out here."

"You used to live here in Palm Shores?" Now she had his undivided attention. The gold-streaked hair of her companion shone in the sun as he watched her.

"That was years ago. My folks owned a motel a few miles from here," Claire explained. "The Palm Shores I grew up in was a lot more primitive than this. No condos. But I still love it here," Claire added. Her love had something to do with the scent of salt air and the cry of the soaring birds. When she had returned there had been a sense of reconnecting she could not put into words. It was like looking into the sea-blue eyes of Dylan Jamison and knowing that he understood her. Something about all these things just felt natural and free.

"So where have you been while the condos have been gobbling up our little paradise?" There was little humor in his eyes, indicating he felt as negative about the "development" of beach islands as she did.

"I'm a musician," Claire replied easily, surprised that she found speaking to this man so effortless. Since her divorce from Wes Raines, she hadn't told anyone much about herself or what she had been through. She maintained a noncommittal cheerfulness with her brothers and their friends, who still treated her pretty much as the kid sister she'd always been. Other than these "safe" relationships, Claire discreetly avoided most men. Her marriage to Wes had meant everything to her—and regardless of how she tried to make it succeed, it had still failed. In the aftermath, Claire preferred to maintain her distance and keep her private life to herself.

"I was married to a singer and I traveled with his band for years," she said, supplying a superficial summary.

Dylan looked up at her briefly. "Was he someone famous?"

"Wes caused a ripple on the charts about four years ago with a song called 'Hurtin' Inside.' You may have heard it. The group's name was Rainstorm. We slipped right back into anonymity after our brief brush with fame."

"Sorry, I don't remember the song," Dylan apologized, then went back to making zigzag lines in the sand with Claire's shovel. "I imagine it was a difficult readjustment—anonymity, I mean."

"We used to laugh and say it was a character-building experience," Claire recalled. "We settled in New York and did a lot of studio work while we waited to be rediscovered. Obviously we weren't," she added with a wry smile. "Things sort of fell apart. When it became too tense, I left and came back here. Now I'm working on a paddle-wheeler that cruises the bay. I'm the on-board dinner music and dance band," she said lightly.

"That's quite a change of pace from New York," Dylan observed as he laid aside the shovel and looked up. The way his eyes remained riveted on hers told her he knew there had to be much more behind the move. If she wanted to add more, he would listen.

"I needed the change," she said simply as she considered avoiding the issue. The perfunctory statement brought a glimmer of impatience to Dylan's eyes. He obviously didn't like glib answers.

"It wasn't quite that simple," she admitted to him—and to herself, as well. "We went through a few lean years while we tried to adjust. Starting at the bottom again bothered Wes more than the rest of us, and he pushed us all harder. Gradually all the relationships—personal and professional ones—suffered. When I filed for divorce and left New York, it was more than a career move. I had to get away." She felt strangely lighter, now that she had added the other details. If she could explain some of it to a stranger, eventually she could talk about all of it with her brothers. "I came back here to regroup." She lowered her eyes momentarily as the tension in her chest increased. The sadness of losing all the dreams and all the good feelings threatened to overwhelm her.

That last year with Wes had destroyed so much of what had been beautiful. The memory seemed like something out of a nightmare, a nightmare that still had the power to torment her, even here. It could wake her from a sound sleep, shivering and struggling to cry out in the night. As Wes's career floundered, he'd assuaged his pride with drugs and liquor and, Claire suspected, other women. When she managed to get work on her own to help with the expenses, Wes became even more unpredictable. The trouble began with words, mean insinuations that she was only playing games, showing off with other performers— mediocre ones at that. He'd say she wasn't good at all, that she had to hang on to someone else. She was nothing by herself. He would explode in anger, kicking a table or throwing a dish. Eventually he turned on her.

The first time it was a loud, heart-stopping slap. Claire was so shaken she couldn't even talk. She'd stared wide-eyed in disbelief, her cheek stinging as tears welled up in her eyes. Wes held her and wept and begged her to forgive him. He swore he would never hurt her again. He said he was worried about money and was having a rough time working up some new music. And because she loved him, Claire forgave him.

But there had been a next time. Then Wes tried to shift the blame onto her for making him so angry that he lost control. She'd come back from work to an empty apartment. When he finally came home later, she asked him where he had been, so he hit her. He'd been drinking. He claimed she should know better than to interrogate him when he'd been drinking. Then he stumbled off to bed. The next time he couldn't even remember hitting her. That time he blamed bad drugs.

Claire tried to accept the excuses, hoping each outburst would be the last, just as Wes kept promising. In times between, she worked harder, collaborating on the songwriting and rehearsing with Wes, struggling to keep his creative urges stronger than his self-destructive ones. Love and hope and trust were difficult to surrender. Then in one dreadful night they were all destroyed. Wes had met her at a club where Claire was substituting for the regular keyboard player. He had a few drinks while she finished up for the night. In the parking lot, he ignored her protests and sent her on to the car while he stopped to make a quick transaction. Drugs again. They drove home in silence. Then Claire went straight to bed, leaving Wes with his purchase in the living room.

An hour later he burst in, his eyes glazed and his breath reeking from liquor. "You're nothing without me," he screamed. "You're getting sloppy with your playing. You mumble when you sing. I'm embarrassed to watch you."

Claire had tried to handle the situation calmly, urging him to quiet down and come to bed. All he needed was to sleep. Instead Wes dragged her onto the floor, beating her with his fists. Bruised and terrified, Claire broke away and raced into the night to the apartment of a neighbor. That was the last time she ever saw Wes

Raines. The next day, when he was away, she packed her bags and hired a lawyer.

But all it took was the strain of a familiar song or the mention of his name to bring back all the memories. Even here at Frenchman's Pass she couldn't escape the reminders. So for now, while she remembered, she would avoid meeting the perceptive gaze of Dylan Jamison. The painful associations were something she would eventually work through on her own.

"If it's regrouping you need to do, you couldn't have picked a nicer spot to come to. There's just enough civilization around to keep you in touch with reality, but it is still beautiful and peaceful here." He spoke quietly as he glanced across the beach toward the water. His steady voice filled the space of time Claire needed. "It's a nice in-between place... for building castles." His last comment elicited a small smile from her.

"If you are still interested in working on that sand castle you mentioned, I could volunteer a couple of hands," Dylan said hopefully. He offered the old red shovel to her in a gesture of conciliation. "You scoop and I'll pat it into a tower." With a slow deep breath, Claire forced her attention to the pastime she loved and became a castlebuilder again.

"I hate to be picky," Claire replied. "But your building technique is all wrong." She eased out of her low-slung chair and stood there sipping the cool canned drink. The simple conelike heap of sand that Dylan was patting into a mound was not at all what she envisioned. "You're working from the bottom up. I like to work from the top down."

"That sounds like a major engineering miracle," he said, laughing. "Sand—suspended in air?"

"It isn't quite that mystical. First I start with a huge pile of sand. Then, beginning at the top, I carve out the shapes I want." She took another long sip of her soft drink, then tucked the can carefully under her chair, where it would be out of the sun. "But before I start, I pick just the right place." She took the shovel. Flourishing it like an Olympic torch, she summoned Dylan to follow her. "The sand here is too powdery," she announced as she started off toward the shoreline, where the fine white sand was slightly damp beneath the surface. This meant it was below the tide line; water would sweep over the area when the next tide came in. "Now this is where one builds a sand castle." Claire circled a flat spot of prime territory.

"You're the engineer...."

"Right." Claire nodded approvingly, then handed him the short-handled shovel once more. "You can be the construction crew."

Dylan laughed. Then with a steady thrust-and-lift rhythm, he started to scoop up the damp sand.

"You have to keep moving out so you get only the fine top sand," Claire directed. "I'll be the bucket patrol and keep wetting it down." She went to get a pail.

Dylan worked effortlessly, with the precision and stamina of a man accustomed to physical labor. Between soaking and stomping the pile, Claire watched the definition of Dylan's arm muscles as the digging emphasized the contours. The slimness of his build belied the power in those arms. And he smiled as he worked, as if the contact with the sand pleased his senses. Within minutes the pile had grown into an impressive mound that would have taken Claire an hour to shovel alone.

"Try to avoid getting too many shells in with the sand," she cautioned him as she moved around the pile, packing it with her feet. "When we get to the sculpting part, shells pull out and leave holes in walls, or they turn windows into gaping openings where you didn't want them."

"No shells," Dylan acknowledged as he picked a few out of the load he was about to throw onto the pile. "Damp sand, no shells." He whistled. "You take this castle building seriously."

"Anything worth doing is worth doing well," Claire said sincerely.

"My mother used to tell me the same thing," Dylan replied with a low chuckle. "Generally it was when I was doing the working and she was supervising." He looked up at Claire with that arresting, lopsided grin. "However," he said, pausing dramatically, "my mother did not have a great set of legs like yours." His appreciative scrutiny did not end with Claire's long legs. His gaze continued upward, over her striped bikini and the expanses of well-oiled uncovered skin. She was tall and lithe, broad shouldered and narrow hipped, a body that still had the slimness of a teenager but moved with the grace and strength of a woman. And her oval face, delicate and ethereal, possessed a certain serenity—until he looked deep into her eyes, sooty gray and suspicious.

The sudden intimacy had apparently violated certain unspoken boundaries, and Claire's shoulders tensed.

"Of course, my mother never looked at me the way you're doing. You have the most cautious pair of eyes I've seen in quite a while." He contemplated her thoughtfully, trying to fathom the pleasant-but-remote expression behind which she had retreated. "I know—I dig, you stomp," he reminded himself before she had to say a word.

"While you dig, I think I'll finish my soft drink," Claire said, backing off toward her beach chair, where her ginger ale still sat cold and dripping in the sand. "I'll round up a few tools." It wasn't the sun that sent the slow coursing ripple of warmth through her long limbs as she strode off, aware that Dylan was still watching her.

During his frank survey, Claire felt a sensual awakening that she had not experienced in a long time. His eyes and his words triggered her carefully suppressed need to be admired. He made her feel beautiful, desirable—and uneasy. Wes still had a hold on her. Even though the divorce was official, she had not lost the feeling that made a sexual response to anyone else seem like an act of betrayal. But with Dylan, there had been no opportunity to second-guess herself. Those sensual feelings were simply there when he had looked up at her and smiled.

Standing by the beach chair, sipping the remainder of her drink, Claire watched, eyes shaded by her visor, while Dylan transformed the mound of sand into a thigh-high mountain of prime building material. Safely removed from his presence, Claire could examine the responses he prompted in her. Up close, it was impossible to be objective.

Dylan stood and circled his handiwork, then walked to the edge of the gulf, scooping the water up to cool his face and wash over his shoulders. Highlighted by the sunshine, his wet body looked sculpted, like an ancient sea god cast out of burnished bronze. Lean and hard and magnificent. The attraction was very clear and very physical. But it was the magnetic force of his eyes that had slipped through the barriers and connected with parts of her that were deeply hidden. With the pleasure she felt, there was also a feeling of helplessness, an inability to draw back from him that was disturbingly familiar.

It had been that way with Wes. He had come into her life suddenly—standing in a spotlight, singing his gritty, rhythmical love songs. Claire thought she was looking into the soul of a kindred spirit. Part minstrel, part poet, he had captured her heart.

The eyes of this castlebuilder were not dark like Wes's were. They were an enticing bluish green that spoke of serenity and sparkled with amusement. But their impact was so immediate and familiar that Claire could feel the tremor begin, the crumbling of the defensive walls that could let this man into her life. *Not again, not yet*. . . . Claire tried to resist so strong an attraction. She was no naive teenager now. She had endured the loss of her one perfect love, and she didn't intend to get swept away again. She had no time to be distracted by a romantic illusion. To her, reality was getting through one day at a time.

"Hey...castlebuilder." Dylan turned and called her, summoning her back to the construction site. "Let's see you put some of your expertise to work. Where are those tools you're supposed to be bringing? Let's get on with this."

Building a castle. That was all they would do. They would share this one day, nothing more. "These are the tools of the trade," she announced as she approached Dylan with her assortment of items held out for inspection—a metal spatula, some Popsicle sticks, a ruler, a couple of small firm-bristled artist brushes and a plastic melon-ball scoop.

"You're kidding." He shook his head in disbelief.

"You'll see how handy they are." She defended her collection against his dubious response. She lay them out in a neat row, then circled the mountain of hard-pressed sand that stood waist high and was wider than her arms could stretch.

"Where do we start?" Dylan crouched beside the pile, his muscular body still glistening from the Gulf.

Claire knelt on the opposite side, facing him. "What we do is imagine that a marvelous castle already exists under all this sand. Moorish or Gothic or perhaps something the Mayan Indians might have constructed. Just let your imagination run wild." She sat down in the sand and stared intently at the un-shaped structure.

Dylan looked across at her, shaking his head in amusement. "I think you'd better do the castle find-ing," he said, giving up. "I still see a mound of sand, and I remember every shovelful. You begin, and I'll take a swim. When I get back, you can tell me what you have in mind.'' With long, deliberate strides, he walked off into the low waves, then plunged beneath the surface. Claire glanced after him, watching as he surfaced and began to swim out into deeper water with powerful strokes of his arms. She forced her attention back onto the sand.

Medieval. Rapidly she began cutting with the metal spatula, outlining peaks of towers and descending tiers of buildings high atop the mound. Each stroke of the spatula scraped away the excess, until a high central keep, a cathedral spire and several lesser towers emerged and the walls of the outer fortifications took shape.

With little half circles from the melon-ball scoop, Claire created a scalloped parapet around the top of the squared castle keep. The parapet provided a low protective barrier behind which imaginary knights and archers could stand to defend their fortress. With the pointed end of the paintbrush, she cut arched window openings in the sides of the tower through which other defenders could survey their foes and release a barrage of stones or arrows.

The evolution of the miniature citadel became increasingly engrossing, artistically and technically. Like a beautiful dawn or a shared smile, the castle was transitory—a solitary gift she could craft and give to nature. It didn't have to be lasting to be priceless.

When Claire began cutting away the next tier of the multileveled castle, a tall shadow fell across the mound of sand. ''I've never seen anything like this,'' Dylan said as he stood dripping wet by her side. He walked around the structure, admiring the emerging design. "Amazing. You have an entire city inside those walls."

"I'm not sure where the ideas come from," Claire replied. She leveled off a terrace that she would eventually fill with tiny sprigs of plants. The ideas formed spontaneously as she touched and tested the sand. "I used to read a lot of fairy tales and legends about knights and sorcerers and quests. Every fairy tale had a castle, so I got sidetracked learning more about them." She spoke with a trace of sadness in her gray eyes. Her mother had shared her love of fantasy and scoured old bookstores, bringing home unusual stories with beautiful illustrations. Since her mother's death, castle building had become inextricably linked with memories and love.

"I've given up the fairy tales," Claire added. "I held out as long as I could, but I finally grew up." The sadness in her eyes deepened. "I found out that handsome men are not always princely, and not all witches have visible warts to warn you they are evil. Then there are the very real potions that can be bought on the streets...the spells they cast are deadly." Again the old images began to sneak out of the dark corners of her mind. "But a castle..." Claire said, forcing herself to suppress them, "has no menace. It is simply what one decides to make it."

"Your castle is marvelous," Dylan assured her. "Regardless of what inspired its creation." He bent down and peered into one tiny carved window. "Now why would a grown man expect to see a tiny face looking out at him from in there?" he said, grinning sheepishly. "And why does it seem as if there should be a few guards pacing back and forth along those walls?"

Claire wished he hadn't said that. She wished he hadn't smiled that way and fallen into the spirit of gentle fantasy with such unpretentious ease. It was just too perfect and he made her heart ache. "Maybe it's the heat . . ." she answered, trying to joke.

Dylan's smile faltered. "I'm a strong believer in possibilities," he replied. "If I can find a castlebuilder who looks like a princess, then her castle must be full of hundreds of little people—whether we see them or not."

"I am not a princess," Claire said quietly. "And I won't be much of a castlebuilder if I don't get going." Once again the conversation had become dangerously intimate, and Claire turned to safer ground. "The tide is not going to wait. . . ." She ignored the slight waver in her voice.

"Just tell me what to work on," Dylan responded diplomatically. He moved to the far side of the mound, giving her some physical as well as emotional distance.

"I'd like to have a walled orchard on this side." Claire sketched light lines in the sand, outlining the perimeter of the structure.

"How about a moat?" he suggested, caught up in the fantasy. "And maybe a couple of guard stations to screen anyone who approaches and check if he knows the password?" Claire inclined her head slightly in agreement as his vision merged with hers and a more elaborate landscape took form. In rapt silence, the twosome worked, each occasionally glancing over at the other, then returning to their task to add unique variations and details to the master plan.

When Claire strolled off toward the stretch of scruffy pines that shaded the nearby park and restroom area, her departure drew only a brief glance from the sun-bronzed builder. She returned with hands full of twigs and tiny foliage and had pulled on a light T-shirt to protect herself from the sun—and from the eyes of Dylan Jamison.

Using the pointed end of the paintbrush, Claire poked rows of little holes in the terrace she'd completed, then sprigged the miniature hedge. Dylan studied her landscaping technique before going in search of some items for his part of the grounds. He returned with a bottle cap and several strips of dried palm leaves, from which he fashioned a miniature wishing well. He even filled the bottle cap with water to make the effect more realistic.

Occasionally their solitude was interrupted by curious passersby strolling along the beach. The jetty was now spottily occupied by fishermen staking out their territory to await the incoming tide and the fish that would accompany it. From time to time, one of them would wander over, watch, then leave the builders to their craft.

After hours of carving and brushing and sculpting, the strain was beginning to tell. "My arms ache," Claire confessed.

"Let's take a break," Dylan suggested. "I'll run across the road and pick up a couple of sandwiches. Even slave laborers had time out to eat," he noted.

Claire collapsed on the sand. "An ice-cold soda would be a lifesaver at this point."

"Then you guard the castle," Dylan told her. "I'll be back in a few minutes," he said, gazing down at her a little too intensely.

"Food...drink," Claire clowned, trying to divert him with her theatrical pleading. "We must complete the moat and the drawbridge before the army of the evil Count Zimbrowski attacks," she insisted.

"Count what's-his-name is the least of your worries," Dylan teased as he started off.

Claire watched his broad shoulders sway slightly as he strode away. He obviously knew she had deliberately evaded another attempt of his to invite a personal response. Yet he accepted each evasion with good humor and a gentle deference. He seemed to tune into her defensiveness and back off just when she was deciding to retreat.

"We're only building a sand castle," Claire muttered to herself as she tried to put the relationship into proper perspective. They were two strangers who had met for an afternoon and cooperated on a childlike project. Then her smoky-gray eyes shifted to the elegant castle that reflected their combined talents. This was no childish effort. Nor could the immediate and undeniable chemistry between the castlebuilders be dismissed as an afternoon comradery. Something miraculous was happening, and it didn't involve merely this structure of sand. Claire had met a man whose presence tantalized and enthralled her. She had begun to feel like a woman again.

But let's keep this simple, Claire cautioned herself

as she reflected over how little either of them actually knew about the other. They had both talked intermittently about safe, happy subjects as they worked. But now she realized she had been the one to give specifics. Divorce. Relocating. Her job. She'd even mentioned her brothers Pete and Robby and how she enjoyed hearing their band play at the Pier. But Dylan worked in relative silence, listening, studying her, but revealing very little about himself.

When he comes back, more working and less talking, she vowed silently. She was determined that this afternoon was going to develop into nothing more than a pleasant memory. Nothing too complicated. Nothing too personal. Apparently that suited him, too. They'd stick to castle building.

When Dylan returned, the large white paper sack under his arm indicated his shopping trip had been successful. "Grouper sandwiches. . . with tartar sauce and pickles."

Claire nodded as Dylan unwrapped the filet-on-a-bun for her. "Excellent. I love them!"

"And french fries. . . and cold drinks from my cooler, of course." Dylan made neat holes in the sand with the two cans, then sat down cross-legged, facing her. "Now how's this for a civilized luncheon?"

Claire moaned in reply. She had just taken her first bite of the steaming fish sandwich. "Delicious," she announced when she had finally dispatched the mouthful. "A feast fit for kings," she concluded with a grin.

"Not kings." Dylan raised his cold soda to salute his co-worker. "For castlebuilders," he corrected, and toasted her.

Claire hastily picked up her soda to join in the toast. "To castlebuilders." They grinned at each other as if they were children sharing a marvelous adventure.

Later they sprawled out in the sand side by side, surveying the unfinished castle and the grounds that surrounded it. Already the sun had shifted from overhead to a lower position out over the Gulf, sending a new pattern of light and shade across the medieval fortress.

"We need stairways," Claire announced seriously. "The tide will be in in a couple of hours."

"Let's get to it." Dylan scooped up the paper bag containing the napkins and other remnants from their luncheon. He loped across the sandy beach to a trash can and deposited the bag, pausing to look inside the rusty can and retrieve something that he tucked into the pocket of his khaki shorts.

"What did you find?"

The smug smile on Dylan's face indicated that whatever he'd discovered was a secret. "Later...." He refused to divulge his find. "When we have it all finished," he promised.

"Intrigue!" Claire joked as she handed him a Popsicle stick. When he stared at the flat piece of wood, Claire reminded him what was next. "Stairs. Press little ledges to make great stairs. And we need some secret passageways—and a stable."

Dylan smiled. "I'll get right on it."

As Claire stooped over the stairway and began to cut in one tiny step slightly lower than the previous one, she felt an inexplicable sense of possessiveness.

This was their creation. She and Dylan had worked well together. If he ever built a castle again, surely he would have to remember her. She would never build one without thinking of him.

"Done." Dylan brushed the sand from a final slender alcove, then stood to inspect the results. "How are you doing?" He carefully walked over to her side, avoiding the scattered tools and low walls.

"I think I've included everything except air conditioning and indoor plumbing." Claire rocked back on her heels and sprigged one final plant atop the stairway wall. It trailed like a tendril of ivy, giving the immediate effect that both the plant and the stairway had been there for generations.

"It still needs a little something." Dylan fumbled in his pocket for the trash-can discovery he had made earlier. "Apparently someone has been dining out at a more expensive place than we have." He held out two tiny plastic banners attached to toothpicks. On one side of the tiny flag was the imprint of a lion's head. On the other side were the words "medium rare."

"Perfect." Claire took one flag and poked it into the pointed roof of the central tower. Dylan placed his with equal caution directly above the main gate. Without speaking, the two workers carefully lifted up all the tools and unused fragments of twigs and plants, smoothing a wide expanse around the moat. Surrounded by a barren landscape that bore no footprint or shell to distract from its beauty, the castle they created acquired a new grandeur.

"Congratulations, partner." Dylan caught

Claire's shoulders and hugged her against his side as they stood admiring the finished product. Then his hand began massaging her upper arm, as if he sensed the dull, weary aching that she felt. For an instant she stiffened, unable to suppress the instinct to recoil from so intimate a gesture. Thoughts of Wes Raines were still tormenting her, making her suspicious of any move that could be construed as a physical overture.

Dylan dropped his arm immediately, then looked down at her curiously. "Are your muscles that tender?"

"I think I got a little too much sun." Her explanation didn't sound as convincing as she had hoped. Claire turned to look at Dylan, catching a glimpse of disappointment in his eyes before he brusquely shifted his gaze out over the Gulf.

"The tide is coming in." She stood staring out at the glimmering water as he was doing.

"Just like always." The low rumble of his voice had a pensive quality that made her wonder what he was thinking. "I'm sorry if touching you spoiled anything." He kept his eyes seaward as he spoke. "I didn't stop to think...." He scanned the horizon more intently, following the flight of a long-legged egret as it moved inland, returning home as evening approached. "This has been a beautiful day," he said, saying aloud what Claire had thought to herself repeatedly. "I didn't realize how much I needed to slow down and just relax. I certainly don't want to ruin anything."

The slight change in the wind, a recognizable coolness that came with sunset along the Gulf Coast, swept in from the water. The day Claire and Dylan had shared was coming to a quiet close. Claire turned away.

"Are you leaving already?"

The disappointment in Dylan's voice stopped Claire in her tracks. It would get chillier as the sun dipped beneath the horizon and the sky put on its light show of deep rose and purple and gray.

"I'm just going to get my warm-up jacket," she assured him. "Enjoy the sunset. I'll be right back."

Claire strode off toward her car and grabbed the cotton zip-front jacket, tugging it over her bare arms. Dylan waited on the beach. He was standing, arms crossed, watching her, with an inscrutable expression on his face. Behind him, spreading streaks of burnt orange low in the sky meant the sun was rapidly slipping lower. Her magical, beautiful day was fading away.

Their magnificent castle now sat silhouetted in gold, its arches and windows cloaked in deep shadows and its parapets and stairways eerily vacant.

Dylan spread out a blanket for them to sit on. He even yanked a sweat shirt over his bare torso. The wind had picked up considerably, and the low, choppy waves whispered of the cool night to come. Sometimes laughing, sometimes pensive, the twosome watched the waves licking closer and closer to their citadel-by-the-sea.

When the first wall began to crumble and melt slowly away with the ruffling waves, Claire felt a sadness gradually settling in her chest. This was goodbye, she knew. This time she didn't want to stay until the castle was all swept away. Like the afternoon she had shared with this quiet, golden man, she didn't want to see the beauty end. She wanted to leave while it was still intact.

"I've got to go now." Claire tugged her eyes away from the castle after one last look. For a moment her gaze locked with Dylan's, and she knew how much she had opened up to him. She had somehow touched souls with this stranger, and both of them knew it. But still they would part. The unspoken ground rules were set: no involvement beyond this day.

Without another word, Claire picked up her beach bag and the macrame chair and trudged off toward her orange Toyota. She couldn't hear the footsteps following her, for the waves now swept in with a steady, swooshing sound and her own heart thundered in her ears. Only after she pulled open her car trunk and threw in her beach gear did she feel the presence of someone else.

Dylan didn't speak. His sea-blue eyes stared into hers, searching for something that neither of them could explain. Then they moved together in one fluid motion. The cool breeze off the water was insignificant compared to the tender heat of their embrace. Like a desperate swimmer clinging to a rescuer, each of them held on to the other, lost in the overwhelming need to hold and touch and kiss. A fiery tremor shot through her when Dylan's deepening kiss invited her to respond. And she did. Eagerly, naturally. This was no longer farewell. Suddenly they were staring at each other, reeling from the force of the sexual bonfire they had ignited.

"Don't leave. Stay with me." Dylan's rasping voice was as breathless as Claire felt.

"Dylan...." She said his name so softly it was barely audible. "I can't...I'm not ready for anything like this." She still held him in her arms and his strong embrace had relaxed only slightly. Their bodies molded together so perfectly that even now they seemed like one. And she trembled.

Dylan looked at her solemnly, as if he were considering protesting. Then a peculiar light glimmered in his eyes. He pulled her closer, only this time the passion was controlled. Claire pressed her cheek against his chest while he stroked her wind-blown hair and simply held her. Gradually the racing of her heart subsided and both of them breathed more evenly. With blinding intensity, they had witnessed their impact on each other. But the time was not right.

"Good night, my castlebuilder." Dylan placed a final, tender kiss softly on her lips. His mouth lingered on hers, savoring the softness without making any demands. Then he watched as she walked away from him, to slip behind the wheel of her car and drive off.

Long after Claire had climbed the stairs to her apartment and showered the sand and suntan lotion from her skin, she lay awake, listening to the muffled sounds of rock music rising from below. Her brothers Pete and Robby had converted the two-car garage beneath her into a well-insulated studio, and tonight their band, Sound Off, was rehearsing. Tomorrow they'd be playing at the Pier and Claire would be back on the paddle-wheeler. The day of castle building would be a pleasant memory and a promise that her life was beginning again. But as the coolsheet slid softly over her naked body, her thoughts returned to the sea-blue eyes and golden body that had pressed against her own.

She had taught herself to be cautious. So cautious.

If I had stayed with him... Claire thought. *If I'd said yes.*

She had no doubt they would now be in a different bed wrapped in each other's arms. They had responded to each other so effortlessly; their bodies fitted together so beautifully. Everything they touched that day had been perfect.

Perfect. That's how it would stay.

Even as she lay there in the night, staring at the patterns that the streetlamps made on her ceiling, Claire knew the golden man had made a genuine contribution to making her whole again. He had awakened a sensual response that had been anesthetized by the violence of a man she had once loved. Dylan with the sea-blue eyes had made her feel again.

It was a beginning.

CHAPTER TWO

"How about singing a couple of songs with us in the next set?" Pete Parnell looked over the sparsely occupied lounge, then brought his gaze back to the face of his apprehensive sister. "Really, Claire." He tilted his head toward the raised platform, where his band was already set up. "The crowd is light tonight. Robby has a cold that's settled in his throat. We could use a little help." He grinned at her hopefully.

"I haven't rehearsed with you guys," Claire protested. "I can't just jump up there and sing any old thing—or any new thing, for that matter." She dismissed his suggestion. "I play smoothies and oldies on the cruise boat," she reminded him as her cautious gray eyes shifted to the lead singer's microphone suspended just above center stage.

"You can't keep hiding all that rock and roll inside," Pete teased. "You know how good it feels to get out from behind your keyboard and strut out a real thumper. You've heard us rehearsing all week," he persisted. She had been in the studio off and on, watching and listening, and the fact that she had not been able to stay away revealed more than Claire realized. "You could do half a dozen songs without breaking into a sweat," Pete insisted.

Claire had to smile when she looked into his eager brown eyes and caught their cunning sparkle. Since she had come back home, neither Pete nor his wife, Amy, had pried too deeply into the problems Claire had buried with the divorce. They knew "irreconcilable differences" had included a great deal of bitterness and had left Claire troubled, but she had gone right out and got a job playing music again. As long as she performed—even though she wasn't singing— they assumed she would be all right.

Pete knew that the dinner-cruise-boat music placed few demands on Claire's talents. She handled the keyboard effortlessly, playing standards and a few upbeat contemporary songs. But the bayside scenery, the food and an occasional dolphin were the main attractions. She was holding back, and Pete knew it.

"Are you sure Robby has a sore throat?" Claire said narrowing her eyes at him. "Or are you guys just setting me up?" She suspected that her brothers had been waiting for a night to spring this on her. For the past three days, Claire had gone about her usual routine, practicing keyboard in the afternoon, then playing on the *Bay-Belle* for the dinner cruises every night. She had tried to forget about the golden man who had helped her create a fantasy castle in the sand. And apparently he had forgotten about her.

But Pete had known all along something was brewing inside her, and he knew if he could only get her to cut loose with a "thumper" or two, he could eventually break down her barricades of reserve. If Claire would sing as he knew she could, she could regain her confidence and her real emotions would be liberated.

"Robby's throat really is sore," Pete assured his sister. He looked from the spotlit stage to Claire. "You belong up there, honey." She closed her eyes and braced herself. With a half-hearted nod, she agreed. She would sing.

"We got us a singer!" Pete shouted when Robby and the three other band members returned from their break.

"You don't know how glad I am to hear that," Robby croaked. "I sound like Joe Cocker singing underwater." He smiled in relief. "And that isn't going to draw a crowd."

"I may not be much of an improvement," Claire cautioned the guys.

"At least you're better looking," Charlie, the bass guitar player, threw in. He glanced at her with his great droopy eyes.

That sleepy expression rarely changed, but Claire knew from the tone of Charlie's voice that he was pleased to have her talent as much as her beauty. Charlie was an old pro who liked to do things right. Robby's singing with a cold would not be good enough. Not even for a small crowd or the late set of a Saturday night.

"Pick a song." Pete slid the strap of his guitar around his neck while the other players resumed their positions. "You should have the same range as Robby—without the cold, of course—so we can slide in with whatever makes you comfortable."

Claire stood a moment, recalling the songs she'd been listening to them play each night when she'd stop in after the cruise boat docked. The *Bay-Belle* was moored at the land end of the long, four-laned pier that jutted out into the protected bay between St. Petersburg and Tampa. The Pier, as both the roadway and the huge inverted-pyramid-shaped building were called, was a striking landmark overlooking the marina and the city beyond. On the third floor of the glass-and-concrete building was the lounge where Pete and Robby played and where Claire came to unwind after each cruise. Tonight there would be no unwinding.

"I like, 'You Know It When You've Got It.'" Claire named one of Robby's upbeat country rhythm songs that spoke of falling in love. The words were catchy, and each time the guys came in on the chorus, there was an infectious burst of enthusiasm that made it a crowd pleaser. The best thing about the song for Claire was that musically it was simple, but it had the building razzle-dazzle style that would let her warm up gradually while the band got used to working with her. Pete pulled the overhead mike closer to Claire so it would pick up her voice more effectively. Then he nodded to Robby, who sat behind his array of drums, contentedly sucking on a throat lozenge.

Robby began with the rocking, down-home beat, bobbing his bushy head as the other instruments joined in. Bizzy hit the light panel right on cue, catching Claire in the glowing center spotlight.

Don't go 'round sayin' that you feel so bad
When you know you're lookin' so good,
Don't waste your time on a second-rate lover
Who ain't treating you like she should. . . .

Claire started the song with an easy, restrained style that didn't intrude too abruptly into the conversations of the patrons sitting at the various tables in the lounge. Then the mischief of the lyrics put a grin on her face as she began punctuating the next lines with her swaying body. By the time the guys joined in on the chorus, singing out, "You know it when you've got it," Claire had begun to sparkle and sizzle, dancing with the beat of the music and giving herself up to the high-spirited song.

"Definitely not dinner cruise," Bizzy cackled as the number ended. "How about 'Heartbreaker'?" He suggested another of their favorite numbers. When Robby and Bizzy sang the number, it had a teasing, pop-rock sound, but with Claire's low honeyed voice, it took on a sensual quality that made it sound innocent one moment, then almost seductive the next. Best of all, it was a good dance song. Soon the smooth rectangular floor in front of the stage was occupied by several couples who stepped and bobbed from side to side with the rhythm.

The sound of the band and its new singer filtered out into the central foyer, drawing into the lounge several of the late-night diners and Pier visitors who found the music appealing. Faced by an expanding audience, Claire glanced anxiously at Pete. This was more than she had bargained for. She had hoped to step aside after one or two songs, but leaving now would put the entire band, and especially Robby, on the spot. "I don't think I have enough songs to fill a set," she whispered once she'd finished "Heartbreaker." "Music, I remember. Lyrics are another thing entirely. My mind has just gone blank.''

"Bizzy has the words to all our songs typed out on note cards.'' Pete kept smiling as he passed her the cards. "You sit this one out while we do an instrumental,'' he suggested. "You don't have to do everything perfectly,'' he assured her. "This is just for fun.''

"'Fun.''' Claire shook her head. That's what the years with Wes had taken away. Everything had become tense, rehearsed, perfect, planned. Tonight for a few minutes, performing had been fun again. Now that the audience was increasing, her professional pride was taking over.

"Loosen up, Claire.'' Pete said, winking at her. "I'm not Wes. I won't get angry if you miss a note. It's just exciting to have you up and singing again. Relax.'' Her dark-eyed brother rarely misread her. He had known for years that the temperamental Wes Raines had insisted on perfection from his band. Part of Wes's troubles came when disgruntled musicians quit. There was no opportunity for spontaneity or for individual creativity under Wes's rigid control. When the Wes Raines group was working well, their music was exceptional, but during the in-between times, or when a singer or musician had an off day, Wes would pour on the pressure and spare no one his criticism. Temperamental and tyrannical, Wes developed a reputation for being erratic and unreliable. That led to fewer and fewer jobs.

"I'll give it my best shot.'' Claire perked up under Pete's easygoing direction. "It is nice to be singing again,'' she admitted. On the stage she could put aside her natural reserve and become the singer, assuming whatever character the song required. She could be that other person, lose her inhibitions and enjoy the pleasure she was giving to others. She was creating something transitory—a fragile bubble of sound and feeling. It didn't matter at all if or when it burst. It had existed because she made it exist. "Like building sand castles," she said, smiling to herself. Like the sand castle, the music—once finished—lingered only as a memory. And that was enough.

When Claire stepped into the spotlight again, the luminescent glow around her began to dispel the unnamed shadows that had haunted her for months. For the first time since she had left New York, she didn't feel the urge to hide away. Grinning shyly, she started right in with a gritty, throaty number that sounded unmistakably like her former husband's style. It was the only hit Rainstorm had ever had and Claire had helped write the music. Most of the words belonged to Wes. But tonight this was Claire's own rendition, marked by a slight bravado. Wide open and honest, Claire sang out her bluesy version of "Hurtin' Inside" to a nearly motionless collection of upturned faces.

When she sang of "Bein' everything you asked, till I didn't know who I was..." she couldn't stop the tears from trailing down her cheeks. But her voice wavered only slightly when she sang "Keepin' up appearances.... Putting on a mask, but all the time I'm hurtin' inside." The image of the slender, pale-haired woman, silhouetted by the light, held the scattering of observers mesmerized. When the song finally reached its plaintive, agonized conclusion, there was not a sound in the small lounge. Even the electronic beeps of the video games were stilled.

Pete Parnell didn't even raise his gaze. He was determined to keep smiling in spite of the bright liquid that had collected in his eyes. He'd got more than he'd bargained for and had been touched by this unexpected magic in Claire's performance. His little sister had grown up a lot more than he had realized.

Before the audience broke into applause, Pete heard Bizzy give a low whistle of respect. Balding and slightly overweight, the Biz leaned over from the keyboard, his handlebar mustache twitching as he spoke. "I think I'm in love," he told Pete.

"And I think this throat problem may be permanent," said Robby, looking over his chrome-and-Plexiglas drums. His slightly dazed expression was the same as the one on Kurt, the bass player, and even droopy-eyed Charlie. They were all feeling that strange electricity that stood their hair on end when a performance crackled with emotional energy.

After the momentary silence, the blast of applause left Claire more startled than anything. It was as if she and perhaps twenty close friends had shared a very special celebration. A coming-out-of-her-shell party, and Claire was the honored guest. For a moment she felt too exposed, too vulnerable. She had actually cried in public. Then she looked closely at the faces. They had been moved and they were asking for more.

At the back of the lounge, Claire's gaze suddenly stopped at a face that was not smiling. Wearing a loose-knit ivory sport shirt and pale khaki slacks, Dylan Jamison regarded her thoughtfully with his inscrutable sea-blue eyes. His cautious gaze locked on to hers for a long, breathless moment of silent greeting. Finally, Dylan inclined his head. A polite, formal gesture that was both greeting and accolade.

When Claire nodded at him, Dylan's lopsided smile erased the days they had been apart. Just a second ago they had held each other. Only a moment had passed since they'd said good-night. Now they would say hello, and they would touch again. The rest of the room seemed to shift out of focus while they looked at each other across the expanse of tables and cigarette smoke. Then the sound of Bizzy playing the lead-in to the next song forced her attention away from the tanned face with the wide-set eyes. Once again, she was that person on the small stage standing in a circle of light. The show had to go on. Claire turned her attention to the music, concentrating so the words would come to her. And they did. So did the persona needed for the delivery.

Tossing her mane of pale-gold hair, strutting and singing with bubbling energy, Claire threw herself into the last two songs. Pete and Bizzy were singing harmony, watching her with sidelong glances, grinning like conspirators who had stumbled upon a secret treasure. Their voices blended like vinegar and honey, sandpaper and satin. The toughness in the male voices set off the clear, mellow sound of Claire's singing. Yet when Claire hit a line she could belt out with a husky, provocative purr, Bizzy and Pete intuitively slid into a lilting falsetto backup.

"I think we've got something, all right," Pete enthused between the numbers. The response within the

two-tiered lounge confirmed it. Even the bartenders
and waitresses joined in the applause that erupted
when the set ended. Then the prerecorded tape piped
in through overhead speakers filled the silence with
impersonal music while the band packed up for the
night.

Claire made her way straight to the man whose face
had remained with her even in her dreams. Flushed
from the exertion and the hot lights, she fanned
herself with her hands. "I haven't had a chance to sing
like that in quite a while," she puffed. "I'm out of
practice."

"If you are, it didn't show," Dylan said simply. He
reached down and brushed a stray whisp of damp,
darkened hair from her forehead. "When I walked in
here, I was expecting to hear your brothers. You mentioned that they worked here. I sure didn't expect
this."

"I'm usually in the audience, not on the stage,"
Claire answered, trying to read the message beyond
his words, the one in his strangely pensive expression.

The overhead speakers blared on while the strag-
glers in the crowd finished the last round of drinks
before closing time. Dylan frowned at the loud taped
music that made conversation nearly impossible.

"Let's go up on the roof and get some fresh air,"
Claire suggested. "I'm a bit out of shape. I need to exercise and build up my stamina again." She led him
out into the foyer, where the elevators were located.

"Have you changed jobs?" Dylan asked quietly as
they waited for the elevator. "Are you working with
this band now?"

"Oh, no. This was a spur-of-the-moment thing tonight." Claire wanted to dispel the peculiar polite distance that had stretched between them ever since she'd left the stage. No sun, no waves. Everything seemed artificial and strangely formal. Both of them were dressed in street clothes, not bathing suits. Everything had been far more natural on the beach. "I didn't expect to sing tonight at all," she added. "It just happened."

"I'm glad it did. I came in here hoping to find out where you were. You're not in the phone book, you know," Dylan said as he pushed the elevator button again and glanced at her cautiously. "I would have met the *Bay-Belle* when it docked, but I got hung up with some phone calls. The boat was moored, dark and empty when I passed. I started playing detective. You said your brothers played here, so I was going to track them down and ask them how I could contact you."

There was still no trace of his lopsided smile, and Claire felt increasingly uneasy.

"Well, your detective work paid off. Here I am."

"You certainly are." He shook his head. "I walked in and you wiped me out."

"I hope that's a compliment," Claire said good-naturedly. "You make me sound like a health hazard."

"Not knowing when or even if I would see you again was beginning to be the health hazard." He lowered his voice as the elevator hummed to a stop at their floor and the doors slid open. Dylan's comment sent a reassuring ripple of pleasure through her limbs. The pieces were all falling into place. She and her fellow castlebuilder were finding each other once more.

"I haven't been able to get you out of my mind," Dylan said quietly as the elevator lifted them skyward. "It may sound foolish, but I missed you." Claire knew exactly what he was talking about. Dylan had lingered in the corners of her mind and had drifted through her thoughts night and day.

"There is a certain affinity between us." Claire tried to put her feelings into words. But lyrics weren't her strong suit.

The elevator doors opened and they stepped out silently, crossing through the set of glass doors that led to the rooftop observation deck atop the Pier. From the deck they could see for miles on all sides. On the landward side, rows of moored boats nestled in the marinas of St. Pete, with the sparkling lights of the city spreading beyond. On all other sides the dark, silent bay stretched out, glistening in the moonlight, with only a few distant lights visible across the water on the shoreline of Tampa. The only sound was the soft rush of the wind.

"This feels more real up here." Dylan took her hand and pressed it gently between his larger, rougher ones. "You look more familiar out here in the open." He lowered his gaze to her lips as if about to kiss her. "I came looking for you tonight just to put what happened on the beach into perspective," he admitted. "I really don't have time for the usual dating routine. My hours are hardly predictable. I guess I was hoping that my feelings about you would wear off, but they haven't. If I thought I was hooked on you before, I'm really in trouble now." His gaze shifted to the deep vee of her jade-green silk blouse, where moisture still glistened in the shadowy valley between her breasts. Then his eyes met hers again— and held them. "I think I'm bewitched," he announced poetically. "Watching you sing reminded me of the old legends about the sea sirens weaving spells with misty eyes and seductive songs."

Claire didn't like the implication that she would seduce anyone, and she was well aware that the siren legends had a sinister side. The man who had seemed to understand her so intuitively on that quiet crescent of beach now looked at her as if she had metamorphosed into a creature not quite real. On top of which his interpretation of the siren implied that she was some kind of threat.

"I wasn't trying to be tempting."

"I didn't mean to suggest you were trying to be anything," he stressed. "You are what you are. I'm just seeing another side of you. There is something otherworldly about you, Claire. At the beach you were like a fairy princess with her fantasy castle. Here you are a beautiful siren. You're elusive—almost magical. All I have to do is hear you sing to understand that."

The cool night air rippled through her pale-gold hair as they stood there above the dark waters of Tampa Bay with a canopy of stars overhead. For a moment it appeared as if both of them were carved in alabaster.

"That person you saw up there was a performer giving a performance," Claire began carefully.

"Singing is a kind of theater for me," she said, trying to explain the difference between her onstage image and herself. "I become an actress up there, and I can charge the music with whatever emotional intensity the words and the music require. That's the nature of the business."

Dylan looked from Claire across the bay to the distant lights of Tampa. "I understand the performance part, but some of what you do is very real. What comes across is too powerful, too personal to be acting." Onstage, the reserve of the princess was replaced by a sensual quality, made much more tempting because the innocence and vulnerability were still there—in the misty gray eyes and the tentative smile.

"I don't know what you've been through or how deeply you've been hurt," Dylan said softly, "but your feelings show when you sing." He put his hands on her shoulders and looked into her eyes. "That's not just my impression. Everyone in that room could feel what you were going through. That was fascinating. One part of me anguished for you. Another part was stunned by your pure talent." His next words were whispered. "You're a singer. You're no dinner-cruise musician, Claire." He smiled again as a new thought struck him. "You're a siren all right. You're a golden haired, gray-eyed mermaid who miraculously survived a storm and wandered onto shore. You can pass as a castlebuilder for a while, or you can play for your dinner cruise. But when you sing, you belong to the songs the way the siren belongs to the sea. And you're very good. One day your songs will take you away."

Claire tried to protest. What did he really know

about her? She had finally found her way back home. She had no intention of going anywhere. She was not driven by any ambition to launch a singing career, one that would put her on the touring circuit again. She was a person, not a product to be marketed. Besides, Wes had made it very clear that she didn't have what it takes to make it alone. He said she lacked the discipline to put her own success first. But success had a way of warping things, and she'd seen too much of that distortion in Wes's career to want any part of it for herself.

She did want something, though. She had seen the look on the faces of the band tonight. She had felt the rapport with the audience. A certain magic had happened during her performance, and it had felt good. But in Dylan's eyes, the magic set her apart. Now apprehension clouded the sea-blue eyes that regarded her. He was seeing her as someone uniquely talented, but someone who was just passing through.

"I'm here now," said Claire, trying to focus on the present. "That's all anyone can be sure of."

"I guess it is," he agreed. "Here and now is fine with me. But when tomorrow does come, I wouldn't try to stop you or hold you back," Dylan said sincerely. "I'm not sure what we can be to each other or how long it can last. All I want you to know is that I wouldn't hurt you. I want to be near you and I want to make love with you as long as you are here. When you feel the calling to move on," he added with a slight smile, "not me—not even castle building will be enough to hold you. Nothing should hold you back."

Dylan's smile disappeared; his eyes narrowed as he slid his hands down the silky fabric covering her arms to pull her closer to him. "I won't hide what I feel right now. I can't let you go without touching you...and wanting you to touch me." He lowered his lips to caress hers. The easy delicious contact of their lips set off instinctive responses. There was no demand in the kiss, just a softly sensuous give and take that spread a pleasant glow throughout her body.

Claire slid her arms around him as he gathered her into his embrace, clasping her tightly against him. What had begun tenderly and tentatively began to build into a series of sensations, a discovery of primal pleasure. Pleasure so familiar, yet new again. Their bodies molded together as they had before with effortless precision, seeking an intimacy and acceptance expressed without words.

"Oh, Dylan..." Claire whispered as she felt the solid muscles of his shoulders beneath her fingertips. She experienced a surge of purely physical longing as curves and muscles touched, communicating in a language all their own, yielding and accepting with natural, sensuous grace. Dylan's lean form felt so perfect against hers, seeming to melt into her one moment, then become taut and controlled the next. Her own body was responding to the closeness, the tenderness, the comfort, and she wanted more. Like a slowly rising wave that would sweep them out to sea, the building swell of passion whispered an irresistible summons.

Until now, they had been alone on the rooftop

observation deck. But the lounge downstairs was closing and several other couples were coming from the elevators for a late night view of the city. "I don't make love in public, and I'm sure you don't, either," Dylan said in a low, intimate voice. His jaw clenched as he held his passion in check. "But if you don't come away with me, we may both embarrass ourselves."

Claire held his hand tightly to signal that she understood. The feelings they were sharing were very private, very intense. Claire moved beside him, turning to face the dark, lustrous water, as if the water held an answer to the conflict between desire and denial. The pressure of the wind and the whisper of the waves only accentuated her sense of well-being. Dylan's arm looped around the curve of her back, holding her snugly next to him. Her fellow castle-builder.

"Come home with me, Claire. Be with me tonight." He offered no tomorrows and demanded no promises. The fire in his eyes was like a beacon in the night, slicing through the darkness of her past, summoning her to a safe harbor. More than anything, she wanted to ride the wave of freedom that his nearness prompted. Yes, she wanted to be with him. Tonight there was no other choice.

If he saw her as a paradox, part gentle spirit who lingered on the beach—part sultry siren who could seduce with a song, Claire could not dispute his vision. Both were parts of her. Regardless how he saw her, here or anywhere else, the sea-blue eyes were offering her a special world—for now. They were filled with a rare and sensuous magic that promised exquisite rapture and asked for nothing more than she could give this night. In the sea-blue depths she recognized a special wisdom that could set her free. Until now, she had been drifting aimlessly, carefully avoiding all the womanly pleasures her body once took for granted.

"Take me home with you." Claire leaned closer and breathed her reply against his cheek. After so much sorrow and so little comfort, she felt the spark of what was possible again. While it warmed her, she hungered for a night of love.

WAITING IN THE HALLWAY while Claire went back inside the lounge to pick up her purse and jacket, Dylan felt the first tremor in his chest. This was risky business. He had come here uncertain what he'd learn about her—an address, a phone number, any trace of the castlebuilder. Anything to see her again, to sort out the barrage of mixed emotions that had buffeted him like summer squalls since they had met. From the moment he had seen her hands touch the sand and begin to coax a fairy-tale castle from a formless mound, he knew he wouldn't be able to forget her. The pensive look on her face had told him she was troubled and she had come to Frenchman's Pass to find peace, just as he had. Only his troubles had been the usual kind—mostly money and business. Hers were distinctly different. And he wanted to help, if she'd let him.

This may not be helping, he warned himself as he watched her stop for a moment to speak to someone on her winding pathway through the lounge. She had left him once before, apparently content to let that one day on the beach be the beginning and the end. He'd half expected that when he did find her, he'd see the same remoteness in her gray eyes that had alerted him when he had said something too personal or looked at her too intently. But when she saw him tonight, her eyes were not remote. They were pure and bright, clear and sharp, cutting through all his caution. She looked for all the world as if she were the one who had found him.

She is so fragile. Again the caution came over him, chilling and chastising. He could perceive the contradictions—her reserve, her vulnerability, her passion, her pain—yet he couldn't pull all the pieces together into the one image that had stayed in his mind. He hadn't dared to imagine their next meeting would be like this. That they would reconnect so effortlessly. That they would be going off together in the night to make love. He didn't act on impulse. And he knew from everything he'd seen of her that she didn't act on impulse, either. Tonight, with each other, it was obvious that the old rules didn't apply. But proceeding without any rules at all disturbed him.

The pale-haired lady with the voice of velvet was not the only one who was vulnerable. She wasn't the only one who was apprehensive about going too fast, feeling too deeply, risking too much. Dylan had come to the Pier tonight looking for more than a memory. He had found a compelling enigma, one he could not resist pursuing, however precarious the journey might be. He just wished he knew what was going on inside her head. Claire seemed willing to trust him, and he sensed how difficult trusting was for her—lowering her defenses, letting someone into her life. Now it was up to him to follow his instincts, to keep both of them from harm.

But it was so easy to get lost in those misty eyes when she looked at him.

CHAPTER THREE

THE HIGH-PITCHED RAUCOUS CRIES of the sea gulls outside were the first Sunday-morning sounds Claire heard. Frantically scrambling after a school of tiny silver herring, the gulls squawked and jostled for position, diving again and again into the rippling melee. Their feeding frenzy awakened Claire abruptly from her languid cloudy dreams.

When she cracked one eye open and saw the bright streaks of light streaming through the window blinds, she knew that the day had a long head start on her. And as for the dreams.... She did not know where they left off and reality began. In the dreams she was not alone. But the rumpled pillow next to her and the newly familiar scent of the man who had slept there were her only companions in the wide water bed. Dylan-with-the-sea-blue-eyes was gone.

"Oh, my goodness...." Claire lifted herself onto her elbow, trying to piece together the night before. But the movement produced a throbbing pressure in her head and the world seemed slightly out of kilter. Claire closed her eyes and pressed her face into her palms, and gradually the sensation subsided. She remembered the wine. And how the nervousness had made her throat dry. Finally everything stabilized, even the steady, dull throbbing in her head, and she slid into an upright position once more. She stared uneasily around the room, then down at the oversized T-shirt covering her body. "Oh, my," she whispered anxiously. Then she brushed her fingertips over the warm sheets and scrubbed her bare feet on the soft carpeting. It was all very real.

Her face slowly deepened into a warm pink flush as she tried to transpose the delicious dream that had filled her night into what she could remember of what really had happened. "Dylan...?" Claire called softly, afraid to confirm that the night had contained all the images and sensations that she imagined. In that fantasy night, the siren and the sea god had loved each other with smiles and sighs and haunting music. But now it was morning, and two very real people had to move into the light.

In the dream, the loving had begun nervously, with a tentative embrace, then with a shiver of desire. They'd sat in the moonlight, sipping wine and talking, and gradually the shyness had slipped away. Once they held each other, the tide of longing crashed on the shore of their souls. Then the golden sea god had led her into the darkness and they had touched each other gently. He'd unbuttoned the silky blouse, his fingers cool like the ocean. Then his open hands, warm like the sun, swept over her skin. For a long moment she felt as if she were floating. She had savored the luxurious, unhurried kisses, losing herself in his embrace. Then she shivered with ecstasy as his lips worshipped her breasts. In a cloak of abandon, the passion built. Naked in the moonlight, with the salty sea air wafting in, they had become one, and they had drifted on a crest of desire.

The sea god was a gentle lover, strong and eloquent with his caresses, becoming powerful and tantalizing as he wanted her more. The lean, hard muscles beneath his velvety skin had trembled, holding back the force of his desire for her. Then the siren's womanly responses answered his summons with a fluttering from within, sending ripples of liberation throughout her body. Making love together became an act of affirmation, a rediscovery—a ritual of nature—as each offered to please and to share and hold back nothing. They had smiled and touched and clung to each other, excluding everything else from their embrace. He offered the warmth of his sun-drenched realm; she whispered the timeless sighs of her ocean domain, and together they wove an in-between world for each other with soft caresses, gliding bodies and a rhythmical confirmation as ageless as the seas.

In the dream, it was innocent and very beautiful, mystical and mythical.

"Dylan, are you here?" Claire wrapped the bed sheet around her and padded across the thick chocolate-brown bedroom carpet. She stepped out into the vast room beyond, a sparsely furnished combination kitchen-dining-area-den that opened, like the bedroom, onto a wooden deck overlooking the Gulf. The night before, when Dylan had told her that "home" was a stilt house on a narrow peninsula of beach on the farthest point of land from the Pier, Claire knew it would take half an hour to cross through St. Petersburg, then pass over the toll bridge that spanned the Intercoastal Waterway linking St. Pete to the islands of the beach strip. Taking care of the transportation details had not been particularly romantic. Claire didn't want to leave her car unattended overnight in the parking space by the Pier, so she had opted to follow him out there.

During the solitary drive, the other Claire, the cautious one, had surfaced again. But the castle-builder Claire kept driving, watching the tail lights of Dylan's pickup truck in spite of the second and third thoughts she had about what she was doing. But the perfectly rational objections with which she attempted to undermine her resolve were no match for the sense of destiny that compelled her to follow this man. Claire had denied herself so much; she held so much inside, grieving for a dream that had died. Dylan touched a responsive chord in her. Not just sexual. The part of her that needed to be held and loved demanded the chance to live again.

Claire and a man who was still something of a stranger to her had come to this tiny strip of land instinctively. From the rustic wooden balcony they had watched the water, listened to the waves, until the cautious Claire had fallen silent. Dylan had offered her wine and there was moonlight, and she had been terribly nervous. But together they had created a magnificent night—a night to remember. Ruefully Claire acknowledged she could remember parts of it more vividly than others.

Now in the light of day, the magnificence seemed to be slipping away rapidly. Without the moonlight, nothing looked the same. The interior of the house was very obviously unfinished. Paint cans and scraps of paneling were stacked along one wall, and an assortment of tools were spread out on the kitchen counter. Bookshelves with no books, closets with no clothes. This was not the dwelling of a sea god, and there was little in the house to suggest what kind of man this Dylan Jamison really was.

Taped to the cabinet, just above a small automatic coffee maker, was a note: "Leave your phone number, please. Had to go out on an urgent mission and didn't want to disturb you. Will call you. Dylan."

Claire looked from the note to the clutter of building material surrounding her. Tugging open one cabinet door after another, disclosing mostly vacant shelves, she finally found several mismatched coffee mugs, paper filters and a can of decaffeinated coffee. There was no milk in the refrigerator. There was nothing but a container of frozen bait shrimp, five oranges, half a loaf of bread and several slices of cold pizza. And a very large bottle of wine, half-empty. She wondered how much of the deficit she'd made. She was no drinker. The throbbing in her head was testament enough. Though the wine had relaxed her the night before, today it just fogged her memory. She'd overdone it. But she'd made her choice, and she'd have to face the consequences.

Claire closed the door, plagued by the troublesome feeling that Dylan could not actually be living permanently in this place. At best, he might occasionally spend some time working or sleeping here. What had seemed like an intimate seaside paradise by night appeared barren, makeshift and unwelcoming by day.

Claire glanced once more at the perfunctory note and inhaled the sour odor of sawdust. One seemed as much of a leftover as the other. She wondered if the urgent mission that had called Dylan away on a Sunday morning was simply a fabrication to let both of them ease out of an uncomfortable situation gracefully.

He isn't like that, she told herself resolutely. There had been such tenderness in Dylan's eyes when he looked at her. Dream or not, the warmth that had coursed through her body when they had moved in silken unison was more than physical. Certainly they were sexually compatible, but there was something far more significant involved. Now Claire yearned to look into the sea-blue eyes and confirm this other truth—one that subtly entwined this man in her tomorrows. He had said he was a believer in possibilities. Surely his possibilities with her extended beyond one night of passion.

Claire dressed hurriedly, then paused on her way out, considering whether to leave a phone number or not. What she had to say to Dylan was too new, too elusive to translate into words and leave behind in a note. It just wouldn't do. Dylan had found her before. If he wanted to, he could find her again. And if he didn't, no piece of paper with a number on it would make a difference.

When Claire stepped down the wooden stairs that led from the deck to the open area below the house, her car sat alone between the huge support pilings, no longer dwarfed by Dylan's truck. Three brown-bellied pelicans squatting in the shadow of the house glared at her curiously before waddling off to one side. Until she arrived, they had been enjoying a quiet midmorning snooze. "Sorry fellows," she apologized half-seriously as the revving of her engine caused them to puff their feathers indignantly and recoil from the noise.

Without looking back, she drove down the narrow roadway that connected the peninsula with the main artery, the beach boulevard. Undoubtedly brother Pete would be at home, eager to talk to her about working a little more with his band. She had spoken to him briefly before she left the Pier with Dylan, and Pete had known she was leaving with the sandy-haired man. Since she had not returned to her apartment above his studio, she guessed Pete might want to discuss more than music.

"How about lending me a hand?" The old fellow in the faded peaked cap directed his request at Claire.

She had driven out to the beach early that day, hoping to "fast walk" a couple of miles before too many people filled the sandy stretch from Frenchman's Pass to the fishing pier farther north. She hadn't heard a word from Dylan, not in three days, and the vigorous exercise worked off some of her tension. Besides, it felt good to get out in the salty air and enjoy the surroundings. Sea air and the sand between her toes put everything into perspective and nurtured that part of her that needed to be close to nature.

Onstage she'd need to be in shape. Pete wanted her to rehearse with his band every evening that she was not working on the cruise boat, but if Claire intended to double-up on weekends and follow the three hours on the boat with a few short sets in the club, she'd have to start training. "Fast walking"—striding up and down the beach rapidly, arms swinging and back comfortably erect—built up the muscles in her legs, developed her breathing and increased her stamina.

The old fellow who now called out to her had been squatting on the jetty, tossing bait fish to the pelicans, when she began her exercise routine. Now that she had returned from one lap, he looked as if he'd been waiting for her.

"I need to get that bird." He jerked one weathered hand toward a rather dopey-looking brown pelican that plodded along the sand waiting for a handout. "He wants the fish," the old fellow said, smiling cunningly, "but he doesn't want it enough to get real close to me. That's a tip-off the poor thing has something wrong with him."

Claire now stood next to the wiry old man whose peaked cap only reached her shoulder. There were nine other pelicans surrounding them, nudging each other and jockeying for position to get one of the fish being passed out. But the one pelican the man had singled out was hanging back, remaining on the fringe of the circle of eager birds.

"You mean he's sick?" Claire eyed the creature closely. As far as she could tell, he looked just like the other ones in the group.

"That's what I intend to find out." The fellow reached into his bucket and grasped a silvery fish. "Only it will take two of us to outmaneuver this bunch," he insisted. "So I figure if you dangle this fish in front of these birds, I'll work my way 'round behind them and lure that one away with a fish of his own. You don't mind handling a fish, do you?" He held the flopping bait fish out for her to take.

Claire wrinkled her nose but grasped the fish firmly by the tail while it jerked from side to side. With one surprisingly quick flick, it slipped from her grip, but her companion picked it up from the sand, washed it clean in the bucket and handed it to her to try again. With an apologetic shrug, Claire grabbed the fish. The old man chuckled at her apparent discomfort but winked appreciatively over her sporting attitude. He took one fish himself, then gave her the bucket.

"Now you get these fellas goin' in that direction." He tilted his head back toward the bridge. "And I'll get this young one to overcome his shyness. Now you can be real stingy with those fish," he instructed her. "These guys can find plenty of food on their own."

Claire waved the first shiny fish from side to side over the heads of the long-beaked birds. Like spectators at a tennis match, they wagged their heads back and forth, following the tasty morsel with eager pastel-blue eyes. With a toss, the fish was caught in midair. "It's like conducting an orchestra." Claire laughed, this time making her arm swing more gracefully in wider and wider loops. From the corner of her eye, she could see that the crafty old man had enticed the shy brown pelican back toward the jetty and was using his fish skillfully, drawing the creature closer and closer to him. Then with an efficient drop and swoop of his arm, he flipped the fish into the pelican's pouch, grabbed the long bill and held it closed, clutching the bird under his free arm while he held the sharp clawed feet together tightly.

"Just turn your back on them and hustle over here," the old man called.

Relieved to get away from the knee-high birds, Claire hastily carried the bucket of fish over to the elderly pelican catcher. "How about this one?" She looked at the bird he held. "Can you tell what's wrong with him?" The pelican wasn't struggling or straining at all. Within the man's grasp, the bird was calm. It sat quietly braced against his hip while the man inspected it.

"He's been hooked all right," he noted. A slender string of clear monofilament fishing line trailed from the corner of the bird's bill. "You grab on to these feet a moment and let me peek inside."

Claire's eyes widened at the prospect of holding the leathery clawed feet with her bare hands, but her curiosity overcame her doubts when she looked into the earnest face of the pelican catcher.

"Just reach over him like this," he directed her on the method of transferring the bird from under his arm to hers. "Then hold him against your side."

Slowly Claire reached over the wonderfully soft feathers and grasped the bird. The pressure of her arm around him kept his wings snug against his sides, and her long fingers held the feet and braced the underside of the creature. The most surprising thing was the insignificant weight of the big, ungainly bird. In spite of his apparent size, he was amazingly light, and the texture of his feathers against her skin was soft and delicate, like luxurious fur.

"My name is Frazer." The old man seemed to be introducing himself to the injured bird as well as to Claire, for now he held the bill handshakestyle and moved around to face the bird straight on.

"My name is Claire," she replied with a slight smile. Holding the bird had given her an unexpected pleasure as she felt the flutter of its heartbeat against her side. Instinctively she stroked the smooth, chocolate-brown neck of the bird, soothing him with her caress as weathered old Frazer opened its bill and looked inside.

"Geez," he muttered as he frowned. He lifted out the fish still trapped inside the bird's mouth. "Couldn't get it down, anyway," he explained. "He swallowed one of those damn triple hooks and it's really dug in there."

Claire leaned forward and peered into the bird's mouth. At the end of the trailing fishing line, a grotesque multipronged hook had pierced the soft skinlike pouch of the pelican and was trapped in his throat like an ugly claw, blocking any food from being swallowed. The remainder of the fishing line was twisted around the points of the hook, tangled and matted like a plastic spider web, full of seaweed and debris.

"The thing was starving," Frazer said softly. "And slowly choking to death on the mess caught in his bill."

"What do we do now?" Claire could see that one jagged point had penetrated clear through the soft pouch and stuck out the other side. The surrounding tissue was inflamed and puffy looking, obviously infected.

" 'We'? " Frazer grinned at her. He was delighted with the eagerness of his new ally. "We take him up the beach a ways to the clinic and get him fixed up."

"A clinic? For birds?" Claire had been back in the area several months, but she had definitely never heard of such a place.

"You don't know about the Seabird Refuge?" Frazer's eyes lit up. "Come on, Lady Claire." He grandly waved her toward a rusty vintage Studebaker parked down from her compact car. "If you have the time, honey," he said, almost dancing alongside her, "do I have a treat for you!"

Claire held the injured bird on the seat next to her as Frazer drove northward along the main beach highway. "If you weren't lookin' for the refuge, you could pass right by and never know it's there. But once you know it's there, it's like a little piece of nature holdin' out against all these fancy big shots." He tossed an angry look at the tall buildings that lined the prime beachfront.

Between two smaller condo units, in an area that still had a sprinkling of private residences, Claire saw the wooden sign—Gulf Coast Seabird Refuge—but only after Frazer had slowed down and switched on the car turn signal. He was right. Unless you knew what to look for, the refuge was an easy place to miss.

The dusty, fenced parking lot in front of the cement-block, split-level house was occupied by several vehicles. The adjacent yard, a sandy expanse shaded by low-spreading Australian pine trees, would not have attracted particular interest if it hadn't been for the assortment of birds perched on every available surface. When Frazer pulled his car to a halt and flung open his door, the tree branches shook and erupted with a flutter of wings.

"Emergency clinic is this way." Frazer lifted the pelican out of Claire's arms and signaled for her to follow him through an open gate leading into the sandy yard. As she kept in step with him, Claire looked at all the wire pens that lined the pathways cutting across the property. Inside the enclosures, birds of every size and shape wandered about, balanced on perches or sat on makeshift nests, barely glancing up at the newcomer.

"Got a patient for you," Frazer greeted the young bearded man who came out in answer to the bell on the door. "How's it going, Kurt?" It was clear from the harried expression on the young fellow's face that things had not been going well.

"Just about like usual, only worse," Kurt said, summoning a preoccupied smile for Frazer's blond companion. "Some developer has moved in heavy equipment on a dredged piece of land south of here. Sunday, they started plowing up hundreds of laughing-gull nests. They had promised to work around the gull's nesting habits. Unfortunately the birds began laying their eggs a few weeks early this year. The bulldozers were already scheduled, so they started plowin' away full blast." He solemnly recounted the current dilemma while he inspected the pelican Frazer and Claire had brought in.

"Can't you stop them?" Frazer asked. Claire was only half listening, absorbed in the handling of the pelican.

"We're doing the best we can," Kurt answered. "D.J. has been negotiating for three days' straight. He started out nice and reasonable at 7:00 A.M. on Sunday. Some local ordinance made them shut down that day. By Monday, he'd telephoned everyone from the wildlife authorities to the state attorney general. That last call got the work postponed indefinitely...well, at least until we can get a ruling on the operation."

"How do we stand?" Frazer inquired as he adjusted an overhead lamp so Kurt could see better as he examined the injured bird.

"We don't know if any laws or regulations have been violated. D.J. flew to Atlanta on his own to meet with the district federal wildlife agents to get a ruling." Kurt nodded to Frazer, tucked the pelican under his arm efficiently and started down the hallway toward a STAFF ONLY area, with Frazer right behind him.

Claire hesitated for a moment before venturing into the corridor after the men. As she passed each doorway opening off the hall, she quickly looked inside each room. What had once been a family dwelling had been transformed into a small animal hospital, complete with cages of recuperating birds, incubation compartments containing unhatched eggs and an operating room where Kurt would work on the injured pelican.

"You said the boss started out reasonable...." A hint of amusement rippled through old Frazer's voice. "How's he doing now?"

"He's passed angry and turned deadly." Kurt

flashed a quick grin. "He's called in the reserves," and he chuckled. "Little blue-haired ladies who know how to get things done when the bureaucracy moves too slow." He added the explanation for Claire's benefit. "Also a few journalists and TV people have been fired up. It's really a grim scene over there. Hulking machines sitting idle next to piles of twigs and smashed eggs. A neatly condensed, very visual comment on the triumph of civilization," he added cynically. "A crew went over this morning to shoot some footage."

"That sounds promising." Frazer solemnly appraised the details of the confrontation.

"There's only one problem." Kurt stroked the velvet neck of the pelican and reached for a pair of sharp-edged metal clippers. "Laughing gulls are not on the endangered-species list. Not yet," he emphasized. "Unfortunately they were inadvertently omitted from the Migratory Bird Treaty. This plowing may wipe out thousands of fledglings that would have hatched over the next month. Worst of all, what the developer is doing isn't illegal."

"But it's wrong," Claire blurted out. The callousness of the act horrified her. "Endangered-species list or not—it's just not right."

Kurt and Frazer turned to look at her. Then they looked at each other knowingly.

"We agree. But what makes sense to us, doesn't always coincide with the plans of the developer. Laws or no laws, this kind of destruction is just mindless waste," Kurt said. "You are quite correct, Miss—" he ended awkwardly, not knowing her name. He smiled to reveal even rows of white teeth above his trimmed beard.

"Pardon my manners." Frazer came forward a step, resting his hand on Claire's shoulder. "Claire, this is Kurt Chambers. He's a one-man fix-it phenomenon when it comes to injured birds. Kurt, meet Claire."

They nodded politely. "Claire," Kurt noted. Then he turned his attention back to the bird and continued working to remove the hook.

Claire quickly pressed for more details about the disturbing plight of the gulls. "This trip that your boss took to Atlanta—will that save these birds?"

"We can only hope so," Kurt answered. "But let's save this one bird today. I know I can do that."

"Are you a veterinarian?" Claire asked as she moved closer to the table where Kurt and Frazer held the surprisingly calm pelican. The steady, precise clipping away at the hook didn't agitate the bird at all. He seemed to sense he was in competent hands, so he stood calmly on the waist-high operating table while the bright light shone down into his throat.

"No, I'm more a technician than a vet," Kurt answered as he slipped the most vicious of the hooks through the tender pouch. Snipping off the jagged point, he deftly slid the curved shaft back through the ragged hole it had created. "But I'm pretty good at this stuff," he added as he withdrew the now-harmless hook from the pelican's mouth and held it up for Claire to see. "We have an excellent consulting vet to do the tricky surgery and set broken bones. We can't afford a full-time vet, but our consultant gave us lessons on how to do the routine work. Like this.'' He continued to speak as he cleaned the wound with antiseptic, then prepared an injection of antibiotics. ''I'm a graduate student in marine biology, specializing in seabirds,'' he explained. ''I got into this the way most of us did—sort of by accident. I came as a visitor, became a volunteer. Now I'm hooked,'' he finished, laughing good-naturedly.

''You are very good at this,'' Claire commended him.

''I get lots of practice,'' Kurt replied solemnly. ''Hooks, fishing lines, plastic bags, parts of metal cans, key chains, plastic forks—you name it and I've taken it out of a bird.''

''Well, you've got a very grateful patient.'' Claire smiled as she watched the brown pelican on the table stretch his wings and waddle from side to side. Obviously the bird was feeling better, but now he had had enough of the bright light and the peculiar antiseptic smell. He wanted to be outdoors again.

''We'll put this guy in a cage and keep an eye on him for a few days.'' Kurt removed a numbered metal leg band from a roll and snapped it into place on the bird's spindly leg. On a file card he copied out the number and neatly wrote in the details of treatment. Finally he pulled out a measuring tape and recorded the size of the creature: height, wingspan, beak length. With the official accounting complete, the threesome left the clinic's operating room with the relieved pelican snugly under Kurt's arm.

''Here's the recovery room.'' Kurt stopped at a former bedroom, now lined ceiling-high with cages.

Carefully he put the pelican in a cage of his own, covering the bird with a towel and adjusting a heating pad to keep him warm. "Helps to prevent his going into shock," Kurt explained as he waited a moment for the bird to settle down. "Sometimes the emotional trauma is more deadly than the injuries. You never know how much they've been through."

Kurt glanced over at Claire, noting her troubled expression. She stood there motionless, staring into the cage, lost in thought.

"We've done our part," he said at last, eager to divert her from her vigil. "Let's give him some time to rest," he suggested. Then he caught Frazer's eye and inclined his head toward the door.

"Now you get the unofficial tour," Frazer said, picking up on the hint. "Come on, Claire." Outside in the compound, the trio strolled from pen to pen, with Frazer and Kurt alternately giving details about the species of birds and the types of injuries suffered.

"This owl obviously isn't a seabird." Kurt lifted the canvas flap and pointed out the elegant white-headed bird high on a perch in one wood-sided enclosure. "But someone took a potshot at him and blew apart one of his wings. We try to release as many birds as we can back into the wild, but a one-winged owl can't fly and can't hunt. So he's become a permanent resident."

Kurt pulled down the canvas shade to cut out as much light as possible so the bird could resume his nap. "If a bird can't fend for himself or if he simply won't leave, then we try to make room for him or we find him a suitable home in some other facility. We send a lot of imperfect creatures to zoos and aviaries. In fact, we have a standing agreement with Busch Gardens to take any crippled animals we can't place. Keeping an injured bird in captivity makes more sense than trapping and confining a perfectly healthy bird that belongs in the wild. It also teaches zoogoers about the kinds of injuries possible and the way creatures adapt. We think we've worked out a pretty realistic and humane system all around."

Set on the acre of land that had once been the side yard of an attractive, split-level residence, the rows of cages offered a diverse exhibit—sea gulls, cormorants, herons, egrets, pelicans, falcons, hawks, vultures and even jays and sparrows. Each bird wore a numbered leg band that matched the bird to a file card recording its history. The other leg bore a second band: blue for birds being held for observation, red for patients who would soon be able to fly away and gold for those crippled birds who would remain in the refuge permanently.

"Who owns this place and who pays for all this?" Claire asked. "Does the state or the county finance it?"

"We're approved but not financed by the government. The state and national wildlife agencies issued special permits for us to do the work," Kurt said, warming to the subject. "We operate as a nonprofit corporation and are supported totally by donations and a few grants we've been lucky enough to secure. Basically we run on a shoestring budget. There are four full-time paid employees," he explained, "one of whom is me."

"The rest of us are volunteers," Frazer added, his piercing black eyes sparkling as he looked up at the tall golden-haired woman. "All it takes to be a volunteer is a little love and not being afraid to grab on to an injured pelican," he added deliberately. "Like you did."

"Frazer should have been in public relations," Kurt joked. "When he's not fishing, and even when he is, he's always on the lookout for hurt birds and willing workers. Unfortunately the injured birds outnumber the volunteers by a large margin. But if you have the inclination and any time at all, we're always eager for helpers."

Claire didn't even have time to think over Kurt's suggestion before the slam of a car door was followed by the bark of an angry voice. "Hey, give me a hand out here. Where is everybody? Kurt? Tammy? Somebody give me a hand." The barrage of orders caught them all by surprise. The two men took off instantly, with Claire close at their heels.

"Here we are," Frazer yelled.

The two men rounded the corner and Claire nearly ran into them when they stopped abruptly. The man they called "D.J." had met them halfway, carrying a Styrofoam ice chest, which he immediately thrust into Kurt's arms. "Hurry up, there's more," he said brusquely. "One of the bulldozer operators decided to tidy up a bit for the press. He tore up another strip of nests trying to get the company name out of the camera range." Bristling with anger, D.J. started to turn back toward the pickup truck. Suddenly as if forgetting something, he turned around, facing the wide-eyed woman standing behind the refuge workers.

"Claire. I want to talk to you," he said tersely, an additional anger smoldering in his eyes.

Now the two men glanced uncertainly from D.J. to Claire.

"Dylan?" Her whisper was lost among the squawking cries of the multitude of birds who fluttered a welcome in the trees above.

"Let's take care of these eggs. Then we'll talk." The businesslike tone in his voice made it impossible to tell at whom the comment was aimed. "You take those in," he directed Kurt. "We'll need to find someone who can lend us some extra incubators." He shifted his sharp gaze to the older fellow. "Frazer, come with me. I brought as many eggs as I could rescue, but I don't want the site left unsupervised. Someone will have to go back to the nest."

Frazer nodded and grabbed another Styrofoam chest, eager to hurry off toward the refuge building and give Dylan a few minutes with Claire.

"As for you...." Dylan turned his stormy blue eyes again on Claire. "I've been chewing myself out for days for putting too much pressure on you. Maybe I asked too much, but I sure didn't expect to have to play another round of hide and seek. I want to know why you skipped out without leaving a number where I could reach you. I called the Pier to get a hold of you through your brothers. Their band doesn't work there until tomorrow night, and their home phone numbers are unlisted. No one would give me a clue. You walk out without a word, disappear for three days and show up here. What kind of games are you playing, lady?''

Claire felt her pulse racing and tried to suppress the impulse to bolt. Too stunned to speak, she stood motionless while the sharp-edged frustration in his voice assaulted her. All the comments about D.J. made by Kurt and Frazer fitted perfectly with this blue-eyed fury confronting her. Logic told her he was angrier about the destruction of the laughing-gull nests than at her. But anger was anger, and Dylan's outburst elicited an involuntary response, a feeling of helplessness and terror more deeply ingrained than she had realized. She wasn't playing games. She'd been accused of that once before—unfairly—by Wes. Without warning, the old nightmare sprang to life. Wes Raines came charging at her, accusing her, cursing her, ready to pound her with his fists.

White-faced and shaken, Claire felt the ground shift beneath her feet.

''My God, Claire.'' Two strong hands reached out and grasped her shoulders. She was only vaguely aware of the sea-blue eyes that swept over her terrified expression. ''I didn't mean to frighten you.'' Dylan held her facing him, speaking softly, as if he were subduing some wild creature. ''Take it easy. Look at me. No one is going to hurt you.''

As they stood there, amid pens full of recuperating seabirds and birds of prey, Dylan could not ignore the poignant similarities between the birds and the frightened woman standing before him. Once again he thought, *she is so fragile. . . .* He knew that. He just had not realized how fragile she was.

When she began to relax and breathe normally, he loosened his hold on her. "Talk to me," he said quietly. "What happened just now? I need to understand. Surely you didn't think I'd hurt you?" His questions came one after the other, and Claire could only shake her head. Then he stopped and waited while her solemn gray eyes met his intent gaze.

"I wasn't playing games. This isn't hide and seek. I didn't know you worked here." She spoke very slowly, as if she were having difficulty communicating. "Kurt and Frazer had been telling me about the birds—all the injuries. And the bulldozer smashing the eggs. So cruel." She realized how dissociated she must sound, but she was unable to separate the images in her head. Everything, past and present, seemed to converge.

"I wasn't sure how I'd feel if I saw you again. I didn't know how you would react. I never imagined you would be so...upset." She settled for a hardly adequate word. "My brain had a little difficulty shifting gears," she said so quietly that he could barely hear the words. "I guess I'm not as resilient as I thought. Angry outbursts have a way of unnerving me." She understated the obvious in a deliberate attempt to smooth over the incident. "I'm afraid you caught me off guard." She tried to smile to ease the tension, but her face felt stiff and unnatural.

"Your being here caught me off guard, too." Other than a few dead-end phone calls he had made trying to find her, he'd had to put his search on hold when the issue of the laughing gulls' nesting site became more demanding. Even while he struggled through a morass of red tape and wildlife ordinances and rescued the eggs that had survived the plowing, she'd never left his thoughts. He had brooded over their night together and the dreams that hadn't come true. Nothing had turned out as he hoped.

Dylan dropped his hands to his sides. "We've got to talk...." He let her move away from him. "About the other night. About this. I'm not angry, I'm just confused. I want to know what's going on."

"I think our talk had better wait," Claire suggested. Her finely boned oval face was still pale. "You've got two others waiting to talk to you and a lot of eggs that need your attention. I could use a few minutes to collect myself."

Dylan looked at her apprehensively, then reached out and clasped her hand gently. It was cool and damp. "You won't disappear on me this time?" he asked.

"I can't. I didn't bring my car," Claire reassured him. "I left it back at Frenchman's Pass. I like exercise, but not enough to try walking that distance in my bare feet. I think I've lost the urge to run," she added with a touch of humor.

"Then I'll take care of a few details and be right back," he promised. "Don't you worry." He leveled a parting look at her before he turned away. "Whatever's bothering you, we'll deal with it. We'll get through this. Castlebuilders are an endangered species." He could back off. He could give her time to find her own direction. He would do anything to see her look at him again with that rare rapture in her eyes. "I'm not going to let anything happen to you."

This was the man Claire remembered. These eyes were the ones that had sought and found hers across castle walls, through a smoky room and even in her dreams. But now the sea-blue eyes looked a bit the worse for wear. The laugh lines at their corners had deepened into jagged creases. Nevertheless, his was a face engraved in her consciousness.

Claire nodded, then watched thoughtfully as Dylan strode toward the building where Kurt and Frazer waited. He moved like her golden seaside idol; that part was still unblemished, frozen in time. But he had shown a distinctly human side that fumed with indignation and crackled with terrifying intensity. The idyllic night they had shared had been a time apart from the real world where frustrations seethed and tempers flared. But the worlds had collided, and she was still feeling the aftershock.

Claire sat on the wooden bench, contemplating the rows of fenced pens and their avian occupants. Nearly all the pens were completely enclosed; even the top was covered with wire to keep inside the creatures who might otherwise attempt to fly off. The red-banded birds were still recuperating, but without the fencing, their instincts might override their injuries. The decision to return to the wild was not left to the birds. Until they were sufficiently healed, the wire top kept them safe. And it kept out the free flyers who came visiting, prevented them from intruding into the protected world of the recuperating creatures.

Claire studied the structures, and a pensive smile formed on her lips. *Maybe I should have stayed on the ground a little while longer myself,* she reflected. A dark-feathered cormorant limped over to peer at her plaintively through the fencing. Red banded—recuperating. He looked as embarrassed at his predicament as Claire felt over hers. His quick jet-black eyes shifted enviously to the free flyers overhead. ''I know the feeling,'' she whispered to him.

She had tried too much too soon. The night with Dylan, she had even needed a couple of glasses of wine to bolster her courage. That wasn't like her at all, but at least the effects of the wine had kept the old doubts and fears at a distance, if only for a night. But they were back.

Her instincts had been right, however the rest of her hadn't quite mended. Like the pelican she'd brought in that day, she'd survived the overt damage Wes had inflicted. Yet she had obviously suffered other wounds she could not see. He still had his hooks in her. She wanted to be in control again. She wanted to try her wings and take chances, but the effort was going to be more harrowing than she had expected.

''It will take time...'' she said to the cormorant, leaning forward to peer into his inquisitive face. ''For both of us.''

CHAPTER FOUR

WHILE CLAIRE WAITED for Dylan to return, she finished her tour of the one-acre facility on her own, walking along the pathways past the remaining tall fenced pens, reading the signs posted on the cages and billboards. Stopping by one smaller, roofed pen, she looked at the red-tailed hawk that was housed separately from the other birds of prey in the adjacent compound. The hawk, named Ariel, was blind.

"You must be the one I'm supposed to check on." The throaty voice came from a slim dark-haired young woman on the opposite side of the cage from Claire. The comment was not intended for the bird—it was directed at her. Wide-set brown eyes and a trace of freckles across a turned-up nose gave a childlike quality to the pretty, sultry-voiced refuge worker. But she was no child; she was in her midtwenties, about Claire's age.

"I'm not one for subtlety, so I'll tell you straight out that I'm supposed to keep you occupied so you won't leave." The woman thrust her hand into a heavy leather gauntlet and continued to talk as she opened the heavy screen door of the cage and stepped inside to get the solitary hawk. "But I also have to exercise Ariel. Dylan said he wanted to talk to you but he'll be tied up for a few more minutes. With the way things are going today, that could mean half an hour. You can wait here, or if you'd like to come along, you're welcome to watch.'' The slightly annoyed look in the woman's brown eyes made it clear she did not like being assigned hostess duties.

"I'd like to watch you and the hawk," Claire answered, intrigued by the idea of exercising the blind hawk.

With a slight nod that settled her dark single braid squarely between her shoulder blades, the young woman stepped toward the hawk, repeating its name and saying, "Let's go." At the sound of her voice, the large bird shifted feet eagerly and puffed its feathers in anticipation. She arched and bobbed her neck while the woman slipped leather loops over her feet and attached a long tether. When the bird stepped onto the gloved arm, the woman brought her outside. "Are you a reporter?" the woman asked Claire, as if that seemed a logical possibility, even though Claire's bare feet and short beige jogging outfit were a bit casual for a journalism assignment.

"No, I just met Frazer on the beach and helped him bring in the pelican he found."

"Oh." The information seemed to soften the remoteness in the brown eyes. "Sometimes an extra pair of hands makes all the difference in the world. Frazer is good at recruiting volunteers. If he hasn't made the pitch, he will. Are you interested in helping with the refuge?" Now there was a trace of a smile on the woman's lips as she started toward the beach with Ariel on her arm and Claire at her side.

"I'm not sure," Claire answered honestly. "This is all very new to me."

"If this is your first time here, you've seen enough to get the general idea. Working here isn't glamorous, but if you like animals, you'd certainly get a lot from helping out. And we sure can use reliable workers. There are a lot of routine things that need to be done—from feeding birds to sanding down the pens to rescuing injured birds. For really big problems like an oil spill, we call up every name in our files. In spite of everyone's good intentions, it often boils down to counting on the same volunteers. I'm in charge of the outdoor rehabilitation. I'm Tammy. Tammy Todd." She offered her free hand in a firm handshake.

"Claire Parnell. Nice to meet you, Tammy."

"Hey, cut it out, you two," Tammy called abruptly to a couple of very indignant pelicans feuding over a twig of red-berried pepper tree. "Nesting time," she explained to Claire. "One of them is swiping a branch from the other one's nest. That means the supply is getting low. Would you pick up an armful of those branches?" She nodded toward a wheelbarrow parked off to the side. "Throw them inside that pen, so the birds will have a few more to choose from. Once all the good branches are gone, they get cantankerous."

Claire did just as Tammy said. She picked up a generous load of the leafy twigs. Then Tammy opened the pelican pen and Claire dumped the branches onto the sandy ground. Throughout the maneuvering, Ariel remained poised and alert on the gloved forearm of the pigtailed young woman.

"Now they'll all start picking through those," Tammy said with a chuckle. "That ought to keep them busy for a couple of hours."

"Those are injured birds building the nests?" Claire paused to watch for a few seconds. She noted the gold leg bands.

"Most of them are permanent residents," Tammy explained. "They are crippled, but they're still fully functional in other ways," she added with a slight smile. "And they have produced some beautiful babies. Those babies eventually fly off to the wild or we ship them to one of the Gulf states where brown pelicans are nearly extinct. Captive breeding is one of our main concerns. The brown pelicans are on the endangered-species list, so we are very careful to encourage nesting. In fact, we're the first place where they've ever bred in captivity. Of course, we have a few freeloaders," she said as she pointed to several squat pelicans settled on the screen roof of the large pens. "We feed our guys at four. Some of the former residents and sundry companions drop in for a snack. Most of them I know by sight."

"You can tell the birds apart?" By now they had moved on to the third pen of brown pelicans, and to Claire every one looked just like the next one—grayish-silver back, chocolate-brown neck, yellow head, olive-drab pouch and pale-blue eyes rimmed in bright-red tissue.

"After you're around them, they become pretty distinct from one another," Tammy assured her. "They have different personalities and habits. Small variations in color become more noticeable. But I do goof up occasionally. Then I try to read the leg band and make the appropriate apologies.''

''But not all the birds here are that tame or that common, are they?'' Claire wondered.

''We deal primarily with seabirds and whatever local residents we find, but the word gets around. Sometimes birds we've raised or treated get hurt and come back here on their own. Ones we've never even seen have shown up, too. People hear about us and bring in all kinds of patients,'' Tammy explained. ''We've had everything from huge parrots to hummingbirds. Some are wilder or more exotic than others. Those are the ones who have the hardest time adapting. We treat any creature, even an occasional turtle. If we don't know how to repair the damage, we can find someone who does.''

''How long have you been doing this kind of work?'' Claire turned to stare at the tanned, earnest face of the woman with the hawk poised on her arm.

''Five years. Since Dylan started this place. I was one of the original volunteers. Now I'm like Ariel here—a permanent fixture—full-time.''

''Is Dylan a scientist of some sort?'' Claire still knew very little about the man.

''No, he just knows a lot about animals, especially birds.''

''Does he work here full-time?'' Claire tried not to make her interest too obvious.

'' 'Full-time?' '' Tammy laughed. ''Dawn till dusk, and sometimes through the night, you'll find Dylan doing something involving birds or the refuge. He really is round-the-clock full-time.''

"He makes his living doing this?" Claire asked dubiously. Birds were definitely nonpaying patients. The refuge facility hardly seemed substantial enough to support anyone financially. Yet Dylan's truck certainly was new and expensive, and the beach house he'd taken her to was on an exclusive waterfront lot.

Suddenly the openness in Tammy's expression vanished, and the polite, noncommittal look returned. "Sometimes we settle for rewards that aren't exactly impressive financially. But if you want specifics, you'll have to discuss salaries with Dylan." She clicked her tongue at Ariel and effectively ended the conversation.

In silence they crossed the low rise of sand dunes and sea oats, where a rustic gazebo separated the refuge compound from the flat white public beach at the water's edge. From the Gulfside the refuge appeared to be nothing more than a rooftop and a few trees wedged between bookends of tall condominiums. A small faded sign on the gazebo read Gulf Coast Seabird Refuge and invited visitors to explore.

Other than a few people strolling by or seated in chairs, watching the waves, the two women and Ariel had the entire stretch of sand to themselves. "Come on, Ariel," Tammy said, urging the hawk to stretch her wings. "Come on, baby. Time to fly."

Tammy broke into a run, racing along the beach with Ariel clasping the gloved arm. Then the hawk spread her wings and took off, stretching the tether full length as she flew. "Ariel, come on, baby. Good girl." The bird sailed above her, guided by the sound of Tammy's voice. With her dark pigtail bouncing in the air and her long legs leaping, Tammy made a wide arc that finally curved full circle as she and Ariel turned back toward Claire. Then they passed her by, heading the other way, sweeping so close that the rush of Ariel's wings sent a strange shiver of excitement through Claire. There was a wildness that defied the otherwise civilized surroundings.

Out of breath, Tammy came loping back, with Ariel perched on the gauntlet once more. "She's ready to go again," Tammy gasped. "I need a few minutes to catch my breath. You want to try?" She held the huge hawk out toward Claire playfully, but her bright dark eyes were serious.

Claire did not move to take the hawk. She sensed the dark-eyed woman testing her. "Not without a glove like yours and a good bit of preparation. What you do isn't an easy act to follow." Claire kept her voice steady, although her eyes never left the hooked beak of the winged creature. "Besides, I don't think Ariel would respond to anyone else the way she does to you. I suspect Ariel is a one-person bird." Claire had observed an uncanny bond between the two.

Unwavering brown eyes studied her a moment. Then a small smile brightened Tammy's face. "You're right," Tammy admitted. "I just wanted to see how you'd react. We can't have anyone skittish working around the birds. They've been through enough as it is. Even Ariel, blind as she is, can sense if someone is frightened of her."

"I'm not exactly comfortable with her," Claire admitted. "I'd be heading for cover if she dropped out of the sky and started for me," she added. "Still, I guess being here has made her pretty tame. If she didn't hurt you, she probably wouldn't hurt me.''

"Don't count on that if you're going to help out around here,'' Tammy cautioned her. "We try to keep the wildness in these birds. Dylan insists on it. They aren't pets—not even the permanent residents. Oh, sure, the birds have favorite people. They have crushes, they get jealous, they have excellent memories, they can be loyal or very fickle and there are people they simply dislike. It depends on your personality. Either you get along, or you don't. You'll find a niche for yourself if you want to.''

"I'm not sure I'm going to get that involved in all this. I just came along with Frazer out of curiosity.'' The concept of the refuge fascinated her, but Claire felt a bit intimidated about taking on the responsibilities of a volunteer. She was just learning to take care of herself. Besides, she liked having her days free; that was one aspect of the *Bay-Belle* job that she enjoyed.

"If you're interested in Dylan, then you can count on working with the birds. This isn't his hobby, it's his life.'' Claire noticed a trace of hostility in Tammy's voice. "He doesn't have time for much else.'' The matter-of-fact way Tammy spoke made the package deal very clear. "Ready to go again, Ariel?'' Tammy turned to the red-tailed hawk. The bird swiveled her hooked beak toward the voice, her proud head tilted slightly. Then with the same burst of speed, Tammy started down the beach once more, with Ariel airborne at her side.

Claire's steady gray eyes followed the jubilant

course of the bird and her mistress. There was a certain majesty in the sight of the two of them—the wild creature and her companion—both defying Ariel's blindness, to soar again. All the birds in the refuge were adapting to flightless wings or sightless eyes or some other affliction. Frazer and Kurt and Tammy treated the creatures with deserved respect—for being survivors. Some part of that caring touched Claire in a way that made her want to help. It would be a way to give back to nature a little time, a little kindness.

There would be other advantages, Claire admitted inwardly. She would get to see Dylan Jamison in the surroundings that were a part of him. Apparently, a very high-priority part. If she wanted to understand the man in a setting he had created, she had an excellent opportunity right here. As Claire watched the hawk soar, she wanted to be a part of this place, too.

"Beautiful creature, isn't she?" Dylan's voice caught her by surprise. Claire turned just as he strode up beside her.

"The bird or the lady?" Claire smiled as her gaze returned to Tammy and Ariel, but every part of her was anxiously awaiting his reply.

"Good point. Both, I guess." He lifted one hand to shield his eyes from the sun and watched the run continue. "Tammy has a gift for this. She's quite remarkable." There was affection in his voice, but no hint of anything that suggested a more intimate relationship.

"Yes, she is. She handles that hawk wonderfully. Ariel is remarkable, too," Claire added. "How did she lose her sight?"

"You've heard of those harmless pellet guns that

kids get...?'' Dylan's sea-blue eyes took on an icy chill as he explained. "Well, they aren't toys and they aren't harmless. This was a right-after-Christmas present that happened about four years ago. Some boys went hunting way out in the woods and apparently shot at anything that moved—including Ariel. We got the pellets out of her, but the optic nerves were permanently damaged. She couldn't exist in the wild like this, so we keep her."

"She's a gorgeous creature," Claire told him. "She seems very confident with Tammy."

"They hit it off right from the beginning. Tammy talked to her all through the surgery. When Ariel came out of the anesthetic, she zeroed in on Tammy's voice—instant bonding. When Tammy calls her, she knows where home is." Far down the beach, the bird and her companion turned back toward the refuge.

"You've been at this five years?" Claire gave him an opening, hoping he would talk about himself.

"I've been taking care of critters ever since I was a kid," Dylan replied. "The refuge is the first organized effort. About five and a half years ago, I picked up an egret with a broken wing. It had crashed into the office building where I was working—plate glass and hard as cement. A veterinarian friend of mine helped pin the wing back together. Then there were a couple of other birds. Those times, I helped. Once I got the hang of it, I eventually became adept enough to put a couple of gulls back in shape. By then I knew I had found my place in the scheme of things. The vet gave me books to study and all the on-the-job training I could stand. I started reading everything I could get my hands on and writing off to state and federal agencies for information and authorization to work with wild birds. Then word began to get around. The cages in my side yard got bigger.''

"The refuge is your own yard? You live in the house here?'' She turned to look at him.

"Technically I'm still here, but not for long. As you can see, I'm being crowded out,'' Dylan said as he smiled down at her. "The house used to belong to my folks, but I inherited it a few years ago. Now we need more room for our work and I need a place of my own again. I started building the beach house you saw. I almost live there. That is my home, or will be.'' There was a remoteness in his expression as he spoke to her. "When I want some privacy, I go there. It is pretty bleak, I have to admit, but it's coming along.''

"It was pretty barren.'' Claire looked away as she recalled the misgivings she'd had as she moved through that unfinished beach house, wishing for some touch of warmth, something to reassure her of Dylan's presence.

"That's why you didn't leave your number? Something about the house upset you...?'' He guessed very close to the truth.

"No, it wasn't just the house. It was the emptiness. It was a lot of things.'' All the words she wished she could say to him, feelings she had, just wouldn't come. If she were to put them to music, the melody would have been a melancholy one. "I don't like notes. I didn't feel comfortable about any of it.''

"Maybe I should have awakened you. There were a few things that I would have liked to say to you,

Claire." He hesitated, and Claire glanced at him uneasily. "But there wasn't time. The trouble with the laughing gulls' nests started then. I didn't want to drag you out of bed just because I had a call. You looked so peaceful...."

Before he could finish, the whir of wings and the steady thud of Tammy's footsteps interrupted them. Flushed and glowing, Tammy stopped a few feet from them while Ariel sailed down onto her upraised arm. "Good girl," Tammy praised the bird as she joined them.

"Quite a workout," Dylan remarked, stepping close enough for Tammy to prop her hand on his shoulder. Now he supported most of Ariel's weight, even though the hawk still rode on Tammy's glove. "Let's get you both a place to perch," he joked as they started back over the sand dunes toward the refuge. His glance at Claire indicated their conversation had only been postponed—not concluded. There was more to come.

Claire fell into step beside them, relieved that Dylan had broken off before he said too much about how she looked sleeping in his bed. She was embarrassed enough about drinking too much wine and making love in a haze. But even if the details were blurry, parts of the experience had been strangely reassuring. She had rediscovered her sensuality. However impetuous she had been and however vague the images were in retrospect, she had ventured again into very intimate territory. In his arms, the old nightmare had not pursued her. There had been something liberating about that night.

Something she didn't want translated into words. Not yet.

For a while, the only sounds were of footsteps on sand and Tammy's rapid breathing. "Here they come," Dylan said as he watched the gliding path of two pelicans descending into the refuge. Airborne, the broad-winged creatures were graceful and elegant. On land, they turned into feathered comedians, waddling awkwardly and waiting for handouts. Several more pelicans followed, queuing up along the screen pen coverings. Then a flutter of gray and white announced the arrival of sea gulls. "It must be a couple of minutes to four." Dylan laughed, glancing at his watch. "Feeding time. Four. On the button."

"I'm the one who's off schedule. I'd better put Ariel back and get the food doled out." Tammy hurried ahead of them.

"Do you have some time? Do you want to help?" Dylan looked at Claire hopefully.

"I'm not sure." Claire hesitated. "I don't want to hurt your feelings, but I'm not sure how I feel about any of this."

"I assume you're talking about more than the prospect of handing out a few fish?" He looked at her solemnly. "The let's-not-get-too-involved syndrome?"

"I'm afraid so." She managed a weak smile.

"Don't worry about hurting my feelings. I've survived so far. I've even accepted the fact that you didn't expect me to be here," he conceded. "So let's get back on track. You came with Frazer to see the refuge. He says you have a nice touch with the bird he found. If my being here causes you to go away, he'll shoot me. He thinks you're a natural. A real animal lover.'' His calm voice began to soothe her.

''I was more uneasy than I let him know,'' Claire admitted.

''He probably suspected that.'' Dylan looked at her evenly. ''What impressed him is that you didn't let your uneasiness interfere with the care of the bird. That takes a special quality. And that is what brought you here. I don't want anything that goes on between you and me to scare you off from the refuge,'' he stressed. ''And I don't want you to miss out on something that may be right for you. Let's separate the issues.''

''I didn't think that was possible,'' Claire said quietly.

''For castlebuilders, there are lots of possibilities,'' he assured her. ''You're a beach person. These birds and this place are just another part of that world.'' He could tell by the gleam in her eyes that she was tempted. All he needed was a commitment, just a small one, to get her back again. The birds would do the rest. ''Try it for a few afternoons. Then you'll know if you want to keep it up. We'll take as much or as little as you have to give.'' His keen gaze shifted to the snowy egret perched in a tall pine overlooking the refuge.

''As for me, I admit I was out of line for bellowing at you. I'm not generally so foul tempered. It's a part of me that slips out occasionally.'' He watched her carefully as he spoke. ''I won't let it happen again with you. We can use the refuge as a free zone, where we can get a different perspective on each other. We'll have a strictly professional relationship here. I'm like the birds," he told her softly, meeting her gray gaze. "I'll take as much or as little as you have to give. We can start with a clean slate."

Claire caught the trace of melancholy in his voice. Dylan's attitude seemed strangely distant, considering how intimate they had already been. He spoke as if that night had never happened, he was willing to dismiss it so casually. Wiping the slate clean. Unlike him, Claire didn't find it that easy to forget and begin again. Apparently the magic in that night hadn't communicated enough. They had been lovers, but they were strangers still.

"There may be no point in beginning again." Claire could feel the walls of self-protection closing in. The more she looked into his sea-blue eyes, the more cautious she became. They were eyes she could lose herself in—and she was afraid to lose control again.

"I'll take that risk. Now how about you. Will you take a chance—with any of us—the birds or me?" He was still smiling, but his eyes were very solemn.

"I'll give the birds a definite yes. I'd like to come here again. I like this place." Over Dylan's shoulders, Claire saw Tammy and Kurt wheeling a dolly loaded with buckets along the path of the refuge. At each pen door, they stopped and unloaded one covered bucket. "I don't know what to say to you, though." She barely whispered the words. "I'm just not sure that I want to get that close to anybody again. Physically or emotionally..." she added uneasily.

He reached out and rested one hand on the gate, as if he were deliberately restraining himself from touching her. "I don't intend to crowd you. I don't take advantage of anyone, regardless of their condition," he added enigmatically. "As far as the refuge work goes, I feel like Frazer—I think you're a natural."

"I suppose that all depends on how the birds and I like one another," Claire said, trying to lighten the mood. Birds were a safe subject for both of them. "Tammy said they have strong likes and dislikes."

"Oh, they'll like you. They have instant rapport with castlebuilders," he assured her. "They may look goofy, but birds are excellent character judges. The question is, will you like them up close, with all their bad habits and peculiarities showing?"

Claire was already asking herself the same question about Dylan. Getting to know the real man might make him seem less a sea god and more human. Claire had cherished the image of the sea god. But an illusion couldn't hold her in his arms. "I liked the pelican Frazer found, and his friends back at the jetty were charming enough. I like Ariel. That's a start."

Dylan's smile broadened carefully to indicate that he understood the underlying message of the truce. "A start..." he agreed. She had conceded as much as she could at this point. He would have to proceed with caution, keeping the conversation on neutral ground. "Speaking of starting, it's time to feed these guys. Come on and toss the pelicans a few fish. They're a bit frantic now, but when they have a full belly and settle back, relaxed and content, you'll find out what they're really like.'' He led her toward the first bucket. "I bet they'll remind you of some of your dinner-cruise audiences." He smiled slightly, then reached for the lid. "They often act rambunctious until the food is served.''

"I'm supposed to go in the pen with all of them?" Claire stopped in her tracks. Fluttering and wobbling, the birds converged on the gate where she would enter. It had been one thing feeding the large pelicans on an open beach, but being closed in on all sides and overhead made the situation claustrophobic. Dylan didn't give her time to back out, though.

"Walk right in and let them have it." Dylan handed her a slick, silvery fish that fitted her palm nicely. "They can't applaud, but they will be very receptive," he teased. Then smoothly he became the professional instructing the novice. "Toss the fish one at a time, headfirst, so they go down easy. Backward, the scales and fins stick out and the poor birds have to flip them forward, then turn them around. That slows down the eating process." His voice was calm and authoritative, and he made feeding them sound so sensible and easy. Whatever apprehensions Claire had about facing forty hungry pelicans faded. "Feed the pelicans until they're satisfied—or until they start dropping the fish. If they're too lazy to try to catch them in the air, then they've had enough. Then go on to the next cage, give these guys a chance to switch places with the ones on the nests and come back in five minutes to feed the next shift."

"They eat in shifts?" Claire asked.

"The ones on the nests won't leave until their mate takes their place," Dylan informed her. "They know the routine, and they'll break you in."

"Dylan...." The call came from the office area. Another woman, this one, a striking, large-framed woman with salt-and-pepper hair who appeared to be in her fifties, stepped around the corner of the building, looking for him. "Someone is on the phone calling from a zoo in Texas. They're interested in taking some of the birds," she informed him in a voice deep and resonant.

"You take it from here," Dylan said quickly as he left Claire standing with the fish in her hand and loped off toward the office.

"I guess it's you and me, guys...." Claire turned to face the assembled group of pelicans. "Headfirst," she reminded herself as she stuck both hands into the bucket and began tossing silvery, edible missiles into the open beaks. Even with the strong fishy smell and the scales covering her hands she felt wonderful.

Fifteen fish later, she began to distinguish one hungry bird from the next. Some had more white feathers on their head than yellow. Some had necks with white stripes in the brown. Some looked arrogant, others timid. A few greedy ones outmaneuvered the others, until Claire caught on to their strategy. Then the shy one with the missing foot got his meal special delivery—handed right to him by the lady with the sunshine hair. And the one with the twisted upper bill moved closer to her. Grotesque as he was, he sensed that the lady wouldn't leave him out.

"Quit being so pushy." Claire nudged aside one

huge bird whose head reached nearly to her waist. "Take your turn like the other guys." Then she turned back to old One Foot, and felt as if she'd been at this for ages.

Two days later, Pete Parnell took one look at Claire, limping off the elevator at the Pier, and groaned. "What the heck happened to you?"

"I had an unfortunate encounter with a pail of fish. I dropped it on my foot." She had concluded her first afternoon as a volunteer at the refuge by mistaking a full bucket for an empty one. When it rolled off the dolly and onto her foot, the error became painfully apparent. To her relief, no bones were broken and no one was around to witness her discomfort. Dylan had been off at meetings the entire day, and Tammy had taken two healthy but crippled roseate spoonbills to the airport to fly them off to a botanical garden in Palm Beach. The two other employees, Josie and Kurt, were busy inside the building. Claire rinsed and stowed the buckets, then hobbled off to her car without stopping in the office to say goodbye.

So she hadn't made a dramatic exit. No one had commended her on a job well done. But Claire couldn't stop smiling in spite of her throbbing foot. If it hadn't been for her, mealtime for the birds would have been very late. She had filled in like an old hand, and the smelly job of distributing the fish had been finished on schedule.

"I thought this refuge was for fixing injuries, not causing them," Pete muttered as he looked down at her sandaled foot. "Did you go to work like that?"

Two of her toes were puffy and turning a purplish pink.

"I have a sit-down job," Claire reminded him. "My foot didn't bother me on the *Bay-Belle*. Getting over here took a little longer than usual..." she admitted. "But the pain is worth it. I had a great afternoon." Her gray eyes sparkled with enthusiasm. "I got to feed everyone, even the hawks and vultures. Tammy makes them balls of raw meat...."

"Could you hold off on the gory details until we finish here and get something to eat ourselves—preferably cooked? I have a feeling that what you were about to go into would spoil late-night steak and eggs for me." Pete Parnell grimaced as he made his request. "I'm more interested in hearing you sing than hearing you recite the seabird menu."

"You'll have to come out to see the place..." Claire insisted. Then, noticing the slightly desperate look from Bizz at the keyboard, she gritted her teeth and proceeded toward the stage, keeping her limp as imperceptible as she could.

"How's Mother Nature tonight?" Robby said, bobbing up into position at the drums. Like his brother, Pete, Robby was vaguely bewildered by Claire's volunteering to help out at the bird refuge, but he found some humor in the earnest way she had assumed her responsibilities to the birds.

"If you're referring to me, I'm not amused," Claire responded. "I'm not Mother Nature. I'm just one of her helpers."

"How about knocking off the chatter and giving Claire a shot at the microphone," Pete said, interrupting the exchange. "I missed dinner tonight and I'm starving. She sings, we finish, we eat. Then we talk." His broad smile was less severe than his rapid-fire orders suggested.

Claire opened the last set with "Heartbreaker," and people got up to dance. Each time she sang it got easier, but there wasn't a moment that Claire wasn't fully aware she wasn't onstage alone. Like the queen's guard, the band protected her, surrounding her with their music, backing up her voice with theirs.

Afterward, in a small all-night diner, with Pete safely through his course of steak and eggs and Robby on his second bowl of chili, Claire told her brothers about her day with the birds. When she finally got around to the dreaded details, such as putting lumps of raw meat and small whole chickens into the birds-of-prey cage, Pete was on his second cup of coffee and ready for anything.

"What are they doing with owls and vultures and hawks out there with all the sea gulls and pelicans?" Robby wanted to know.

"Birds are birds. When one is hurt, they fix him," she explained. "Most of these birds are victims of some man-made problem—from hitting power lines and glass buildings to outright malicious acts such as gunshots and poisonings. Some of the stuff people have done to the birds is really sick. Some is just careless."

"Spare me the gruesome parts. I've heard enough about birds." Pete looked at her evenly. "How about tellin' us about the Birdman." It had been almost a week since Claire had left the lounge with Dylan and not returned to her apartment until the next morning. Pete was still bristling with big-brotherly concern.

"Dylan wasn't even there today. He had appointments away from the refuge. He was meeting with the Fish and Wildlife agents to work out a solution between nesting gulls and the construction company." Her bright smile showed no sign of having been disappointed by his absence, but it had bothered her. Tammy had said that as the refuge had grown, Dylan had been increasingly swamped with meetings and paperwork. The rescuer of hurt critters did double-duty as administrator. More of the routine work with the animals had to be delegated to the others. Claire understood perfectly, but that didn't get rid of the gnawing sensation that something wasn't quite right.

"I like that," Robby huffed. "The volunteer does the dirty work while the boss sits in air-conditioned meetings. I'd think he'd let you start in real easy so you don't get turned off."

"They don't have the luxury of starting someone off 'easy.' They use the old sink-or-swim technique. One of the regular workers tells you what to do—once—and then leaves you. Frankly, I like the dirty work," Claire answered enthusiastically. "I like working in the cages without anyone having to help me. It's kind of like you guys asking me to step in for a few songs..." she added with a knowing smile. "If you survive the shock, you're hooked."

Instantly she remembered that was precisely what Dylan had said that night at the Pier. He was "hooked." But now he had extricated himself quite neatly. He had left the choice to her, and she had chosen not to be too involved. Suddenly his missing every hour of her first scheduled day on the job seemed more than coincidental.

"Well, I've got another hook for you to grapple with," Pete informed her. "There's a job opening up out at the beach. The new management at the Mariner Club wants to try us out for one night the first weekend in May. Original stuff along with some of everything else—from top forty to Broadway tunes. If we manage to land a steady gig, we'll need a female singer. Full-time."

"That means a lot of new music." She considered the implications carefully. "If you're looking at me, I've already got a job, and I'm not very strong as a singer. It's a very big club, and I'm just not up to that kind of pressure."

"I bet you thought the same thing before you took the raw meat into the hawks," Robby said dryly. "Still, you did it for the birds."

But when Claire caught Pete's sheepish expression, her smile faded. "I have a feeling there's something else you need to mention. What have you done?" She eyed him suspiciously.

"I guess I opted for the sink-or-swim technique myself," Pete confessed. "The birds aren't the only ones out on a limb. I said we had a great female lead singer who also writes some of her own music. Without you, we're just another band with a bunch of hairy guys."

"Pete, you really don't know what you're asking," Claire said, trying to reason with him. Singing lead, she would have to carry the show in a room far larger than any she'd performed in before. She'd have to come up with some flashy solos. Part of the time she'd be out there in front—on her own. That was something Wes said she could never do.

"I'm asking you to go for the money. The big places pay a lot more, and the exposure is great publicity. Some pretty influential folks stop at the Mariner. Word gets around. This kind of job puts you in a position to be noticed, and that could mean records and videos."

"It's worth a shot, Claire," Robby insisted. "All you have to give up is your current job, your sanity and about twenty hours a day for the next two weeks to get an act together. It would help if you could come up with a couple of songs, too." As outrageous as the list sounded, the summary was close to the truth. Now was the time to get serious.

"You two are crazy." Claire looked from one brother to the next.

"Hopefully our kind of insanity runs in the family. Even a short hitch with a big club like the Mariner will get you on your feet financially. Maybe even more than that. The timing is right. You've got the talent. We've got our foot in the door." Pete shook his head. "A chance like this is a rare thing. Surely you can devote two weeks to something more challenging than shoveling bird droppings or hanging around with some beach bum who fools around with birds."

Claire sighed longingly for the simplicity of her afternoon at the refuge. "Right now, the bird droppings and the beach bum are sounding better and better."

"So's your voice," Pete countered very seriously. "The more you work with us, the better you sound—stronger and more controlled. Two more weeks and you could take on a big room in top form. We all could. Let's go for it. The worst that could happen is we work our buns off and miss. But we'll improve our overall performance in the process. Wouldn't you like to find out how good we can be?"

"I'm not consumed by curiosity," Claire muttered dryly. But she was wondering if she could do it, if she could perform under those conditions. Then she caught the disappointment in Pete's expression. He had visualized something spectacular for them. Something he believed was possible. If only she'd try.

"I'm not going to quit my job on the *Bay-Belle*," Claire insisted. The job provided the stability she needed. But the fact that she was showing some interest in Pete's deal brought a smile from both brothers. "I can't risk everything for a one night tryout. I will simply ask for the night off and get someone to sit in for me. And I'm not going to give up my time at the refuge. I promised them two afternoons a week. I won't go back on my promise. But if you can schedule rehearsals around my commitments, I'll work with you."

"All right." Robby cheered. At this hour, his outburst produced dubious looks from the other diner customers, sitting glumly clasping their cups of coffee.

"I just hope the birds don't mind my singing while I pitch them their dinner." Claire could imagine the pale-eyed pelicans turning from side to side to stare at her. But she was thinking of another pair of sea-blue eyes. She remembered what Dylan had said—one day her songs would take her away. And he would let her go. Instead there was a chance her songs would bring them closer. The Mariner was only minutes away from the refuge. His world and hers would not be miles apart. Dylan would have to pass by every night if he was heading for his beach house. And in time she might call to him again with a siren song.

IT WAS WELL AFTER MIDNIGHT when Dylan climbed the stairs of the beach house. Driving back from town, he'd tugged open the neck and unbuttoned the front of his pale-lavender shirt. Now he tossed the gray suit coat and striped tie on the back of a chair, then moved into the dark living room. All day long he'd been the epitome of "the successful professional," meeting with the city council, several wildlife agents, attending a businessmen's luncheon and studying maps of the bay area, looking for undeveloped land to purchase so he could expand the refuge. Having played the role all day had reminded him of another time, a time when it had seemed very important to look businesslike, professional—to succeed.

To a substantial degree, he had done that. But the world he found himself in had been tense and impersonal and computerized. And once he'd mastered the job, he felt the walls closing in. His environment lacked something essential that he discovered quite by accident when a bird bumped into a window. And there were those who said he was a fool for giving up a brilliant career. Now Dylan pulled open the doors and let the sea air blow in, breathing deeply of the fresh breezes. Opening the refrigerator door, he stood silhouetted in the rectangle of bright light, staring at the partially empty bottle of wine. And the hectic pace of the day began to slip away.

Quite by accident.... That was how he'd met her. Building castles in the sand. And he had discovered something else essential that was missing from his life. Her injuries were far more complex than a broken wing that could be mended with a metal pin. She was vulnerable, talented and very frustrating. She didn't know what she wanted. She wasn't ready to get involved, so she said. But a part of him insisted he'd be a fool if he gave up.

Holding his glass of wine, he stared out over the inky water. A few night fliers cut across the sky, skimming low over the water in search of food. Barely touching the water, they would scoop up what they could and move on, hardly rippling the surface. Then somewhere farther on they would dive again. Dylan watched them as he had so many nights before, finding something tranquil and reassuring in their nightly ritual. Creatures of the sky. Of the sea. Touching. Taking only what they need. Leaving again. She was like that. Barely touching down. And he didn't know what she needed, or when she would leave him. But she'd already made ripples in his mind, ones that kept bringing back images of her. Images such as eyes wide with inexpressible anguish.

Taking a long slow sip of the wine, Dylan knew that he couldn't stay away from her. He'd done all right today, booking himself up for hours of conferences while the others had the refuge to themselves. Claire was there. Hopefully making discoveries of her own, touching, caring, taking for herself what she needed to ease the pain inside. But he had to see her, to watch her mend and grow strong, knowing that the day would come when she would take to the sky. And he would have to let her go, regardless of the ripples.

CHAPTER FIVE

"I SEE YOUR BIRDMAN made the Sunday paper," Pete said as he passed the Outdoors supplement to Claire. "You didn't tell me that the guy had money."

Claire looked at him quizzically. Ensconced with the newspaper and a glass of orange juice in a huge ivory macrame hammock strung between the two large oak trees in his backyard, Pete was enjoying his day off and the warm weather. He was also enjoying teasing his sister.

Claire glanced at the earnest face staring up at her from the cover page. "Public Defender—for the birds," the caption read. The story documented Dylan's past week of legal maneuverings with the wildlife authorities, the developer and the construction company in the crusade to save the laughing-gull nests from further devastation. Sinking down into a lawn chair, Claire scanned the pictures of the construction site and started to read the small print.

"Former systems analyst and computer whiz kid..." the description of Dylan began. "Jamison stepped out of the high-tech world of computer programming into the modest surroundings of the Gulf Coast Seabird Refuge, but the man is not your amateur bird-watcher." The article stated that in his years as a top-rated systems analyst, Dylan had developed several innovative software packages for computerizing hospital and medical-center records. The revenues from those would continue to pour in for years. In essence, at twenty-nine, Jamison had retired a wealthy man. For the next five years he had been turning his expertise to programs of another kind—protective ones to preserve wildlife, particularly threatened or endangered species.

"He sounds like a cross between J. Paul Getty and St. Francis of Assisi," Pete remarked with a low chuckle.

"He does, doesn't he," Claire murmured without looking up from the columns of print. She was desperately trying to reconcile what she knew of the man she'd met with the person described in the paper. This previous career of Dylan's intrigued her. He had only mentioned once in passing that an egret had crashed into the building where he was working, but at the time Claire had never given it a second thought. She had viewed him only in the context of the refuge, not high-tech business.

Whoever wrote the article obviously supported Dylan's efforts to make a sanctuary and hospital for injured birds. There was even a clear pitch for funds in the explanation that the refuge was a people project, not a government-funded one. Volunteers, private contributions and community support would make or break the refuge. Although Jamison had started the facility by donating his own premises and much time and money, he would not sustain the operation on his own.

Being stewards to nature's fragile gifts is everyone's responsibility. Supporting the refuge is just one way. We all can do something to protect our environment, whether we pick up litter on a beach or put up a bird feeder. Possibilities are unlimited and information is available. We'll be glad to get anyone started. Once an individual gets involved in protecting any aspect of our natural surroundings, the satisfaction is priceless.

That was Dylan's official comment.

That's true in my case, Claire reflected silently. He had let her into his refuge and had let the magic work upon her. And what she was able to contribute to the refuge gave her a sense of accomplishment that nothing else had.

The writer then told about the educational efforts of the refuge—from tours and slide shows for school children to programs for civic organizations and seminars in rehabilitation and rescue techniques, given monthly on the refuge grounds. Then it leapt into a projection for the future, describing Jamison's dream of establishing a larger facility, an educational and research-oriented zoological park in the area, where ill or injured land and sea creatures could be treated and returned to nature.

"We have been successful with captive breeding of several endangered or threatened species," Dylan was quoted as saying again. "We can establish that type of program for other species, as well, and make our information available internationally." That was the link with his past. According to the article, Dylan intended using his expertise with computer programming to document the research and rehabilitation techniques and make those findings instantly accessible through a computer network. Now the countless file cards documenting treatments, breeding and releases took on a new significance. For a man who believed in possibilities, the concept was exhilarating. And whoever wanted to make the dream a reality could help—with time or money or both.

"I'm impressed," Claire said as she finished the last paragraph. She scanned the page, noting the name of the writer. Gallagher. The guy was good.

"If I were you, I wouldn't let this Birdman out of my sight. A rich beach bum who fools around with birds is a whole new story." Pete studied Claire's face, looking for a reaction.

He got none.

"Does St. Francis have some drawbacks that the article failed to mention?" Pete persisted. "What is going on between you two?"

"Nothing at all lately," Claire replied honestly. "We made a pact of noninvolvement and he's sticking to it." Silently she wished he had been around the refuge more. They would have had time to work together and talk and sort out what had happened between them. She felt like an outsider, learning all of this about him from a newspaper.

Pete's brows pulled into a frown. "If you change your mind and decide to get involved, you may have to step in at the end of a long waiting line," he warned her. "This article will shake loose some admirers who may have other ideas. Dylan sounds like a real prize."

"This isn't a contest," Claire replied more philosophically than she actually felt. "This article can't change the way I feel about him or myself."

But the article had changed everything. He was no longer just a regular person with a streak of dedication, making a small contribution to conservation. He was bigger than life—handsome, educated, brilliant— with a vision far beyond the seashore refuge. He was successful and had chosen to pursue a dream. Money had made the difference.

"Right. It isn't a contest." Pete dropped the subject. "How do you feel about doing a little work? I have some lyrics I want you to hear. I've got the first few bars. All I need is the rest of the song and a bridge that's a grabber. Maybe we can put in some hours and get it far enough along to use for the performance."

"Let me hear what you've got." Claire put aside the paper with a certain sense of regret. Things had been simpler when her brothers disapproved of the beach-bum birdman and had wanted to keep her away from him. The man in the article—wealthy, clever, and dedicated—had now become highly acceptable, eligible and publically very visible. Dylan had his vision, and there was no reason why the vision should include Claire.

"Music, words, fame, fortune..." Pete said, trying to tease her out of her solemn silence. "Let's go work on a song."

"Let's do that," she agreed. What Claire wanted was something familiar to fill her mind with, something to make her feel good about herself—and music could do precisely that.

"HERE COMES ANOTHER ONE." Tammy Todd pointed the hose at the heavy plastic pool in the center of the pelican pen and gave it a shot of clean water. "Another ecology-minded female coming to check out the highly eligible Dylan Jamison."

With her shirt sleeves rolled up to the elbows, Claire scrubbed away the grime with a heavy brush. Only fleetingly did she look up at the red-haired woman coming into the refuge compound. Her high heels and peach dress made it obvious that she had not anticipated the terrain. Even the entry pathways of shell and sand made her step gingerly toward the main building. "A real outdoorsy type if there ever was one," Tammy whispered sarcastically.

Claire looked up again. The young woman was stunning, but her long fingernails and picture-perfect auburn hair wouldn't last long around the refuge. Pete had said the article would bring out the women, and he was right.

"Would you tell me where I can find Dylan Jamison?" The lovely redhead balanced on her toes as she stopped by the cage where Tammy and Claire were scrubbing the bird pools. She looked up apprehensively into the overhanging branches, checking for birds before stepping nearer. The tight, polite smile on her face matched the tight, polite look in her eyes.

"He should be in the office—second door to the left once you round the building," Tammy replied civilly. But from the mischief in her eyes, Claire could guess what her companion was thinking. Just turning the pool slightly, then hitting it with another blast from the hose would send a spray ricocheting over the lady in peach.

"Thank you." The clipped, precise reply was more automatic than sincere.

"Why do I feel grungier than usual?" Tammy muttered as the crunch of heels marked the departure of the woman. "I bet those hands have never held a dead herring."

"You and I are just lucky." Claire laughed, but her gray eyes followed the attractive woman.

"Sure we are...." Tammy aimed the hose dangerously close to Claire. "But every once in a while, I'd like to try being gorgeous instead of so darned lucky. The best I was ever called was 'wholesome' and occasionally 'cute.' But once I hit twenty-two, 'cute' lost its appeal. That woman was never cute."

"But maybe she hasn't much of a personality..." Claire said without any real conviction.

"What would she need with a personality?" and Tammy grinned good-naturedly. "That would border on overkill. Surely something is left to the laborers."

"Right now the only thing left is another cage with a dirty splash pool," Claire reminded her, and with an expert flip, she emptied the dirty water onto the ground and set the pool down, ready to be refilled. While the water gurgled into the pool, Claire stood and glanced toward the office again. Self-consciously touching her hair, she wondered what the lady in peach had to say to Dylan Jamison.

"We're from Channel Six." This time when Claire and Tammy looked up from their scrubbing they stared into the lens of a video camera. The camera was poised on the shoulder of a tall young man with deep-set eyes and dramatic cheekbones.

"All we need is a little information." The man who did the talking was slightly older than the cameraman and impeccably groomed. He was obviously the one who intended to be in front of the camera. "Dylan said we could shoot some footage for a spot we're doing on the refuge expansion. He suggested we talk to Tammy. Are either of you Tammy?"

"I am if that camera isn't running," Tammy said as she stood and brushed a strand of hair from across her forehead. "If it is running, she's Tammy." She pointed a finger at Claire.

"I'm Phil Stockman, and the camera is not running," the older man said in his best announcer's voice. "Dylan said you can point out the real tear-jerkers, and he and I can do the voice-over later."

"'Tearjerkers'?" Tammy stared at him. Dylan wouldn't say that.

"You know, the heavy-duty cases. The birds that have sentimental appeal. Endangered species, and all that. I want a story that gets people talking, and to do that you gotta have heart." His perfectly aligned smile widened and the silver temples of his flawlessly trimmed hair glistened in the sunlight. Claire's and Tammy's glances met as both wondered if this slick showman had any heart at all. Behind the announcer, the cameraman stood in silence, scanning the compound with obsidian eyes.

But with a blend of self-discipline and detached poise, Tammy nodded understandingly. "I think I know what you're after."

For half an hour, Claire continued scrubbing and sweeping the pens alone, until another volunteer, a high-school student, came to pitch in. Gradually Claire was getting to know more and more of the other volunteers. "Just call me 'Robinson,'" the tall dark-skinned youngster said. And within a minute, they were working side by side, filling the buckets with fish for the afternoon feeding.

"Do you want to be on TV?" Tammy came over to Robinson. "These guys are shooting a heartrending spot for the news show on Channel Six. The tall one with the plastic face thinks it might be effective to have a black, all-star athlete in the picture." She didn't disguise Stockman's intent.

"That narrows things down considerably. What do you think?" Robinson stretched to his full height and looked down at her. "Think it will do some good?" His dark, intelligent eyes shifted from her to the cameraman near Ariel's cage.

"Every bit helps." Tammy shrugged. "As Dylan says, we're here to help the birds. Every move we make publicly can add a pound of fish or a new incubator to the budget. I say go for it. Let's see the charm."

"Okay." Robinson agreed. "This one is for Tex." He straightened his shoulders resolutely and stuck a genial smile on his face.

"Who is 'Tex'?" Claire asked abruptly, disturbed by the exchange. This do-it-for-the-money attitude was a part of Dylan's philosophy that sounded calculated and mercenary, a part that had been discreetly overlooked in the very flattering newspaper article.

"Tex is a pelican that Robinson found six months ago when he was walking on the beach to build up his leg muscles. Robinson's leg muscles," Tammy said, clarifying whose legs needed the therapy. "He sprained his knee in preseason basketball practice and walking on sand helps. Anyway, he found Tex flopping around with a broken wing and brought him here. Tex has mended and flown the coop, but we still have Robinson. He's used to this kind of public-relations work."

"This happens often? People just drop in and start filming or interviewing?" Claire quizzed her friend. Suddenly she remembered when they'd first met. When Tammy had asked Claire if she was a reporter.

"The more often they do a story on the refuge, the better for us. We get used to having them around. We do our best to give them what they want, but we don't have to like them all." She tilted her head meaningfully toward the pretentious Phil Stockman, who had spoken so coldly about "tearjerkers." "What Dylan insists we do is get out there and educate the people. Generally some significant good comes out of any article or feature."

"I suppose that is important," Claire conceded reluctantly.

"The public has a short memory," Tammy added. "One article may prompt a flurry of action. Like the Sunday feature," she explained knowledgeably. "Then amnesia sets in. But the bills for the fish still have to be paid. These reporters keep us in the public eye. Some of them do it more graciously than others." Her steady dark eyes radiated a wisdom that took

Claire by surprise. Tammy knew press relations as thoroughly as she knew pelicans.

"I'm not sure that I could handle them the way you do," Claire admitted. "I don't like people like Stockman."

"Around here we have no choice. Dylan wouldn't tolerate any rudeness that could cause a negative comment about the refuge. You never know if someone like Miss Peach-and-Flimsy might drop a donation in the coffers or turn out to be an excellent fund-raiser. Even if Stockman is making himself look good, we benefit. And if he likes the results, he'll come back." Tammy glanced at her watch, then began stacking pails of fish onto the dolly for delivery. "So you learn to grit your teeth through the not-so-nice ones and take great pleasure in the sincere folks, and you do it for the birds."

"I'll try to remember that," Claire promised.

"There is a closet behind the surgery room, where you can go and scream if things really get to you," Tammy added mischievously. "There have been times when I've closed the door and made some colorful comments."

"And Dylan?" Claire asked. "Does he go into that closet?"

"Usually he's pretty calm. Sometimes I wonder how he keeps the pressure from getting to him. We know he's had enough when he takes his fishing gear and wanders off for a day. When he comes back, he's got everything sorted out. He's a very private person. Don't let his public image fool you."

Claire followed Tammy and the dolly-load of fish in

silence, remembering the day she and Dylan had met at Frenchman's Pass. He had come there to fish. Now she wondered what troubles he had been mulling over while they'd built their sand castle.

"Smile, you're about to be on 'Candid Camera,'" Tammy whispered. "Feeding the birds always looks impressive on film." Stockman and the tall fellow with the camera were heading their way.

"But I won't," Claire said as she tried to duck behind the buckets. Tammy had already claimed that spot. Then the sound of Dylan's voice made them both get to work, bearing the buckets into the cages.

"Come on, folks." Claire began pitching the fish out to one enthusiastic group of pelicans. From the corner of her eye, she could see Dylan standing in earnest conversation with Stockman, and between the two men was the lady in peach.

Once the filming of feeding time was complete, Claire and Robinson rounded up the empty pails and returned them to the storage area. Stockman and Dylan settled on the benches by the nesting pens and began taping the voice part of the interview.

"Her name is Rebecca Stroud, and she's a real-estate agent," Tammy informed them, poking her head around the corner. "Josie says that Ms Stroud has a piece of property she wants to show Dylan as a possible site for the zoological park. I might add, she's the fifth real-estate agent to call in since the article, but she's the only one who showed up in person. Apparently Dylan is interested in seeing what she has to offer."

Robinson was the only one to find the last comment amusing.

"I have to clean up and get to work." Claire hurriedly washed her hands, wishing to be on her way. Still grimy, with her hair smelling distinctly like fish, she had no intention of lingering where the contrast between her and Rebecca Stroud would be more apparent. She had told Pete that this was no contest and Dylan was not a prize to be vied over. But she felt a sense of possessiveness that sheer logic couldn't overcome. In the darkness of a magical night she had formed a bond with him. Still, she smiled politely, hiding the mixed feelings that seeing him with that woman stirred. Claire had commitments elsewhere. What Dylan and Rebecca had on their agenda was beyond her control. Besides, she was the one who had insisted it be that way.

WHEN CLAIRE WAS SUMMONED to the telephone in Pete's kitchen the next morning, she hoped to hear Dylan's voice. But it was Josie, the office manager, who had called to enlist her aid.

"I know this is not your day as a volunteer," Josie apologized. "But we had a call for a pickup down at the Bayfront. Someone spotted an injured egret by the Dali museum. They have the bird cornered, but no one can leave the museum to drive her all the way out here. Do you think you could help?" From the pained silence on the other end of the line, Claire could imagine Josie's crow's-feet crinkling deeper as she grimaced.

For the past hour Pete and Claire had been laboring over the phrasing of the song they were collaborating on, and their efforts had reached an impasse. "I'll make a quick run out there," Claire responded. She and Pete could definitely use a break. With a little encouragement, she knew she could persuade him to go along. "Call and tell them I'm on my way," Claire suggested. "Is there anything special I need to do?"

"Wrap the bird in a blanket so she can't thrash around and hurt herself," Josie stipulated. "Just talk to her, honey. You'll do fine." Josie's deep voice had a reassuring sound. If she thought Claire could handle the egret, then Claire knew she could.

"How would you like to assist in a rescue mission?" It took a moment for the question to penetrate Pete's consciousness. He sat with his guitar on his knee, playing and replaying the same few bars, squeaking out unintelligible syllables in Claire's key.

Flapping her elbows, Claire moved closer. "Bird hurt. Take to refuge." She bent low, using sign language to emphasize her words. "You come."

"You think the Birdman will be there?" Pete brightened at the thought. "I'd really like to meet this guy."

"No one mentioned if Dylan is there or not. But I have an egret to pick up and deliver. Take your chances. You'll see the refuge. We just need an old blanket," she told him.

"You're the expert," Pete replied with a touching show of brotherly pride. "I'll drive."

Forty minutes later, Sara, as they'd named the elegant egret during the drive, had been injected with cortisone and tetracycline, fed liquid food and was ensconced in a tall fiberglass holding cage. Her left leg had been shattered by a blow that Kurt guessed was from a thrown rock. Since the egret was a wading bird, they wanted to save the leg. With splint and medication, the beautiful bird had a fighting chance. Peering out the metallic grid front, Sara lolled her head to the side wearily as Claire looked back at her, softly singing the tune that had finally fallen together during the trip. Outside, Pete and a bearded volunteer named Chuck, a carpenter who had helped build the frameworks and wood coverings for many of the smaller cages, were discussing the occupants of the various pens.

"Nice tune, but I don't think she'll be able to duplicate it in the wild." Dylan's voice startled Claire from her solitary vigil with Sara. "She's a wild bird and she'll be mended sooner than you think. We really don't want to do anything to take the wildness out of her." The reprimand in his voice was softened only slightly by his smile.

"I just wanted Sara to settle down. Singing seemed to work in the car." Claire didn't see any harm in singing.

"Sara...?" Dylan seemed displeased again. "I prefer that any bird who will obviously be returned to the wild have no name—just refer to it by the end numbers on its leg band. This may sound a bit cold, but we can't personalize every relationship with every patient. Using numbers helps keep the workers from becoming too attached to the birds—as well as the reverse."

"Am I doing anything right?" Claire replied testily. "I can't sing to calm her. I can't give her a name. How about the pools in the bird pens? Did I scrub them the wrong way?"

"I'm not trying to be overly critical," Dylan replied evenly. He'd been attempting to keep things strictly professional, but the scene he'd interrupted was an intimate one, filled with a tenderness that he envied and a possibility for sadness that he dreaded both for Claire and for him.

"I have been through this before with other workers," Dylan continued in his matter-of-fact delivery. "People do get attached to these creatures. If they're released or shipped off, there are emotional repercussions, a real sense of loss. The ups and downs are very rough as it is. I'm just suggesting this as a precaution that comes from years of experience. No names." His expression was guarded; the words he spoke came back at him, emphasizing the difficulty he was having keeping his own distance. "You're doing very fine work here. Your pool scrubbing is exceptional." He smiled stiffly. "I've heard only good things about you. I'm sorry if I sounded so negative." Here he was, apologizing again.

In her unassuming manner, Claire had fitted into the refuge scheme smoothly. It was Dylan who was having trouble. While part of him melted at the sight of her, another part made him react coldly. After all, he had to protect himself. This time he'd obviously overdone the chill factor.

"I'll say you're negative," Claire huffed. "Before you notice anything else to complain about, I'll be going." She cast a parting glance at Sara. "But it's too late about the name. I can't take her name back," she said firmly. "Robinson had Tex. Tammy has Ariel. I have Sara. That's just the way it is." She delivered the rebuttal with only the slightest tremor in her voice, but in spite of the bravado in her words, the look in her eyes was more hurt than angry.

"Have it your own way," Dylan shrugged as she brushed past him. He kept his hands stuffed in his pockets to keep from reaching out to stop her. He'd handled everything all wrong—again.

Out in the refuge compound, Pete was waiting and Chuck, the carpenter, was nowhere in sight. "Has the famous Birdman shown up?"

"He's inside the recovery room."

"Don't I get to meet him?" Pete sounded disappointed.

"Just don't call him by name," Claire replied sarcastically. "He might think you're forming some kind of an attachment." The words were barely out of her mouth when she realized that Dylan had come out of the room after her. He had heard everything she said. From the stormy look in his eyes, he was not amused. And she couldn't care less.

"You're Claire's brother. Nice to meet you." Dylan stepped forward and politely greeted the dark-haired eldest Parnell. "I heard your band at the Pier."

"Pete, this is Dylan," Claire said, making the introduction. "The Birdman."

"It's a pleasure." Pete returned the handshake. "Read the article in the newspaper. I sure wish you success. You have a very interesting setup here."

"Thanks for helping us out," Dylan replied. "We appreciate your helping Claire bring in the egret."

"Whatever her number is. . . ." Claire muttered.

Dylan gave her a reproachful look, but never responded to the barb.

"Actually, helping you helped us get a song straightened out," Pete informed him. "Claire and I had been working on the song for days. We picked up that hurt egret, and even with all her pain, she didn't make a sound. She just looked at us. It was downright eerie."

"I know the feeling." Dylan nodded grimly. He'd nursed many of the sad silent creatures.

"I mean, parrots squawk all the time. When Claire said we were bringing in a hurt bird, I expected shrieking all the way. But Sara...not a squeak." Pete pursed his lips to conceal how deeply he was moved, then went on about the bird and the song. "Sara just sat between us, looking pathetic. If she could only have told us what to do for her. Or who hurt her."

"You used that in a song?" Dylan asked.

"You'd have to know musicians to understand how Sara got us thinking. The song is definitely not about birds," Pete admitted. "This is a love song about how hard it is to put feelings into words. Getting things right seems easy when you're just thinkin', but when you need to say it, the words don't always come out so good." He fluttered one hand in the air, as if he knew he was rambling and wanted to get to the point.

Dylan nodded thoughtfully. He'd had problems putting his own feelings into words lately.

Pete went on, anyway. "We use music to say things, but poor Sara doesn't even have that option. Anyway, we felt the connection. Sara didn't have a song and neither did we. Claire started humming the music and words came out. Still rough, but real strong. The music kept Sara real still, but it had us both nearly cryin'," he admitted with a tight grin. "Inspiration from a bird." He bobbed his head appreciatively. "Nice timing, though. We needed to get the song finished. We'll be trying it out in a couple of weeks at the Mariner just down the beach a bit. You should come in and hear us. Bring Sara." He laughed. "We'll polish it up and dedicate it to her." In his enthusiasm, Pete didn't see the protest in his sister's eyes.

"You're moving to the Mariner?" Dylan said with obvious interest.

"Actually, just for a tryout, a one-night shot," Pete explained hastily. "We've added another fellow to the band—a fiddle player—and Claire is singing lead. I've been telling her she's too good to hide out on that paddle-wheeler or in a little lounge."

"I said something similar myself," Dylan observed. "I just didn't know that things were happening so soon. I wish you all success." He directed the comment to her with the same politeness he used with other people. But she knew she wasn't just "other people," and she disliked the irritating, impersonal tone.

"We're talking about a tryout here, not a road tour," Claire interjected. She hadn't wanted to say anything to Dylan until it was all over—if then. For she felt this was a very personal mission, an opportunity to prove something to herself.

"I'll make it a point to stop in that night." Dylan's eyes locked on to hers. "I'll always be able to say that I knew her when. . . ."

"I'll still be here. I have no intention of giving up the distinction of being a great pool scrubber," Claire quipped. "I'm not leaving," she advised him. "If the job comes through, I'll be working less than five minutes from here. I'll still have my two days a week with the birds."

"Until some big producer drops in and sees you in action," Pete said hopefully. "Then the sky's the limit."

Both of them, Pete and Dylan, had visions of her going on to bigger and better things. Claire could tell by Dylan's expression.

"And I'm not talking birds," Pete joked.

She wanted to put things in perspective so both of them would know how premature their view of her success was. "Before I rush right out and order my Rolls-Royce, I think you'd better get me back to town so I can change clothes and go to work. Unless, of course, you don't expect your lead singer to pay rent."

"She has a point," Pete said with a chuckle. "But she also has a heck of a lot more. She's gorgeous. She can deliver a song. All she needs to believe in is herself."

"I knew right off she had possibilities." Dylan's words had that pensive quality she had picked up on before.

"Back to reality, you guys. If making a steady income is to be one of my possibilities, I have to get to work," Claire insisted. "I'll be back tomorrow for my regular duty," she informed Dylan. Then, as an afterthought, she added, "Boss. . . ."

Dylan considered her stubborn reply. Then a curious light flickered in his eyes and one corner of his mouth pulled up into a trace of a smile. He was changing tactics. "Tomorrow afternoon I have to go scouting through that piece of property we're looking at," Dylan commented. "I spent most of today there with a surveyor, locating the outer boundaries. Now I need to see the rest. Maybe you'd like to come along and look at nature untouched—and help me count nests and water holes. We need to study the terrain closely to know if it's what we want." Claire was aware the suggestion that she come along was a peace offering.

"I'd like to see the site," she said cautiously. "But my rounds here come first."

"Then I'll see you tomorrow, after you finish here." Dylan stood in the walkway, watching as Pete and Claire left together, walking to the car.

"Nice guy," Pete concluded once they were out of Dylan's hearing. "I think you're a bit brusque with him, though. Did you two have an argument, or something?"

"We have a difference of opinion," Claire conceded. "He's determined to treat Sara and I as 'short-timers.' She gets her leg fixed, I sing my songs and we're both gone."

"He may be right." Pete opened the door for her. "If that's what you want...."

"I don't know yet what I want," Claire admitted. "I know I want to succeed at something. But I'm not sure what that something is. When I find out, I want to make my own decisions, without either you or Dylan or anyone else hovering over me, saying, 'I told you so.'" She could have added Wes Raines to the list, but she kept that thought to herself.

"No 'hovering.'" Pete nodded.

"And don't tell him how gorgeous and talented you think I am. It makes me feel like some windup toy on display. Turn the key and watch the show. That's show biz. I just don't think people like us are in the same orbit as people like him."

"Sorry again."

"And I wish you hadn't invited him to watch us perform. I'll be nervous enough."

Now it was Pete's turn to get testy over the deluge of criticism. "I'm beginning to wonder if I should have gotten out of bed today. All I was trying to do was make conversation with him." Pete sighed with exasperation. "Next time I'll tell him you've got tattoos and you're an ax murderer."

"I'm sorry." Claire suddenly realized how petulant she sounded. "That isn't-she-wonderful talk embarrassed me."

"Yeah, well maybe I was a bit pushy," Pete conceded. "I was just trying to help."

"I don't need help. I need time—just like Sara."

Pete reached over and grabbed her hand, giving it a squeeze. Then he cleared his throat and pursed his lips. Claire still seemed bent on working everything through by herself. Even though he could sense something special in the air whenever Dylan's name came up, the lady was not talking.

But Pete would stick with her. He'd be there if she needed him. For now, there was nothing he needed to say. So he leaned back and whistled a song for Sara.

CHAPTER SIX

THE MINUTE CLAIRE saw the vaguely familiar car parked next to Dylan's truck in a clearing on the overgrown stretch of land, she knew she'd made a mistake. She'd come clear across town to spend a few hours studying the site with him, but apparently she would not have Dylan or the prospective refuge area to herself. The red-haired woman in slim white jeans and leather deck shoes was there before her.

Dressed in work clothes and knee-high rubberized boots borrowed from Tammy, Claire stepped out of her car and walked toward Dylan and his companion. Tammy had warned her that scouting the area would be hot and difficult work, so Claire had dressed for the jungle. Rebecca had dressed, instead, for the yacht club.

Chafing over the contrast, Claire moved as gracefully as she could over the uneven terrain. Then her foot sank ankle deep into the soggy tire marks, and she was stuck. While Claire struggled to work her foot free without losing her balance or her boot, Dylan studied a map of the area. But Rebecca Stroud glanced up in time to see Claire teeter and then drop backward on her fanny in the mud.

"She seems to be having some trouble," Rebecca

said dryly, resting an elegant hand on Dylan's shoulder to direct his attention to Claire.

"Oh, brother," he groaned, shaking his head as he trudged toward her to offer his hand. "I see you've already confronted one of the problems. The land is low and tends to hold water. We're talking about a lot of landfill to make it suitable for building."

Although his manner was cool and businesslike, he had smiled when he saw her, which suggested more than mere amusement at her predicament. His rough hand enfolded hers, and he hesitated a moment as he looked down at her. With a strong, smooth tug, Dylan pulled her to her feet, minus one boot. He steadied her with one hand and yanked the boot out of the mud. When he bent close and slipped it onto her foot, she braced herself on his hard, sculpted shoulders and a scene from Cinderella flashed through her mind. She even had a face for one of the wicked stepsisters, who in this production was wearing white slacks and deck shoes.

"I'm glad you came." Dylan stood and glanced at her briefly. Then his eyes shifted to the east. "It is a beautiful piece of land, isn't it?" He kept a grip on Claire's arm as they moved onto firmer ground.

"I really haven't had a chance to notice," Claire replied, diligently rubbing the mud from the seat of her pants. Now her hands were covered, as well.

"Rebecca Stroud, this is Claire Parnell," Dylan said, introducing the women. "I asked Claire to help me walk the site," he explained. "She's one of our newest volunteers."

Claire started a handshake, then saw the condition

of her hands. With a slightly embarrassed smile, she retracted her hand and simply nodded.

"Nice to meet you," Rebecca said pleasantly. "You were at the refuge when I came to see Dylan. I'm sorry this excursion started out so unfortunately." She looked at Claire's soiled and disheveled appearance as if she were observing a lower species of life. "But I suppose that comes with the work." Her comments came out effortlessly, with a glibness that indicated little real interest.

"It seems so," Claire agreed glumly.

"Rebecca brought a schematic of the land to help us keep our bearings." Dylan directed Claire's attention to the outspread paper on the hood of the car. "Pelicans are already using the mangroves near the water as a nesting area." His callused finger traced the area. "What I want to know is what other birds are nesting around here. From looking at the old roosts, we can tell how long they've been coming here. If we cut a path straight through toward the water, we'll get an idea of the variety of wildlife that calls this home. That means snakes, too. You were smart to wear those boots."

Claire felt her stomach lurch at the mention of snakes. In zoos they were fascinating enough, but without a cage or a pane of glass separating them from her, Claire was terrified. "What kind of snakes are you anticipating?" She knew at once why Tammy had insisted she wear the metal-toed, heavy boots.

"Brown and banded water snakes—they are harmless. There may be a few water moccasins. They'll get out of the way when they hear us coming." He looked at her calmly. "There's no real danger."

"So you say . . ." Claire mumbled, unconvinced.

"Just send smoke signals if you want me to call in help," Rebecca suggested.

"You mean you aren't going with us?" Claire tried not to sound too relieved.

"I have some other business to attend to," Rebecca replied. "This is not the side of the real-estate business that I specialize in," she added with another amused glance at Claire's appearance.

"This isn't exactly my line of business, either," Claire told her. "Are you sure we'll be back in time for me to clean up and get to work?" She turned to Dylan anxiously.

"You work at night?" Rebecca turned wide greenish eyes on Claire again. "What kind of work do you do?"

"I play on a dinner-cruise boat. I'm a musician."

Rebecca's gaze dropped pointedly to Claire's mud-caked hands. Her own hands were lily-white, with perfectly oval fingernails painted salmon to match her silk shirt. "Maybe I should put in an emergency call to my manicurist," she remarked. "You'll need her help."

"I can manage on my own," Claire said, stiffening defensively. A manicurist was an indulgence she had never been able to afford.

"I'll get you back in plenty of time," Dylan promised. "Let's douse ourselves with insect repellent and get going."

"I'll be in my office." Rebecca rested her hand on his arm once more. "Call me when you get back. We'll have dinner and discuss your findings. I'll do a financial breakdown and we'll see what kind of financing is possible.''

''Fine with me,'' Dylan agreed.

Rebecca flashed a sultry pink smile at Dylan, but didn't bother with Claire. With a toss of auburn hair, she turned and walked off.

Claire tried not to sputter out some indignant comment. She attempted to assure herself that theirs was just a business dinner, but she couldn't shake the image of Rebecca's slim hand reaching out and touching Dylan with increasing frequency. Claire wished she could remember how his skin felt beneath her own fingertips.

While Rebecca backed her car out onto the shoulder of the main road, Claire found herself hoping for a sinkhole to swallow one of the tires. Or the whole car. Anything that would ruffle the glamorous lady's composure. But when the car moved off easily with the traffic, Claire was left nursing a bottle of bug repellent and a smoldering feeling of frustration.

Dylan was grinning as if he were a kid about to go off on an adventure. He'd hacked down hiking sticks and worked quickly to remove excess branches, but he left a forked end in case something should slither across their path. Only the serpent Claire imagined wore a salmon silk shirt and an icy smile.

The interior of the undeveloped land was canopied with ancient, moss-hung oak trees and dense Australian pines. Low palmettos and vine-tangled bushes carpeted the ground. Primitive and wild, the foliage muffled the distant sound of traffic from the interstate highway and put them back into a time untouched by progress. Low and soggy, the ground sucked and pulled at their shoes as Dylan and Claire moved in single file toward the heart of the land. As they inched along, the continual squawk and flutter above them or the scuffle and swish through the undergrowth clearly confirmed that they were not alone. Claire scanned the ground constantly, dreading that one of the twisted roots she poked or stepped over would prove to be something else and move, coil up and strike. But each time Dylan glanced back or offered her his hand through a particularly tangled passage, Claire forced herself to smile bravely and move on.

"Egret. . . ." Dylan pointed up to a collection of twiggy nests high in the trees. "Heron." He indicated a blue-gray flutter above them. "Watch. . ." he whispered, pulling her close to him. "It's the changing of the guard." He motioned toward one heron, who was bowing, stretching and spreading his wings in an elegant display for his mate on the nest. "Actually, it's really called a 'nest-relief ceremony,'" he explained. "He's telling her he's ready to take over if she wants to have a break. When she returns, she'll go through the same ritual, never rushing the other. Herons are very gracious. If they're nesting here, we should also find some ibis."

Still holding her arm, he steered her deeper into the undergrowth. "There's some water ahead," he told her. "Wading birds often roost in clusters. And it's the right season for nesting. This is a great natural rookery," he observed, obviously encouraged by his findings. "There's quite a variety of indigenous wildlife."

"There's also quite a potent smell," Claire noted queasily. By now, cut off by the canopy of greenery, the air barely moved beneath the dense overhanging trees, and the bird droppings from many nesting seasons contributed to the oppressive odor.

"We aren't exactly taking the scenic tour of Busch Gardens," he muttered. "But you don't have to endure all this stoically. It's all right to complain about the stink or the snakes or the humidity. We came here to look, not to move in. Say what you think."

"I think I should have mentioned that I'm terrified of snakes." Claire finally said out loud what had kept her stomach in knots throughout the trek. "I think I'd like to go back." She could feel the clamminess creeping over her. "Never mind. It's too late," she reported dutifully. A relentless cold wave of sweat swept over her. "I think I'm going to be sick."

But Dylan caught her arm, stabilizing her as he propelled her steadily out of the rookery into the open air. Rapidly they retraced their steps to the clearing where the vehicles were parked, and Claire collapsed dejectedly on the ground next to the truck. Leaning against the tire, she stared at her mud-splattered pants.

Dylan pulled open a can of soda and offered it to her. Then he opened one for himself and sat down next to her. "A lot of people are afraid of snakes. And that smell back in there is one of Mother Nature's lesser delights. You were determined to hang in there for some reason, snakes or no snakes. What I want to know is what were you trying to prove? And to whom? Me or you?" His piercing sea-blue gaze locked on to hers.

"I think it was just the principle involved," she said at last. "I've lived in Florida most of my life and I've never walked into a mangrove swamp or any other kind of swamp, for that matter. I felt that I should. At least once. I wanted to see if I could."

"Is that your usual mode of attack? Steel yourself to do something you don't know if you can do?" His steady gaze held hers, unwavering and cool.

"Why do you say that?"

"I've been thinking about the night at the beach house and your sitting there with the wine. It took four glasses before you finally loosened up. And you were the one who refilled the glasses," he pointed out.

"I did?" Claire tried to recall that part of the evening. She remembered wine and the lovemaking and the pounding in her head the next day. But four glasses. No wonder the near-empty wine bottle in the refrigerator had prompted such a dissonant response.

"Fortified by the wine, you were so soft and loving. . ." he said in a curiously cold voice. "Were you trying to prove something then, too?"

"What happened that night was something else entirely." She was determined to protect that memory and get the conversation back to something less personal.

"What do you think in retrospect?" The creases in Dylan's tanned face deepened as that lopsided smile softened the remoteness in his eyes. "The mangroves, I mean."

"I'm glad I went in there. I don't feel in a particular rush to go back. But I could, if I had to." There was beginning to be an unmistakable double meaning in everything she said to him.

"Good. If you want to go along on an offshore rescue mission, you'll run into this kind of setting. We're always climbing through branches to free a bird tangled in fishing line or to pick up a chick that's tumbled from a nest. The smell, the heat and the possibility of creepy crawlies are all part of the deal. You've got courage. Perhaps tentative and highly specialized, but it's courage nevertheless," he said, assuming his refuge-director persona.

"Is that supposed to be a compliment, sir?" she asked, tilting her chin defensively.

Dylan let out a slow sigh as he looked at her, obviously realizing that with the two of them sitting side by side in the mud, his attitude was overly official. It was happening again. She had him off-balance and he'd started sounding like "the boss" again. He felt the same helplessness. How should he treat her, how could he get through to her and how should he respond to the constantly fluctuating moods that made her so irresistible.

Then, in spite of the ordeal, the perspiration, the bug repellent and the mud, Dylan leaned forward and kissed her. The kiss was gentle and light, but to Claire it was immediately familiar. The soft pressure on her lips lingered a moment, then intensified as she let him pull her closer, lifting her across him to cradle her in his lap. When his hand moved up her side and rested against her breast, the heat penetrated even through the rugged fabric of her shirt, and she felt a tingle of anticipation. To be loved again. To be caressed. The hunger was still there, just beneath the surface.

Claire balanced her cold drink precariously in one hand and reached up with the other, holding on to the next gentle kiss and seeking more. The gesture was the same as the one she'd made before, on his balcony that magical night. Dylan grasped her wrist and lifted her hand away without breaking the sensuous contact of their lips.

"Do you remember when I lay next to you and held you close to me," he said softly. "Do you remember my touching you like this?" The erotic rumble in his voice started a responsive flutter deep inside her.

Claire shook her head slightly. Dylan stiffened, then moved back and stared at her.

"I didn't think you did." His voice sounded slightly ominous. "You were too well fortified for that. Now that makes it even more flattering." His voice sizzled with indignation. "Let me tell you how wonderful that night was." His words were as sharp as razors, cutting through the haze of passion that had begun to envelop them. "When you took off in the morning like a scared rabbit, I felt like a barbarian. As if I'd pushed you into something you couldn't deal with. You came all the way out to the beach house, and I thought we had broken through whatever walls you had built." Without physically moving, he had become inaccessible, distant. "Our romantic glass of wine multiplied—and four glasses later you seemed to want me. But what became increasingly clear was that there was more involved than I'd ever anticipated. Before I could make love with you you were gone. Unconscious. Sound asleep."

"Is that what happened? That's all?" Claire stared at him. "But I thought—" Her eyes widened in bewilderment. This was not the enchanted tale she had clung to.

"You thought what?" He glared at her. "That I went on and made love to you, anyway. Is that what you thought? Is that what made you skip out the next morning without leaving a note?"

"I thought we made love with each other," she countered. "I thought we did and it was. . .lovely."

"So 'lovely' you couldn't even remember?" he snapped. "You think I could have done that to you? I was making love with you—not simply having sex. Then after you were asleep I remembered you said you weren't much of a drinker. I wondered why in the heck you came all the way out to the beach then deliberately drank too much wine. I had a very confusing conversation with myself trying to figure things out. You trusted me with your body. Couldn't you have trusted me enough to talk to me, tell me what haunts you? I wasn't going to do anything that could make things worse. So I did the gentlemanly thing."

"What was that?" Claire asked, half-dazed by the shifting realities. She was anxiously trying to reconcile the highly vivid images, erotic memories with this new version of that night that Dylan was unfolding.

"I gave you the benefit of the doubt. I figured you had troubles that you hadn't quite resolved. And I guessed the wine had more clout than you expected.

So I put you in one of my T-shirts and tucked you back in bed.''

"And that was all we did?" Claire still couldn't believe it.

"That covers the important points." He glanced away momentarily, holding back the few details he wished to keep for himself—the softness of her breasts, the feel of her skin as he undressed her, the way she curved into his body while she drifted off to sleep.

"I remembered so much else." She couldn't look at him. Her face felt hot with the admission. "When I woke up, it looked as if you'd slept in the bed with me. I thought—" She saw a flicker of amusement in the sea-blue eyes.

"You must have been dreaming," Dylan insisted. "Not the in-bed part. That was true. There's only one bed, and we both spent the night in it. I told you that I'm not one to take advantage of a situation. But I want more than you can give, lady," he whispered. "I want to be inside your head. And we're not there yet." He sat her upright, putting some distance between them.

"I don't want to start something out here that I don't intend to finish. That night taxed my restraint to the limit. When I got called away the next morning, we were both spared a lot of embarrassing explanations."

"I wondered if you'd sneaked out early because there was nothing to say," Claire confessed. "But I didn't want to believe you were like that."

"And what was I supposed to believe about you,"

he almost shouted. "Why didn't you leave a number? Why did you sneak out?"

"I was embarrassed. I was hurt. Maybe I was scared. I'd never spent the night with anyone—except with Wes. I was confused and my head hurt." Her dismal account brought a slight smile to his lips.

"You didn't do anything to be embarrassed about—except drink too much. That, and give me one heck of a restless night," Dylan admitted. "Trying to sleep next to you didn't make me feel any better, no matter how understanding I tried to be. When I saw you at the refuge I knew the place could give you something I couldn't. You belonged there. I didn't have to be part of the deal. I still don't."

"And all this time I thought we had been so intimate," Claire said quietly. "I couldn't understand why you seemed so distant. Now I'm beginning to think that you don't want me as one of the refuge workers—I'm an inmate," she said bitterly. "I don't want to be on your list of rescued critters."

"You can be whatever you want to be," he answered with restraint. "But unless you open up to me, I can't deal with whatever it is that drives you back into yourself. Unless you can trust me with all of you, I don't want to be another testing ground." He glanced away, his expression remote. She could imagine how different this had all been from his perspective. They had both felt used and misunderstood.

The long silence was broken only by the distant squawking of nestlings demanding to be fed. "I'm sorry for all the trouble I've been," Claire said softly. "I wasn't just looking for a challenge that night—or just now. You're not a test for me, Dylan, and I'm not a tease.''

"Not dressed like that you aren't,'' Dylan said with a glimmer of humor. He didn't look at her face. He was observing her dirty jeans and muddy boots.

Then they both laughed, and Claire felt strangely liberated. They'd brought a lot out into the open. They had penetrated the walls of misunderstanding that had been separating them. She leaned against him, listening to the thunder of his heart, a low, melodic rumble that she knew she'd heard before. And she knew she hadn't just been dreaming. When she looked up at him, her face flushed and eyes sparkling, Dylan stopped smiling. And the softness in his eyes was the stuff dreams were made on. She wanted him to lower his lips very slightly and kiss her again.

Then Dylan whispered softly, "No. No more tests of willpower today—mine or yours. You have an audience waiting and I have a dinner engagement. This isn't the time or the place."

In that instant, the light of laughter was gone. Reality had returned to end their wilderness sojourn. The serpent she had dreaded raised its auburn head and coiled, smiling, somewhere in her mind.

"Of course you're right," she said as she glanced at her watch. Even her watch was streaked with mud. "We both have other things to do." The terseness in her voice was prompted by the intrusion of the outside world and Rebecca Stroud into what had been a very intimate reunion of sorts. She was deftly reminded of her proper place.

"There is a real world out there," Dylan noted with

a slightly patronizing touch. "Regardless how tempting castles and mangrove jungles may seem."

"Then I'd better not keep the real world waiting," she commented with a rueful smile. Claire had found such comfort in the lovemaking she thought they had shared that she regretted finding out what had really happened. She knew some of what she remembered was true, but the siren and the sea god were only illusions. She hadn't broken free, not as she had hoped.

"By the way, I really don't want you naming the birds," he reminded her just as she stepped away. "That part of my philosophy still applies. You're the one who'll get hurt."

"I'll take my chances. I told you before, I can't take back anything that's happened, including Sara's name," Claire answered immediately. Her wide gray eyes sparkled with defiance. "Give her my love. I will still sing her to sleep." Then she strode off toward her car.

"Lucky bird..." Dylan muttered as he watched Claire's car pull out and disappear into the late-afternoon traffic.

THE NEXT MORNING, the green-eyed serpent had moved out of the jungle and into the newspaper.

"The Birdman made the society page," Pete said, stepping into the studio where Claire was working alone. She'd spent the morning with the earphones on, singing along with the music the fellows had taped earlier. That had become their rehearsal strategy; those who could only make a single session taped their portion. Then anyone who missed out or wanted additional work on a number could come into the garage-studio and play back the tapes. With the Mariner try-out only a week away, Claire used the mornings to work out the kinks.

"Your friend. . . ." Pete held the paper in front of her. "With some woman." He intended to sound as disapproving as he did. Claire looked at the picture of Dylan and Rebecca, then switched off the controls. Sliding the chair back from the keyboard, she read the caption. "Fund-raiser planned at Dali museum for refuge expansion."

"Apparently Dylan liked the land you two went exploring yesterday," Pete noted. "His taste in women isn't bad, either," he added pointedly.

Claire simply read on. The Jamison-Stroud business dinner the night before must have been productive and considerably more formal than Claire had imagined. And at some point, the twosome managed to stop by the Salvador Dali Museum by the bayside and have their picture taken. How convenient that a photographer from the *Times* had been on hand.

Rebecca Stroud, board member of the museum, is hosting a cocktail reception at the museum Friday evening. There will be a slide presentation by refuge president Dylan Jamison. Funds from a raffle of several Dali lithographs will be donated to the refuge-expansion fund. Jamison has taken an option on a hundred acres of undeveloped land on Tampa Bay in northeast St. Petersburg. Ms Stroud will be contacting other civic organizations to enlist their aid in raising funds for the expansion.

"The article fails to mention that Rebecca Stroud is the real-estate agent who is selling the acreage," Claire added for Pete's information. "If the deal goes through, she'll have a nice commission to show for her civic-minded efforts. Behind that perfect smile is a brain registering dollar signs," she finished cynically.

"Let's hope she's content to walk off with the commission and not the buyer," Pete said as he leaned close and studied the picture. Rebecca's hand was resting on Dylan's arm. The gesture made Claire's fingers itch.

As the BAY-BELLE made its way down the bayous and inlets along Tampa Bay that evening, a party was under way near the waterfront in the low, modern Salvador Dali Museum. Elegantly dressed guests roamed the lighted promenade and visited over cocktails and hors d'oeuvres on the neatly landscaped grounds. Some paused and waved at the passing cruise boat and others swayed to the music Claire played. But when the boat passed on, the guests went inside to meet the "Public Defender of Birds" and view the slides of his work. A show that Claire would have liked to attend. However, the engraved invitations signed by Rebecca Stroud had been mailed only to the affluent members of the community. None had been sent to her—or any of the refuge staff.

At the Pier lounge, Claire was welcome.

"Claire, I want you to meet Brett Westbrook." Pete pulled out a chair for her when she arrived for the final set. "We've been talking about shooting a video of our show at the Mariner Club tomorrow."

"I saw you out at the bird refuge," she said to Brett.

"I was helping Tammy clean the pens." He had been the one behind the camera when Phil Stockman had come to do the news spot on "tearjerkers" undergoing treatment at the refuge.

Instantly the color in the fellow's face deepened. "That was not one of the better moments for journalism," he apologized.

"I'm relieved to know that at least one of you has some sensitivity," Claire said, sitting down next to him.

"Brett's into music videos, which is real convenient for us," Pete explained. "Tomorrow night he'll record our performance and edit it. Regardless of how that one night turns out, we can make up a video package we can take around to some record companies and cable-TV stations. A video just might get us some attention. I think we should cover our bets."

"That means, if anything goes wrong, it's going to be immortalized on film. You're braver than I am." Claire looked from one brother to the next. Both Robby and Pete appeared unperturbed. Least concerned of all was the dark-eyed cameraman.

"Don't worry," Brett advised her. "I'll have a second cameraman working on the wide shots. I do the zoom work. Out of all the footage I can get a good video."

"How about it?" Pete leaned forward and asked her.

"The idea of having a camera on me makes me nervous," Claire confessed. "But I understand how effective a video can be. I guess we shouldn't let a chance like this slip by. I have no objections to doing the videotaping," she told him. It would be one more adventure she had never been on.

"The taping isn't as obvious or as awkward as you may think. I don't have to move in real close with the camera," Brett explained. "The telephoto and zoom lenses can do it all. What you'll see," he said as he stirred his drink, "is a tall guy moving just beyond the lights. The other fellow will be stationary somewhere above the rear tables. You won't even see him."

"Good, that makes it less threatening," she commented. "We already leave the amplification and mixing to the sound men. Now I guess we'd better leave the filming to the specialists."

Brett smoothly shifted the subject to scheduling. "If you're rehearsing and doing sound tests tomorrow, I'll come out and line up all the shots. When the show starts, it will all go like clockwork."

Just as he spoke, Claire glanced up over his shoulder. Apparently the reception at the Dali museum was over and some of the guests had decided to drop in for a nightcap at the nearby Pier. Among the first to step into the lounge were Dylan Jamison and the auburn-haired Rebecca Stroud.

Brett turned to see what had caught Claire's attention. "Ah...the Birdman," he said with mild amusement. "All dressed up and out on the town." In his black tuxedo, Dylan looked strikingly handsome, and the white shirt against his tan seemed to emphasize his rugged profile. This Dylan exuded an air of confidence and sophistication that had the others in his party circling around him deferentially, including Rebecca.

Claire couldn't put into words the sense of invasion she felt. She had experienced something like this when she'd showed up at the new site and found Rebecca there—only this was worse. This intimate lounge was Claire's territory, her world, one that Claire didn't think Rebecca should have been brought into. Certainly not by Dylan.

Before she could articulate her anger, the music came to rescue her. The instrumental was ending and it was time to get back on stage. Brett stood and pulled out her chair, smiling down at her all the while.

Without looking again at the back tables, Claire steeled herself for the next few songs. Some of them were fun, rocking dance numbers she had to be up for. They were flashy pieces, but nothing too personal. But to close the show, she had planned to sing the love song that Robby insisted on calling ''Sara's Song.'' If Dylan had come alone, ''Sara's Song'' might have communicated something of her difficulty in putting feelings into words. But the red-haired beauty in the aquamarine silk tunic had been holding on to his arm possessively since they'd arrived with their group of friends. Nothing would make Claire sing that song now.

''We're dropping 'Sara's Song,' '' she whispered to Pete.

He immediately began to protest. But when he looked into his sister's eyes, he reconsidered. Those stormy gray eyes said the timing wasn't right, and he didn't ask why. ''Replacing it with what?''

'' 'Turnabout,' '' Robby butted in. He was in heaven when Claire did a ''torchy'' number, taunting and hardhearted. They'd pulled out and polished up this one in case they needed it for the Mariner.

Claire hesitated just a second. "Turnabout" was all about getting what you deserve, and that put a gleam of mischief in her eyes. She nodded to Robby and he passed the word. If Dylan chose to take the words to heart, he might realize the faux pas he'd made. Regardless of whether his association with Rebecca Stroud was strictly business or something more intimate, he had overstepped his bounds by bringing her here. Even if the message didn't sink in, the song was still one of her theater pieces. The words would sneak up on him and curl his socks.

With a rush of adrenaline brought on by Robby's drums, Claire strutted into the first of several "thumpers" they'd planned. Her wavy pale hair gleamed under the lights, framing her head with a shimmering halo effect. And not once did her eyes light on the table where Dylan was. But when she got to the last song, the room fell silent. After Bizzy's delicate lead-in, the face that turned toward the audience was not angelic. There was a sultry smile and a flash of fire in the wide gray eyes. Even the tension in her tall slim body was designed to be sexy. Claire was in her element. She started low, throaty, with only a trace of musical backup.

> The nighttime lonelies will be
> Comin' after you
> They know where you'll be
> Now you're missing me
> Like I was missin' you.

Then the drums came in subtly. Jess played tears on his violin. Bizzy grimaced and bent over the keyboard, teasing anguish out of the electronic marvel. The lady sang the blues, but the words smoldered red hot.

> Baby...
> The midnight sorrows will come
> Knockin' at your door
> Won't you let 'em in
> Think of me again
> Like you did before.

The song gave Claire a role to play and just enough drama to hide behind. Her delivery was slightly teasing and somewhat menacing. She had borrowed a bit from Bette Midler's bluesy, tormented style but Claire gave her song a poignancy that was her own.

> Turnabout is fair play
> Reaping what you sow
> Don't come turnin' my way
> I've got somewhere else to go.

> Ya' know...
> The nighttime lonelies will be
> Comin' after you....

When one by one the instruments fell silent again and Claire's pure voice pierced the room for the final lines, she could feel the new power in her voice. She was good. Not even the presence of green-eyed Rebecca Stroud could diminish that.

"You sound great." Dylan came forward alone and stopped on the dance floor by the front of the platform, intercepting Claire as she stepped down. Above them the recorded music was playing over speakers, as Pete, Robby and the other band members gathered their equipment. The live entertainment was over, but a few couples still remained on the small dance floor.

"Can I have this dance?" Dylan held out his hand.

With a slight shrug Claire accepted, still feeling very much as if she were part of the show. She let him hold her at a distance, and slowly they circled the smooth dance area.

"I thought you came with someone," Claire said, looking up at him. "I wouldn't want to keep you from your associates."

Dylan's smile widened. "I had a feeling you knew we were here. The last time I saw you perform you didn't ignore that side of the room."

"I wasn't ignoring anyone." She glanced over his shoulder, noticing that one of the other men in the group that had come with Dylan had invited Rebecca Stroud to dance. Together they were coming toward the small area where Claire and Dylan were. "I had to concentrate on my work."

"I like it better when you look at me." Dylan's low voice brought her attention back to him. "Not just when you're singing," he added. When she resisted his attempt to pull her closer, he simply shook his head and held her. "I did not bring Rebecca here as my date and I didn't intend to show up with an entourage," he informed her. "These are all folks who helped put together the reception and raffle. Afterward they suggested going out for a drink. I'm afraid I was in a bit of a dilemma. Either we could come here, or I could miss seeing you. So we all came. Rebecca was quite curious to see you perform."

"Am I supposed to feel flattered?" Claire moved a bit closer to him as other dancers—including Rebecca and her partner—joined them on the floor.

"You don't need to feel anything but very proud of your performance," he whispered against her temple. "You were wonderful. But now I wonder what was going on in your head. For a nice, wholesome woman that last number was a bit steamy. Am I supposed to take the last song personally?" He seemed to find the possibility amusing.

"It was a last-minute choice." Claire avoided a direct answer. "Robby likes it and so did the audience."

"Will you do the song tomorrow?"

"No. We have some others planned." Her answer sounded evasive. "A few of them are a little steamy, too."

"May I show up to watch?" Dylan eased back and looked at her closely. "You know, you've never told me how you feel about having me in the audience. If my being around bothers you, just tell me straight out. I don't want you to feel uncomfortable because of me. I told you before, I won't get in your way."

Before Claire could answer, the light touch on her shoulder pulled her away from the sea-blue eyes that were studying her expression.

"Your group has a nice sound," Rebecca commended her. "Dylan said that two of the band members are your brothers. How satisfying to have a musical family.'' Coming from Rebecca, who leaned gracefully in one man's arms while gazing up at Dylan, the remark seemed calculated to sound gracious. For Rebecca words flowed easily, but that didn't necessarily mean she meant them. To Claire, Rebecca's comment reduced musical ability to a genetic trait as uncomplicated as eye color.

"I'm glad you enjoyed the music,'' Claire replied with equal diplomacy and a deliberately bland expression. Then, since there was nothing else to say, she moved back into Dylan's arms and Rebecca danced reluctantly away.

"Charming. You're both so charming,'' he murmured sarcastically. "Now that she's here, you're suddenly cuddly and friendly. Are you proving a point again?'' The displeasure in his voice made it clear he wasn't going to be used. If Claire hadn't felt like snuggling before, he didn't want her to do so now, not for Rebecca's benefit. "Where's all that integrity I thought you had?'' He let the space between them widen.

"I'm sorry,'' Claire said sincerely. "I have no reason to be upset. I know better. But she does get under my skin.''

"Is this a personality clash or a territorial dispute?'' He had hit the nail right on the head.

"Both.'' Claire answered bluntly. "And we're both out of line.''

"Would you like to elaborate?'' Dylan grinned at her. He finally had some reason to be encouraged.

By now a break between the recorded songs accentuated the awkwardness of the moment. When Claire glanced toward her table, Brett Westbrook was already approaching them. "No. I would not," she whispered as Brett zeroed in on her.

"Last dance. Ours?" Brett's hopeful expression greeted her.

"Sure," Claire responded without looking up at Dylan. She already felt foolish about her behavior. She had revealed more than she'd intended to both Dylan and to herself. Now she had no desire to explain anything to anyone. "Dylan, you may remember Brett from the Phil Stockman taping." She introduced the men as the music resumed.

"Sure do. Nice job you did." Dylan responded.

"Brett is going to do a video of our performance tomorrow night. Pete hopes to use it to promote the group."

"That makes good sense," Dylan replied politely. "I'd like to see the tape when it's finished."

"We'd better see how it turns out first," Claire suggested. The idea of showing the tape to Dylan made her even more nervous. This was no refuge promo. This one was promoting her.

"I'm sure it will be good," Dylan said.

"You bet. The lady is in good hands, starting now," Brett joked, slipping his arm around her waist. Dylan stepped aside so Brett could escort her onto the floor.

The next glimpse Claire had of Dylan was him dancing with Rebecca. His back was toward her, so she couldn't see his face, but Rebecca was smiling.

When the dance ended, Claire, Brett and the five

band members, carrying an assortment of instruments and music, formed a procession heading toward the exit. Only briefly did she glance over at the group that Dylan had come with.

Dylan and his companions were standing together, still conversing, but Claire knew that the lounge was ready to close and they would be leaving soon. He was shaking hands with each of them, his lean form marked with a masculine grace that the black tux emphasized. And once again Rebecca Stroud had her arm linked in his.

He had said he'd come to see Claire perform, but he hadn't asked for any more than that one dance and a few answers she didn't wish to give. For a moment she considered hurrying over and asking him to join Brett, her and the band at the restaurant. But tonight was business. He didn't fit into her world and she didn't fit into his.

This is how you wanted it... Claire reminded herself. No involvement. No strings attached. Like the no-name birds destined to fly free, she and Dylan had a no-name relationship. Neither had the right to make claims or expect commitments. But for something without a name, the pain was very real.

CHAPTER SEVEN

FROM THE MOMENT Claire stepped into the empty cavernous Mariner ballroom the next morning and saw the gaping stage across one end, she knew the ambience was all wrong. Robby and Bizzy were deep in conversation with the two technicians from Turn of The Century, sound specialists, while Pete was pacing off the platform, marking the places where the instruments and microphones would be set up. In a darkened, glassed-in booth high on the wall behind her someone was experimenting with the lighting system, transforming Pete into colors varying from green to pink.

The room was far bigger than Claire had envisioned; the decor, stark and functional—like an airport terminal between flights. Unoccupied chairs encircled bare tables like ghostly sentinels, waiting. Crossing the carpeted area onto the central dance floor, her heels clicked against the slate surface, sending staccato sounds echoing through the area. Every click echoed, "Wrong, wrong, wrong."

From the stage the view was even less reassuring. Even at night, with the softer lighting and the room filled with people, from onstage, it would still look like there was a landing strip separating the performers from the audience. The dance floor was a stage in itself, another platform for another type of showmanship. The tables were so far away. There was no intimacy, no atmosphere like in the lounge at the Pier. The faces of patrons two tables back would disappear into the darkness, making everything remote and everyone anonymous.

"What do you think of this place?" Pete grinned enthusiastically when he came over to meet her.

"I think it's very big." Claire propped her hands on her hips and stared out over the emptiness. "Maybe we should have hired a chorus line and some acrobats."

"Don't worry. We don't have to put on a floor show," he said confidently. "The audience can do that." He stuck his thumb at the dance floor.

But Claire was already studying the stage, trying to imagine how much more flamboyant her delivery would have to be to hold an audience of this size. Wes had always said she couldn't carry the show— not on her own.

"I'm glad I've been getting so much exercise at the refuge." She paced the stage, getting the feel of the vast space she would occupy. "Carrying buckets of fish back and forth over an acre of pens gives one a comparable experience," she joked as she took long strides.

Pete stood there, watching her intently. He had deliberately kept Claire from coming onto the vast stage until the last day. Get the music down. That had been first. He didn't want the room to dictate how she delivered a song. Now she would loosen up—improvise; it was too late for her to worry.

For the rest of the morning and well into the afternoon, everyone worked steadily on technical details, checking and rechecking the equipment. Then, for an hour they walked through the performance, playing and singing some of the material they would use, chasing away the emptiness of the room with their mellow sound. The video team planned their maneuvers for the filming.

By late afternoon the air crackled with excitement. ''Win, lose or show, we're ready,'' Pete declared. ''Be here at eight. We go on at nine.'' Some of them decided to go out to eat. A few went home. Claire headed out the back door, straight for the beach. She needed time to herself to let all her reactions settle.

Knees pulled up under her chin, she sat and stared at the waves as bits and pieces of conversation drifted through her consciousness. She could hear Pete encouraging her—could remember the tenderness in Dylan's voice after he saw her singing. But the images kept shifting—beach, stage, refuge, swamp, the Dali—separate settings like separate worlds, each with different meanings and different possibilities. Like countless seashells stirred and tossed by the waves, the memories churned, and for once the water offered no peace.

By show time she was calm, composed, and ready, at least outwardly. Claire was a pro, and she was going to prove it.

Even several songs into the set, Claire couldn't shake the feeling of detachment that she experienced in the big room. She kept scanning the audience for a familiar face, some kind of human connection. There was none. She was playing to a roomful of strangers, and Claire knew she was partly to blame. Dylan would have come if she'd asked him, but she hadn't. She had wanted to do this on her own. And he'd gotten the message. Apparently he'd passed the word on to the others at the refuge—none of them had come, either.

Under the lights, Claire couldn't see beyond the first tables. Even Brett Westbrook was concealed behind his video camera, and he was no more than a moving shadow. Regardless, the performance was slick and professional. Technically, the show was flawless. But it still didn't feel right.

"We did good," Bizzy declared after the first long set. The band members had gathered backstage to take a breather.

"I have one thing to say," Charlie began slowly. "Being good and being comfortable ain't the same. I don't feel like we belong here. At least I don't." He looked genuinely dejected.

"I'd feel better if they'd glance up occasionally and actually listen to the words," Claire added. "The audience is too far away to get any interaction. I get the feeling that if six other bodies showed up there for the next set and played loud, no one would notice any difference."

Pete took a slow breath, which he held. Then he sighed and nodded. "Anyone else have something to say?" He looked from one solemn face to the next.

Robby wobbled his bushy head of hair from side to side. "I was sitting up there listening to how good we sounded and wondering what we'd do if they offered us the job. I don't know if I'd like this night after night. It's like being a kid and having to be on our best behavior. 'Sit up straight, act nice, don't make a fuss.' Besides that, we're just part of the background, and that's no fun.''

"If the place doesn't feel right, then I guess it's not right.'' Pete sighed. "I'm the one who got us into this. And even I agree with you,'' he admitted. "This place is something special, big and snazzy, but it isn't us. However,'' he said as he straightened his shoulders, "we have one more set to do. Let's go out and make it good—and do it for us. We'll still come out of this with the video. We've got some fine new material. And we've still got our job at the Pier to go back to. Unless we gave it a shot, we'd never have known what we know now.''

"I'm glad someone here can be philosophical while all that money slips away,'' Bizz muttered glumly. "I kinda like the place. But if the rest of you vote no, then I'm with you.''

"Show time. . .'' Pete announced as he checked his watch. "Let's cook.''

As soon as Claire read the Sunday paper, she knew why none of the refuge workers had attended the Mariner performance the night before. Headlines in the City section reported the death of seventeen pelicans and two roseate spoonbills whose bodies were found near a sewage dump site. Twelve other severely ill birds had been taken off for round-the-clock treatment by the staff of the Gulf Coast Seabird Refuge.

Ten minutes after reading the grim report, Claire was on her way out to the refuge to help.

"We've been up all night." Tammy didn't have to explain. Her reddened eyes and bedraggled appearance told Claire how strenuous the night had been.

"We couldn't save them. . . ." Large tears welled up in Tammy's eyes as she slumped in an armchair in the corner of the recovery area. "Too many bacteria in their organs—too many pollutants destroying their bodies. The poor things had been feeding at the site regularly and were poisoned by all that crud being dumped into the waterway. Dylan has taken the birds to a microbiologist to have autopsies done. He's bumping heads with some pretty important city officials. They're trying to discount pollution as the cause, but he's calling in every state and federal agency to lower the boom for dumping violations."

"We're talking major warpath." Kurt came around from the surgical area to add his comments.

"I thought Dylan knew all the public-relations angles," Tammy continued, "but Rebecca Stroud has a few things to teach him. She's been calling all over, getting information on disposal regulations, and she even contacted some newsman who did a story on the impact of new developments on sanitation. This is right down his alley. He had a television crew out here filming the treatment of the birds. Then they talked to Dylan about the need for expansion onto the proposed site—getting birds and people into an area that is safe for them. With the hearings coming up, it will sure make the city look bad if they seem reluctant to approve the zoning changes. Rebecca sure can capitalize on a sad situation.''

''We've got to give it to her,'' Kurt responded, ''that woman knows how to nail the right folks to get things done.'' In spite of his personal feelings, he was obviously impressed with Rebecca's cunning.

''Is there anything I can do?'' Claire asked, knowing her efforts could never be as spectacular as Rebecca's. When she came into the compound, she'd noticed several other volunteers industriously doing the things she generally did—cleaning the pens and freshening the water pools. Apparently she hadn't been the only one to come in for extra duty.

''Tell us how it went at the Mariner last night.'' Tammy seemed eager to get off the subject of birds. ''Did you like the place? Did you and Sound Off get the job?''

''We were good enough,'' Claire said honestly. ''But we decided during a break we really didn't like the space. The manager was disappointed, but he has lots of other bands who'll step in. So back to the dinner cruise and the Pier for me.''

''Sorry it didn't work out.'' Tammy sighed. ''If it hadn't been for all this, I would have been there.''

''Me, too,'' Kurt added. ''We forget what life is like out there in civilization.'' With that, he began squawking and flapping bent arms like wings.

''Last night was a little too civilized,'' Claire replied. ''But we're having a video of the performance edited. I'll bring in the tape and play it to you and the birds,'' she promised. ''But for now, I'd be glad to do something while you two go home and get some sleep. I hate to say it, but you look dreadful."

"You don't have to tell me," and Kurt chuckled.

"I may not look good to you," Tammy grunted, "but Dylan is coming by in a few minutes to take Frazer and me on a rescue run along some of the nesting sites in the mangrove islands. If we find any tangled birds, they'll think I look marvelous."

"But you're so tired already," Claire protested.

"Yeah. . .but it has to be done today," Tammy said with conviction. "A tangled bird doesn't care if I've had a long day. He only knows that someone cares enough to free him."

The earnestness in Tammy's eyes caused a twinge of envy in Claire. For Tammy, just as for Dylan, her work was her life—her source of joy. There were times when Claire had felt that way about her music. Before Wes Raines.

"Maybe I can go on the rescue in your place?" Claire suggested. "I've survived the guano test," she added with a smile. "I'd like to help."

A slow smile spread across Tammy's face. Even with the sprinkling of freckles and the tan she looked pale and drawn. "You know, I just bet you could handle it. And I can hide upstairs for a couple of hours and get some sleep. Get some cages, and take them down to the beach," Tammy directed. "You take them empty and hope you won't need them, but you usually do. Also, get the garbage bags." Tammy's matter-of-fact instructions made the preparations sound routine, but the mention of garbage bags were a grim reminder. The dark plastic bags were for the nonsurvivors—the birds they were too late to save.

"I'll stay and man the fort," Kurt promised. "Frazer went to answer a call, but Robinson said he'll go on the rescue. We'll hope for an uneventful, mundane afternoon. The weekend fishermen have been out, though. That means more hooks, lines and sinkers. No tellin' what will show up."

"I'll see you when we get back," Claire called to them as she set off to locate Robinson and get him to help her lug cages and supplies down to the path toward the waterfront.

"Here comes Dylan in the boat now." Tammy stood still and listened a second. "Hurry."

Dylan cut the motor and glided silently up toward the sandy beach. He'd been expecting Frazer and Tammy.

"We're the second team," Robinson informed him as he waded out to the boat. "We're giving the first-string team a little relief." Dylan looked as if he could use some relief himself. The stubble of a beard outlined his chin, and his eyes, shaded by his wide-brimmed fishing hat, were heavy lidded and bloodshot.

"We will do, won't we?" Claire stood knee-deep in water behind Robinson with a cage balanced in her arms.

"You'll do, all right." Dylan looked from the tall black Robinson to the slim blonde behind him and smiled. "Okay, crew," he said with a chuckle. "All aboard. We have some birds to save."

THREE HOURS LATER, grim-faced and streaked with perspiration and dirt, Dylan, Claire and Robinson carried their precious cargo into the refuge. In addition to the fledgling pelican that had fallen from his nest and two birds badly mangled by fishing line, they had one other slightly shrunken body of a pelican that had been suspended in a crooked mangrove tree where he had become trapped.

Like the others, he had apparently tried to beat a fisherman to his catch and had taken hooks, bait and the fish itself into his belly. Rather than lead the flapping pelican into shore, the fisherman had cut the line, so yards of line trailed behind the bird as he flew off. Those yards caught on the tree limbs when the pelican went home to roost and made a monofilament prison that the helpless bird could never leave. He had starved to death within inches of his mate and their nest of young.

Halfway through the treatment of the two larger birds, Frazer's rusty voice bellowed to them from outside. Claire continued to work silently, clipping the tight knots of line from the birds, while Kurt raced outside to find out what was wrong.

Then Dylan's voice sounded clearly above the others. "Get Ben Grimes over here. We're going to need him."

"Two more are in the patrol car," Frazer called out.

The rapid-fire exchange sounded ominous.

"Some lunatic is loose." Kurt's voice crackled with an uncharacteristic viciousness.

Claire heard the door to the clinic open and footsteps coming quickly her way.

"This is pretty ugly," Dylan came up behind Claire and rested his hand on her shoulder. "Maybe you'd better step outside while we get to work."

Claire held the bird she had been working on snugly against her side and walked over to put him in the recovery cage. "I'd like to stay and try to help."

The scrape of the outside door was the only sound that marked the arrival of the new patients. "Here's the first one." Kurt carried the large brown pelican to the surgery table. "Frazer is bringing the other two."

Under Kurt's arm was a mature pelican whose eyes were wild with panic. Where the bird's upper bill should have been was a ragged stump. Someone had deliberately sawed off the upper mandible.

"There were others like this?" Claire gasped.

"I've read about mutilations like this in California," Kurt fumed. "But I sure never thought I'd see anything like it. What on earth are we supposed to do?"

"We'll give them antibiotics for now and pump some nourishment into them," Dylan directed. "When Ben gets here, we'll see if he can suggest anything. Before we worry about repairing the damage, we have to stabilize them."

This time when the door swung open, Claire hurried over to relieve Frazer of his patient. Clasping the bird's wings and feet and holding him on her lap, she sat trying to soothe the frightened bird until his turn on the surgery table came up. *Three of them....* The viciousness of the act descended upon her like a lead weight. Deliberately someone had done this to the goofy, friendly birds who could not utter a whine of protest or cry for help.

"Are you okay?" Dylan asked Claire as he crouched close to her while they waited for the arrival of the vet, Ben Grimes. Dylan rested a comforting hand on the silvery-gray back feathers of the mutilated bird.

"I'm all right," Claire replied, breathing evenly. "I'm all right."

"Let's have the next bird," Kurt called from across the room, interrupting their quiet conversation. "This one doesn't look good, Dylan." The pelican he had treated lay on a heating pad with a towel draped over his back. "Blood pressure is low..." Kurt observed. "I think the poor fellow is exhausted. He's giving up the fight."

As they stood watching, the bird began gasping, opening what remained of his upper bill with each breath. Claire looked from one face to another— Frazer, Dylan and Kurt all knew the signs. The bird was dying.

"Get the next one on the table." Dylan turned on her brusquely. "Let's get the antibiotics into this one." Stone-faced and tense, he injected the medication into Claire's pelican, then with equal efficiency dosed the third bird. "Where the hell is Ben...?" he muttered angrily. But there was a catch in his voice that his anger couldn't disguise, and his eyes glistened. When he lifted the dying pelican and carried him down the hall, he went alone.

"I DON'T KNOW WHY they don't put the poor things out of their misery." The reporter took one look at pelicans 417 and 418 and decided that the disfigured birds should be terminated. The police report of the mutilation had piqued his editor's interest, but he'd been the one roused from his Sunday-afternoon ball game. The fellow had arrived at the refuge complaining.

Frazer glowered at the man. "I hope none of your relatives is hurt in a car accident and some idiot says the same thing about them. Put them out of their misery..." he grumbled, then walked off.

The fellow stared after Frazer, then pulled out a note pad and jotted down a few lines.

After Ben Grimes arrived, Claire and Frazer had stepped outside to give the others more room to work. Now only she stood sentinel, waiting to hear the results of the examination.

"Whatever happened to 'survival of the fittest'?" The reporter tried his rhetorical technique on Claire. "If these birds can't survive on their own, then it's Nature's way to let them die."

Claire just looked at the reporter blankly, then shrugged. Nothing about these mutilations fell into the category of "Nature's way," but as long as that note pad was in the reporter's hand, she wasn't about to open her mouth. She certainly wouldn't want him to print what had crossed her mind.

When the flash of red hair in the parking lot heralded the arrival of Rebecca Stroud, Claire discreetly moved off toward the office. If Rebecca was such an expert with the press, she could have this fellow all to herself. But as Claire peeked between the venetian blinds, watching the exchange between the two, she could tell by the expression on Rebecca's face that the conversation wasn't going well at all.

"Get me Gene Bell of the *Times* on the phone," Rebecca snapped as she stalked into the refuge office.

Claire had ducked behind the counter and was busily stacking refuge brochures.

"Just give me the phone," Rebecca insisted impatiently.

"Gene, this is Rebecca Stroud." Instantly the voice became liquid honey. "I have a real public-interest story for you. The most gruesome thing has happened out here on the beaches, and I do wish you'd send someone very special out to cover it. One of your Outdoors staff would do. Apparently some sadist is on a rampage damaging the pelicans, cutting off part of the beak and leaving them to die. The birds are at the Gulf Coast Seabird Refuge. Yes... thank you, Gene," she cooed. "I'll be here. And Gene...thank you." With a perfunctory thud, she put the receiver back on the cradle. Then with a steely look she stepped outside again.

When the phone rang this time, Claire was the only one available for rescue duty. "I have five sea gulls in my swimming pool," the elderly woman said. "It's a covered pool, but the door was open and the birds came in and ate all the canapes that were set out for a cocktail party. Now they keep flying into the screen enclosure. They won't go out the door. My aerobics class is coming over in half an hour and I'd like someone to get the birds out."

"Can't you chase them out?" Claire asked curiously.

"My dear, I'm eighty-four and just had a new perm. I'm not chasing the birds."

"I'll bring the net and come right over," Claire said, chuckling. For the first time all day she had something to smile about.

"Would you pick up a loaf of whole-wheat bread on the way," the woman asked sweetly. "One with fiber...to make new canapes."

"Fiber..." Claire repeated, rolling her eyes. "Right."

IT WAS ALMOST DARK when Claire returned to the refuge. The sandy parking lot was vacant, and Dylan's pickup truck had been pulled inside the fence, next to the clinic. Other than a few herons gliding into their treetop roosts and settling in for the night, the compound was very still. But when Claire tried the clinic door, it was unlocked.

"Dylan...?" Claire poked her head into the clinic and called his name.

The surgery area was all in darkness, but in the back room, the recovery room, a dim light was on.

A shift in the shadows near the cages in the corner startled her, but it was Dylan who moved into view. "I'm here."

"I left before anything was settled. What did Dr. Grimes say could be done for the pelicans?" Claire walked toward him.

"There's only one still alive," he said in little more than a whisper. The diffused light from the hallway deepened the lines in his face as he stood with his hands stuffed into his pockets, staring into the cage of the lone survivor. "Old 418 is hanging on as best she can."

The weariness in his voice compelled her to reach out and slip her arm into his in a gesture of comfort, but Dylan remained tense and preoccupied.

"The other two suffered from shock and exposure," he went on, relaxing slightly. "Their bills were cut closer in. Ben said that even if they survived the trauma, there wasn't enough mandible left to try a reconstruction. This one has three inches to work with. If she makes it through the night, I'm taking her to California tomorrow. There's a vet on the coast who has successfully attached artificial bills on victims of mutilations there."

"Do you think there'll be more mutilations?" Claire stared up at him.

"More than likely. Both the police and Ben agree that whoever is responsible will keep at it. It gives the perpetrator some perverse thrill." His sea-blue eyes turned to meet hers. "He'll go on until he's caught, or frightened off, or gets enough of a thrill to hold him for a while. If he stays in this area and if there are more, I don't ever want to feel this helpless." His voice vibrated with outrage. "None of us, not even Ben Grimes, can repair this kind of butchery. It's a heck of a specialty, but we located the fellow who knows how to handle these cases."

"Why doesn't he come here?" Claire's question brought a half smile to Dylan's lips.

"That was my first idea. But he's got a full schedule already, plus someone would have to pay his plane fare. That won't look good on the budget. I can take a day of personal leave, pay my own way and be back before I'm even missed. And no one will have reason to gripe." He pulled one hand free from his pocket and put his arm around her shoulders. "I've been told that I need to pay very careful attention to my public image," he said half-jokingly.

"I thought you were doing quite well at that already," Claire said, intending the comment to have a bit of a sting.

"There are those who are still unconvinced," he replied, ignoring the barb. "Apparently Frazer had a run-in with a reporter who thinks our work is frivolous."

"I saw that one briefly myself," Claire told him.

"So did Rebecca. She was the one who made the point that since we are attempting to mount a massive fund-raising drive, this isn't the time to be doing anything that can be misconstrued as indiscriminately spending refuge money. This California trip will be at my own expense."

"I see." Claire stiffened slightly. She could imagine Rebecca Stroud using her sweet-as-honey technique on Dylan. What disturbed Claire was the fact that Dylan couldn't see through her. Preserving his impeccable public image would be feathering more than nests in the new refuge expansion. Rebecca's own nest could be refurbished nicely by the huge commission she would make if the land sale went through.

"There was another reporter who showed up late today," Dylan added. "He's doing a very thorough story on the mutilations. Frankly, I'd have preferred to keep the thing quiet for a while. There's always a chance of another weirdo picking up the idea and going out to commit the same crime.''

''But I suppose Rebecca Stroud thought the article could be helpful.'' Claire guessed precisely how the red-haired woman would manipulate the incident for her own purposes.

''She did suggest the story could raise the public awareness,'' Dylan acknowledged.

''It could also raise her commission,'' Claire said, blurting out what she'd been thinking.

''Ah. . . .'' Dylan narrowed his eyes and nodded. ''So that's what's bugging you. Well, brace yourself, lady. This is strictly confidential. You are not to breathe a word of this to anyone until Ms Stroud chooses to make it public, but she isn't keeping any commission coming to her from the sale of the land. She's donating the money to the refuge.''

Somehow this unselfish side of Rebecca had been missed in Claire's few encounters with the woman, and listening to Dylan come to the real-estate agent's defense made Claire feel foolish, as if she were a jealous child calling names and pointing fingers. She felt the heat of her cheeks as she reddened with embarrassment. Regardless of how she felt about Rebecca, she had misread the woman, at least in part, and voicing her opinion had only made matters worse. ''I guess I put both feet in my mouth,'' she apologized.

''That's one condition that could interfere with your singing career,'' Dylan observed dryly.

''There isn't much of a career to worry about,'' Claire answered with a shrug.

"Really? Things didn't go well at the Mariner last night?" he asked as he took Claire's shoulders and turned her to face him.

"The performance was fine," Claire told him. "But the place wasn't, so it's back to the drawing board," she said, summarizing the evening succinctly.

"Is the *Bay-Belle* still on that drawing board?"

"I don't know. It's nice there. Nice and safe," she admitted. "I'm just not sure where I should be. I've been second-guessing myself for so long, I really don't know what I want."

"I think you do," Dylan said, smiling slightly. "But something is holding you back—keeping you from trying. One day, when you're ready to talk, I'd like to know the whole story."

"What 'whole story'?" Claire avoided his penetrating gaze.

"The story of your life. The cause for all that caution you exercise." He took her chin in his hand and gently lifted her face so she would look at him. "Trust me. I'll help."

"I am not one of your case studies," she answered tersely. "I have no broken parts."

"None that show," he said softly, "except in your eyes. You can hide whatever's hurting you from the rest of the world, Claire, but you can't hide it from me. Your story comes out in bits and pieces when you sing. You show your feelings when you touch a lost or injured bird. But you whisper another story to me with your body every time you let me close to you."

Claire suddenly felt as if the bronze-skinned man

had looked into her soul. She felt exposed, totally vulnerable. She placed her hands on his chest and gently backed away. "My songs are just songs," she said softly, trying to sound convincing. "It's all part of the act."

"I doubt if Sara would agree." He obviously had succumbed to calling the egret by name. "Look at her," he said as he walked over closer to the cage where the elegant white bird stood silently in the shadows. "She wants to hear that lullaby you said you'd sing. When you sing to her, you're not acting."

"She wouldn't understand the words." Claire moved to a side table and busily arranged some files that were already in order.

"How about humming to her the way you did the other day?" He was referring to the love song "Sara's Song." Claire had dropped the number first from the Pier, then from the Mariner show and still had not performed the song in public. "Sing it for us." He turned and looked into her eyes. "The little bit of melody I heard sounded pretty. We could use a song to cheer us all up."

"I can't sing that one," Claire said in a very small voice. With the band she could pretend that it was just a song, but there was no way she could look at Dylan and sing the words without revealing far more than she dared. Saying the song belonged to Sara kept Claire safe.

"One day I want you to sing to me, Claire. Look me in the eye and sing just for me." Dylan stepped between Claire and the table and removed the files from her hands. "I want you free from all those memories that keep reaching out to foul you up and hold you down. You're like that seabird trapped in the treetops. Only your strings are invisible ones, and I don't know where to reach to cut you free."

The image of the imprisoned seabird seemed hauntingly appropriate. Like the bird, Claire had come home with invisible hooks, but the strings of her past trailed along. She had brought her prison back with her. Only one night in Dylan's arms had she dreamed she had broken free. Then the prison closed in and held her tighter than before.

"Sara, the seabirds and I have a lot in common. You are very wise," she whispered.

"Not wise enough to know where to touch you to stop the hurt. Not wise enough to keep from wanting you." He bent down and kissed her lightly on the lips. Then his arms enfolded her like gentle wings, holding her against his firm body, letting her feel the steady beat of his heart. And as the heat from his body sent a comforting warmth throughout her, she wanted to be closer. She wanted to break free again.

"I want you to want me," he whispered roughly into the tousled confusion of her hair.

Claire wrapped her arms around him, feeling the hard muscles of his back, taut beneath his shirt. And her senses responded to his taste and scent and movement so totally that her body curved against his instinctively. The sureness of his strength and the sweetness of his kiss brought back visions of the sea god.

But her mind filled with other images: Dylan's

public world where someone else fitted in; a manicured hand resting on his arm and keen jungle eyes
that saw very clearly the way to this man's heart was
through making his dreams a reality. Rebecca could
use her social ease, her business skill, her influence to
help Dylan acquire his wilderness. Claire only had a
castle of sand and a troubled heart. Not enough to
build on. Not enough to hold him. Love was not
enough. She had failed once before with a love and
had nearly been destroyed. But the powerful force
that drew them together once more tantalized her,
and she could feel the restraint slipping away. His
hand fitted into the curve of her back and lifted her
against him. With a vividness that took her breath
away, she remembered how it felt when they'd
touched each other for the very first time.

"Dylan. I do want you...." She felt his embrace
tighten at the sound of her words. "But...."

Dylan moved back, looking down at her wearily.
He placed one finger on her lips gently to silence
what she would say next. "Stop with the first part.
That's what I wanted to hear." He forced the words
out in a controlled, precise voice. "That's what I
wanted you to feel. Want me. And remember every
detail."

"'Remember'?" Claire braced her arms and
stepped from his embrace. "Just what does that
mean?"

"I'm giving you some help fighting those invisible
strings—memory for memory. Something has divided you into neat little compartments with trapdoors
that snap shut. You really might let me make love to

you tonight, but you'd be full of doubts in the morning. You just don't trust me enough. Not yet. You touch the creatures in my world, but you won't invite me into yours. You couldn't bring yourself to ask me to the Mariner—or to tell me to stay away. So you said nothing.''

Claire still had nothing she could say.

''I think you want me and you want to succeed with your music, but you can't let yourself go all out for anything. There is always a 'but' gnawing away at you. I won't settle for that—not for long. Now all I wanted was a beginning. I want you to want me,'' he said evenly. ''Without the 'but' and without the wine and without the repercussions the next day. I want you to let me into all the nooks and crannies of that complicated mind of yours. And before I can move in, you have to get the ghosts out. Take a good look at my face,'' he insisted. ''Just make sure that the ghosts that spook you look like someone else, not me. And let all the 'buts' get attached to someone who deserves them. I don't. When you go to sleep at night, I want my face in your dreams, not someone else's.''

''I can keep the faces separate,'' Claire protested. But in her heart she knew Dylan was right. Somewhere in her mind she was putting Wes Raines's face on him, imagining the hurt again, dreading the anger and the disappointment and trying not to let the songs say too much.

''You've been very good at keeping things separate,'' Dylan said, stepping away from her. ''Too good at times. I just want you to know that I'm not.''

"What do you mean?" She looked at him apprehensively. He had moved toward the rows of cages and peered in at the injured 418. Now he straightened his back, stretching the stiffness out, rotating his neck to ease the exhausted muscles.

"It means it's time for you to go home, Claire. I'll have to discuss this with you when I get back from California. Tonight I have another lady on my mind." Abruptly he walked off down the darkened hallway, leaving her standing amid the cages.

For an instant Claire thought he meant Rebecca. But then she saw what had prompted Dylan's comment. Pelican 418 had perked up and was bobbing her head from side to side, peeking back at her. The lady on Dylan's mind had lots of personality, but she was no beauty.

"If this cot were big enough and if I had more energy, I might consider keeping you here." The sound of wheels on the hard floor preceded Dylan's return. "I'm not sure if 418 is hearty enough to witness what I have in mind." He began setting the cot up right in front of the cage. Then he stood there unbuttoning his shirt while 418 watched from her cage.

"I am going to get naked." He pulled the shirt open and slid out one tanned, muscular arm, then the other.

Claire couldn't pull her eyes away from the rise and fall of his chest. Just watching him, she could feel her breasts responding, her nipples becoming fuller, more erect. "I'm beat. I've got to get some sleep. And I am going to try desperately not to think of your body or your big eyes or your cool hands on my skin. And if 418 will doze off again, now that the crisis is over, I'm leaving at dawn to take my lady friend out to the coast for a nose job."

When he unbuckled his belt, Claire looked up hastily. "I think I'll be going."

"I think you'd better." His voice rumbled low and soft through the muted darkness of the room. "Think of me in the night."

He didn't have to say that. Claire was already imagining the emptiness of the wide bed that waited for her.

"And don't forget to say good-night to Sara before you lock the door."

The raspy sound of the zipper broke the silence as she crossed the room. "Good night, Sara," Claire whispered hurriedly. Then, as she closed the outside door, she heard the squeak of the springs on the old cot. "Good night, Dylan," she called softly.

"Sweet dreams . . ." came the reply. And she knew that a lopsided smile was all he was wearing.

CHAPTER EIGHT

"How could any human being think this way?"
Tammy stormed about the office, waving the newspaper column written by the reporter who had been
blatantly undercut on the mutilation story because of
Rebecca Stroud's maneuvering. When the wildlife
reporter Rebecca requested came out to the refuge to
do a sympathetic coverage of the crime against the endangered pelicans, the first reporter had known he
was caught in a power play. So he had submitted his
comments in the form of a letter to the editor, recom-
mending euthanasia, as a more humane solution for
the victims. And he had sparked a controversy. In the
two days since Dylan and 418 had been gone, the
refuge and the debate over treatment was mentioned
on the news in the bay area and was even given a brief
spot statewide. Visitors and contributions to the
refuge had increased, but the response was not all sup-
portive.

"He actually thinks that survival of the fittest
means that we should let the injured birds die without
treatment. That we should just kill them quickly with
an injection," Tammy fumed. "I suppose 'Mother
Nature' was responsible for filling their throats with
fishhooks and cutting off their circulation with

monofilament fishing line,'' she huffed. ''Those birds were butchered by a human being. The others were poisoned. There is nothing *natural* about any of it. But if we use human technology or human medical advances to save these birds—suddenly we're tampering with the grand scheme of things and wasting our time and other people's money.'' As she stormed over the so-called natural approach to treating the animals, her dark braid snapped from side to side like the tail of a caged panther.

''What scares me,'' Josie said as she swept her salt-and-pepper hair back and propped her reading glasses on top of her head, ''is that this reporter is serious. He thinks that being dead is better than having an artificial bill or a crippled wing. And there are others just like him. I bet there's a reception committee waiting for Dylan at the airport. And this jerk will be with them, wanting to know the cost to the penny of that darned fiberglass bill.''

''Her Highness plans to be there to head them off. Rebecca Stroud will take care of everything.'' Tammy was still chafing over the woman's insistence that she meet the plane, instead of one of the refuge staff.

Josie turned to the silent figure at the desk who was reading over another piece of writing—the rebuttal letter that Kurt and Tammy had composed. ''Well, how's it sound?'' If the angry reporter could have his view published, they intended to publish theirs.

''I think it sounds very good,'' Claire said. ''I like the point about captive breeding—producing healthy young by crippled parents. Very effective.'' She grinned.

"I think you'd better let Dylan take a look at the piece before you submit it," Josie added.

"I'll bet his self-appointed PR adviser, Rebecca, will want to read it just to make sure it's consistent with our image. I want you to know that she came by and picked up his suit to take to the airport," Tammy muttered sarcastically. "I guess she plans to have Dylan change before he's interviewed. Pelican 418 will be sitting in the baggage depot all by herself."

"If Rebecca is starting to get fussy about how he dresses, wait till she gets to us," Kurt said, glancing at his torn jeans and camouflage T-shirt. "We may be next. She could have us all dressed up in matching uniforms," he said with a chuckle. "We're going to be on television, too."

"Very funny," Tammy replied.

They were to be on television all right, but not for public viewing. Earlier that morning a local businessman had donated a used video-surveillance system to the refuge. He was upgrading his video unit to accommodate three large warehouses, and the donation of the smaller, outmoded system was tax deductible. The system was going to be very helpful. Once installed in the refuge, everyone, particularly the birds, would be on the screen around the clock. From the front office, Josie or any other worker would be able to monitor the entire facility during the day, and in the evenings, Dylan could switch the system upstairs.

"If we're all going to be TV stars, I think we'd better get back to work on the wiring," and Claire summoned Tammy outside.

There was still the matter of strategically placing

the cameras in several of the larger pens so the behavior of the birds could be observed without disturbing them with a human presence. Claire had to work the *Bay-Belle* later in the day, so if they wanted to take advantage of her electronic talents, they couldn't take any more time with the letter.

In the corner of the pen for wading birds—herons and egrets and ibis—Chuck was mounting the Plexiglas box that would protect the unit from the weather.

"Dylan is going to be knocked out by this," Tammy said as she clasped one remote camera against her chest. "He'll never believe we installed this without his help. We'll have everyone under observation anytime we want. There's a lot of stuff we miss just because the darn birds are smart enough to wait till we're not looking. Now we'll always be looking." Observing, recording, never intruding and never tiring, the cameras could add volumes to their knowledge of seabirds.

"Where'd you learn so much about wiring?" Chuck asked Claire with more than a casual interest. He'd watched the slim, gold-haired volunteer set up the inside units, then connect the remote cameras one after the other.

"When I worked with a road band, we had a lot of electronic equipment," Claire explained. "What I know, I just picked up out of necessity."

"Well, I'm impressed," he said before moving on to the next site.

"I'm impressed, too." The voice that caused her to spin around was Dylan's. From the way he was looking at Claire in her white shorts and T-shirt, he was evidently admiring more than the wiring.

"I thought your plane didn't come in till three!" Tammy blurted out in surprise. "Where's 418?" Then her dark eyes grew wider. "And where's Rebecca? She and your blue suit were planning to meet you. I think she had some kind of interview set up."

Dylan glanced down at his crumpled gray slacks and zip-front jacket. He had a huge manilla envelope stuffed with papers under one arm and an overnight bag in the other. "No one mentioned anything to me," he said, shrugging. "We finished ahead of schedule and I switched to an earlier flight. I'll have Josie call Rebecca's office. By the way, my girlfriend with the new beak is in her cage in the airport limo." He tilted his head toward the air-conditioned car waiting in the parking lot. "I brought her home in style."

All work stopped while the three workers went to get 418, and Dylan stepped into the office to tell Josie he was back and have her inform Rebecca Stroud. Outside, carrying the caged bird like Cleopatra on her barge, Chuck led the procession into the refuge, with Tammy and Claire following.

"She looks wonderful...."

"What a schnozzle...." Kurt said with a cackle. "I like it."

The long narrow shaft had an open channel on the upper edge that neatly fitted over the stub of 418's natural beak. Stainless-steel bolts had been put through from one side to the other, securing all three layers. Except for the small, rounded tops of the bolts, 418's new fiberglass beak was the same drab grayish-brown as her own. The only thing missing was the hook at the end of the beak. That detail had been omitted to keep the bird from putting too much pressure on the artificial beak. Even with the repair, the new apparatus would not work well in the wild. But around the refuge she'd be able to function almost normally.

Dylan met them on the back patio, bringing with him an armful of cold drinks to toast the returnee. Pelican 418 put up with the attention and the impromptu celebration for several minutes, then, with an impatient wobble of her new beak, indicated she'd had enough. Kurt scooped her up and took her inside while Dylan held open the door.

"Nice job on the surveillance units," Dylan commented as he stepped back onto the patio. "Who's going to tell me how it works?" He was in such a good mood that Tammy and Claire simply grinned and looked at each other. The letter to the editor could wait.

While Tammy explained about the placement of the video system, Claire checked the angle of the remaining camera. Dylan nodded and glanced over at the gray-eyed lady with the wire clippers, pliers and the screwdrivers.

"Another hidden talent," he commented to Claire.

"Speaking of talent...and videos." Tammy brightened in the midst of her commentary. "Where's the one they made of your performance last weekend." She poked an accusing finger at Claire.

"It's still being edited, I guess," Claire replied while she clipped a thin red-coated wire. "I haven't seen anything. Brett Westbrook insisted that Pete help him edit. I guess he figured Pete could be more objective than me.''

"Well, when it's ready, we all want to see it," Tammy insisted. "We can plug the video into all this stuff and play back on all the monitors. We could send the sound into the recovery room for musical therapy." Tammy was only half teasing.

There was an awkward pause in the conversation that very clearly indicated the two women were avoiding something important. "Okay...what else has been going on?" Dylan looked from one semi-innocent face to the other.

"We'll tell you right after we fill the bird pools," Tammy said, then motioned for Claire to follow her. Like escapees making a swift exodus, they retreated to the far side of the pens. Dylan stared at them in bewilderment, then shrugged and stepped into his office, closing the door.

By the time Claire finished the first pool, Rebecca Stroud had arrived.

"This should be good," Tammy said, nudging Claire. "Let's go hear the PR specialist smooth this one over."

They raced into the rear entrance of the main building, waved for Kurt to follow them, then tried to appear nonchalant as the three of them strolled into Dylan's office. Rebecca Stroud, in white slacks and a tropical print blouse, was leaning over Dylan's shoulder as he sat at his desk, reading a newspaper clipping.

"The longer article is very positive." Rebecca pointed a manicured fingernail at the lead paragraph of the article she had brought in. "As far as this other reporter is concerned, I think we should just ignore him. We have other things to play up.'' The ''we'' made Tammy's eyes widen.

''Kurt and I have already decided what 'we' will do.'' Tammy picked their letter off the desk and passed it to Dylan. She didn't even glance at his red-haired companion. ''We are very angry about his comments and we intend to say so.''

Tammy sat on the corner of Dylan's desk to wait while he read the rebuttal. Rebecca looked down at the muddy boots swinging casually so near her crisp white slacks and stepped toward the window.

''That pretty well says it all,'' Dylan said when he'd finished. ''You've covered the issues without focusing on the sensational aspects.''

''The letter is quite good,'' Rebecca remarked after Dylan stood and handed it to her to read, ''but hardly objective, especially since it's signed by two full-time refuge employees. I think it isn't wise to get into a public fray.''

''But we have rights as individuals...'' Kurt argued.

''In this case, your rights aren't in question. Your motives may be. The letter could be construed as self-serving. That won't look good for the refuge,'' Rebecca insisted. Sharp green eyes shifted from Tammy to Kurt, then softened as they turned to Dylan.

''Would it help if I signed the letter, instead?'' Claire asked. ''I'm not on the payroll.''

Only the slightest touch of surprise gleamed in Rebecca's eyes. ''That may open an entire other can of worms,'' she replied. ''Some of the organizations that support the refuge are churches and ladies' groups.

Dear Laura,

Your special introductory offer of 4 free books is too good to miss.

Please also reserve a Harlequin Love Affair subscription for me. If I decide to subscribe, I shall receive six new books every two months for £7.50* post and packing free. If I decide not to subscribe I shall write and tell you within 10 days. The free books will be mine to keep in either case.

I understand that I may cancel my subscription at any time simply by writing to you. I am over 18 years of age.

Name _____ Signature _____

Address _____

_____

_____ Postcode _____ 9L5S

Laura King
Harlequin Reader Service
FREEPOST
PO Box 236
Croydon
Surrey
CR9 9EL

NO
STAMP
NEEDED

They are very sensitive about the character of the staff."

"So?" Tammy stared at her.

"Claire is an entertainer. She sings in bars. There's a connection with drinking and loud music—not to mention other possibilities. However unfair, having the letter signed by a bar singer isn't a wholesome image for the cause."

Rebecca felt the icy chill in every glance that came her way. Claire reached out to place a calming hand on Tammy's shoulder, knowing that an explosion was likely.

"I'm just telling you how it may look. I didn't expect you to agree." Rebecca refused to back down. "We are dealing with a sensitive issue in a very public medium. Entertainers don't have a particularly savory reputation."

For a moment no one said anything.

"I hate to admit it, but she has a point." Dylan looked at Claire with a somber expression. "If this reporter is backed into a corner he may not let the issue drop. He might pick up on anything to come back at us—and that includes Claire. We're dealing with a kind of prejudice, and the issue is credibility." Stony silence greeted Dylan's remarks. He turned to Kurt and added, "Think of how certain facts could be distorted."

Claire felt her mouth go suddenly dry. Coming from Rebecca, the remarks only made her angry. But if Dylan agreed that a performer could besmirch the image of his precious refuge, she didn't want to be around him at all.

"If he said anything mean about Claire, I'd drive

the pickup truck over him a few times," Tammy said, bristling.

"Now just simmer down. Let's think this through without everyone getting his feelings hurt." Dylan tried to play peacemaker, but Claire had already put up the defensive walls.

"If it will end this arguing, I'll sign the letter."

Rebecca's proclamation was a conciliatory gesture designed to appease everyone. She needn't have bothered. Kurt glared at her. Claire frowned and turned toward the door. Tammy became rigid, like a cat ready to pounce.

"Wait a minute," Dylan barked. "Rebecca, please do us a favor and step outside for a moment while we have a short conference."

With a fleeting, tight smile, the red-haired woman slipped past Claire and did as he asked.

Once she was out of earshot, Dylan turned to the others. "This is mushrooming into something all out of proportion. Rebecca is on our side. What she says makes sense."

Tammy rolled her eyes in exasperation and crossed her arms over her chest.

"No one is trying to rob you and Kurt of the credit for writing an excellent letter," Dylan hastily clarified. "But since you are both highly professional refuge staff members," he stressed coolly, "I'm sure you can appreciate Rebecca's point."

Both Kurt and Tammy refused to respond.

"It isn't who sets the record straight. What matters is that the information in your letter gets to the public. Rebecca can do that. She's from a family with a reputation for supporting a variety of community projects. This reporter won't go after her, or he'll be stepping on some very sensitive toes.''

"I wish they were hers," Tammy grumbled.

Claire stared down at her hands, determined not to say anything.

"As much as it may go against your grain, I think you should let her submit the letter in her name. None of us has time for this kind of hassle." His eyes shot from one silent listener to the next. "We have more important things to spend our energies on. I'm going upstairs to change clothes. You think this out, let Rebecca know what you decide and we'll all get on with our work." He walked out, leaving them standing stonily in a semicircle.

Kurt cleared his throat and shifted from foot to foot. "Well, what are we going to do?"

"I've got to get ready for the *Bay-Belle*," Claire said wearily, and started for the door.

"You mean you're leaving us just so you can sing your sexy songs in some sleazy bar—a floating one, no less," Kurt teased. "Take me with you, please!"

Even Tammy giggled at that one. For a few seconds the tension melted away.

"I surrender. Hand this to Joan of Arc out there." Tammy held out the letter to Claire. "Tell her to sign her John Henry and send it in."

"Okay. But only because it's a good letter. And it's for the birds." Claire gave Tammy a quick hug, knowing the irony of the phrase wouldn't be missed.

"I'll say it's for the birds." Tammy forced a tight smile.

"See you on Wednesday," Claire said. Then with a quick nod to both of them, she walked outside.

Rebecca Stroud was waiting on the patio and turned to hear the outcome of the conference.

"Would you please sign this and send it in." Claire kept her smile polite and her gaze brave and unwavering. Then she strode off toward her car. She found her steps accelerating as the knot in her chest moved into her throat and threatened to burst out in a sob. "For the birds...." She gritted her teeth and struggled to maintain her composure. But no matter how she tried not to cry, slow tears trickled down her cheeks as she drove away.

THE BALMY BREEZE off the bay that evening carried Claire's music softly over the water, drifting through the rigging of moored yachts in the marina and winding amid the elegant shoreline palms that waved their umbrella arms to the airborne melodies. The paddle-wheeler moved serenely over the water away from shore giving Claire the distance she needed tonight—emotional as well as physical. For the patrons aboard, the cruise gave them a few leisurely hours where music and good food and the gentle rhythm of the boat lulled away all other concerns. And there was nothing to do but enjoy it.

Claire first played the melody inadvertently. In the break while coffee was served, she sat behind the keyboard, fiddling with the adjustments so her synthesizer sounded like violins, and the first phrase of a song was born. Intact. Words and music. Like a brilliant sliver of light, the spark of creation broke free. Just for an instant.

"Sit here with me, facing in the wind...."

Though just a phrase, Claire knew the rest would come eventually.

"Share your freedom, gentle friend...."

There was no coherent pattern or form yet, and the images drifted through her mind disorderly—sea gulls and egrets, beaches and waves, castles on the seashore and faces. Wes. Dylan. Tammy. But she knew the message had to do with letting go and trying again.

Bar singer.... Claire's hands trembled over the keys, feeling the indignation once more. Somehow it was all connected and all simmering inside. The feelings and the images were coming together in a song. If she didn't rush, didn't try to force herself, the images would free themselves in time.

FOR SEVERAL MINUTES after the boat docked alongside the pier, Claire went through her usual routine of dismantling the amplifiers from her synthesizer and hauling the electronic equipment to her car. "Let me give you a hand with that." Dylan stepped up onto the upper deck and came toward her.

"What are you doing here?" she said, looking up in surprise.

Dylan's white slacks and open-necked shirt gave him a casual, comfortable look, but the half smile he wore when he approached didn't match the concern in his eyes.

"I caught a glimpse of you when you left the refuge this afternoon. You looked upset. I thought maybe we should talk." He studied her face, trying to read the emotion behind her veiled expression.

"That depends on what you have to say." She busied herself with the equipment.

"First I want to thank you for the excellent job you did installing the surveillance system," he began politely. "I can see now why you need to be such an expert with wiring. You've put a lot of money into this equipment." Dylan studied the assortment of dials and tone adjustments above the keyboard of her synthesizer. Carefully he stepped over the curlicues of wires connecting the console to the amplifiers.

"You're right about that," Claire replied, trying to appear nonchalant. When he picked up a few loose pages of her music and deftly tapped them into a neat stack, his uncalculated gesture of concern softened the set of her shoulders. At least he cared enough to come by. "This kind of equipment is very expensive. When Wes and I divorced, our custody battle was over things like YAMAHA and OBX and Moog. He got the JBL speakers and the stringed instruments. Fortunately I came out with all this."

"You must have had a good lawyer," Dylan joked. But the sudden change in Claire's gray eyes made his smile less certain. Even the presence of these inanimate objects could distort the present with visions from the past. Suddenly he felt as if someone else, an unwelcome intruder, had joined them on the upper deck of the old boat.

"My attorney knew what to do, that's for sure," she admitted. "He knew these were the tools of my trade, as well as Wes's," Claire replied quietly. "That part was all settled out of court, actually." What she didn't add was that the leverage in the out-of-court settlement was the filing of assault charges that her lawyer held over Wes Raines. Play fair or go to jail.

"I'll carry this to your car," Dylan said, offering to haul the keyboard.

Claire nodded, leading the way with an armload. With every step down the stairway to the lower deck, she waited for him to get to the real reason he had come there.

"I know what happened at the refuge today didn't seem fair. I don't want to leave it hanging." His voice, low and smooth, surrounded her in the darkness of the stairwell.

"Do you mean the letter or bar-singer business?" Claire tossed the question back at him coolly, taking each step down carefully.

"Both. The whole thing was very complicated and not as important as everyone thought. None of it was personal," he insisted.

"Not 'personal. . . .'" Claire stopped at the bottom of the stairs and turned to glare up at him. "Not 'personal'?" she repeated in a flat, uncompromising voice. "You have to be kidding."

Dylan stepped down next to her, his expression controlled. He definitely was not kidding. "Neither the Pier nor the *Bay-Belle* could qualify as a dive," he said evenly. "They both have bars. You're a singer. But what Rebecca pointed out is the way some people might choose to interpret that, given a little help by an angry reporter. That's hard, cold reality. Nothing personal. You can't hide your head in the sand."

Claire turned away as he spoke and walked slightly

ahead of him, down the gangway and out into the nearly vacant parking area.

"I played for a boatful of people tonight," Claire reminded him as he caught up to her, falling into step. "That is hardly hiding. I've had a run in or two with reality before, and if I get hurt, it's personal."

"I'm not so sure," he said cautiously. "That nerve Rebecca hit may have been overly sensitive. You wrap a cocoon around yourself then go to work and do an excellent job. But you're inside that cocoon, and all you see is the beauty. That part is very personal. But Rebecca's comment was about the outside part, the job description, not the person, and if the label hurts your feelings, I'm sorry. I just don't want you to wear that cocoon when you're with me—or at the refuge with the birds. I don't want you on the defensive there."

"Until Rebecca arrived on the scene, I never felt the need to protect myself at the refuge," Claire answered as she thrust the key into the car door and opened it. "The only predators were the hawks and vultures," she added pointedly, "and they stay in cages." Silently she loaded her keyboard, then slid the amplifier inside.

Dylan stood very close to her. "There's more to it than Rebecca," he stressed. Clasping her shoulders gently, he turned her to face him. "Whatever hurt you and still makes you so defensive happened long before I met you that day on the beach. Long before Rebecca showed up. Something or someone has done a job on you, and I want to get to the bottom of it. What went on between you and Wes?" he asked bluntly. "What did he do to you?"

Claire looked up at the questioning sea-blue eyes, wondering in what ways she had let the truth show through to him. His hands on her shoulders were warm, strong and comforting. He was waiting for an answer. None of the easy explanations worked with Dylan. He had asked her to trust him, to let him know what she was thinking or feeling. To open up.

"The break wasn't as civilized as it may have sounded. Part of the trouble we had was tied up with the music business. Creating and performing are part of the good times. But the bad times are pretty grim. There is always the dark side—liquor, drugs, groupies." Claire took a deep breath and looked away. "Wes had his dark side, too. When the pressure got to him, he did drugs and drank. He also hit me."

The words were simple enough to say but they opened up the secret parts of her that refused to go away. All the humiliation, the pain, the unspeakable sorrow that she'd tried to leave behind.

"He did what?" Dylan's voice was glacial.

Claire moistened her lips with the tip of her tongue and spoke very precisely. "Wes hit me. Very hard. There were three or four incidents over the last year we were married."

"Was the divorce the end of it? Does Wes still threaten you in any way? Are you afraid he might hurt you again?"

Claire shook her head thoughtfully. "No, I'm not afraid of that. There are a lot of feelings left over."

"How do you feel about him now?" Dylan's face was drawn and tense, but his eyes held her with a questioning urgency. "Do you still love him? Does he still have that kind of a hold on you?"

"I don't think so," Claire answered. "That last year he wasn't particularly lovable or loving." But there had been times when she had seen flashes of poet in him, periods of creativity, when her heart had felt hopeful and her body had responded to him with a passion that could illuminate that darker side and comfort them both—for a while. That tug-of-war between intellect and passion had kept her with him.

Dylan took a deep breath and let it out slowly. "But you really aren't sure," he said deliberately. "Something there isn't really over yet. And you can't go on until you know what it is. What do you think about, what did he say or do that pulls you back into yourself?" He was searching for the invisible strings that were still holding her down.

"I'm trying to sort that out. I have a lot of unanswered questions," Claire admitted. "Sometimes I wonder how I could have changed things. There are a hundred 'if onlys' that I've run through. And I wonder now how I could have ever loved anyone who could do that to another person." Her sad eyes glistened with tears, but she swallowed hard and tried to blink them away. "I don't know how he could have done that to me."

"How could anyone hurt Sara or 418 or Ariel?" Dylan reached up and brushed away the lone tear that had slipped past her control and trickled down her cheek. "But someone did. And the birds can't even cry out or ask why. They are loving, trusting creatures, just like you were. The problem is with the attacker, not the victim. In your case, you were accessible. You were there. Maybe that's all he needed. The violence changed things. But it's over, or should be. What concerns me is what's next. And my interest is becoming increasingly selfish.'' The seriousness with which he spoke made her apprehensive. He released her, sliding his hands into his pockets, holding back once more.

''What's next? That's what I've been asking myself,'' Claire's tense, clipped words echoed the confusion she felt. ''Now the storm is over. All the parts are broken and scattered. They didn't get divided up neatly into his and hers in the settlement.'' She pressed her hands over her heart in a touchingly expressive movement. ''Some of Wes is still here. The memories still come back, good ones and bad ones.''

She watched the disturbed glimmer in Dylan's eyes, knowing how it hurt him to hear her say that. But she had to tell him the truth. What had begun between Dylan and her was too fragile, too precious to tolerate less than the truth. ''For a while I was too numb to care about anything,'' she admitted. ''I didn't want to care for anyone again. But I'm feeling things now, and I get pretty scared. I'm trying to think things through and not make mistakes.''

''And not get hurt again,'' he finished for her. ''I can understand that. I can understand a lot of things better now.'' Dylan seemed so solid, so sure of himself. He fitted into the universe so naturally. But Claire was still looking for something to bridge the gap between his world of peace and hers of uncertainty.

"I'm still trying to understand," Claire said pensively. "I've never even told Pete this much. The only one who knew was my lawyer. That's why I got all the equipment I needed. Wes had to agree to settle and not bother me again, or he'd go to jail." While they talked, the last few crew members had disembarked from the cruise boat and passed by, leaving the two of them alone in the parking lot, standing between Claire's car and Dylan's truck. Dark and empty, without music or direction, the *Bay-Belle* tugged at her mooring lines.

"Now where do we go from here?" Dylan asked her.

"That's another question I ask myself." Claire walked back toward the water and stood staring at the dark, shiny surface. Dylan came and stood next to her, listening to the soft splash of the waves against the hull. "I've been working on my music. I think I've got a new song," she told him without lifting her eyes from the bay. "I think it's important. I need some time to let it come to me."

"And when it does?"

"Maybe I will have some answers for both of us."

Dylan nodded and kept his hands clasped behind his back, thinking how like the seabirds this lady was. A rare breed—endangered. How he wanted to hold her again and feel her body welcoming him into a world where gray eyes replaced the sun and moon. But he wanted more than her body. He wanted all the beauty in her soul, shining in her eyes and sparkling in her voice. She had finally opened up to him and established a bond that was more than physical. They had touched in other ways tonight, and the wounds they had opened still had the power to hurt.

Thoughtfully Dylan nudged his toe against a tiny plant with starlike white flowers that had somehow managed to squeeze through a crack in the seawall. In spite of the cramped space and the effects of sea air and saltwater, the little plant was holding on, determined. Like the egrets and herons, the gulls and pelicans, whose natural territory was being cramped by civilization and whose lives were threatened with the by-products of progress, the plant was still alive and thriving—despite the odds.

"I can't function in a vacuum, Claire," he said at last. "And I can't watch my step or my temper every moment of my life—or qualify my decisions—to keep you from hiding again. I'll be as open with you as you are with me."

Like the tiny plant, she had to find her own way. He couldn't protect her, and he couldn't alter reality to make things easier for her.

"I don't like paying for some other man's mistakes. I make enough of my own. I've been doing a lot of thinking about our day at the beach and our night at the beach house and other times when we're together. Promising starts—poor finishes. I try to be cautious, but a lot of this is out of my control. Something like the bar-singer business and the letter comes up, and we suffer a major setback. We both deserve something more."

Claire stood very still, not liking the tone or content of this conversation. She couldn't promise that there wouldn't be other setbacks. She couldn't promise anything.

"I know you need time," Dylan continued evenly, "but I'm just not sure that's all it will take."

There was nothing Claire could say. Answers still eluded her. And the questions were painful.

After a long silence, Dylan reached into his pocket for his ignition keys. Claire could think of nothing to say to keep him from driving away from her tonight. He was right. Promising starts, poor finishes. They did both deserve something more.

Silently Claire walked to her car. With the door open, she hesitated for a moment, her hair a pale halo in the moonlight. Then she looked back at him. Dylan still stood there, motionless, watching her.

The gentle evening breeze swept his whispered words to her. "Good night, castlebuilder."

To Claire, it sounded more like goodbye.

"MORE PELICAN MUTILATIONS ON SUNCOAST." The headline in the paper was just the beginning. Twenty-four hours later, a national TV news team brought its crew to the refuge, and Dylan and 418 made both the evening and late-night newscasts.

"It is possible to repair the bills of some of these birds," Dylan pointed out to the off-screen interviewer. "As long as the bird is healthy and a sufficient stub is left to use as a base for attaching an artificial one." He was sitting on the low wall by the refuge patio with 418 nestled complacently in his lap. The soothing rhythm of his hand on the creature's back was unobtrusive, but his touch communicated a constant reassurance to the bird.

Claire sat on her bed with knees drawn up to her

chest, watching the small television on her dresser. Dylan's streaked tawny-gold hair blew in the breeze, spilling several sun-bleached wisps onto his forehead. The camera did not pick up the softness in his sea-blue eyes. The accent was on the craggy lines of his face and the purposeful set of his jaw. Keen and confident, he explained the apparatus that had saved 418's life. And he emphasized that regardless of expense, he would attempt to repair the beaks of the latest victims, hopefully with equal success. And all the while the comforting hand continued to stroke 418. With mingled feelings of pride and longing, Claire reached out and touched her fingertips to the cold hard screen, wishing she could smooth back that tousled hair—a gesture she would not trust herself to do face to face.

Along with the close-ups of bright-eyed 418, the network of footage showed the two latest victims, each with grotesquely gaping lower bills and the ragged remainder of the upper one. A third victim of the mutilations had died. When they showed Kurt holding the lifeless pelican, Claire clicked off the TV. She'd had enough.

By the next morning, when she met Tammy in the parking lot of the refuge, it was apparent that the show was not over. "Make sure you keep smiling," Tammy cautioned her. "We have wildlife agents, newspaper photographers, a crew filming the public-information spots and folks from the Audubon Society all scheduled for today. Add that to a boat designer who is great with fiberglass, and you have a real hodgepodge. But never fear," she added sarcastically. "Rebecca Stroud has taken over the hostess duties.

We have coffee and donuts for everyone—except the birds. They still get fish—which, incidentally, arrived frozen and we need to start thawing.'' Without having to go through the main gate at all, they turned toward the storage shed, where the iced fish awaited their attention.

"Where is Dylan?" Claire asked. She hadn't heard a word from him in two days, except for the very public ones spoken on the televised newscast.

"He's everywhere," Tammy answered. "He's been on the run since this began. Right now he's gone to the factory where some fellow named Walker Hall builds fiberglass boats. Hall saw the news last night and offered to help. Apparently he's some kind of inventor. He designs industrial parts and he has some molds he offered to adapt to produce the artificial bills locally. As grim as the whole thing may be, these mutilations are generating a lot of publicity and some of it is getting to the right folks."

"I just hope the one doing this to the birds isn't enjoying the air play he's getting," Claire remarked. "I wonder if that's why he does it—for the publicity."

"That's what Dylan keeps muttering about." Tammy doused a block of frozen fish with the hose and set it in a bucket to defrost. "We have forty patients with fishhooks in the past month, and no one notices. That's too mundane. Add a bit of lunacy, and suddenly everyone wakes up. A nut like this is newsworthy."

"Are there any clues about the person?" Claire had seen the photo of the mutilation site—a strip of grassy beach next to a long wooden fishing pier on the Gulf. The area was near a section undergoing renovation, where older low motels had been demolished for the construction of high-rise condos. A construction worker arriving in the morning had spotted the damaged birds and called the police.

"The police have a few clues," Tammy said absently while she sprayed another block of frozen fish. "From the footprints they found they know he wears a size-seven jogging shoe, is about 160 pounds and walks with a slight limp."

Claire stared at Tammy in amazement. "All that from a footprint?"

"Several footprints. And he smokes. There were the remains of hand-rolled cigarettes where he stood and waited for the birds. Other than that, no description. No one saw him."

"So what can be done to stop him?" Claire slid the last package of fish into a pail, then lined it up with the others.

Tammy passed the bar of lemon-scented soap so they could take turns scrubbing their hands under the hose. "Dylan suggests organizing a citizens' alert. You know, asking folks who live along the beaches to keep an eye out for anything peculiar or for anyone who fits the general description. He wants volunteers to go from door to door, passing out information and helping recruit people."

"Do you think he'd let a bar singer help?" Her touch of cynicism made Tammy chuckle.

"You could specialize in the places that have lounges," Tammy joked. She took her turn with the soap as Claire held the hose.

"I think I'll pass," said Claire with a smile. "What

I will do is drop in and see Sara before we slosh out the pens.'' Deftly she turned off the water and looped the hose over its rack.

''Sara's coming out today.'' Tammy beamed. ''I checked her over, Dylan gave her his okay, so we're putting her in the outside pen. If you like, you can do the honors.''

''Now?'' Claire asked eagerly, wiping her hand on the seat of her pants. Sara had been cooped up inside with the splint on her leg while it healed. Getting her outside into the sunshine sounded wonderful.

''Why not?'' Tammy agreed.

Claire and Sara never even got out the door of the clinic before the film crew stopped them. ''Could you tell us about this bird for the camera,'' one earnest fellow asked. ''Stork, isn't it?''

''She's an egret. Her name is Sara,'' Claire answered carefully. ''But Tammy is in charge of outdoor rehabilitation. She can tell you a lot more.'' When Claire turned around, Tammy was gone. Her camera-shy friend had seen the crew converging and had ducked out of view. ''I'm just a friend of Sara's,'' Claire concluded quietly, stiffening in front of the blank, single eye of the camera.

''Looks good, looks very good.'' The young man watching on the video display liked the camera angle on Claire. ''Now just go on with what you're doing,'' he told her. ''We'll follow along and get some shots.''

''Keep a close-up on the face,'' he ordered the cameraman.

''Tammy, you come out here!'' Claire called into the silent interior of the clinic. ''I don't know what

I'm supposed to do." Nervously she moistened her lips with the tip of her tongue.

"I'll tell you what to do."

When Tammy answered, her voice came from the opposite direction Claire had expected. Tammy had skirted the building and come out behind the film crew. Safely off camera, she gave instructions, while Claire complied, delivering Sara to her new surroundings, a huge tree-shaded pen where several other egrets strolled about.

"Nice, real nice." The shot of the seabird hesitating by the lady's side, then gingerly stepping away as Claire nudged her gently toward the other birds had a poignancy that the camera loved. The trace of an enchanted smile on her lips and the gleam of a tear in Claire's eye would end the spot eloquently and leave a lump in everyone's throat.

Oblivious to the film crew, Claire urged the elegant egret along, but the bird paused again, looking regal with her lacy feathers ruffled by the light breeze. "Go on, Sara," Claire whispered. "You're on your way."

It was the first of their farewells.

CHAPTER NINE

By the time Tammy and Claire took a break for lunch, the rear patio of the refuge had been transformed into an open-air picnic ground. Reporters milled about restlessly, waiting for Dylan to return. The film crew spread out along one low wall, munching on sandwiches and sipping Cokes, while facing the crew, on the roof, a flock of impudent sea gulls of varying types and sizes watched with their bright dark eyes for any tidbit that might fall to the ground.

"The darn things remind me of vultures," one of the fellows said with a chuckle. He moved his sandwich from side to side, and the pointed beaks and spindly legs shifted in anticipation.

"Whatever you do, don't throw them any food," Tammy warned the men. "They'll descend like locusts on you—rather, on all of us. Their squawking will bring in more. These are perfectly healthy birds," she pointed out. "Don't fall for their begging routine."

But one man was too softhearted to listen, and he pitched a crust of bread into the air. When the birds descended en masse, Tammy didn't bother to say, "I told you so." She simply shook her head, grabbed her lunch bag and signaled for Claire to follow.

While the gulls squawked and fluttered around the others, the two women took their lunch out to the wooden beachside gazebo.

"I'm really embarrassed by all this," Claire confided to Tammy. "You're the one who supervises all the rehab work, and they keep taking pictures of me. I don't think we're being very honest and I feel uncomfortable. I'm only a part-time worker—just a volunteer." In addition to her own discomfort, Claire was already dreading the reaction that the publicity might prompt from both Rebecca and from Dylan. She was still very much a bar singer and this time, her face and not just her name would be made public.

"You are very photogenic," Tammy replied, "and I'm not. If these spots are going to be shown all over the state, we need to put our best face forward. That means *yours*. Besides, you're not just a volunteer." Her piercing dark eyes assessed her blond companion. "We all know that. You're part of this place. Whether you like it or not, you're hooked. You just keep doing what they ask, and Dylan or I will supply all the voice-over—off camera, of course."

"But I don't like to get the credit when I don't deserve it. You should be the star."

"I've been the star and I almost got an ulcer." Tammy shook her head. "With everything else I've been responsible for lately, I'd fall apart with a camera focused on me. Really—" she looked earnestly at Claire "—I can't stand doing the publicity bit. Even Dylan doesn't like it, but he knows how to grin and bear it. When he tells the same details for the umpteenth time, he's as patient and convincing as he was the first time." Tammy's expression bordered on desperation. "Please."

"I still don't think it's fair, but if you're bothered that much, I'll be your stand-in," Claire assured her. "But this may not sit well with Dylan."

"I'll take care of Dylan," Tammy promised. "And anyone else who says anything." She was already anticipating another round with Rebecca.

"Then you'd better start now," Claire said, lowering her voice to a whisper. As she glanced over Tammy's shoulder, she could see Dylan coming along the pathway between the low dunes and waving sea oats. Right behind him was a tall, younger man, perhaps thirty, with brown curly hair and tanned as dark as Dylan.

"He's absolutely gorgeous," Tammy whispered appreciatively, trying not to be too obvious as she stared at the newcomer. "Severely able bodied."

But Claire was watching the easy sway of Dylan's shoulders and the purposeful, confident strides that brought him closer. He wasn't as fine featured, nor was his smile as perfect as the younger man's, but Dylan had a grace and power that made him distinctive. And because Claire didn't want him to recognize the emotion she was feeling, she looked away, pretending that her peanut-butter-and-banana sandwich held a strange fascination for her.

"This is Walker Hall," Dylan said, introducing his companion. "The boat builder. He needs to measure the injured pelicans and take a mold of their upper bill so he can start on the new beaks." He was aiming the information at Tammy. "It may take some time and I don't want to draw any attention to the pelicans. If you take over from here, I'll pick up with the reporters and film crew."

Tammy munched on her bologna and cheese, trying not to let her pleasure become too apparent. When she swallowed the bite, she agreed to be liaison between the handsome fellow and the birds. "I'll take over the inside work if you'll stick with Claire and the film crew. I left her holding the bird, so to speak," Tammy joked. Her cheeks reddened slightly as her glance shifted from Dylan to the young man. "Someone had to be on camera, and I didn't want it to be me. Fortunately Claire was here and she looks very good on film," she concluded.

"I assume she would," Dylan replied with a terse smile that indicated he was not displeased with the switch. "At least this way we won't have to wait to get the footage of a star being born," he added. "I do remember vague promises of another video...." He left the statement dangling.

"I didn't forget the video," Claire countered evenly. "They're mixing in the sound. Pete said it would be finished tomorrow." Claire folded up her napkin, which she tucked inside her paper bag. "First I get a preview. Then I'll bring a finished copy out here. You'll see the show eventually."

Dylan's smile stretched into a satisfied curve. "Good. If you're interested in giving another performance, we may have something else lined up. Something that may get you some very impressive network exposure," he added.

"I don't understand."

"These public-information and news spots are one thing, but I just agreed to something that will help us much more. In return for using the refuge in a commercial, an oil company will donate money to the expansion project," he said, stating the plan simply. "A lot of money."

"A commercial—for an oil company? Isn't that getting into questionable territory? As in, conflict of interest?" Tammy asked pointedly. "I know the oil company wants to look good and the money may be tempting, but I've seen enough victims of oil spills to know there is a bit of a compromise involved here. What about your policy of sticking to unconditional donations—no-strings contributions."

"Nothing will be compromised," he assured her. "The commercial is intended to highlight some positive efforts in preserving the environment, and our work here is being honored. We aren't promoting their product or the company. I'll have final approval of the content," Dylan added. "The spot will go prime-time nationwide. We couldn't afford that kind of public access on our own budget."

Tammy gave a disgruntled sigh and crushed her napkin into a wad. "That oil company will still have its name and trademark right up there with our pelicans. This still doesn't sound right to me," she insisted. "But then I'm just a lowly employee here. I've said my piece."

"You usually do," and Dylan chuckled. But his humor did not erase the wary look in Tammy's eyes. "Agreeing with me has never been a job requirement here."

"How fortunate for me," Tammy responded with a toss of her braid. She turned to the dark-haired onlooker, who had been observing the exchange with a slightly bewildered frown. "Come on, Walker," she addressed the man. "Let's go where we're appreciated."

"I do appreciate you," Dylan called after her as she and Walker Hall moved away. "But I also appreciate what this can mean."

"Sure, sure," Tammy muttered, unconvinced. The lean boat builder looked uncertainly from Dylan to the dark-haired young woman at his side. With a slight shrug and an amused smile, he waved a hasty goodbye to the twosome left behind.

For a moment, while Dylan stood staring after them thoughtfully, Claire studied his profile. Tanned and windblown, he looked almost boyish, but Claire couldn't forget for a moment that he was a grown man.

"You don't look too enthused, either," Dylan observed as he turned to Claire again. "Does the idea of taking oil-company money strike you as offensively as it does Tammy?"

"I can see her point," Claire conceded. "I'm trying to see yours. What would I be doing in this commercial?" Claire's gray eyes clouded with uneasiness. She was willing to help the refuge, but there was a great deal of difference between a public-information spot and a commercial. If Tammy balked at the concept, Claire would proceed with caution.

"Probably nothing different from what you've been doing today," Dylan answered. "Caring for the birds. Giving a glimpse of what goes on here."

Claire took a sip of her cold drink, disturbed by the fact that she would be doing something he was so skilled at—only she would be doing it with less composure. "Why don't you do the spot yourself. You're the one with the press following. You're the celebrity." She didn't try to disguise the criticism in her comment. His penchant for publicity had taken on an element of cunning that reminded her of a green-eyed redhead, and she didn't want to be the focus of yet another dispute.

"To get us this far, someone had to be the celebrity," Dylan said matter-of-factly. "The public is interested in seeing something they can relate to. If a picture is worth a thousand words, then I'll give them that picture—a bird or the Birdman—whether I like the notoriety or not. Pictures are much more eye-catching than neat little paragraphs about pollution and fishing lines. But if one brings attention to the other, here's my face." He leaned forward slightly, pointing to his face, the determined set of his jaw matched by the determination in his eyes. "I've learned what works. But there is such a thing as aesthetics, and this spot needs to be special. If I could choose between seeing me or you on the screen, there'd be no contest. You'd win."

"What about the public image of the refuge? I haven't changed jobs," Claire noted coolly. "I'm still a bar singer."

"That point is wearing thin," Dylan shot back crossly. "Something spontaneous and natural happens between you and these birds, just like when you sculpt in sand or lose yourself in your music.

Sometimes it happens between you and me." He didn't have to elaborate. "If that magic comes across on film, then you'd be doing all of us a favor." His sea-blue eyes flashed with impatience.

"I hope Rebecca agrees with you."

Dylan studied her closely. "I'm talking about a thirty-second spot on the work here, not your life history. If you wish to remain anonymous, we won't even mention your name. And this time we aren't countering an attack."

He let out a slow breath and his attitude became more personal. "When they approached me with this idea, I knew what they were after," he said in a far softer voice. "I could picture the whole thing in my head—cages, trees, birds, the recovery room—and you were there. Remember how you look at a pile of sand and see a castle? This film already exists. I think you understand." For an instant, they stared at each other in silence, feeling the closeness of that first afternoon envelop them again.

"Okay. I'll do it," Claire agreed quietly.

"Fine. I'll get a shooting schedule set up for the commercial. In the meantime, we've got that video crew waiting on our patio to finish up the public-information spot for Channel Six. I need to look over what they were working on today. Then I've got a meeting with some bankers." He stared out over the Gulf for a moment longer, drinking in the sparkling beauty with his eyes and filling his lungs with a deep breath of sea air.

Lately everything was so hectic. That single golden day of castle building on the beach at Frenchman's

Pass seemed a lifetime ago. Claire tried to think of something to say, something safe yet important enough to let them talk longer, as they had that day. Interested, but not intrusive.

"How are things progressing on the land purchase?" Claire asked as she stepped up beside him and looked out over the blue-green water. There had been rumors of bank assessments and zoning questions, but no one in the refuge office knew the specifics. Rebecca Stroud was taking care of most of the paperwork. On her trips in and out, she left the forms and messages neatly sealed in envelopes for Dylan's attention only.

"If Rebecca can get the zoning commission to rezone the entire area as 'greenspace,' then we'll be able to go through with the purchase. She's taking care of the technicalities. There are zoning ordinances to decipher...." He shook his head. "What with state and federal wildlife regulations, it's complicated. But all this attention the mutilations have stirred up should make the rezoning procedure move along faster and easier. Rebecca has put together quite a portfolio of information. She even has pictures of the injured birds to take to the commission members."

"And a picture is worth a thousand words. That should make quite an impression on them," Claire noted, realizing that she sounded more and more bitter.

"True. But it takes more than sentiment to impress the loan officers at the banks. I'll have to put up the beach house and the land here as collateral," Dylan added. "Over the next few years, if private donations or corporate contributions don't pay off the loan, the bank will just foreclose."

"You mean you could lose the refuge?" Claire hadn't realized what a personal gamble he was taking. "And the beach house?" Claire's mind quickly conjured up images of his unfinished home on the tiny strip of beach farther south and the land here that he was giving over to the birds. Regardless of what other income Dylan had, he was jeopardizing something irreplaceable—his waterfront land.

"We could end up with another condo here," he acknowledged. "And they could flatten my beach house and stick up a high rise. On the other hand, we could pull in the funding and pay off the loan and have it all—including a zoological park and a rookery out where we were hiking by the bay. The bottom line is money. I told you that I couldn't live in a vacuum," he said as he turned to face her. "I mean that professionally, as well as personally. Physically, this place is too small for the work that needs to be done. Even if we limited this spot to captive breeding, at the rate natural rookeries are being wiped out by housing developments, we'd still be fighting a losing battle. We need space—unspoiled— for a major research center."

Dylan turned back to look at the busy, crowded acre that was the refuge. "Rebecca has made her point. Undeveloped land is scarce, even swampy places like I need. If I don't take that land now, someone else will. They'll fill it, clear out the birds and put up an industrial park or a massive apartment complex. I don't have much choice other than to make my offer. Rebecca is holding the land on a sixty-day option.''

"How much money do you need to raise in the sixty days?''

"The entire package is two hundred acres at five thousand an acre. The selling price is a million. But that's way down the line. A simple five hundred thousand would get us off the ground for the down payment and initial building costs. That's the combined value of the land that the refuge and the beach house are sitting on.''

" 'Five hundred thousand'?'' Claire was stunned at the figures.

"I put up my land as a guarantee now. We try to raise contributions to cover it. That's where individual donations make or break us. You'll reach a lot of individuals if you do the commercial. National exposure. Millions of people will see it. More attention means more money. We rely on the press. Every article about the refuge or even the mutilations makes people aware of what we're doing here and brings in donations. We have individuals and organizations offering to hold fund-raisers. Rebecca set up the Dali museum event—that brought in a few thousand. There are ways and there are people willing to help. We just have to keep working.''

"I'm one of those people willing to help,'' Claire added a bit defensively. "Maybe I could do something on the *Bay-Belle* or when I work with the guys at the Pier.'' She wasn't sure how the management would take an appeal for contributions, but she was willing to make the proposal to them.

"Your part in the commercial will help," Dylan replied. "Being here and working with Sara helps. Money isn't all that matters," he told her.

"But it does matter."

"Of course it does," Dylan said solemnly. Once again his attention shifted back to the main building. "I'd better put on my celebrity face and do my best," Dylan declared. He had not missed her gibe over his press status. "And you'd better come, too." Stepping out of the gazebo, he headed across the rise of sand between the beach and the refuge.

Claire was about to start out after him when a voice from the beach stopped her.

"Excuse me...miss? Could you tell me where you report a hurt bird?" An elderly gentleman hurried up to the gazebo. "There's a big black bird flopping around on the beach just up the way." His bald head, rimmed by an open-crowned visor, was smooth and tanned nut-brown. His fine-lined face, shaded by the hat, was wrinkled with concern. "The wife and I spotted it from our condo." That explained the huge binoculars clasped in his hand.

"You report it right here. I'll come with you," Claire offered. "You go on ahead," she called to Dylan, who had heard the man and was coming back toward them. "I can handle this. Really. One picture is worth a thousand words, remember." But he didn't stop. "Go!" She waved him back toward the video crew.

Dylan hesitated, then nodded. She was handling

this with a quiet confidence that he liked. He was excluded, but that wasn't important. She was doing precisely what he'd hoped she would; she was taking charge.

"This way, miss," the old man summoned her. "Right down this way a bit. The wife is down there keeping an eye on the poor thing."

"Which condo do you live in?" Claire asked the man as they headed up the beach.

"There. Third floor front." He pointed to the taller of the two on the north side of the refuge.

Claire noted the vantage point he had and smiled. "You must have an excellent view of the shoreline."

"Real nice view. Used to be a dentist. Worked all my life looking into folk's mouths. Can't tell you how much I enjoy just sitting and watching the water and the birds for hours on end. Pure heaven," and he chuckled.

"For hours?" Claire's eyebrows arched with interest. "Since you're already so observant, perhaps you could help us. We're organizing a committee for the protection of seabirds. I suppose you've heard about the dreadful mutilations of the pelicans."

"Why, yes...." The old fellow straightened his shoulders as if he'd just been summoned to battle. "The wife and I were just talkin' about that this morning."

Arm in arm, Claire and the rescuer hurried off down the beach in search of the big dark bird. She had her first recruit for the bird-watch. And from the way he spoke of "the wife," she guessed she had two.

CLAIRE CARRIED A STACK of printed flyers from the Gulf Coast Seabird Refuge on board the *Bay-Belle* that evening. It took her a few minutes to work up the courage to go into the office, but once she'd set up her equipment, she reached the point of no turning back.

"I've been working several days a week as a volunteer out at the refuge," she explained as she passed the information out to the crew and the gray-haired woman who managed the paddle-wheeler. Claire had always thought the crew a little remote, but she felt the invisible barrier vanish as she spoke, bolstered by her eagerness to talk about a cause that touched her deeply. Her gray eyes glimmered with relief and enthusiasm as she was besieged with questions.

Yes, she had seen the mutilated birds that made the news. Yes, she knew Dylan Jamison, the Birdman, quite well. Yes, the new fiberglass bill was working and they could see 418 if they came out to the beach-side compound—and yes, the do-it-yourself tour aided by the informative signs was unhurried and free. No, there were no solid leads on the culprit who had sawed off the upper beaks and left the birds to die. Then she told them about the beautiful Sara, who'd been picked up on the bay along the usual route of the *Bay-Belle*. By the time the passengers for the night cruise were beginning to arrive in the parking lot, Claire had recruited the crew and manager into the bird-watch program. She also had permission to add something new into her usual routine. She could do a promo for the refuge during the return trip every cruise, and a canister would be kept by the cash register at the bar for donations.

Talking to the passengers was not as easy as Claire had hoped. Performing as "the entertainer" gave her a format to follow and a protective persona that made her feel secure. However, when she took the microphone and tried to explain the refuge and its work, she saw all the faces turn toward her, and she was suddenly onstage without a song or music, just words. She was reminded of an old nightmare, where she was on her own and couldn't perform at all.

"For the birds...." She remembered the phrase that had become her, Tammy and Kurt's unofficial motto. It had helped each of them through some rough spots; maybe it could get her through this. Then she remembered Dylan calmly and convincingly relaying information and always making it seem fresh and new. "I'm really not a public speaker," Claire said with an unexpected tremble in her voice. "But I'd like to tell you about a very special place on the Gulf, a clinic for seabirds...." She began with difficulty, but she kept going.

Much later, when the tension had relaxed in her throat and her hands were no longer cold and damp, Claire answered questions from the audience and passed out the last few brochures about the refuge. And when she told them of her very first rescue and the trip she and Pete had made with the silent, injured egret, she knew she had broken some of the invisible strings that had hurt for so long.

"We'll come out and visit Sara."

"This is for 418."

"Is the refuge open on Sundays?"

The comments of the disembarking passengers were punctuated by the clinking of coins and the rustle of checks and dollar bills as they were deposited in the canister. Claire waited until she'd packed up all her equipment into her car before returning to the *Bay-Belle*, emptying the donations into a large envelope, then stuffing it with her sheets of music in her purse.

"Is that how they pay you on this vessel? Pass the hat for the minstrel?" The raspy voice and the touch of sardonic wit halted her in midstep. Like a phantom from a dream, Wes Raines stepped out of the darkness and stood waiting for her at the foot of the gangway. His dark eyes gleamed with amusement and his close-trimmed beard framed a smile that had once been the touchstone of her universe.

"This is for some friends of mine," Claire managed to reply without stumbling over the words. After she left New York she had never expected to see him again. But if she had considered the possibility, she would have imagined a different scenario—something cold and dramatic, where they would meet in passing and move on. But his presence was calm and unspectacular, as if there were nothing extraordinary about Wes's being in this setting.

"How have you been, Wes?" They had not been face to face since the night she had left him raging through the apartment and shouting after her.

"I'm doing good." He nodded, watching her intently as she stepped onto land next to him. "You're lookin' great. Got a nice tan," he observed.

There was no trace of menace in his attitude, and Claire found the friendliness of the conversation unnerving.

"I spend a lot of time outdoors," she answered calmly. Instead of being overwhelmed by a barrage of old emotions, Claire looked into the face of the man she had loved, married and fled from, and felt nothing—not even a hint of fear. "What brings you back to St. Pete?" Claire felt like an observer, watching the blond-haired woman wearing her face converse casually with the dusky-voiced Wes Raines.

"It was a long, cold winter and I'd enough of the North. I did a little touring with some groups. I've been working on some songs and I'm getting ready to put a band together, so I thought I'd start looking back here," he explained. "A lot of good musicians have settled around here, so I figured I'd come down for a while and see what I could round up. I seem to recall it worked out pretty good once before," he said, smiling. All the while he kept his onyx eyes riveted on her face, as if he were taking in every detail, trying to match what he saw with what he had allowed himself to remember. "You're still as beautiful as an angel," he insisted. The gravelly voice reverberated through her, insinuating its way into the parts of her mind that were still his.

"I don't want your compliments, Wes," Claire replied evenly, resenting the ease with which he thought he could come back into her life. "There really isn't anything I want to hear from you. I don't mean to be rude, but we didn't exactly part on friendly terms. I don't know why you've come to see me, but I wish you hadn't bothered. I have some people waiting for me at the Pier, and I'd better be on my way." She stepped around him and walked toward the parking lot.

"I came to find you because I had to. I still love you, Claire." Wes caught up with her before she reached her car. "I know it's been a long time and you have a lot of reasons to hate me, but I still love you. I've tried to put you out of my mind. I know what I did to you and I'm sorry. But I had to come and see you again. It isn't over for me."

Claire didn't look back at him. She concentrated on aiming the key into the lock and opening the car door. She had the eerie sensation of déjà vu; this had all happened before. She had listened to him say the same things and she had believed him. And in spite of all the time and all the hurt, a part of her still listened.

"Did you hear what I said?" He stood close to her, but he didn't touch her at all.

"I heard you quite clearly," she answered, finally turning to look at him, trying to ignore the longing in his eyes. "I was always one of your better listeners. You do have a way with words, Wes. You always did. But the problem was that the words weren't always pretty and they weren't necessarily complimentary. I heard them then just as clearly as I hear you now. When you started punctuating your comments with your fists, I committed everything to memory. So I'd never be taken in again."

"I was wrong. I was scared and crazy, and I know how wrong it was. I know I had all sorts of excuses, but I can't excuse hurting you. I'm ashamed of what I did. But I can't stop loving you." The pain in his eyes testified to the truth. "I still remember all the good times."

"Your memory must be more selective than mine," Claire said without anger. "My memories are all mixed together. I've been trying to sort them out and put them away so that one day the bad ones won't spoil the others. But they still do." Standing this close to him, seeing the luster in his black eyes and the rhythm in every movement he made, Claire could remember how it once was. How he flashed his handsome smile, sang his seductive songs and won her heart.

"You don't have to be satisfied with just memories," Wes said hopefully. "We still have a chance."

"I've taken enough chances with you," Claire said, standing firm. "I put my whole life in your hands—and you broke it into little pieces. I'm still putting me back together."

"I could help. I've been getting some practice at picking up the pieces myself," he said with a wry smile. "We don't have to go fast. We could try being friends. We could try making music together. You know we made a good team."

The charisma and the charm were still there. The Pied Piper had come back to town and was working his spell. But for Claire, fairy tales didn't always end happily, and she resisted the enchantment that he offered.

"I don't think so." She stopped him. "I'm doing all right on my own."

"I heard you playing as the boat came in." Wes nodded as he glanced back at the moored *Bay-Belle*. There were still a few crew members aboard, closing up for the night. "You're playing good. Real nice clean sound. The music comes in across the water with the breeze. I miss hearing you play." The pensive look on his face reminded her of all the times they had sat around after a performance, doing a postmortem over what went well and what songs still needed work. Wes knew how to make good music. He'd been her mentor as well as her lover. Claire had always valued his expertise as a musician, and a part of her still responded to his praise, just as another part had been nearly destroyed by his criticism and cruelty.

"I'm singing, too," she added, less defensive than she had been. "Pete and Robby have a good group of guys playing with them, and they're in the mood to get into something a little different. I've been singing the late set with them at the Pier. We've been getting some new material put together and trying it out."

"You're going there now? They're at the Pier?" His dark eyes narrowed with interest as he realized that the people waiting for her weren't having a strictly social gathering.

"Yes. I really have to get moving. They'll be wondering what's keeping me." Claire was getting through this reunion nicely, but she was glad there was someplace she had to be right now.

"Is it all right if I come and listen. I won't interfere," Wes promised. "I'll just watch." His comment echoed of another time. Onstage together, their talents had meshed beautifully. They had been a good team, complementing each other physically and musically—light and dark, satin and sandpaper. But when they worked apart, even out of necessity, the troubles began.

The night of the final beating, Wes had sat in the audience watching critically, and he never smiled. And in some way, that negative presence haunted every audience she faced—had even extended to haunt her moments with Dylan. Claire remembered what Dylan had said about putting the right faces on her ghosts. If she looked out in the audience tonight and saw Wes sitting there—if he were unable to shake her confidence or hurt her—she could exorcise that ghost; she could put an unwanted image aside and move on. It was a chance she had to take.

"Sure. Come and see the show. We have some new material, but we also do some of our old songs." She wanted no surprises for either of them.

"It will be like old times," he promised her, flashing a too-perfect grin.

"No. It's not 'old times,'" Claire cautioned him. "This is new times."

"You're right." He nodded soberly. "'New times.' I'll see you there." Wes went over to his car while Claire slipped behind the wheel of her own. As she drove out to the end of the Pier and saw his headlights in her rearview mirror, she knew he'd been following her in one way or another for a long, long while. He'd been a shadow whose dark image she still hadn't been able to shake. But tonight she was bringing him out into the light. If she took a good look at what was really there, she could stop imagining. . . .

Pete and Robby stood with arms folded over their chests and stared at Wes Raines as he entered the lounge with Claire. She stopped at the bar to get a glass of plain water, then introduced Wes to the bartender, who added a slice of lemon and a cherry to decorate her drink.

"What's he doing here?" Pete said, managing to plaster a genial expression on his face.

"It's been a while." Pete greeted Wes stiffly when he joined them.

"Yeah. Yeah, it has," Wes answered. He looked cautiously from Pete to Robby, trying to determine how precarious a situation he was in. But all he saw was a slightly bewildered, very polite welcome.

"Wes stopped by the *Bay-Belle* tonight," Claire hastily explained, knowing that both her brothers would have been dragging Wes off if she'd given the least indication his presence was unwelcome. "He came to hear us play."

"Okay." Pete grinned. His smile widened, but the rigid set of his shoulders remained. In spite of Claire's easy manner there was a lingering trace of apprehension in her eyes. She could hide it from other people, but Pete had a special radar when it came to Claire. Nothing was wrong, but it wasn't quite right, either. "Let's do the set, then." He rallied the band members while Wes settled into a seat near the window. Then Bizzy hit the lights, and the lady with the pale-gold hair stepped into her other world.

On the first few numbers, all that was required was

for Claire and Sound Off to give a good rendition of
a few songs currently on the charts. But when they
shifted from tunes by other performers to some of
their own material, every song became a personal
battle—a tug-of-war—with Claire pulling lyrics and
melodies away thread by thread from the quiet
bearded man who sat watching her with solemn onyx
eyes.

Without moving a finger and completely unbe-
knownst to him, Wes had a hold of every image,
every emotion, every gesture. All that he had been to
her, all they had meant to each other became a thousand hooks snagging on phrases and digging deeper
each time she resisted.

Dylan had said something wasn't quite over between Wes and her. The words of her song had a ring
of truth that could apply to both Claire and Wes.
Wes hadn't been able to get over her, and she was
still struggling to get free of him.

> Don't you see I made a difference
> I changed all your forevers, just by lovin' you.
> Even when you're far from me
> I'll linger in your memory
> My voice will echo in your night
> And no one's touch but mine feels right
> From this point on, I am a part of you—
> And everything you do.

Robby loved this song. He lowered his fuzzy mop
of hair, pale and shimmering, the color of his sister's,
and bent into the drums. The song was loud and

raucous, with a bouncy acceleration that let him pour on all the percussion. But Pete picked his guitar, never taking his eyes off Claire. He watched the emotions registering on her face change like patterns of a kaleidoscope. One minute, triumphant as fireworks; the next, as soft and lovely as a rainbow. But the dark clouds kept drifting in.

"Why not ask Wes to do a number with us?" Pete made the suggestion while Claire sipped a glass of water between songs. She almost choked. "Hey," Pete went on, "if you want a test by fire, why not jump in. Get it over with. Maybe singing together will be like signing a treaty," he explained. "Onstage is one place you two never had trouble."

"I don't want to go back to that," Claire answered simply. "The onstage magic has a way of making things look better than they are," she answered carefully. Now was not the time to tell Pete how rough times with Wes had been. "Wes and I had a lot that was an illusion. Private lives often aren't as civilized as public ones. He isn't in either part of mine right now, and I'd like to keep it that way. Working with Wes again is too civilized and a little risky. We might get dependent on each other. I want to keep my perspective, and I can't do that if I let him too close. I can't quite explain it," she said to counter his questioning look, "but I'm coming out of this on my own."

"Then pick your number, hotshot." Pete backed off. "What do we end with?"

Claire remembered the few times she had tried to

sing Sara's song and hadn't been able to. While the dark eyes of Wes Raines followed her every move, she was thinking of another pair of eyes and another kind of magic—of splints and stitches and tethers and fiberglass bills. Like Sara, she hadn't totally healed yet. She was stepping out cautiously, and maybe she needed to be nudged. Before she tried to sing just for her blue-eyed audience of one, she would try the song here.

"We'll do this one for Sara," she said softly.

Pete grinned and passed the word down the line. When word got to Bizzy, he went into a delighted frenzy readjusting knobs on the synthesizer to get the delicate effect he wanted. Then Jess tucked the electric violin under his chin and began the intro, soft and slow. Claire stood in the spotlight, singing all alone. It was a song of beginnings.

> Don't really know how to say it.
> Words don't come easy to me.
> But I know how I feel and the feeling is real. . .
> My love's just a melody.
>
> Talkin' in dream comes so easy to me
> I can say how I feel in the night
> But day comes my way and the words slip away,
> Still the feelin' inside's so right.
>
> Music is the language of love,
> When your body's moving close to me.
> Music is a symphony with you.

The song had a sound unlike any of the others they'd done that night. Like a lullaby, the music was hushed and soothing. Like a promise, it ended with a smile.

When the song was over, Wes Raines stood up and walked toward her. Gently he offered her his hand. When she accepted the handshake, he looked at her sheepishly, then opened his arms. The gesture was warm and affectionate—no longer reminiscent of a passion they once shared. Claire hesitated, then stepped into his embrace.

"Pretty song." He kissed her forehead. "I wish I'd written it."

"Pete and I wrote the song."

"I wish you'd written it for me," he said solemnly. "But you didn't." The implied question was meant to be purely personal.

"No, I didn't," Claire answered.

"And I'll bet it really isn't for any Sara."

He'd guessed correctly, but Claire wasn't about to let him know that. "You'd lose the bet. There very definitely is a Sara, and I sing it to her."

Wes looked at her pensively. "The bet isn't the only thing I've lost. But I know from that song that you've got a whole lot of heart. There's someone more than that Sara on your mind. Whoever he is, if he ever hears you sing it, he'll be a damned fool if he lets you get away."

Wes turned to the others in the band, his arm still around Claire's shoulders. While he shook one hand after the other, commending each of the band members for a job well done, the tall figure in the doorway stood watching.

"Who's the guy with the beard?" he asked the bartender.

"I don't really know. Wes something-or-other. He came in with Claire."

Dylan had reached the lounge in time to see her standing like an ivory goddess in the pale column of light. He hadn't disturbed the tranquillity of the moment by coming all the way in. Leaning against the bar, he had heard only the last few lines of the song, and when it had ended, he watched another man hold her in his arms. Someone else had heard the siren song and come home again.

CHAPTER TEN

DYLAN SHOVED ASIDE several small boxes of books and a larger box, full of shells, from which a gnarled branch of driftwood protruded. He'd spent three hours with Rebecca and the symphony board members, then come back to the upper floor of the refuge to finish packing. It was well after two in the morning before he'd let up. He had been trying to ease the hollow feeling inside by pushing himself until he was exhausted. Now, finally surrendering to a gnawing curiosity, he slid the video cassette of Claire into the VHS unit. The luminous glow from the screen shifted colors as a rapid-fire sequence of freeze frames showed, in a style that was almost documentary, each of the members of Sound Off taking his place on the stage.

But then the image became soft, pale gold and beautiful—a slow motion, close-up shot of Claire swirling around in the semidarkness behind them all. The hard-rock music broke out, and with a shake of her head, Claire came forward, swaying and prancing in a synchronized burst of energy. With all the intricate camera work and razzle-dazzle of a network video concert, angles shifted, images grew under the eye of a zoom lens, action slowed or halted entirely.

Exquisitely orchestrated, the editing of the video had been skillfully done. Dylan had to admit the video was a slick product, and it held him transfixed. The Claire on that stage had a disconcerting quality, a polished veneer, brassy and sophisticated that contradicted everything he knew about her.

Impatiently he switched off the video, removing the finished tape and replacing it with the uncut and unedited footage from the refuge. Amid the varied shots of birds and nests and lab equipment, the face and hands and body that had made the music sparkle now gave another eloquent performance without sound. This Claire was more familiar. As he witnessed what the camera had recorded, Dylan realized how much she'd changed since that day they'd met at Frenchman's Pass. The sureness with which she had carved arched windows into castle walls now was shown in the confident way she grasped the wings of a pelican and tucked the bird under her arm, gave an injection or fed a motherless bird from a syringe.

At the refuge her cautiousness had given way to an unguarded enthusiasm that reflected her concern for the creatures that needed care. Even under the artificial circumstances of doing each task for a film team she radiated a naturalness that this other video, this performance at the Mariner, obscured.

In the solitude of night, Dylan switched one tape for the other, trying to come to terms with this complex woman. All were a part of her. Her voice, her dazzle, her vulnerability and her gentle comradery with the creatures of the refuge. And somehow she was putting it all together.

Then he remembered that other moment in time, frozen in his memory as he had watched from the shadows. The radiant lady and the dark-eyed, bearded man from her past smiling in an embrace. The song had to do with love and music, and the man was Wes. She was putting it all together—even a relationship with a man who had hurt her and sent her running for sanctuary. Together again. If she could forgive and forget, give that old love a new chance and go on with her life, Dylan knew he would be happy for her. But there was no place in all the visions for him, and no comfort in the cassettes of tape that gave him any warmth at all.

"HERE IS FIFTY-THREE DOLLARS and ninety cents," Claire announced as she placed the money collected aboard *Bay-Belle* on the desk in front of Josie Flynt. "And the names of two people in the old northeast section of St. Pete who are willing to pick up any birds in their area." She placed the list next to the money. "And—" she dragged out the final presentation with a dramatic flourish "—T-shirts. This one is for you."

The shirt itself was nothing impressive, just plain white trimmed in blue. But the message on the chest brought a fog-horn hoot of delight from Josie. "I love it." She laughed as she held the shirt over her very ample bustline.

"For the Birds...." The refuge motto sounded impudent and catchy. And below, a goofy pelican with a slightly bemused expression perched atop a sign reading Gulf Coast Seabird Refuge.

"Now this is nifty!" Josie proclaimed approvingly. "I want a bunch of these for my grandchildren," she enthused. "They'll go crazy over them." Then her eyes zeroed in on the bag still bulging with Claire's other acquisitions. "Are they all the same?" Her eyes twinkled with a greedy delight. "Show me all you've got," she insisted. "I'm a dyed-in-the-wool comparison shopper."

"The motto is the same on all of them," Claire assured her. "Some of the artwork changes." As an example she lifted out a bright yellow one with a hawk on it—unmistakably Ariel. "This is for Tammy, and this is for Robinson." His was designed like Josie's, but in green and white, his high-school colors. "We can get all sorts of them if we want," Claire noted. "We could order a bunch and swap them for donations."

"Good idea. Now show me your shirt," Josie demanded. "While I'm making out my shopping list, I want to see everything."

Claire reached into the bag for the bright aqua T-shirt with the delicately feathered egret all in white. It could have been just any egret, but the artist had added a whimsical expression, a leg splint and a tiny leg band inscribed SARA. "This is a one-of-a-kind designer fashion," Claire said proudly as she held up the shirt.

"Hardly...." The disparaging tone of the newcomer announced that she was no T-shirt aficionado. Rebecca Stroud took one look at the assortment of shirts draped over chairs and desk tops like an exploding rainbow and frowned. "I don't think the connection between the motto and the refuge is something Dylan would want publicized," she remarked. "Generally there's a very negative connotation in saying that something is for the birds."

"Not around here." Josie clasped her shirt possessively. "Here we have a very nice way of turning negatives into positives," she declared. "I think the shirts make that point very succinctly. Besides, they're cute."

"I'm not sure that 'cute' is the image Dylan is after." Then a knowing smile added a further chill to her aloof expression. "But surely you asked his permission before you used the name of the refuge? Otherwise you may have infringed on certain legal rights."

"I'll ask him whenever I see him," Claire answered, lifting her chin and meeting Rebecca's icy stare. "If he wants to press charges for my oversight, then he certainly has plenty of evidence. I don't intend to leave town anytime soon. I just thought that as long as we're into fund raising, we may be able to appeal to a lot of kids with these. And since kids go to the beach a lot, it may do some good."

"Kids aren't particularly generous when it comes to fund raising," Rebecca informed her. "You're aiming at the wrong income bracket."

"'Income bracket' isn't the highest consideration on my priority list. And I'm not aiming at anything right now," Claire answered brusquely. "I am simply giving some shirts to my friends—and I'm making a proposal that will give the small donors something to show for their efforts."

"And something to show off," Josie added to the defense.

"I still think we could strive for a little more class." Rebecca raised one arched russet eyebrow.

"I think I'd better get to work." Claire broke off the debate before she got really angry. Then she adopted the same arrogant tone that Rebecca used with all the refuge staff. "Have Dylan call me at my office when he has a chance," she directed Josie haughtily. "You know, the storage shed next to the fish freezer. In the meantime I'll be in pen four, rearranging the droppings as artistically as I can."

Rebecca's flawless ivory skin turned crimson as she watched Claire flounce across the room and disappear out the door.

Josie discreetly folded her T-shirt and tried not to laugh out loud. "Did you have a message for Dylan, also," she asked politely.

"I have the final notes for the zoning meeting, which is at eight tomorrow," Rebecca said through clenched teeth. "Afterward I've arranged a dinner with the members of the symphony board Dylan and I met with last evening. Some investors have agreed to sponsor a performance, with the profits going to the refuge. We need to finalize the date."

Josie noted the information dutifully.

"When do you expect Dylan?"

"Whenever his homing instinct brings him back," Josie replied, straight-faced.

"Then have him call me at my office." Rebecca's parting instruction was all Josie needed to lose her control. When Rebecca closed the office door and left, the throaty, resonant laugh of the office manager broke out as an unrecorded postscript to the exchange.

CLAIRE DIDN'T LIKE to call the refuge emergency number, especially after hours, but enough was enough. She stopped in the lobby of the Pier to make a quick phone call before she went upstairs. Several messages she'd left for Dylan had gone unanswered and there had been no response from him to her T-shirt proposal. Now she had another good idea she wanted to suggest, but most of all she wanted to end the days of "just missed him" that had been going on for nearly a week.

"Finally...." She sighed with relief when he answered the call. "How are you, stranger? I know this is the emergency number, but I want to know what's going on with you?"

"I'm in the midst of moving," Dylan answered hesitantly. "Other than the usual overlapping meetings and occasional few minutes in which I actually touch down in the clinic, everything is pretty normal."

She could tell by his voice that he was tired, but there was another element, a kind of preoccupation, that made her uneasy.

"Am I interrupting something?" She knew no other way to ask. She hadn't expected Dylan to keep his life in limbo, waiting for her to sort out hers. And with Rebecca Stroud constantly hovering around, the possibility was always there that she or some other woman would be eager to share his company. Dylan hadn't existed in a vacuum before she came along. Their relationship without name or rules wouldn't keep him from others who didn't need four glasses of wine to get up their courage. Josie had remarked repeatedly that Rebecca had been keeping Dylan booked up with appointments that generally included her. There was no doubt in anyone's mind that the red-haired real-estate agent had every intention of making Dylan her personal property. In addition to locating a prime location for the expansion and giving him all the professional advice he needed, she was dedicating her personal time to assist with the symphony night. Josie had sniffed indignantly that she suspected more than music was on Rebecca's agenda. Now it was well past ten o'clock and very possible that Rebecca's strategy was working.

"You're interrupting a very intimate encounter between me and a corned-beef sandwich," Dylan told her sardonically. "I'm between trips to the beach house and I stopped at a deli."

"Are you too exhausted to come in to the Pier? I've got some interesting news. I've also got some other things I'd like to talk over with you. But if you're too busy, they can wait until tomorrow. If I don't 'just miss' you again." She made the comment pointed enough to let him know she suspected he was avoiding her.

"How about you coming out here when you finish?" Dylan wanted her on his territory when she talked to him. If what she wanted to talk about had to do with Wes Raines or music or anything that would confirm what he had already concluded,

Dylan preferred to say his goodbyes where they had met, by the beach. They spent other parts of their lives in front of audiences of one kind or another. Here everything would be all wrapped up in a neat package—beginning and ending—in a world not public at all. No one would know the details or suspect the hurt.

"I may be late," Claire told him.

"I'll still be up working."

"At the beach house or the refuge?"

"The beach house."

"See you later, then." Claire placed the phone back on the hook, remembering a time when his voice had been more welcoming. He had said, "Come home with me," and the drive out there had seemed like a thousand miles.

Dylan was in the parking area underneath the house when Claire pulled up behind his truck. Covered with perspiration and sawdust, he was bent over a cagelike contraption he'd been working on. "This isn't going to please the bankers, and it sure won't help the resale value of the house," he declared as he lined the cage up between the chalk marks he'd drawn on the cement. "But the darn thing will make it easier to handle the birds."

Claire stared up at the hole he'd cut in the wood floor, eight feet up. He had attached heavy hinges so the outlined section could be opened and closed like a huge trapdoor. From what Claire could remember of the beach house, the opening took up most of the bathroom floor—in a rectangular shape as wide as she could reach. "You're going to have birds in your bathroom?"

"Only on special occasions," Dylan replied with a smile. "I'll still be bringing in some cases that I just don't want to leave overnight. If the choice is to stay at the refuge or bring the bird here, where we both might have a little serenity and get some sleep, I'll bring it home with me." They were talking about seabirds, but when their eyes met, there was a hesitation as both of them realized the significance of his comments.

Abruptly Dylan turned his attention back to his work. Claire stood watching him in silence, wondering why he was still working this late at night. She had the feeling that the cage was simply a convenient diversion, something to concentrate on instead of talking to her. Once she caught on to what he was doing, she knelt to help him, holding the cables in place while he connected one to each corner. Finally he twisted the last of the pulley cables tight, then clipped it off neatly with heavy pinchers. Then he stood and stuffed the pliers in his back pocket.

"What next?" Claire asked. Dylan looked at the trapdoor. Then he looked at her.

"I guess that's it for tonight. I can't do any more without a ladder, and it's at the refuge. Maybe tomorrow we'll have elevator service to the penthouse," he joked. "Now we can talk. Come on in."

Dylan picked up a few tools and scanned the remaining work area, never quite letting his eyes meet Claire's. Even his remarks about the elevator system were delivered with a cheerfulness that didn't ring true. When they climbed the stairs and stepped into the kitchen, Dylan put all the tools on the counter, then shrugged apologetically. "I'm really sorry about this mess—me and the house. I have a tendency to get carried away with my projects. If you aren't in a hurry, I'll take a quick shower and wash off this grit. How about some lemonade?" he offered politely.

Claire contemplated the dusting of sawdust that coated the pale hairs on his arms like a haze of springtime pollen. The thought of touching his body, washing the gold dust away, crossed her mind, and the effect on her was disquieting.

"If you can't wait...." He misunderstood her hesitation.

"Oh, I'm in no hurry," Claire assured him, forcing a response that sounded overly bright for one-thirty in the morning. "I don't mind waiting for a few minutes. I think I'll take you up on the lemonade and sit on the beach." The prospect of sitting there, listening to the shower, knowing how near he was and how his skin would glisten with droplets of moisture started another gentle flutter inside her, more tender, more pervasive than sexual desire. Claire wished she could reach out and touch him—to make the distance between them go away.

Dylan seemed eager to retreat. "Lemonade is in the refrigerator. If you don't mind, just help yourself. I'll just be a couple of minutes. If you like, I'll meet you out on the beach."

Outside in the moonlight, Claire could see the flock of black-and-white-feathered seabirds swooping low over the Gulf, gliding along the edge of the water, dragging their lower beaks in the water. Again and again the birds would scoop up their food, then rise en masse, turning in perfect synchronized flight, to disappear in the darkness. Then they would dart across the ribbon of shimmering silver moon water and repeat the gliding pattern. Eventually a few of them settled on the beach a short distance off, snuggling low like her, facing into the wind. There was something primitive and pleasing about the night breeze on her face and the silent company of the seabirds.

"Skimmers...." Dylan settled next to Claire on the sand and named the birds she was studying. "A real fly-by-night crew," he joked. His presence became even sharper when he sighed in contentment and leaned back on his elbows, talking in a low voice. "They like to feed at night because the small fish get courageous and come up near the surface. These fellows fly in low and sweep them up." A shift in direction cooled the light wind off the Gulf. Dylan zipped his jacket, but the slightly spicy scent of his cologne escaped and mingled with the breeze.

"Clever birds." Claire couldn't ignore the pleasure his presence evoked. Side by side, facing the dark water, she felt a delicious rightness, of being one with nature—and Dylan was a necessary part of that oneness.

"These birds are not always clever," he continued. "Skimmers are a bit lackadaisical when it comes to nesting time. Instinct overrules whatever passes for good-old common sense. They just pick out any old flat place—sometimes smack on the side of a causeway with cars whizzing by. They scrape a hole and drag in a few twigs and that's that.''

"The traffic doesn't bother them?" Improvised nests and unprotected locales sounded dangerous.

"No, but it really bothers the wildlife officers who have to rope off the nesting sites and put up markers to keep people from disturbing the birds. Skimmers are a protected species. In this case, they need all the help they can get.'' Along with the humor in his voice was something warm and compassionate and terribly appealing.

"Speaking of helping...." Claire turned and grinned at Dylan. "I have an idea for raising money for the expansion.''

"I know. I saw the shirts.''

"And...?" Claire pressed for an opinion.

"I like them. However...." When he paused, Claire braced herself for the next comment, assuming that Rebecca Stroud had made the case for the opposition.

"They're not classy enough," she muttered, anticipating the rest.

"The birds don't care about class. They're just interested in staying alive," he said quietly. "That's not what's bothering me. I thought they were very clever. I just wondered why there wasn't one for me.''

"I couldn't think of what to put on yours," Claire admitted. "Everyone else was easy.''

"Now how am I supposed to interpret that?" For the first time since she'd arrived, he really looked at her. His sea-blue eyes, calm as the Gulf before them but unsettled beneath the surface, searched her face for something more than an answer about the logo on a T-shirt.

"Dealing with you is very complicated," Claire replied honestly.

"Really."

She deliberately avoided contact with him as he sat up.

"And it would be less complicated if you didn't have to deal with me at all, I suppose?" His eyes shifted back to the horizon and the shimmering surface of the water. "If that's what you want, I can arrange that."

"You seem to have been doing precisely that all week. Being inaccessible. I felt like I was scheduling a business conference when I called tonight. And even here, you kept working on that cage until I thought you'd drop. I don't know what's going on, but if you want to keep it business only, okay, we'll talk T-shirts. But if you are upset about something else, something personal, then I deserve to know. I said I needed some time, but I didn't expect you to stop talking to me or not to answer my messages. You've been avoiding me. I'm not the one who's counting anybody out." She kept her voice low, but nevertheless it crackled with impatience. "You talk to me."

The no-nonsense tone she was using brought a curve to his lips, and his blue eyes sparked like summer lightning offshore.

"Okay. The T-shirt idea is excellent. Get the figures to Josie, and we'll get some made." Dylan chose his words cautiously. "From now on, I'll answer your calls, and we are talking." He delivered his reply point by point.

"And what about the other issue, you and me?" Claire demanded.

"Maybe I have been avoiding you. I think the rest is up to you." He clasped his hands over his knees and stared at them. "I don't know what you want for yourself. I don't know what we can have between us. Our other commitments don't mesh too well. I watched your video the other night. I don't touch that world at all."

"If you saw the video, then you know why I wasn't devastated when that job didn't come through. The intensity was a little too high for me. She's a very talented lady, that one on the tape. Technically impressive." Claire appraised her own performance with objectivity. She critiqued that onstage persona as if she were a separate being. "But *she* wasn't me. I was told once that I couldn't handle that kind of show, not singing lead and not having my keyboard as a crutch. But *she* did it. And I can't tell you how important that was. I learned something very illuminating."

Dylan sat motionless, listening.

"Finding me again means I may make some mistakes, and I may listen to others who make mistakes, too," she admitted. "Even Pete thought we were right for the Mariner, until we were actually there. And we weren't right at all. So if I drive you crazy trying parts of me that don't work out, just try to understand that when I finally work out who I am, I won't be secretly wondering if I missed anything. I'll know what my options truly are. You succeeded at one career, then changed to another—by choice,'' she stressed. ''And you found a kind of satisfaction that I don't have, not yet. I'd like that chance, and I'd like to succeed at what I try. But I want to do the choosing, and I finally have the opportunity to make my choices very carefully—personally and professionally.''

''And have you made any decisions so far?'' he said smoothly, with no perceptible emotion in his voice.

''Why do I have the feeling you think you already have the answer to that one?'' Claire leveled her gray eyes at him.

''I dropped into the Pier the other night. I saw you with a fellow. The bartender said it was Wes. So I left.'' His face remained deceptively calm.

''That was Wes, all right. Apparently he had some loose ends, too. He came back to see what he could do with them. I don't know what you think was going on, but you missed the important part.'' Claire's honey-soft voice merged with the salty air. ''That was when I went home all by myself. You were right about a lot of things. I had all these leftover feelings, and I still do. But seeing him again helped. I didn't feel trapped by the old options. I didn't have to leave alone, but that's what I chose to do. If I'd known you were there, my options would have been very different.''

''You still care about Wes?'' Dylan's question sounded more like a statement.

''Yes. I didn't want to admit it, even to myself, but

I do care. Not in the old way, but there is a lot of sentiment still there. Maybe what I'm feeling is just nostalgia. But even that isn't as dreadful as I had thought." She picked up a broken piece of seashell and began tracing patterns in the pale sand.

"Having Wes show up made me realize that the clear-cut lines I drew don't have to exist. Divorcing someone doesn't mean forgetting any of the bad parts. But it doesn't mean losing all of the good ones, either. I'm not coldhearted, even though things would be a lot less painful if I were. So you saw us saying hello again. Without the anger, without the fear—and without wanting to be with him. That made me like myself a lot better." She tossed the seashell into the water, then watched the ripples circling outward from the spot where it landed.

"How involved is this 'hello' part going to be?" Dylan leaned back, watching her profile silhouetted in the moonlight. The past was no easy adversary— no nightmare he could simply chase away. Now the past had form and texture, in the person of a dark-eyed poet who spun webs of words. Wes had had a chance to learn from his mistakes. If he'd learned well, then regardless of how Claire viewed her relationship with him, Wes had all the old heartstrings to play upon. And he was a master at his art.

"Not involved in the way you mean," she replied. "What's over is over. Wes plans to be working in this area, so we'll cross paths every once in a while. But we are talking about two separate paths," she stressed. "I have a whole other set of concerns."

Dylan looked at her curiously.

"That brings us to point two of my fund-raising plans." Claire turned to look at him. "Since we're talking about seabirds and the beach is their stomping ground, I think we should have a concert on the beach, right out in their natural surroundings. The aesthetics are right, the weather is beautiful and the audience is almost guaranteed. We can get the local radio stations to promote the concert, and we'll invite a lot of music groups to perform. We can hold it right out in the open, where all the birds can watch." Her hands inscribed arcs in the air as she unraveled her vision for him. "We'll have a monumental sandcastle building contest—or sand sculpting, or both. With prizes and T-shirts and a beachful of contestants. And for a perfect ending, we'll give a concert for anyone who comes to watch or compete."

"Hold it, hold it..." Dylan said to slow her down. "You've got a strange idea of fund raising. All I hear is expenses. Who's going to pay for all the prizes? Who buys the T-shirts? Who pays for the staging of this concert?"

"Actually, Wes said something that started me going," she confided. "He said that my predeliction for sand castles was catching on, particularly out in California. They have huge contests there with castles and sculptures. Some of the work is fantastic—absolutely beautiful pieces of art. Friends of his were hired to set up their band on the balcony of one of the hotels out there and the music blasted out over the beach while everyone dug in the sand. I wouldn't want to duplicate the balcony or the volume of noise—I have something more tranquil in mind. But

there are hotels right down on the beach who may go
for an idea like this. If we asked around and made it
clear that the profits were going to the refuge, one of
them might take a chance."

From the gleam of excitement in her eyes, Dylan
knew that she visualized the whole affair. Like one of
her castles, the whole thing already existed in her
mind. Archers and guards and princesses had been
supplanted by musicians, sand builders and seabirds,
but the vision was there.

"And prizes and T-shirts?" he questioned her.
"Who pays for them?"

"You always said that the little guy should put
something toward caring for our wildlife," Claire
went on eagerly. "We don't have to have one sponsor. We ask stores and restaurants to donate prizes.
Bigger businesses can pay for a certain number of
T-shirts, and we put the refuge logo with the pelican
on the front and the name of their business on the
back. Anyone who enters the contest donates a few
dollars as an entry fee and gets one of the T-shirts
and lots of cold drinks. We're offering advertising,
prizes and a deductible donation all in one. And best
of all, all summer long the beaches will be populated
by folks in refuge shirts reminding everyone to look
out for the birds." She carefully emphasized each
point and concluded with a triumphant smile.

Dylan stretched out in the sand, staring up at the
moon, with both arms tucked, pillowlike, beneath his
head. "Not exactly evening dress and symphony
hall," he said, laughing softly, "but it does have a
unique appeal." The silvery lightness in his voice was

a dead giveaway that he was enthralled with the image she had created out of nothing but words.

"The birds aren't interested in class, just in being alive." She tossed some of his words back at him. "The symphony is nice, but it misses a whole lot of people. Why should we be snobbish. The guys and I make very good music. We'll volunteer to do some songs. We know a lot of other performers who would do the same, especially since this is sure to attract a lot of press coverage. Everything I've talked about is very visual. If you want pictures to promote the work at the refuge, this will get them in newspapers and on TV."

"So all we need to start is a place to hold this sand-castle contest." He rolled onto his side, facing her. The way her mouth tilted up on both ends hinted that Claire had a prospect in that area. "All right. Where would you suggest?"

"That's the other news I have to tell you." She tried not to look too hopeful. "I've turned in my notice at the *Bay-Belle*. We have a trial week at a hotel on the beach. Apparently word got around that our stint at the Mariner was good. We've been offered a booking at the Don CeSar. Just a week. Then either side can change its mind," she added warily.

"I thought you didn't like a big place." The Don CeSar was a landmark on the beaches, massive, Mediterranean and ostentatiously pink. Like an elegantly frosted birthday cake, it sat facing the Gulf with tier after tier of balconies and windows basking in the sun. The grande dame of the beaches, the "Pink Lady" wore brocade and flowers and chandeliers with a flair that made her stark, high-rise competitors seem like too-slim, too-spare, unattractive sisters.

"There is a pretty good-sized lounge there," Claire explained quietly. "With lots of stained glass and green plants and comfortable chairs. But it doesn't feel big. When you look out the windows you can see the beach." She had been out to the Don earlier in the day with Pete and she'd liked what she'd seen. In fact, she'd loved the place. Claire just didn't want to get too excited until she'd actually played there.

"There are terraces and a huge raised deck across the back of the Don," she added. "With steps down to the beach, then a wide stretch of white sand for miles in either direction." She had said from the beginning that she wanted to come home, and to her that meant somewhere near the Gulf. If anyone could understand how essential that proximity to the beaches was to her, Dylan would. "I think the Don may be the ideal place."

"It's worth a try," Dylan commented casually. He tried to sound objective, but he had noticed the remarkable luminous glow in her eyes when she talked, and he knew there was a special affinity between her, the magnificent old building and this particular job.

Like the Mariner, which dominated the next beach community farther south on the strip of keys, the Don was one of the largest resort hotels on the beaches, but she was buffered from the commercial strip by residential housing. Moorish and Mediterranean, her lofty turreted roofline and arched windows had made her a highly visible landmark. But it was her serenity and unrushed atmosphere that whispered of an elegance only she could offer. Flowers filled her gardens and decorated her arcaded hallways; fountains sparkled. Imported tapestries, tiles and chandeliers exuded the romance of foreign lands. Here the painted dowager entertained her sophisticated and powerful connections. For years she was hostess to a cosmopolitan clientele and she cultivated a reputation for excellence. And when she found something particularly fine, she shared it with her friends. If one of her patrons saw promise in a singer with a voice as golden as her hair, the Pink Lady would introduce her protégé to yet another world.

"No one could ever criticize the Don CeSar for not being classy enough," Dylan observed with a pensive smile.

"Let's hope that under all that class is a sense of humor." Claire rolled over and stretched out on the beach beside him. "I'll wear my Sara T-shirt when I go to talk to the manager about the concert idea. Either they'll like the T-shirt or they'll faint."

"Or something in between," Dylan added wryly.

For a moment, they simply lay there in the moonlight, grinning at each other under the stars. And slender, delicate threads of communication reached out, invisible yet very real, bridging the distance between them wordlessly. Then the grins melted into smiles, as warm and intimate as a caress. The smiles softened as they leaned forward, touching only slightly with a slow, thoughtful kiss.

"I wouldn't throw you out if you came to me in

your Sara T-shirt," Dylan said with a huskiness that the humor did not disguise. His voice echoed with tenderness. When she was so close, so vibrant and guileless that she seemed to charge the air with her electricity, all the wisdom that told him she was just pausing a moment between her past and future couldn't stop him from claiming a fragment of that time for himself.

"I didn't wear my Sara shirt tonight," Claire answered, wishing she had. "It's in the wash." She fluttered one hand apologetically, as if dismissing the silky cocoa-colored blouse she had on.

The comforting touch of his hand, slipping up her arm, bringing her closer, sent a delicious shiver of anticipation through her, like a thousand tiny fingers untying knots of tension and reserve. She savored the sweetness of the next kiss, feeling the dreamy sensation that promised more.

"Forget the T-shirt. I can use my imagination...." He moved close to her, pulling her against him. Gently his lips came down with feather-light kisses to brush over the tip of her nose, her eyes, the corners of her lips, finally covering her mouth in a tender, silent invitation.

Deep inside Claire heard his words again: "Want me." He had asked nothing more than that. To have her want him—his face, his moods, his touch—no one else. As the pleasure of the kiss gave every muscle a luxurious wantonness and her graceful body willingly entwined limb for limb with his, Claire breathed unevenly through half-parted lips, whispering his name softly. "Dylan." To his silent inquiry the language of her soul was answer enough.

His hands glided over her body so slowly, pressing her into him with a restrained, controlled power, making the contact of chest and hips and thighs more exquisite for being unhurried. In the dark solitude of night shore, he explored the strong lines of her back, the narrowing of her waist, the curve of her hips. The enrapturing movement brought the warm pulsing of his body against every part of her.

"Dylan...." Claire trailed one hand over him, reaching under the fabric of his jacket, touching his hard, bare back and the solid curve of his shoulder. The skin-to-skin contact stopped his breath momentarily. If he'd been waiting, questioning, giving her time to retreat again, he knew that was not what she wished. He kissed her again, deeply, longingly, as his hand sought the softness of her breasts. Carefully he unbuttoned the chocolaty silk blouse, nudging aside the lacy cup of her bra, covering and embracing the smooth surface with his palm. Now his breath escaped, rich and warm, mingling with Claire's as her breasts firmed at his touch.

Easing away from her so slowly, Dylan moved downward, kissing the hollow of her throat, the arch of her collarbone, the rise of her chest, breathing her name against the silken skin. The light, lingering touch of his lips tantalized her, and she wove her fingers through his hair, lifting toward him, seeking the sweetness of his mouth upon her breasts.

"Dylan..." she murmured with pure pleasure.

The next rendition of his name was less erotic. "Dylan. Are you out there?"

Both Claire and Dylan became motionless, listening.

"Dylan?" There was nothing soft about the bellowing sound that Frazer made as he stalked out onto the beach. Flashlight in hand, he cut slender lines across the darkness. "Dylan!" The last bark brought a hoarse and breathy response.

"What the hell do you want, Frazer." Dylan pulled himself away from Claire and sat up stiffly, staring back toward the beach house.

"We got trouble." Frazer stepped in the direction of Dylan's voice, but when the flashlight beam hit the faces of the two moon watchers, Frazer discreetly turned it away. "Oh, boy." He stopped. "I'm sorry to butt in like this." He didn't come any closer. He just stood there uncertainly with the flashlight making anxious, jerky zigzags on the ground.

In the darkness, Claire sat up behind Dylan's shoulder, hastily buttoning the front of her blouse and shaking the sand out of her hair.

"What's the trouble?" With a low sigh Dylan stood up. Then he turned, offering his hand to Claire. He could tell by Frazer's gestures that the matter was urgent.

"That damned guy has been at the birds again. Only he's getting really mean. We can fix the upper bills, so he's switched to slashing the underbill. We've got some very sad-looking birds on our hands." He kept shifting from one foot to the other as Dylan and Claire came near.

"How do you know it's the same guy?" Claire was the first to ask.

"Same cigarettes, same jogging shoes. 'Cept now he's doin' his dirty work late at night instead of early morning. Maybe now that there are folks tipped off, it's easier for him to hide a knife than a saw. Whatever the reason, he's at it again. And the birds are really hurt bad."

"Where are they?"

"In my car. I heard the news from the police while I was night fishing. They'd called the refuge and left a message on the recorder, but I figured I could find you here. It was on the way to the clinic...." He shrugged uneasily. "I didn't mean to interrupt."

"I'll get my truck and follow you in." Dylan put a reassuring arm around Frazer's shoulders. "Let's go take care of the birds." Dylan steered them back across the sand, keeping his other arm around Claire as they walked, holding on a little longer to the closeness they had shared.

"Do you want me to come with you?" she offered.

"Not this time," Dylan answered dully, checking his longer strides to match hers. "I don't know what kind of damage he's done to these birds, but from what Frazer says, I'd rather you stay out of it for now. We may take a while. You can stay here if you want. I'll come back when I can." He didn't sound particularly optimistic.

"I just need to know I'm welcome. When the birds are taken care of, I'll be back."

"You're always welcome here. And you don't have to bring that T-shirt. I'll definitely remember where we left off." He smiled fleetingly as he paused between his truck and her car. Then he kissed her gently and, with a slight inclination of his head, indicated she should get into her car. "Lock the door," he cautioned her. "Stay safe."

"Good luck, you guys," Claire called, then waited to pull out as first Frazer then Dylan pulled off into the night. She followed them to the turnoff on the main beach road, trying not to let the mental pictures of the latest patients become too vivid. Slashed with a knife. She shuddered at the cold-blooded viciousness of the act. "For the birds..." she muttered angrily. And she thought of the bright-beaked skimmers, stalwartly facing into the wind. "Go after this creep," she whispered to no one in particular, her voice trembling slightly in the silence of the car. "Someone has to stop him."

CHAPTER ELEVEN

THE NEXT MORNING, Claire waved down Tammy Todd in the parking lot of the refuge. "What in the world is going on?" The lot was so packed with cars and vans that Claire had to drive a block down the beach to find a parking space on a side street.

"It all has to do with the latest round of mutilations," Tammy replied grimly. "When Dylan and Frazer were in here working last night, they had the video units running. They spotted someone tampering with the back gate. Unfortunately, since the cameras are set to watch the birds, they only got a shot of the guy from the waist down. Claire, he was wearing jogging shoes, and when they turned on the lights, he ran off with a decided limp." With the last detail she gave Claire a significant sidelong glance.

Claire came to an abrupt halt. "You mean, it was him?" she almost whispered. "He actually came here?"

"The police can't be sure, but we were all spooked. Kurt said it could have been someone trying to get to our drug supply or steal some of the equipment, but we aren't taking any chances. We're setting up a round-the-clock guard on the refuge."

"Looks like you've already started," Claire noted,

tilting her head toward the congested parking lot.

"This has a lot of people upset," Tammy said quietly, while her dark eyes somberly scanned the area. "We've got everyone from the news media to the symphony board here in person to get a look at the injured pelicans. Even the not-so-sensitive Phil Stockman is back with his video crew to do an update. Between Stockman and Rebecca, the poor birds are going to get a complex."

"What is Rebecca doing?" Claire asked as they entered the compound, wondering who had let her in on the latest crisis.

"She brought a photographer to add some shots of these birds to the display before the symphony benefit this Sunday. The foyer of symphony hall will be hung with wildlife pictures. Some of them will be beautiful shots of the birds that live in this area of the Suncoast. The others are ones of injured birds. As the patrons browse, the display will appeal to them on both ends of the emotional spectrum." Tammy sighed resolutely. "Rebecca doesn't miss a trick. And she gets results," she admitted. "This morning she dropped off a check from one of her father's business associates. A thousand dollars. One lump."

"And I brought in forty-two dollars from the *Bay-Belle*," Claire said, shrugging good-naturedly. "In lots of little lumps."

"Every bit helps." Tammy hooked her arm through Claire's and marched around to the rear of the clinic, where they could slip into the hallway to the recovery room without confronting either the press or the observers.

Baby-bird season already had them swamped with foundlings fallen from nests and the runts of many hatchings who were too small to compete with their larger siblings. Both the foundlings and the runts had to be dropper-fed or syringe-fed until they were strong enough or large enough to feed themselves.

While Tammy mixed a fresh batch of bird formula from mashed hard-boiled eggs, high-protein baby cereal, warm water and liquid parakeet vitamins, Claire set out the eye droppers and needleless syringes. The long tubes would ease the mushy substance down the right side of the infant bird's throat until its small crop was filled. A half hour later the process would be repeated for the tiny birds, and every half hour after that throughout the day and into the night, for the chirping of the tiny voices rarely subsided.

While they worked on the assembly-line procedure, Claire and Tammy could hear the voices in the clinic and the outer office beyond. Every so often the low rumble of Dylan's voice would be heard patiently responding to a question from the press. And when Phil Stockman began taping the voice over the video he had made about the mutilations, Dylan went through the entire story once more, without diminishing the conviction in his voice.

"There he goes again," Tammy whispered. "He must have answered those questions twenty times today."

"Maybe he should write down the details and make photocopies," Claire suggested. "Then he could get on with the other work he has to do."

"When people come here, they want to hear the

details firsthand, preferably from Dylan,'' Tammy answered. ''You don't get much sentiment from a photocopy.'' She squirted the last of her mixture into a trio of openmouthed mockingbirds. ''Nothing like a little human interest to get folks involved.''

''Speaking of getting involved....'' Claire smiled knowingly. ''I've noticed that Walker Hall's fancy fiberglass bills on our pelicans have stirred a lot of public interest—and I also hear that Mr. Hall himself has generated a little private interest in your life.''

''You can't believe everything you hear.'' Tammy tried not to smile, but the laugh lines at the corners of her eyes gave her away.

''Okay, let's have the real story,'' Claire teased her as they walked into the next room to wash up. ''Is this the start of a serious romance?''

Tammy hesitated, then shrugged. ''I doubt it. The man is good-looking, but he's a workaholic, just like Dylan. Only Walker's always thinking about racing yachts and keel design. We went out a couple of times sailing and stayed up late watching a few movies on television.''

''A few movies?'' Claire grinned. ''That's nice and cozy.''

''Well, I don't think that watching some old Bogart films is the kind of thing to base a relationship on. Besides, I don't like competing with a boat bottom for his attention.''

''I see your point,'' Claire acknowledged. Then she moved on to another kind of competition that might interest Tammy more. ''Did Dylan say anything to you about my idea for holding a sand-castle contest and a beach concert?'' Claire knew that would generate revenue far more impressive than ''passing the hat'' on the *Bay-Belle*, as Wes had dubbed her efforts at collecting donations.

''I think it's a great idea. Even Rebecca likes it,'' Tammy said quietly. ''She offered to handle the publicity and contact businesses for sponsorships.''

Claire looked at Tammy in surprise. ''Oh, she did.''

''There's more,'' Tammy said, leveling her eyes on Claire. ''Her father's company will be a sponsor. She's ordering five-dozen T-shirts with Stroud Real Estate printed on the back.''

''Four days ago she said they weren't classy,'' Claire commented smugly.

Tammy rolled her eyes. ''Rebecca didn't know then how much Dylan would like the idea. Now she's reconsidered. She wants her sixty shirts in aqua and white, just like yours.'' The tight, nicey-nice smile that Tammy used to imitate Rebecca was meant to tell Claire that the choice of colors and design wasn't arbitrary. There had been a deliberate message in the selection.

''Like heck she does,'' Claire muttered. ''My Sara shirt is just for me. I'll have a special order made for her—with a vulture on the chest.''

''Actually, vultures are charming, straightforward creatures compared to her,'' and Tammy giggled. ''Rebecca waited until Dylan was out of the room to place her order. However, the vulture idea does have a nice touch. They both have a remarkably similar red hairdo.''

''I'll straighten out the T-shirt orders,'' Claire said

calmly. "Unless Rebecca has volunteered to take over that, as well."

"Josie and I noticed that Rebecca only volunteers for jobs that keep her with Dylan or those that make her look very good to the public," Tammy declared authoritatively. "This beach contest will give her an excuse for calling up all sorts of potential clients," she added with a cagey wriggle of her eyebrows. "But you-know-who will be sloshing out the bird pens and staring at the video screens all night."

"Definitely not Rebecca," Claire acknowledged with a disgruntled frown. "The job isn't classy enough."

"Right."

"Who has volunteered for night duty?" Claire asked. The funny-you-should-ask grin on Tammy's face was directed at her.

"Not me. . . ." Claire shook her head. "I already work nights, remember."

"We just need you for the very late shift, midnight to dawn, so the rest of us can get away from all the chirping and get some sleep. We need someone capable and responsible. Robinson and some of the other school kids can help, but they can't take that night shift. Women with young kids to take care of can't stay here all night. Most of our volunteers have daytime jobs and can only work weekends. And the regular staff is frazzled as it is. We both know that Dylan will do it if everyone else falls through, but he's finally moved into his beach house. He needs a little time away. That leaves you and a few others who just may be able to fill in until things calm down. In other words, we need you.''

"I do sleep occasionally," Claire reminded her friend. "Starting Monday, we're going to play at the Don CeSar. I've quit the cruise boat and decided to go full-time with Pete and Robby's band.''

"There! That's even better," Tammy insisted. "You won't have to drive all the way back into the city for those nights. Just come out here, bring a late-night snack, stretch out on the sofa upstairs and keep an ear open. Dylan has wired in an alarm system. You can sleep. If anything is wrong, the alarm will wake you. Then in the daytime you can go on back to your place and recover.''

"You won't need me at all during the daytime?" Claire was beginning to understand how this night-time schedule would work, and she didn't like it.

"Exactly. You happen to have odd hours already. Rebecca pointed that out." Tammy looked at Claire curiously. "She figured that as long as you're used to the late nights, you could adapt to the system.''

"And how did Dylan respond to her suggestion that I take the night shift?''

"He said to ask you, naturally. He didn't make the suggestion. Rebecca did, with her big lashes fluttering so nicely and her voice so soft and concerned," Tammy said scathingly. "Unfortunately it does sound logical." Tammy's intelligent eyes shifted to Claire. "I don't exactly know what's going on between you and Dylan," Tammy said quietly, "but if there is something, watch out. Rebecca isn't planning on giving you the edge. She can't keep dropping in here every day and she can't keep him booked up with appointments every night. But she's always thinking ahead.''

"By keeping us in opposite time frames...." Claire saw the underlying impact of the schedule switch.

"She also brought invitations to the symphony for Kurt, Josie and me, but strangely enough she had no extra tickets for the volunteers. Does that tell you something?'' Tammy questioned her.

"It tells me that I'm not going to the symphony.'' Claire tried to sound unperturbed. "We'll be rehearsing that day, anyway.'' Claire finished rinsing off the syringes and eyedroppers and put them away until the next round of feeding. Then she followed Tammy along the hall into a small storage room where the latest victims were squatting in their cages. On the surface Claire was serene and composed, but inside she was fuming.

"After all the picture taking, Dylan had Kurt and Frazer bring the pelicans back here, where they could rest.'' Tammy kept her voice low. She didn't turn on the overhead light, but the hall gave enough illumination to see inside the three cages. "Aren't they sad.''

She and Claire bent down in front of the cages, looking in at the glassy-eyed pelicans. On each one, the olive-drab soft, stretchy tissue of the underbill bore a jagged dark line where the knife slash had been made. Neatly pulled together by rows of even, dark stitches, the gaping holes had been painstakingly repaired, but the scars, visible and otherwise, would always remain.

"We have to stop this lunatic,'' Tammy muttered.

"But how do you catch someone who hides in the dark and ambushes the poor birds?"

"We can go back to recruiting folks for the beach bird-watch," Claire proposed. "I have a couple of folks organizing groups in the neighboring condos, but there are hundreds of others on the beaches that we haven't hit. And we haven't recruited at the bars or restaurants or grocery stores. Give me some brochures and I'll canvas the boardwalk at Frenchman's Pass. There are some deep-sea fishing ships that come and go at all hours. Let me try them."

"Did I hear someone say 'fishing'?" Frazer's bright beady eyes peered into the dimly lit room where the women were talking. His wiry little frame was dwarfed by both of them when they stood. "If you're goin' fishing, count me in," he insisted.

"I'm going fishing for some help to catch the creep who did this," Claire informed him. "Could I interest you in a little promenade through the shops at Frenchman's Pass? If we split up, we could do the entire area there in an hour, then finish off with the fishing boats when they come in from their day trips."

"If you folks are going to hold a conference, could you bring it out in the hall?" Dylan stood silhouetted in the doorway, looking in at them. "We have some very tired birds in there." His disapproving frown softened only slightly when Claire stepped out with the others. "We also have more reporters." He rubbed his hand wearily over the stubble of beard that made his face look even more worn. "Everyone outside, please."

There was another television news team waiting for

them in the parking lot. "I know everyone else has worked you over pretty good." The woman reporter from the cable network had heard about the prior interviews. "Is there anything you'd like me to cover? Anything more you'd like said?" Because Claire was the first one out, the question was aimed at her.

"You could talk about the kind of callousness it takes for anyone to hurt a single defenseless bird." Claire spoke quite clearly. The images of jagged scars and the exhausted faces of her friends tormented her. Fighting back a deluge of tears, Claire trembled with anger. "Or you could talk about the few seconds it takes to injure a creature, and the countless hard hours and elaborate work required to repair them. And you could tell them about someone so perverted that he actually gets his kicks from maiming pelicans—and urge people to band together to stop him."

The female reporter rested a hand on Claire's arm in a gesture of support. "Whoa. Why don't you tell them?" The crinkled smile lines in the woman's face deepened.

"Oh, I'm nobody important here," Claire said, backing off. "I was just making a suggestion. Dylan is the one who does the talking."

"I've done enough talking." Dylan wouldn't replace her. "And you are important. Go ahead," he urged her. "You do the talking today."

IN THE SMALL APARTMENT, a can of beer sat dripping, spreading a circle of moisture onto the end table. A half-eaten pizza lay on the open cardboard box, the spicy aroma mingling with the sweeter scent of a hand-rolled cigarette. The viewer sat motionless, staring at the face on the screen—a gray-eyed woman whose sun-reddened cheeks were totally devoid of makeup. Still, she was striking. But it was the challenge in her eyes that interested him. She was talking about the birds again. The dumb birds. He had already clipped the articles from the papers, and he'd hurried home to see the evening news. He had made the news again. He was getting famous. Just like Jack-the-Ripper.

But the pretty woman on TV wasn't impressed. She was "disgusted." That was the word she used. And when she talked about him, she called him a coward. She talked about the stupid, ugly birds as if they really mattered. She kept on and on about how quiet they were—how they couldn't even whimper when the coward attacked. And she said that a big one weighed only six pounds.

She was organizing people to catch him. She called them bird-watchers and she gave a number where they could call to volunteer. She gave a description, but he could take care of that. The police estimated the assailant's weight was one hundred sixty.

Stupid cops. They were five pounds off.

But she kept calling him a *coward*. A coward twenty times bigger than some bony creature who couldn't cry out in pain.

Stupid birds. Stupid broad.

She didn't understand—the birds were nothing at all. Losers. So stupid they'd walk right up to anyone. *Coward. Coward.*

She was picking on him—on TV. She was trying to embarrass him, to make him feel like a freak. And no one picked on him.

They never gave her name. They said she was a volunteer. But he cracked open another beer, and he learned every detail of that face. Every self-righteous comment and faked pause burned into his memory. He had her pegged. Some fancy uptown socialite who never worked a day in her life. Now she was moaning over those useless birds. Lookin' down her nose at him as if he were nothin' at all. She could have her army of busybody volunteers. He'd still get her.

He drew in a stream of smoke and held it for a long time. Nothing, but nothing would keep him from getting even.

No one called him a *coward*.

Certainly not some air-head blond.

WES RAINES WAS IN THE AUDIENCE when Claire sang at the Pier that night.

She came into the lounge only to be greeted by an unexpected round of applause. The cable network had put on their interview with Claire. They had shown the interview repeatedly, and the impact had been obvious.

"Miss Bird-watch of the Suncoast," Pete said, announcing her arrival. Smiling proudly, Robby rattled off a drumroll. Claire looked bewilderedly around the lounge and turned scarlet. She was used to the applause coming after she performed, not before.

"You're getting to be a regular celebrity." Wes pulled out a chair and greeted her after she'd completed a few songs. He'd ordered a large iced ginger ale just the way she liked it, with a twist of lemon, and had the drink waiting for her. "What's this I hear about your doing a concert at the Don CeSar?" Almost immediately Claire could feel the muscles in the back of her neck tighten. His solicitous attitude was too eager; the question came too quickly to be casual conversation.

"Actually, we're contracted for a week's trial run starting next Monday." She hastily corrected the rumors he had heard. "The concert is something else entirely. It's a fund-raiser for the Gulf Coast Seabird Refuge, and it's still in the idea stage," Claire explained. "I stopped in to discuss the idea with one of the managers there, but he hasn't confirmed anything. He had to discuss the proposal with some other executives. If they do go for the idea, then as soon as we can set a date, we'll combine a sand-crafting contest with a twilight concert."

"And you and the boys provide the music?" Wes's dark eyes stared thoughtfully into hers.

"We'll just be one of the groups performing." Claire corrected him. "The plan is to have several bands play. That way we could have music for any tastes—depends on who we can line up to perform."

"How do you get on the schedule?" His dark beard framed a genial smile. "More specifically, how do I get on the schedule?"

"There is no schedule yet," Claire answered. "But if you want to perform—and if the concert idea goes through, I'll put your name on the list of volunteers."

"'Volunteers'?" The smile wavered slightly. "You mean, you're doing the concert for free?" he said very softly, but the trace of a strain was there.

"It's a benefit for the refuge. Everything is donated, even the music. A concert like this will make the news statewide, perhaps even nationally. On one night's pay, you can't buy that kind of coverage." Claire didn't like the way she sounded, but she made the same points that Pete and Dylan had made. Publicity made money. Free publicity made even more money.

"Right," Wes agreed. "Sign me up, then," he directed her. Once again he had resorted to the amiable attitude that had once been so irresistible.

"When there is a list, I'll sign you up," she promised. "I have to admit, after all this fuss over that TV interview tonight, I think our chances of pulling this off are improving."

"If the Don won't stage it, someone will," Wes said confidently. "You've latched on to a very marketable idea. You'll make any sponsor look like the paragon of ecological virtue," he professed with a delicate balance between cynicism and poetry. "They know they can't buy that kind of coverage." When he caught Claire's response to his comments, he deftly inserted a ripple of low, raspy laughter. "Business is business, Claire. I know you're too softhearted to see things that way," he said softly. "That's one of the things I think of the most." He lowered his voice. "How soft and sweet and innocent you are." The erotic timber in his voice wound around her like a tantalizing trail of warmth.

Claire stared down at the ginger ale on the table between her hands. "I don't want you to talk to me like that," Claire said in a low voice. "I'm not so innocent any more. And being soft and sweet didn't give me much protection. If we can't have a drink together and talk without getting very personal, then we just won't talk.''

''I can't help it if the old memories get the best of me,'' Wes replied apologetically. ''I'm trying. I just need a little time to get straightened out.'' He placed his hand on her arm and left it there. ''Don't give up on me,'' he urged her.

''Then don't try to manipulate me.'' She looked him in the eye.

''I'll behave.'' He shrugged sheepishly and tilted his head like a puppy caught with a shoe. Claire regarded him closely. She could remember the many times that he had done the very same thing, and she had laughed and loved him all the more. She was reminded there had been gentleness and affection and passion. Once upon a time.

''I have some more songs to do.'' Claire excused herself. For an instant with Wes, they had resurrected the good times. She had stepped back into a time when warm looks and tender touches and music had been enough to fill her days and nights. And she was tempted to hold on to that time for just a little while. But that was the old Claire, whispering doubts and giving in and compromising. Holding back instead of going forward. There was another Claire, struggling to stay above it all. And that one had a job to do.

''Thanks for the cool drink.'' With a slight smile she turned away, while Wes watched the lady move into the light.

CHAPTER TWELVE

"I'D LIKE A WORD WITH YOU, if you don't mind."
Rebecca Stroud met Claire in the corridor of the Don
CeSar. "I thought we'd better talk so we could coor-
dinate our efforts."

Claire stared at her uncertainly, trying to figure
out what Rebecca really wanted.

"What efforts are we coordinating?" Claire asked
as they turned into the entrance of the lounge.

"I'm talking about the sand-crafting event,"
Rebecca replied with typical efficiency. "Can you sit
a moment so we can discuss this privately?" She had
noticed Pete and Robby across the double-tiered
lounge, working on the stage setup. "How about
here?" She directed Claire to a chair well out of the
boys' hearing.

"What do you think we need to discuss?" Claire
was getting edgy putting up with Rebecca's super-
visory attitude. "I do have work to do."

"This won't take long," Rebecca insisted, flipping
open her folder and scanning her pages of neatly
aligned notes. "I just want you to clear everything
with me before you commit us to anything," Rebecca
informed her. "I know you have contacted several
groups to play that night, but something like that

can't be conducted just by word-of-mouth. We don't want to be held liable.''

"I don't understand," Claire replied. When the management gave the okay to hold the contest and concert on a Saturday two weeks off, Pete, Robby and Claire had simply called up some friends and lined up different groups who could take shifts playing during the afternoon and evening as the contest closed and the sun set. Their band had also taken on Wes Raines as the new soundboard man. ''We don't need contracts if they're donating their time,'' Claire explained. ''These are friends of ours.''

Rebecca gave her a patronizing stare. ''Dylan doesn't know your friends. Neither do the executives here. The reputations of the refuge and the Don are involved. Friends or not, a contract keeps details straight. We don't want anyone making claims or trying to get reimbursed after the event. Get the terms in writing first. I'll need the names and addresses of the groups you contacted.''

''Fine. I'll get the information from Pete.''

''And I don't want you to contact any media people without checking with me.'' Rebecca continued down her list of notes. ''There is no sense in both of us handling media relations. Between the staff at the Don and me, we can line up all the coverage.''

''Is that all?'' Claire asked flatly. Rebecca had volunteered to oversee the sand-crafting event. After the success of the symphony performance, which had required little supervision and brought in seven thousand dollars for the refuge, Rebecca had turned to the sand-crafting event, obviously eager to impress Dylan once again.

"There is one other thing." Rebecca leveled jade-green eyes at Claire. "I want you to be very careful about your public comments. Since the recent television coverage, you seem to have become a spokeswoman of sorts for the refuge."

"And you want the bar singer to behave herself..." Claire shot back at her.

"Exactly." To Rebecca, the request seemed perfectly reasonable.

Claire stared at the red-haired woman for a moment. Half amazed, half outraged, she kept her hands on the arms of the chair, resisting the impulse to throw something. "Rebecca...." A hundred possible comments flew to mind, most of them very descriptive. But none slipped out.

"Dylan has the refuge on the verge of becoming a major development," Rebecca stressed. "With the right backing and this piece of property on the bay, he can create a refuge that will be a viable attraction. It will draw visitors, tourists and locals. I intend to see that happen." Rebecca kept her voice low. "I know what can be done with the land, and I know how to raise the funding."

"I'm sure you do." Claire slid back her chair in a gesture of dismissal. She didn't have to listen to this woman.

"Right now, you may have Dylan a little dazzled by your songs and your sentimental attachment to the birds." Her condescending words were etched in ice. "But that won't last. He's a realist. He needs someone who can do him some good—someone who can get this project moving. After you've made your little media splash, the excitement will die down. You'll have nothing more he needs. I'll be the one who is indispensable. People tend to drift back to their own kind," she added pointedly.

Without uttering a syllable, Claire stood and walked away. Her skin felt cool and clammy, as it had the afternoon trudging through the mangroves, dreading she'd see a snake. Now she had. Face to face she was confronted by a viper, with cunning green eyes and a cold-blooded heart pumping out evil. A monster. The woman was a monster. Beautiful, sensuous, efficient, clever, manipulating, ambitious—and evil. Yet Claire could see how Dylan could be taken in. An outsider would think Rebecca was unselfish and ever so helpful. Rebecca was a spellbinder. She had a lot to offer any man, as long as his dream connected in some way with her own ambitions. What those ambitions were, Claire didn't know. But Dylan was part of her plan, a part Rebecca didn't quite possess but wouldn't relinquish.

Claire moved across the lounge, staring mechanically at her brothers, still reeling from Rebecca's words. She had told Pete that her relationship with Dylan was not a contest. She'd been wrong. It was a contest. Without realizing what she was doing, Claire had been yielding points by default—letting Rebecca make huge gains while she struggled with the ghosts from her past. And Rebecca played the game well. She had staked out the territory and held the critical vantage points. But if Claire really wanted him, the contest had to turn serious.

Now she was ready to do battle. And she had to win without attacking her adversary.

"IS EVERYONE READY TO GO?" Tammy bounced into the refuge office, looking for the others.

All the staff had agreed to meet there at eight so they could go to Claire's first night at the Don together. This time Claire had given them all an invitation—written and signed and posted in the office. But the envelope in Dylan's hand wasn't one Claire had passed out to them, and the officer at his side wasn't one of the refuge regulars.

"What's wrong?" Tammy stopped and stared at the roomful of people.

"Looks as if the weirdo didn't like what Claire had to say about him." Frazer spoke first.

Dylan broke away from his discussion with the police officer and signaled for Tammy to come nearer. First he showed her the envelope, now sealed in plastic. It was addressed to Claire, but had been ripped open. Then he handed her the contents of the envelope in two similar plastic bags, sealed and labeled by the police.

"Oh, my...." Tammy studied the advertisement announcing Claire Parnell and Sound Off appearing at the Don CeSar. The black-and-white photo of the group had been cut out of the newspaper, and a jagged red line in marker was drawn across Claire's throat.

Inside the other plastic bag was a bloody bird

feather and a penciled note, "You'll get yours," printed in irregular letters. Unsigned. The blood had soaked through the envelope enough to catch Josie's attention, but it was Dylan who had decided to open the envelope without asking Claire.

"This is really sick," Tammy groaned.

"What do we do now?" Robinson hovered at Tammy's shoulder, studying the evidence.

"We go to the show and watch Claire perform," Dylan suggested. "When it's over, I'll tell her about this."

"We could be dealing with a prank," the officer noted. "We'll notify the security people at the Don just in case we're not. And we'll have a patrol car in the neighborhood to check out her home routinely. Other than keeping an eye out for her, there isn't much we can do."

"I think we should keep her away from here for a while," Tammy suggested. "If he comes looking, he won't find her here." All the color had drained from Tammy's face and her eyes were wide and anxious.

"I'll stop in at the Don every night and make sure she gets home safely," Dylan declared. "Frazer, if you can stay on late tonight, I'll change my schedule and move back in upstairs for a while. I'll take the late shift on guard duty here, instead of Claire."

"What a dismal way to start an evening," Josie muttered. "What a rotten thing to have to tell Claire." Then for an instant her eyes flickered with a new light. "Are you sure we have to tell her?" The idea brought a hopeful smile to her face. "Couldn't we let it go until tomorrow?" All eyes turned to the uniformed officer who now had possession of the plastic bags.

"If you had been threatened, wouldn't you want to know?" He aimed the question at all of them. "Just in case something does come of this, the lady should have all the information. She needs to be careful. She has to know what she's up against if she's going to protect herself." He noted the grim faces registering agreement. "But I'll wait till the show is over to talk to her myself. You can have part of the evening. That's the best I can do."

Frazer stayed behind to monitor the surveillance setup. His wizened face puckered into a brave smile as he watched the others leave. He'd catch the show another night. Right now he'd like to catch something else.

"We have to look as if we're having a good time," Dylan insisted as Kurt, Josie, Robinson and Tammy slowed down before entering the Don. He rested one hand on Tammy's shoulder and the other on Kurt's. "When the performance is over, we'll talk about him. Until then, we'll listen to Claire. Ready...?" His intense gaze shifted authoritatively from one companion to the next.

Tammy and Kurt nodded. Josie took a deep breath.

"Let's boogie." Robinson set his jaw firmly and produced a passable smile. "I want to hear my lady sing."

"So do I," Dylan said quietly as he led the procession into the lounge where Sound Off was warming up. When the lady took her place onstage, there were faces she knew—smiling faces—and the place felt like home.

The Claire on this stage was less flamboyant than the one they had all seen on the videotape, and the songs were softer, with a gentler rocking rhythm. In the front right corner of the room, Wes ran the soundboard like a gifted conductor—modulating, adding echo, manipulating the sound, orchestrating the performance. Not quite a part of the band, but essential to them, he demonstrated his technical skill by making the job look so easy. The effects he produced were masterful.

Dylan sat with his hands clasped beneath his chin studying Claire closely. Like a beautiful bird, tall and graceful, honey colored from head to toe, she swayed and danced on her platform, riding on the music. One of nature's creatures, she pirouetted with exquisite grace in a courtly promenade that claimed the territory as her own. But in the dim corner there was Wes Raines. Instead of pulling strings, he was pushing levers. Instead of holding Claire down, he was helping her soar.

"I kept pushing her in front of the camera, instead of me," Tammy moaned. "If only I hadn't."

Dylan reached across the table and patted her arm. "I did the same thing," he said softly. "I told her to do that interview. I wanted her to let out her feelings. I wanted to make the strongest impact. I'm responsible. The final choice was mine." His eyes were drawn back to the lady on stage. "If anything happens to her . . . ."

Then silently another presence settled upon the

group that gathered. Like an unseen chill sliding into their midst, the man who sent the letter was back—invisibly encroaching on them and hanging in the air like a foul stench.

From the stage Claire could see throughout the entire room. Like a creature homebound at dusk, Claire kept her internal radar zeroed in on one special table, where the refuge group watched. And the blue eyes of Dylan Jamison homed in on her. But midway through her first set, the expressions on the faces at that table became somber.

"Okay, you guys." Claire started in on them the instant her numbers were through. "What's going on?"

Five stoically polite faces attempted to look innocent.

"Did something happen to Sara?"

No response.

"He didn't hurt some more birds?"

Blank looks.

Finally Dylan let out a slow stream of air and raised his eyes to meet hers. "We were trying not to let this spoil your first night," he began slowly. "But someone—we suspect him—sent a letter to the refuge. Not exactly a letter. A clipping from the newspaper that contains a threat."

"How could a clipping 'contain a threat'?" Claire pressed him to be more precise.

"This could wait." The instant Dylan reached over and took her hand in his, Claire knew the threat had been directed at her.

"Tell me," Claire insisted, ignoring the cold knot that had formed in her stomach. Then she sat there, watching with somber gray eyes as Dylan told her of the envelope and the contents.

"I'm sorry I got you into this." He still held her hand. "It had to have been that interview—the one with Lucy Hyatt. We'll drop you from the others. No filming. We'll reshoot the public-information footage and call off the oil commercial. We don't need to put you—"

"Hold it," Claire told him. "We are talking about this same cowardly creep who sneaks around at night hurting the birds. He's not going to dictate what I can do. And neither are any of you." She looked from Josie, to Kurt and Tammy, Robinson, then back to Dylan. "I'm home. I'm finally somewhere I want to be. It's going to take more than a magic marker and a bloody feather to get me off his case."

"But he may really try to hurt you," Tammy warned her. "He's a real sick person."

"This isn't the time to prove another point, Claire," Dylan stated with conviction. "This one can be really risky. He could be serious."

"I'm the one who's serious," Claire argued. "He's the one who better crawl back under his rock. I won't let you cut me out of the commercials or anything else. He's picked on the wrong person. I've been afraid before." She looked at Dylan, knowing he would understand what she was talking about. "This guy isn't going to win." Her words were defiant, a subtle challenge.

"I think we'd all better talk to the police." Tammy licked her lips nervously as the brittle silence became insufferable.

"I think you're right," Dylan agreed.

As if on cue, Bizzy played an intro on the keyboard, signaling Claire back to the stage. It was time for the next set.

Claire gave her friends a quick smile and squeezed Dylan's hand before she let her fingers slip away from his. "You'll like this one," she insisted as she took the platform.

Her pulse was racing. The cold knot was still there. She was frightened, but this time Claire had curbed the instinct to flee. That much she could control. She had seen the terror in the face of each of her friends, a terror spawned by the imagined horrors that this unseen perpetrator could inflict on her. "Put the right face on your ghosts," Dylan had told her. She was doing just that. She was putting a coward's face on a one-hundred-sixty-pound male in jogging shoes. If he didn't like it, too bad.

Claire took a sip of cool water from Pete's glass, swallowed hard, lifted her chin and moved under the microphone. She started in with Robby's favorite, "Don't You See I Made a Difference," and she dedicated the song to the five stoic friends at the table and to the bird-watch volunteers.

> Little pebbles
> Make big ripples,
> My friend, they reach far and wide
> Makin' waves
> In the water
> Pushin' out against the tide.
>
> Don't you see I made a difference.
> Just by lovin' you . . . .

This time the words had a new meaning. It was an upbeat, happy song, and it was going to be her anthem. No more backing down. She had things worth fighting for—whether her foe sent her a threat by letter or stared at her with eyes of green ice.

After the performance, Wes, Pete and the band joined Dylan and Claire in the Don coffee shop; the others from the refuge went home. It was time for a conference. With two tables pulled together end to end, they sat listening to the uniformed officer and the Don security chief detail what they could do and couldn't do for Claire's safekeeping.

"Until we know more about this guy, we're just going to have to wait him out." The officer shrugged apologetically. "We don't even have a fingerprint we can use. So the next move, if there is one, is his. We'll all be alert, not take chances and lie low."

"I'll have my men shadowing your coming and going," the sandy-haired security chief offered. Dressed in casual sports clothes and deeply tanned, he looked more like a guest at the resort than an employee. This was intentional. Without a distinguishing uniform, he and his staff could mingle unnoticed amid the lounge patrons and stroll inconspicuously about the grounds, on duty but not obvious. "We're pretty good at spotting people who don't belong here."

"I don't want to cause a big fuss over this," Claire insisted. "I want to keep this job. If we disrupt the usual procedures, we may seem like more trouble than we're worth."

"Our job is to keep an eye on things—discreetly,"

the security chief assured her. "Your job is to sing," he added with a smile. "We had you covered from the time your band played the first note tonight. And nobody even noticed."

"What about when she isn't onstage?" Robby wondered aloud. He was still fidgeting anxiously with his drumsticks, trying to grapple with the severity of the threat to his sister.

"I'll take her home in my car every night," Dylan offered. "To make sure no one bothers her."

"I can do that," Wes Raines volunteered with an edge of possessiveness. "We're on the same schedule, anyway." Throughout the meeting, he had sat across from Dylan, watching every look that passed between Claire and the blue-eyed man who ran the bird refuge.

"I can make sure that Claire gets home all right." Pete leaned forward as he spoke, effectively overruling the others. "We can handle this ourselves." That meant family. Neither Dylan nor Wes looked pleased, but neither protested.

"Lately this guy's been doing his stuff at night," the officer pointed out. "That may mean he has a day job—or he works shifts. It may mean that he just likes to sneak around in the dark. In either case, so far days seem to be no problem. Just exercise a little more caution whatever you do."

"So I'll be at the refuge tomorrow," Claire informed Dylan. "Line up the filming for the commercial. After that, I'm going recruiting for the bird-watch."

"I really don't know if that's a good idea," Dylan

said, shaking his head. "I'd rather you stay where someone can keep an eye on you. Just in case...." He softened the comment as he caught the glint of defiance in her eyes.

"I'll stick to apartment buildings and condos," Claire said. "I'll have lots of people around." She managed a confident smile.

"Don't get too carried away," the police officer cautioned her. "If you go on TV again and say anything bad about him, you may only antagonize him."

"Right. We wouldn't want to do that." Claire seemed to agree, but both Pete and Dylan looked at her closely. Inside her head they knew the wheels were spinning.

FOR TWO DAYS there were no other letters, no further incidents with the birds. There had been innumerable times when Claire had glanced in her rearview mirror or looked over her shoulder, but she chalked that up to nerves. No one had bothered her. Except for her unofficial bodyguards.

"Will you guys quit hovering!" Claire burst out in exasperation as Frazer paced by the gate for the third time and Kurt insisted on straightening the water hose. At the refuge someone was always close, watching and chatting unnecessarily, just so she wouldn't be alone. "I usually do this by myself." Claire sent Frazer and Kurt back into the refuge building. "Please give me a break."

Washing down the splash pools didn't require an extra hand, and Claire knew that both men had been putting in long hours. Kurt had a shipment of antibiotics and equipment to uncrate. Frazer and Dylan were alternating on the night shift, sleeping in the upper room of the refuge while the surveillance system monitored the grounds and the occupants. But the prowler in tennis shoes hadn't returned. This was hatching time, and the influx of new pelicans added to the unpredictable events that kept everyone moving in a different direction. No one needed the extra duty of watching a grown woman rinse out and refill plastic pools for the birds. And for five glorious minutes, Claire had the cages and the herons and egrets to herself.

Josie strolled toward the pen where Claire had finally been left alone. "Remember all those laughing gulls that built their nests on that sandy development?" She grinned as she talked, her deep voice rumbling with delight. "Well, when they ran those bulldozers and plowed away hundreds of nests, they left a very flat, very bare stretch."

"I know." On the rescue trip, Dylan had taken the boat close to the area, and Claire had seen how barren and flat the land was. The bulldozers had been removed by court order and work on the development had to wait until the eggs hatched. Once the young fledged, the laughing gulls would lose their claim on that space. Then the bulldozers could take over.

"Dylan just called in. Guess what's happening there now?" Josie was clearly bursting to tell her. Without waiting for the guess, she went on. "The gulls are just beginning to hatch in the undisturbed part. The bulldozed area is so bare that those rascally skimmers have settled there. Right out in the open. They're scraping a few shells and twigs together and nesting.''

"Now they'll get bulldozed?" Claire dreaded that the black-and-white night flyers who had shared that moonlit beach with her and Dylan were now the next victims on the list.

"No!" Josie's guffaw cut through the compound like a foghorn through the night. "The arrogant little things are on the endangered-species list. Absolutely. They are protected. The developer will have to put off his work until their round of nesting and hatching is over.''

"How about that?" Claire braced her hands on her hips and grinned.

They had scored a small victory, but one with a nice ironic twist.

"Dylan said to tell you about the skimmers," Josie added. "He also said the filming of the commercial would be Friday. He couldn't get the film crew any earlier. So if you want to go canvas a few condominiums for the bird-watch, you can go today or tomorrow. He just wants me to remind you to be careful." She delivered the message with a motherly concern. "Please be careful." The last comment was her own.

First Claire changed into more presentable white shorts, her Sara shirt and a wide-brimmed white straw hat. Then, armed with refuge brochures and a stack of T-shirts, she walked purposefully along the beach. She climbed the steps into the first patio-pool area where residents in low lounge chairs were spread out, baking in the sun. "Hi. I'm Claire Parnell and I'd like a moment to talk to you about the seabirds."

She began each spiel with a line she'd practiced to perfection. If she could get that much out, generally her nervousness would go away and then she was ready to sail into the rest of her presentation. Two iced teas and three condos later, she was out of T-shirts and her brochure stack had dwindled to two slightly dog-eared leftovers.

In the La Serena Condominium, a huge beige-and-burnt-orange Spanish-style building too large for her to cover in this trip, she stopped to see the resident manager in his office. "If you want to be on the program at the next condo meeting, you'll have everyone there. Sure beats standing out in the hot sun." He looked at the perspiration beaded on her temples, then bought Claire a Coke. When Claire accepted, he jotted her name on his calendar the evening of the condominium-association meeting.

"We have a new wing going up next door." He tilted his head to the south.

Claire simply nodded. Years ago there had been wide beach, dunes and sea oats on this spot. A mazelike conglomeration of small beach cottages with screened porches and weathered wood siding had huddled under clumps of scruffy pines. Now La Serena stood where the dunes had been, and the new wing would totally cover the area. Progress—but at what price. Claire glanced toward the nearly completed construction with an ambivalence that made her remain silent.

"If you want to take a peek, you're welcome to explore. The work crew is off today. Something about union hours." He had misread her attentiveness. "It's a shortcut. You can stay cool."

"Thanks." Claire accepted his offer. Then, with the can of soft drink still in hand, she walked off to the new wing. She remembered seeing the sign from the street. Prices started at one hundred thirty thousand per unit. And for a few minutes she could stroll through as if she belonged there.

In the lower floor, the predominant color was apricot. Carpets, wallpaper, bathroom fixtures. Even the kitchen appliances were done in the rich lush color. And in every unit one wall had floor-to-ceiling glass doors angled to get a view of the blue-green Gulf of Mexico. The angled design also effectively screened each unit from the next, so the illusion was one of ultimate privacy. Thick walls separated the individual condo units so no sound from one would intrude into the neighbor's world. Once the air conditioning totally muffled the outside sounds, the occupant would have his own retreat where he could view the majesty of the seashore. And the occupants of the twenty-five other units would each have a cool silent cocoon just like this one. It was a far different world from screened cottages and dunes.

Curiosity moved her along corridors, past open elevators that were not yet functional, to the larger upper units, where the view was through two sets of glass doors, with a balcony added. Stepping past propped-up stacks of uncut wallboard, buckets of joint compound and nails, and easing between upright wall studs that would ultimately divide one room from the next, Claire stepped out on a balcony and let the breeze sweep over her. At this height, she guessed there would always be a breeze. And the feel of the breeze through her light T-shirt reminded her of Dylan's beach house and the dream of the siren in the night and the sea god holding her, caressing her naked body gently—like the wind.

As she started down the stairway, her footsteps making hollow sounds in the unpainted stairwell, she noticed a peculiar sweet aroma that made her stop. Cigarette smoke. Somewhere below, another casual visitor had stepped in out of the sun, only this one had brought something other than a soft drink. Claire scraped her feet and called out, "Anybody there?" Then she started down again, hoping the sly smoker would get the message and go on his way. Instead she heard the dull scrape of footsteps.

At the next landing she could hear the erratic footfalls more clearly. Then they stopped.

Whistling loud and clear, Claire started down the next flight of stairs. Then she spotted a man in an orange hard hat, standing in the hallway, clasping a hammer. He was turned slightly toward one closed door, apparently examining the frame.

"Hello," Claire said quickly. "The resident manager told me I could look around."

The man didn't turn to face her at first. Nor did he respond to her greeting. Instead he glanced the other way, down the empty corridor. Then he started moving slowly toward the stairway where she stood. He just kept coming with a slightly irregular step. Not quite a limp, but an uneven stride favoring one foot.

"I've been watchin' you, Miss Do-Good," he smiled contemptuously, still clutching the hammer by its throat, raising it like an iron claw above his fist.

The blue-and-white tennis shoes cinched it.

It was him.

She tried to scream, but the sound that came out was choked, barely audible, like a moan in a nightmare. Panic—hot and electric—charged her body.

Skidding over strips of discarded wiring, bent nails and the powdery dust from the wallboard, Claire bolted up the stairway. He had been following her. Now he had caught her alone. Leaping several steps at a time, Claire zigzagged down the stairway, not looking back. She didn't have to. She could hear him coming after her, his shoes hitting and squeaking with each stride, longer and heavier than her own.

Claire cut along the second-floor corridor, using a long stretch of newly carpeted hallway like a race track to gain some distance. Then she wheeled into the end stairwell, grabbing on to the railing and pulling herself around and down again. The door at the end of that lower hall was blocked—braced shut from the outside by two-by-fours, as if he knew he could corner her there.

Desperately Claire lunged into the second doorway, squeezing behind an uncrated refrigerator—apricot. Holding her breath and standing very still, her heart hammering in her chest, she listened to the uneven slap of shoes. Moving. Stopping. Moving again. He had come the other way, intending to head her off. Claire scanned the room, looking for anything she could use as a weapon. Something to swing at him if he came close. A coil of copper tubing lay like a burnished serpent on the apricot carpet, and suddenly the images flashed through her mind— Rebecca Stroud—and bulldozers—and the arrogant skimmers who nested where they pleased. Of Dylan as the two of them had sat on the sand by the beach house, facing into the wind like the birds. She had promised to come back with or without her T-shirt. She had a song to finish. It couldn't end like this.

Next to the copper tubing lay a crowbar, pronged like a talon on one end. The odds were improving. And in spite of her terror, Claire gritted her teeth in an angry and bitter grin. "For the birds. . ." No one was going to push her around.

Brandishing the crowbar with both hands, as if it were a battle ax, Claire took a wide stance in the center of the room, facing the open door. With a determination that both thrilled and frightened her, she knew she would take him on. She was ready to fight for her life.

"I'm in here you slimy coward," she yelled out as the footsteps halted. "If you want me, you'd better be ready to swallow your teeth first." She sounded impressive—like a pirate, or maybe Sam Spade.

The shadow outside inched forward, tiptoeing to the door. First she saw the orange hard hat. Then she saw part of his face as he peeked past the doorframe, looking in. When he saw her glaring back at him, he jerked out of sight. And he stood there, waiting.

"You just try it, coward." Swaying from side to side slightly, like a baseball batter waiting for the pitch, Claire adjusted her grip, ready to put the hooked end of the crowbar where it would do the most damage. "I'll give you ten seconds to get out of my way. Then I'm coming out. Move it or lose it, buster." Her voice came through without a waver, but trickles of perspiration trailed down the backs of her knees and the bend of her elbows glistened with sweat.

"One..." she barked out. "Two...." Her eyes burned from staring. She couldn't blink. Not now. At five he shuffled. At seven the shadow moved away.

At eight she could hear him start to run with long uneven squeaks against the floor.

At ten she sat down on a paint can, cradled her head in her trembling hands and sighed.

CHAPTER THIRTEEN

"THEN IT'S OFFICIAL." Josie brushed back a strand of her gray-streaked hair and tried to look businesslike. "Robinson is bodyguard." School was letting out for the summer and the roster of paid employees was expanding.

"Semiofficial." Dylan qualified her statement. "From this point on, Robinson is technically Tammy's rehabilitation assistant, full-time, all summer. But whenever Claire is doing anything connected with the refuge, even attending condo meetings, he's her shadow." He turned uncompromising blue eyes on Claire and her tall, stony-faced companion, Robinson. The young guardian nodded. "You don't go anywhere without him, do you agree?" Dylan waited for her to answer.

"I agree," Claire said glumly. Since her run-in with the fellow in the abandoned condo the afternoon before, she was ready to admit that the threat on her was more than a bluff. Only now the anonymous letter writer had a face, or at least a portion of a face. Claire had given his description to the police artist and a composite drawing had been made. The hunt was on. The Don CeSar's security chief had passed copies of the drawing to his staff. The refuge workers had the picture posted inside each entrance. And Robinson showed up with two friends, other basketball players, who volunteered to patrol the compound while they worked with the birds. But Claire found it all ironic. She hadn't won; it had been little more than a standoff. She had chased off the attacker; he hadn't harmed her at all. Instead he had taken away her privacy and her freedom to come and go as she chose. His specter lurked everywhere. It wasn't fair.

When Dylan asked her into his office and closed the door behind them, she knew there was more and what he had to say wasn't going to be good.

"This won't affect the sand-crafting contest, will it?" Claire kept her voice low as she and Dylan stood in his inner office. Already the local disc jockeys had begun pitching the event as a special summer festival where sun, surf, sand and seabirds were cause for celebration. Rebecca Stroud was having flyers printed to be posted throughout the bay area. The roster of sponsors and the list of prizes was increasing as more merchants were recruited for the event. Boxes of T-shirts had been ordered—all yellow and white—sun and sand colors—to eliminate controversy. Throughout, cool and well organized, Rebecca was overseeing the details with the thoroughness of a general plotting military strategy.

"I don't know." Dylan answered without looking at Claire. "It depends on what happens in the next week. If this guy looks like he could endanger anyone or disrupt the event by pulling something, you may have to keep out of sight. I don't want him to get another crack at you. In the advance publicity, we're dropping you from the program.''

"But you can't," Claire protested. "I want to be there. I want to help. It was my idea." In the midst of her last comment, she realized how childish she sounded. Regardless of her intent, everything was coming out "I."

"It's for your own protection." Dylan looked at her at last. There was an inexplicable sadness in his eyes. "You don't need to prove anything to anyone," he said quietly. "You stood up to the guy once. That's enough. Don't let him turn it to his advantage. Don't let him set you up. You won the battle. Don't lose the war."

Claire stared at him closely. Since the envelope had arrived, Dylan's expression had taken on a somber quality. Her encounter at the condo had deepened his attitude of concern, until it hung like an ominous storm cloud, charging the atmosphere between them with a strange gloomy tension. Claire tried to understand, knowing that Dylan's integrity was somehow involved. Only now he felt responsible for what had happened to her and what could happen. If she stood her ground and fought him on this issue, she might win another battle but lose a far-more-intimate war.

"We'll wait and see." She softened the tone of her voice. "If the sand-crafting event pulls in the crowd we anticipate, then that's good enough for me." That was the civilized kind of thing Rebecca would have said with her polite smile. When the worry lines at the corners of Dylan's eyes tilted into the first crinkles of a smile, she knew she'd spared him a confrontation he'd dreaded. He had never been quite sure what to do with her, but he didn't want to argue with her. "Thanks for being careful with me." She leaned forward and kissed him softly on the corner of his mouth, a kiss tender and light, like a fleeting summer breeze.

He didn't expect that.

"I do want to be very careful with you." He reached out and slid his hands over the still-sunburned surface of her arms. But his touch was gentle, and Claire looked up at him, unresisting and safe within his grasp. The half smile on her lips was an invitation, a gesture of conciliation—a promise of peace.

"Maybe I've been too careful," he whispered as he accepted, lowering his lips to meet hers. Tenderly his lips grazed hers, hovering again and again, barely touching their velvety softness, as if he were testing himself, or perhaps her. Claire couldn't tell if either one passed or failed. She felt only the moist tracing of his tongue, searching, seeking and venturing deeper. She welcomed the sweetness.

His strong arms folded around her, lifting her on tiptoes as he pressed her against the length of his body. It had been like this the first time, when they'd been castlebuilders who had shared only an afternoon. There had been that same tremble inside her, like the tiny heartbeat of a creature newly born, full of wonder. She could feel his heart beating louder as the softness of her breasts molded against the hard cage of his chest. "Claire..." he breathed against her lips. "Be very careful." He wasn't just asking her to take care with a nameless enemy. He was asking her to take care with him.

Claire slipped her open palms over the tense muscles in his shoulders, feeling in the hard contours more than their physical strength. And she sensed the message—it was all right; his shoulders were strong—strong enough to depend on when she needed to. Soft enough to cradle her head in the night. "If I bring my T-shirt—" she leaned back and looked up at him "—could I come here tonight and be with you."

Dylan's eyes, dreamy with desire, held her suspended—captured like a mermaid in a secret lagoon. "I'm not going to like myself for saying this." He managed to temporarily put aside his hunger for her. "But I don't want you here. I don't want you to be anywhere near this place at night. However," he said, smiling at her, "I definitely do want you." He bent low again, lightly kissing her upturned face. "This is a postponement, not a rejection. Something has to be done. We have to find somewhere safe."

Instantly both of them smiled again. The beach house.

"I've got the duty here tonight," he said without releasing her from his embrace. Claire buried her face in the curve of his neck, softly placing a kiss there. "Tomorrow Frazer is on the schedule. Tomorrow night I'll take you home from the Don. I'll be your bodyguard. I'll guard every inch of you." His hands moved caressingly down her back, sliding over the flare of her hips and drawing her against the tautness of his lower body. The contact sent a warm glow of erotic pleasure throughout her, all the more tantalizing, because this was just the beginning.

"This time I don't want anything or anyone to find us. Not tomorrow. That's for us. But oh, how you'll be with me tonight," he moaned good-naturedly. "In more ways than one. I'll be working upstairs with Brett Westbrook, editing the footage for the public-information spots. I'll have you here on all that tape. And when I finally turn off the lights... you'll still be with me." Once more he touched his lips to hers, breathing in her sweetness.

But the voice that came from the other side of the door was not so sweet. "Dylan...." Josie summoned him. "Ms Stroud is on the phone. She has the posters. She wants to know when she can drop them by here."

Dylan pulled away from Claire. "Business," he said quietly. "She got them done free of charge. You can't beat that." Claire let him go without protest—and without muttering what she was thinking. Indispensable Rebecca was using another of her numerous contacts to impress Dylan. One more point for her, Claire calculated coolly.

"If you like, Robinson and I can pick them up for you," Claire volunteered, as nicely as if she'd been coached by the green-eyed viper herself. "We can post them at the beach shops all the way back."

"Great," Dylan agreed instantly. "I've got plenty here I need to do. Josie," he said, stepping out of the office, "tell Rebecca that I'm booked up the rest of the day but I'll send someone by to pick up the boxes. Just leave them in her outer office and we won't even have to disturb her."

Josie relayed the message with undisguised smugness.

"HEY... ROBINSON. Good to see you." The balding man who greeted Robinson in the parking lot of Stroud Realty was someone Claire vaguely recognized. "How's the knee doing?" The older man clapped Robinson on the shoulder with a comradely air.

"Just fine, Mr. Crawford. Just fine. I'll be walking on sand all summer, so I'll be in prime shape for the fall." Robinson slid one box of posters into the back of Claire's car and stood up. "Mr. Crawford is head of our high-school booster club," Robinson informed Claire. "This is Claire Parnell. She works with me at the Gulf Coast Seabird Refuge."

Burt Crawford's eyes lit up. "You're the one I saw on the TV," he told her, smiling and nodding as he wagged a finger at her. "That bird slashing is very bad stuff." He pursed his mouth. "Bad stuff. I intended to send in a check, even if I am from the opposition." He began groping in his jacket pocket for his pen and checkbook. "I'll do it now, if you don't mind the wait."

"What makes you the opposition?" Claire stepped out of the car and walked around to talk to him. She'd pulled out a T-shirt, extra large, to give him in return for his contribution.

"You folks and your birds are picking up some land I wanted. Or at least your boss has an option on it. Rebecca offered me the south end a couple of years back. Then it was about a quarter of the current acreage and not worth much. But the other parcels in the surrounding area were tied up in some estate, or other. Apparently she's got the whole package now."

He hesitated for just an instant as he caught Claire's eye, then added, "Just tell your boss to keep a close eye on the adjacent land. I wouldn't be surprised if the corporation that has it under wraps has a red-headed woman on the board of directors," and he winked pointedly. "I just wonder if they're keeping any of it in their back pocket, so to speak. No matter. If the price is right and you folks want it, that's business. If your boss doesn't pick up the option, I just might." He chuckled as he talked. "I might as well be buying more property on this side of the city—those darn birds are roostin' on my other land. They've got us stymied for another six weeks."

"You own the land where the laughing gulls and the skimmers are nesting?" Claire stared at him. Now she knew where she'd seen him. Crawford was pictured in the newspaper, standing by the idle bulldozers after the state had ordered operations on the sandy development to stop until the birds left. This smiling fellow was the ogre who ordered the devastation of the gulls' nests.

"I'm that ruthless fellow." He shrugged, reading her thoughts. "Building houses for the people and moving out the birds." He was quite familiar with his dual-edged public image. "I was out of the state when the plowing began, but I'm not shucking my responsibilities. I should have had one of my supervisors do an on-site check first. Or given the birds a calendar. Hindsight won't undo anything, but this may help get you on to something else.'' He grinned again, then scribbled away at the check he'd begun. When he ripped it off the stub and passed it to Claire, he paused, looking at the T-shirt she was carrying. "Do I still get the shirt?" he asked her slyly. In spite of his good-ole-boy demeanor, he hadn't missed any detail.

"Oh. . . . '' Claire held the shirt out to him. "Sure. And thank you for your contribution.'' Then she glanced at the amount on the check and her mouth dropped open. Ten-thousand dollars. "You can have the whole dozen,'' she insisted, reaching into the passenger seat for the remaining shirts.

On the way back to the refuge, they made eighteen stops along the way, with Robinson loping into each restaurant, gas station, or resort-wear shop to pass out the sand-crafting-contest and concert announcement. The poster only said, "live music,'' and Claire gritted her teeth each time she thought about the possibility of being bumped from the program. But she kept remembering Burt Crawford's genial face. The eyes were too bright and too cunning for him to let information slip out idly. He had implied that Rebecca Stroud just might be part of the corporation that owned the land optioned for the refuge expansion and there could be more involved than anyone suspected. If anything he told her was supposed to be a secret, Burt Crawford wasn't keeping quiet. He wanted someone to check it out. Unfortunately that someone was Claire.

She was frowning by the time she made the last stop, brooding that Rebecca Stroud had Dylan fooled with her generous offer to donate her commission to the refuge. What if the commission was just the tip of the iceberg. If Rebecca was part of the Bay Trust Corporation she would still get her share of the sale price. The allegation had the ring of truth, but Claire didn't want to be the one to tell Dylan. Someone else had to help him unravel Rebecca's scheme.

"Robinson..." Claire began when the young man returned, folding his long legs like a grasshopper into her compact car. "What do you know about corporate structure?" She began not so subtly. "And land transactions?"

Robinson gave her an inscrutable look, then shrugged. "Practically nothing. But my Uncle Gene is a tax attorney," he said with a slight smile. "You want someone to do some snooping?"

Claire laughed as she handed him Crawford's check for ten-thousand dollars to give to Dylan with the remaining posters. "Maybe we could ask your Uncle Gene to follow up on what Mr. Crawford said. I bet he could find out who's behind Bay Trust and who owns the land Rebecca Stroud is handling."

"I bet he could." Robinson nodded. "For a T-shirt or two." He shot Claire a crafty look. "Large," he added succinctly.

"That can be arranged." Claire laughed as they swung onto the interstate highway and headed for the Gulf.

WES RAINES WAS NOT ALONE for long as he ran the soundboard at the Don that night. Halfway through the first set, Claire and Pete were singing when Rebecca Stroud strolled in, looked up at the band briefly, then scanned the room. Her scrutiny ended with Wes at the soundboard. She headed straight for him.

When the set ended, Claire looked at the two of them, each holding a tall, cool drink as they moved away from the wide panel of dials, colored knobs and sliding levers on the soundboard. In her pale-beige, loose-knit top and slim pants and with her flare of auburn hair catching the light, Rebecca reminded Claire of a match ready to strike fire. The way Rebecca's smile flickered and faded, then sparked again, sounded a primitive alarm inside Claire.

"I see the Dragon Lady is here tonight," Tammy commented as Claire joined Kurt and her at a small table by the window. "Now what could she possibly be discussing so intently with your ex?"

"Maybe they're planning an assassination," Claire finally said. "If there's reason to think this creep may cause trouble, I won't be performing the night of the sand-crafting extravaganza. I'm beginning to suspect where that suggestion came from."

"I'm sure she's only 'looking out for the interest of the refuge.' " Tammy mimicked the comment that usually prefaced one of Rebecca's less-pleasant announcements.

"I can always show up incognito and enter the castle-building contest, though." Claire raised one eyebrow and smirked. "I have talents she doesn't even suspect."

"I really wish you two would stop griping about her," Kurt said impatiently. "She is doing a lot for the refuge. Let's give her credit for putting in the hours. She doesn't have to, you know."

Tammy and Claire looked at each other and sighed. "Men . . ." Tammy huffed. "They're so gullible."

Kurt reached toward Tammy and draped his arm across her shoulders. "Next slow song, if you want to dance with a gullible man, I'm willing." Without the protection of titles and scheduling that the refuge provided, suddenly it all came down to a man and a woman. Tammy looked at the bearded face that she'd seen over many an injured bird, and she turned bright red. He wasn't gorgeous, but he was nice looking. He wanted to dance. Suddenly good-old Kurt would never be the same to Tammy again.

"Sing us a slow song," Tammy said, turning to Claire. "This might be interesting."

" 'Might'?" Kurt chuckled. "This man has hands like a surgeon."

"I'm more interested in how the feet move," Tammy teased him. "I'd have to know you a lot better before we get to the hands."

"I'll sing you something nice," Claire promised. Then with a quick sidelong look at Wes, she crossed the dance floor to the stage. And when the music began, Rebecca Stroud didn't even bother to look up.

"I think we've got a way of getting around the concert problem." Wes walked to the car with Claire and Pete after the show. From the way Wes's eyes shifted from brother to sister, Claire suspected his revelation had been provoked by a red-haired woman. "If we send out the word that I'll be singing with the band, then we'll still be set on the program. When the weekend rolls around, if this guy is loose, we'll play it by ear. Either I go on, you go on or we go on together.'' He made the whole thing sound perfectly reasonable. "Either way the band gets the publicity.''

Pete nodded, but only as an indication that he would think about it.

"There could be some pretty good coverage on the concert,'' Wes added. "No sense on missing out. Plus Rebecca Stroud says her father knows some bigwigs in the recording business. A couple of them have condos on the beach. She's invited these guys to come down.''

Pete smiled tightly. "Yeah, so she said. She asked for a copy of our video from the Mariner to get them interested,'' Pete said. "So I gave her one.''

"When was this?'' Claire demanded.

"Couple of days ago. She told me she was trying to get a couple of record producers interested in showing up for the concert. It couldn't hurt,'' Pete said to counter the frustrated look Claire gave him. "A copy of the tape was only eight bucks.''

Claire rolled her eyes. The eight dollars was not the point. Once again Rebecca had made herself seem generous and reasonable. But Claire was not fooled. "If she's so interested in furthering our career, may I ask whose idea it was for you to sing with Sound Off for the concert, instead of me?'' She aimed her question at Wes.

"I guess Rebecca has been asking around. She just found out that I sing. She didn't even know we used to be married. My stepping-in for you seems like a good idea.'' He gave her one of his rascally smiles.

"You don't mind, do you? I'll only step in if it isn't safe for you."

"You're darn right I mind," Claire answered sharply. "But I wouldn't dream of depriving you of your Good Samaritan deed. You go ahead and plan on singing with the group. Just leave a couple of numbers free for me. Unless this creep is firing mortar shells onstage, I'm going to sing two of my songs. And they aren't going to be for any record producer. One of them is for Sara."

"What about the other one?" Wes narrowed his eyes slightly.

"I'm working on it," Claire answered.

"So work...." Pete chuckled. They had reached the car. Across the parking area, one lone observer nodded. It was one of the security guards who strolled out just ahead of them to check the parking lot each night. With the same quick nod, Pete unlocked the car door and let Claire in the passenger side. "See you tomorrow," he said to Wes. Then across the roof of the car he whispered, "If you're gonna sing with us, don't crowd Claire and lay off the smokes."

They didn't say anything until Pete pulled into the driveway of his house, where Claire's car was parked.

"Oh, brother...." Pete spotted the flattened tires first. They got out and circled her car; every tire had been slashed.

When he walked upstairs to check Claire's apartment, the dead gull lying on her doorstep made him curse loudly. "He's been here," Pete spat. "Come into the house. I'm calling the cops."

"Hello."

"Dylan. . . ." Claire could tell by the grogginess in his voice that he'd been sleeping. "I hate to bother you, but something else has happened."

There was an immediate change in his voice. "What's the matter? Are you okay?"

"I'm all right," Claire assured him. "But he knows where my apartment is. He's cut the tires on my car. He killed a gull and left it on my doorstep."

"I'll be right there."

"Wait. . . you don't have to come all the way in."

"Pack a bag. I'm coming to get you. Now." There was no room for negotiation. And for once Claire didn't even want to protest. Someone else could be in charge—just for a while.

"Here we are again." Dylan took Claire's hand and led her between the tall support pilings and up the plank stairway into the beach house.

He had driven back out to the beach cautiously, cutting into cross streets and checking that no one could have followed them. Even when he turned into the single roadway that circled past the beach house, he passed his property and parked next to another house farther down, instead. They had walked out onto the beach and come up along the empty, moon-lit beach before turning in.

"You'll be safe here," he said as he flicked on the lights and carried her bag into the bedroom. "The phone works, but the number is unlisted. Even the mailman doesn't stop here. This isn't officially a residence yet." He came back through the kitchen and locked the door leading down to the parking area below.

"Now how about a glass of warm milk and a couple of aspirin? You look like you could use some sleep. I'd offer you some wine," he said, attempting a smile, "but I threw it out."

In his haste to come and get her, he'd yanked on a wrinkled pair of khaki shorts and a sweat shirt with the sleeves cut off. His long muscular arms, tanned and hairy, stretched down to a forlorn-looking pair of deck shoes that had taken him on countless rescues. But this rescue had hit him with a different impact from the others, and even now his tense expression suggested a barely restrained rage—and a terrible sense of helplessness. There was no visible enemy, no one to strike out at.

Claire reached out to touch him. She ached to take away the solemn look in his eyes and make him smile again. He hadn't let her down, and he needed to know that. If he could find the dragon to slay, he would be her knight-in-shining-armor. But he couldn't. Modern dragons didn't come into the open and fight fair.

"I don't think I want that glass of milk." Claire brushed the tousled strands of gold-streaked hair from his forehead with her fingertips. "And I don't need the wine. I just want to hold you. I want you to hold me."

Dylan looked down at her, his face lined and worried and his eyes registering a myriad of conflicting emotions. "I don't think I can just hold you," he said softly. "I've been saying no to myself for so long where you're concerned. I've been holding back, waiting to give you time to find out what you really need—what you really want. But holding you...."

Claire silenced him with a gentle kiss. "I know that tonight, right now, I want to be with you. I want you to guard my body, all night long. And I'll guard yours."

Dylan's rough hand touched her cheek in a wistful gesture. Then his thumb traced her jaw and slid down to rest in the hollow of her throat. He could feel her pulse, throbbing so lightly, as he remembered the picture with the red mark slicing across her neck. Keeping her safe was all he cared about. "Castlebuilder, it will be my pleasure." He reached past her and clicked off the kitchen light.

In the moonlight, with the sea wind whispering in through the open windows, the siren and the sea god slowly discarded the trappings of the world they wished to leave. They reached out for each other, feeling in the contact of soft skin upon rougher skin a contradiction that issued a tantalizing summons. More. The softness of the siren disguised shoulders and long limbs of deceptive strength—the harder body of the sea god shielded a gentle heart. And the discovery was an affirmation of what they were both beginning to understand about each other.

Dylan lay next to Claire on the water bed, covering her with slow, languid kisses and lovingly guarding every inch of her naked body. His rough hands trailed over her skin, making tiny muscles tighten in anticipation then shiver as the roughness stirred a bolder response. He had wanted her to desire him. He wanted her to be sure.

Claire pressed both hands upon his chest, pushing him back against the softly undulating surface of the water bed. Rising above him like a goddess from the sea, she covered his face with kisses, letting her pale golden hair trail over him like honey-colored mist, closing off all other time. This night was theirs alone. Her fingertips caressed the smooth column of his neck, glided over chest muscles and teased his burnished nipples until they were erect. Like a mirror, reflecting gesture for gesture, Dylan's hands clasped her breasts, touching and caressing as their eyes burned into each other like beacons on a primitive shore—calling the siren, summoning the sea god to a ritual of passion and an act of love.

And when they moved as one, controlling the motion, clinging to each other, murmuring and sighing in a language ancient and instinctive, Claire could feel his beating heart, taste the richness of his kisses and savor the power of him, rolling beneath him, holding on. Arching to him, she strained to break free, to let her body feel the release that was nature's gift to lovers. The sea-god dream was gone. The reality of Dylan loving her, being loved in return, filled her senses with exquisite rapture. The sweeping waves that had held them nearly breathless, now broke and carried them along, sending out countless ripples of ecstasy.

Gradually the motion subsided, fading by velvet kisses and satin sighs into a hushed serenity as they lay, still embracing, in pleasant exhaustion. Claire nestled in Dylan's arms and smiled contentedly. She could feel his breathing become more even as he held her close. The sound of their mingled breath soothed like a lullaby, easing them to peaceful sleep. Outside near to shore, a night heron, wading in the surf, gave a raucous cry and orange-billed skimmers sailed low over moonlit waters. The waves whispered their ageless song.

IN THE MORNING there was no need for a note. Dylan woke her with a gentle kiss just below her earlobe.

"Good morning."

Dylan's greeting was a husky murmur. But when she stretched out her fingers and toes, he was not beside her. The next kiss came from above her. Claire looked up at him, fully dressed and grinning down at her. He pointed to the steaming cup of coffee he'd put on the bedside table. "I've got to go. Time to evaluate the recoverees and get their records set. We're taking a batch out for release tomorrow. I wish I didn't have to leave now, but I must."

Claire brushed the hair out of her eyes and wriggled into a semiupright position, leaning back against the pillows with the sheet pulled up over her bare breasts. Dylan passed her the cup of coffee, then moved back, retrieving his own cup and sipping from it, looking over the rim with eyes still rich with wonders from the night.

"I called Frazer. He's coming over here for the day. I don't want you here alone. If that's okay with you." He seemed uneasy about making too many assumptions.

"Today I just want to sit on the beach and dig in the sand. I'm not sure Frazer will find that particularly fascinating."

"He'll be bringing his fishing pole. He'll be fine." He took a long sip of his coffee, looked at her, paced to the other side of the window, looked out, paced back.

"I'll be fine, too," Claire insisted, trying to ease the look of concern on Dylan's face. "You can leave. Don't worry about me. I'm the one with the crowbar, remember?"

"And he's the one with the hammer. There's no telling what he's planning," Dylan answered, still haunted by the newspaper clipping of Claire and the dead gull left on her doorstep. "Or where he might turn up next."

"After today, I'm not playing hide-and-seek with that guy." Claire tucked the sheet snugly around her and sat upright in the bed. "I've got too much to do. If he wants me, I'll be out in very public places, with lots of witnesses. Tomorrow we're shooting that commercial. I have an afternoon meeting with the La Serena condo association to present my bird-watch program. The guys and I will have a few practice sessions. Wes may be performing with Sound Off at the sand-crafting concert. That means breaking in a new soundboard man."

"You mean Wes is going to be singing instead of you or with you?" Dylan put his cup down. "Or will you alternate?"

"You may have to check that with Rebecca," Claire replied. "She seems to be the one making the decisions." She kept her voice calm. "I guess it depends on our weirdo out there."

"How do you feel about Wes's stepping in like this?" Dylan watched her sitting there in his bed, her cheeks still pink from slumber.

"I think it will be good for his career," Claire said objectively. "He hasn't put together a group of his own, and I think the concert will remind folks how good he can be. Taking over for me may launch Wes on his own again. But I know where the stage begins and ends, Dylan," Claire said, cutting right to the heart of the matter. "No matter who plays the music or who sings, I know what's real."

"Right." Dylan nodded. His jaw was still set, but he smiled. He was a believer in possibilities, and they often included ones he didn't particularly like.

"See you tonight." Claire slid from the bed with the sheet toga-style and kissed his lips softly. "Now go on and take care of the birds. I have a castle to build."

"Maybe I should wait till Frazer gets here."

"If you keep hanging around, I'll go in and take a shower, and I'l be all naked and warm and wet...." She started across the room, letting the sheet slide slowly down her back. "I don't think Frazer would appreciate it if he showed up and you and I just happened to be...."

"I'll go." Dylan surrendered. "While I still can. But I'll call you later on. And I'll see you tonight. You phone the office once Frazer gets here. Then I'll feel better.'' With a reluctant tilt of his head, he took another long look at her. ''Tonight...'' he said finally. Then he swung the heavy wood door closed behind him.

''Lock it,'' he called to her, peering through the small square window set into the door. ''And don't open it to anyone but Frazer—or me, of course.''

''Of course,'' Claire agreed. ''No one but you... and Frazer.''

WHILE CLAIRE MOUNDED THE SAND, one scoop at a time, the wind gusted in over the beach, whipping up little whirls and tracing wavelike patterns across the sand. Each time the water came crashing in, a cluster of tiny speckle-backed sandpipers scampered out of the way. Then they tiptoed back on little black legs, poking among the overturned shells for tidbits. The game went on and on throughout the afternoon, ebb and flow, as it had countless other afternoons on other beaches. Finally, with a flutter of white-rimmed wings and russet bellies, the sandpipers took to the air, wings beating frantically against the force of the wind until they caught the current. Then the desperation was gone and the small birds sailed on effortlessly. Claire watched them as they rose higher and higher.

''Sandlings...'' Frazer said as the birds passed overhead.

Claire nodded. Then, with a quick smile at each other, she and Frazer went back to their efforts, she to her castle and he to his fishing.

Seabird
I'll fly like you
For your wings have taught me
To fly with you
Upon the breeze that's caught me. . . .

The words started drifting into her consciousness as Claire sculpted in the sand and the wind tossed strands of golden hair over her cheeks. She didn't have her old shovel or the familiar assortment of tools she liked to use, but she had rummaged around in Dylan's storage shed and found some things that would do. While Frazer stood hip deep in the surf, delighted to have someone to break the silence occasionally with while he fished, Claire carved away on a tower. And the wind was a constant companion, tugging at her thoughts as it played with the designs she crafted. She kept thinking about all of those who happened to come together and touch one another's lives to make subtle differences in the patterns left behind—Ariel, Sara, 418, laughing gulls, skimmers, the sandpipers. Dylan, Tammy, Kurt, Frazer. They were all seabirds.

Come and sit here with me facing in the wind
I'm so tired of feeling low
So tired of feeling all alone
Tired of being on my own. . .
. . . stay with me a moment, gentle friend

And the song kept coming in quiet waves.

Seabird
If I hold you softly in my hand
Seabird
I feel your pulsing heart, free and wild
   You touch the earth, but free you fly
   A fragile creature of the sky...

I want to fly like you
Leave my fears behind me
Try like you

When Frazer reeled in his fishing line and called out that he'd been cleaned out of bait, Claire was ready to go inside. She wanted to get the song down on paper while it ran through her mind—nearly complete. There were words to rearrange and edit, chords that weren't quite right, but she had the feeling. And the message was one of freedom.

CHAPTER FOURTEEN

"Is this Dylan Jamison's residence?" The woman's voice was clipped, indignant and obviously Rebecca Stroud's.

"Who is calling, please?" Claire said with studied politeness.

"Rebecca Stroud."

"Oh, yes, Rebecca," Claire responded. "This is Dylan's place. He isn't here right now. Would you like to leave a message?" She didn't think there was any need to identify herself. The silence on the other end was acknowledgment enough.

"Yes. Have Dylan call me when he returns."

"I'll do that," Claire said.

"He has my number," Rebecca slipped in smugly.

After Claire put the phone back on the hook, she muttered softly, "I sure hope he does." If Robinson's uncle was as efficient as he was reputed to be, Rebecca's number would become increasingly clear to Dylan. And the board of realtors would be very interested in scrutinizing the ethics of the transaction.

WHEN CLAIRE LOOKED OVER the head of the dancers on the floor, she could tell it was Dylan standing in the shadows, watching her. He was dressed in his dark suit, midnight blue, and something about his stance indicated he had not been there long. Arms crossed against his chest, he was not enjoying the music; he was anxiously waiting for the set to end. Shrouded by the darkness, the expression on his face was hidden. But when her song ended, he stepped toward her and took her hand.

"I'm not going to be able to take you home tonight." His mouth was drawn in determination. "I've been asked to appear at a federal hearing—a conference on wetlands and mangrove forests. The Federal Department of Natural Resources has established a fund to buy endangered lands. The tract we optioned qualifies for funding, but I have to go to Washington and submit the proposal. I'm booked on a flight out tonight." His eyes were cold and somber. "It took me all afternoon to assemble the information for the presentation. I kept trying to call the beach house, but no one answered. When I finally got Frazer, he said that you'd been on the beach all day and had come in here early. I don't want to go like this, but the sooner I speak to the committee and get this proposal submitted, the sooner I can come back."

"But do you have to leave now?" She studied his eyes, trying to penetrate the remoteness they held and fathom their darkness.

"I'm afraid so. Fortunately Rebecca has been through the government-funding red tape before. She has all the paperwork ready, and she knows some of the answers that can speed up the process. She's going up there with me to help out."

"She is," Claire said dully. Indispensable Rebecca was making her own points. "Did you know the conference would be this week?" Claire felt a chill spreading over her.

"I knew it was coming sooner or later." Dylan answered. "So did Rebecca. I just wasn't sure which days it would involve. I wanted to be away from you as little as I could. I didn't say anything earlier because of this maniac who's loose. You had enough to worry about."

"How long do you think you'll be gone?" Claire forced the words out through lips that had suddenly gone dry. He was leaving her. And he was taking along Rebecca because she could help him get what he wanted. Rebecca would have him in a world where she knew how to get things done, while Claire remained behind. Claire would have felt less desolate if they hadn't been so close, if she hadn't felt his arms around her through the night and trusted him to keep her safe. Even after that he could leave her. And the gnawing sense of betrayal came from the fact that he had known this would happen and had decided to keep it from her until now.

"A couple of days, maybe three. Rebecca will be back earlier. I'll be here for the sand-crafting event. Josie and Kurt and Dr. Grimes will handle the routine at the refuge. The oil-company film team will be covering tomorrow's bird release for the commercial. Tammy will stick with you and supervise that."

He had tried to anticipate every detail. The only part he had overlooked was her reaction to his sudden absence.

"I've talked to the police and the security people. They're confident you'll be safe here. What concerns me is the rest of the time."

"I told you this morning, I have a very busy schedule. Between the refuge work and my music, I'll be with people all the time. I'll be fine." Her face had become a mask, displaying a calmness and confidence she did not feel. But she was determined to convince him she was able to handle disappointment.

"What about the beach house?" He kept his voice low. "There are no people there."

"Are you throwing me out?" She looked at him warily.

"No. I just don't like the idea of your being alone there." He lifted his hand and stroked her hair as if he were touching moonbeams.

"You want me to invite someone to stay over?" Claire asked with a touch of sarcasm.

Dylan didn't appreciate her attempt at humor. "I'm leaving and you're making jokes."

"I'm sorry," Claire apologized. "But it really isn't such a bad idea. The beach house, I mean. If you have to be gone, I could still stay there. Frazer and I got along very well today. We could manage there while you're gone." The beach house had become a haven, a sanctuary where she felt at home. And now every inch of the beach house held some mark of Dylan Jamison. If she could stay there, at least a part of him would surround her.

Dylan began shaking his head. "I don't like the idea. Even with Frazer. If that lunatic should follow you...."

"But we'll be careful," Claire promised. "He won't know where I am." Her wide gray eyes betrayed a desperation that her voice smoothly camouflaged.

Dylan regarded her intently, then sighed. "Okay. You stay there. Let me call Frazer," he said softly. "And let me talk to your brothers. We'll get something worked out."

"I'll take care of the details myself," Claire insisted. "You have a plane to catch." She glanced away, trying to stem the rising tide of tears that threatened to undermine her brave facade. And all she could think of was Dylan's admonition—not to name the birds. He'd warned her that if she did, if she got too attached to them, then when they were released to the wild, she would have to suffer the impact of the loss. In the serenity of the beach house they had become lovers—and the no-name relationship had been transformed into something magical and real—and necessary. Then abruptly he was flying away with Rebecca, into temptations he might not anticipate.

"This isn't how I wanted it to be." Dylan turned Claire to face him.

"But this is how it is," Claire answered. "You go to Washington and do what you have to. I'll do what has to be done here. Good luck with the proposal. I'm sure you'll give an excellent presentation. I hope the funding comes through." The conversation was all polite and civilized, and Claire managed to conduct herself accordingly.

"I'll call you," Dylan promised.

"Have a good trip." Claire stood on tiptoes and

kissed him. Quickly and gently. But she could feel the knot in her chest beginning to tighten, and her chin trembled slightly. Before she made a spectacle of herself, she had to let him go.

He was still there when she began the next set. She could see him standing in the hallway, motionless, studying her. She strutted across the platform singing out the ironic lyrics, noting that this would be the last glimpse of her that he would carry with him.

"Don't you see I made a difference. . . ."

She couldn't even look at him. She just tossed her head and danced with the beat.

> Even if you're far from me
> I'll linger in your memory.
> My voice will echo in your night,
> And no one's touch but mine feels right.
> From here on, I am a part of you,
>   and everything you do.

Claire didn't see him leave. Whether he waited until the song ended or not, she didn't know. She didn't want to know the precise moment he slipped away. She just held on to the microphone and dove right into the next number, hoping the music would sustain her and that some part of her would go with him. She didn't need to see if the hallway was empty. The emptiness was already inside her.

TAMMY USED THE RESCUE BOAT to pick up Claire the next morning. While a cruiser carrying the film crew waited farther offshore, Tammy motored into shallow water and Claire scrambled aboard. The transfer of the cages into the boat was quick, and impossible for the general public to anticipate or track down. And it allowed the film crew to get some remarkable shots of the two women, one dark and freckle-faced—the other pale gold and tanned, riding the waves with the cages of birds due for release.

"I sure wish this didn't have to be Sara's turn." Tammy spoke above the roar of the motor. "I know how you feel about her."

Claire looked at the goldy eyes of the white-plumed egret staring out at her. Then she patted Tammy's arm. "Just slow the boat for a minute," she insisted. "The noise has her frightened. I think I'll hold her."

Tammy looked as if she were going to argue. Then she bent low, looking in at Sara. Quickly she cut the motor. When the roar began again, Sara was snugly cradled on Claire's lap, her long neck pressed beneath Claire's breasts and her head tucked under Claire's arm. That muffled the sound of the motor, but still Claire could feel the egret's rapid heartbeat. When the low stretch of mangrove island came into view, Claire realized the racing heartbeat was matched by her own. She tightened her mouth into a line of firm resolve. Even if Sara had been a no-name bird, sending her off wouldn't have been easy.

"Just take her out there and put her on that flat stretch of beach." Tammy sat next to Claire and Sara and pointed out the spot. The film crew had already waded ashore, ready to record the release. While they found an unobtrusive vantage point to shoot from,

very calmly Tammy went through exactly what Claire
was expected to do.

"Don't rush her," Tammy said quietly. "She'll
take her time. She may be reluctant, but she'll go.
Eventually, her instincts will take over. It's a
beautiful thing to see," she stressed. "It's as if she's
listening to something we can't hear. You'll know
when it's happening." Then she reached over and
squeezed Claire's arm. "You'll feel sad," she said
knowingly, "but for all the right reasons."

The spongy bottom of the mangrove island sucked
against Claire's tennis shoes with each step she took.
Higher on the shore, the ground was firmer and
coarse sand spread between the aerial roots of the
low-sprawling trees.

"Take off the shoes..." the film director called
out. "We like the primitive look."

Claire kept Sara clasped against her chest and
slipped her feet out of the shoes. With her free hand,
she tossed them one after the other into the boat to
Tammy.

"Okay. Let's go." The cameras followed Claire,
and no one spoke. Higher in the scraggy pines that
protruded above the umbrellas of mangroves, a few
gulls squawked and resident herons and egrets
stretched their wings in a protective display, de-
fending nests and fledglings from the featherless in-
terlopers.

"What the heck's she doing?" The director kept
his voice low as he called to Tammy in the next boat.

Kneeling on the sand, Claire cradled the creature,
stroking the back of the beautiful white bird.

"She's singing to her," Tammy said in a matter-of-fact voice. Even though she couldn't hear the words or the music, Tammy knew Claire was singing her lullaby to Sara for the last time.

"Right...." The director nodded bewilderedly, then signaled to his men to keep on filming. Then Claire eased the bird onto its stiff legs.

Sara walked several steps away and stood with her back to Claire, her elegant neck arched high, balancing on one long black leg. On the other, the silver band caught the sun. "You can't fool me. I know it works," Claire chided Sara for her lame act. "Go on, take a walk," she urged the bird. Sara's sharp yellow bill swung from side to side as her inquisitive eyes shifted from the boats to the film crew, then up into the treetops. She pecked at a shell, looked around, and inched back closer to Claire.

"No deal..." Claire said evenly. "This is where you belong, my friend. Take a good look around. No fences. Just open skies for you. Go on. Be careful this time."

Sara shifted feet. Then she arched her neck again. She didn't move. Rigid as a statue, she waited. Only her feathers rippled in the gentle sweep of the breeze. It was happening. Just as Tammy said. Sara heard another song. One beyond the reach of civilized ears.

The egret stepped farther away, wading into the water to stand motionless again as the waves lapped against her sticklike legs. She peered into the shallows amid the mangrove roots, where tiny shrimp and burrowing shellfish thrived. She fluffed her feathers, preening to the unheard music. Without looking back, she spread her wings. Then she was air-borne. Starting off low over the water, her long legs barely missing the surface, she banked into a slow curve, circling to the east, gaining altitude gradually.

"Go, Sara...." Claire stood and called after her. "Go, baby." She shook her fist in the air, punc-tuating the cheer. Patches of wet sand clung to her long tanned legs, and she'd given up trying to hold back the tears. She was sad. Right down to her bare feet in the gooey sand. But it was a marvelous feel-ing. One Claire could never hope to put into words. But when she saw Dylan again and she told him of this moment, he would see the wisdom she now possessed. He would know she'd learned to bear the pain of letting go without losing the joy. But he'd have to understand her side. She would never give in; she would always sing the birds lullabies and she'd always give them a name.

ROBINSON'S SIZE-THIRTEEN SHOES stuck up between him and the television screen like paddles on a giant fan. Only his weren't moving. Opened into a vee, they framed the screen as he sprawled back on the floor of the beach house, devouring the huge bowl of popcorn Claire had popped.

Frazer had settled back on the sofa, trying to stay awake while the cable-channel broadcast of the con-gressional hearings ran on and on and on. He hadn't succeeded. Snoring softly, he was asleep.

"Here it comes," Robinson called to Claire. In the summary of events from Washington, the portion on the Department of Natural Resources was about to be covered. Dylan had left a message at the refuge that there was a chance a portion of his testimony would be shown.

"There he is." Robinson leaned forward while Claire stood behind him, listening to the voice of a reporter reviewing the main issues covered in the "Endangered Lands" discussion. The camera was on Dylan, sandy haired and sun bronzed amid an assortment of paler individuals with indoor lives. Even his tan suit, earthier a color than the others, gave him a distinctive difference from the grays and blues that predominated. Yet he was at ease there, leaning forward comfortably, nodding to a question, then apparently giving an answer. But the only audio was that of the reporter listing Dylan among six participants called to Washington that week.

When the camera panned back to pick up the onlookers who were attending the hearing, another glimpse of color stood out among the monotone audience. The auburn hair of Rebecca Stroud caught Claire's eye the same instant that Robinson rocked forward, pointing at the screen.

"What's she doing there?" he demanded in an outcry slightly muffled by the fistful of popcorn he'd just begun.

"Dylan needed her assistance with the funding-committee interviews," Claire explained without moving her eyes from the smiling woman sitting several rows behind Dylan.

"I'm surprised they're still on speaking terms," Robinson commented. "I told him a couple of days ago that my Uncle Gene found her name on the board of the Bay Trust Corporation. He said he'd have his attorney look into it."

"Then why hasn't Dylan done something about her?" Claire asked with a frown.

Robinson didn't even attempt an answer.

When the on-camera reporter announced another topic and the scene switched to another hearing room and another commission, Claire stood staring blankly at the television set. Robinson gave up and went home. Frazer continued snoozing contentedly on the sofa, oblivious to everything.

Long after she had gone to bed, Claire lay awake in the wide water bed, staring at the ceiling, wondering just how far Dylan Jamison was willing to go "for the birds."

REBECCA STROUD WAS BACK in St. Petersburg two days later. Dylan wasn't. When Claire came in to rehearsal Thursday afternoon, Rebecca was waiting, and she'd brought along a friend. Slightly balding, conservatively dressed, the fellow stood to greet her. "I'd like you to meet Harry Hughes," Rebecca said, introducing him to Claire. Pete and Wes were already at the table, and from the expression on each face, it was obvious they had been talking and some of the talk had been about her.

"Harry produces records for IMPAC," Rebecca informed her. The multimedia company was known for being progressive and innovative—one of the prime movers-and-shakers in the music business.

"I am very impressed with what I saw on that video Rebecca sent me," Hughes told Claire. His brown button eyes studied her closely as if he were looking for something in particular. "We've been discussing taping a couple of numbers live so we can get you and Wes together before an audience. We want to see how you come across separately and together. We're very interested."

Claire stared at Pete, then at Wes. "'Separately and together'?"

"I like you solo, but I don't want to miss anything. There's been a lot of good duos lately. I've heard that you and Wes work well together." Hughes nodded at Rebecca and Wes. Apparently they'd been his source of information. Pete tilted his head, silently cautioning Claire not to make waves. IMPAC was a big operation and she had caught their interest, with or without Wes.

"We'll be doing the sand-crafting concert," Claire replied stiffly. "If you want crowd interaction, you should get it there."

"We've definitely decided it's too risky to have you participate in the concert Saturday," Rebecca informed her casually. "The security people here are already taking on additional help to supervise the contest and handle parking. The police are assigning officers for the usual crowd control. But the event is drawing such a lot of interest that the estimated attendance is huge. If this strange man is still trying to harass you, we can't hope to protect you in a crowd of young people."

"We thought we'd do the taping here, tomorrow night," Pete finally spoke up. "Friday nights there's a big audience. We'll just have to revamp the program a bit."

There had been no duos planned. As stand-in, Wes

had practiced with them, but with the understanding that he'd sing lead only if things looked like trouble.

"Then we'll have to get to work," Claire answered coolly. "I'd like to have the new song ready for you to hear." She was determined to conduct herself like a professional and not to give any indication that missing the beach performance upset her. Now was not the time to act temperamental. Besides, she wouldn't give Rebecca the satisfaction of knowing she resented her behind-the-scenes collusion with Wes.

"Then it's settled," Rebecca concluded smugly. "I'm sure Dylan will be pleased at how well everything worked out. I'd hate for him to come back and have to deal with any unnecessary complications. We had enough to look after in Washington."

Claire was determined not to pick up on any of Rebecca's comments about being with Dylan in Washington, but the "we" reference made her toes curl. Rebecca had mentioned she had been interviewed by several officials and had addressed one of the committees in order to elaborate on the financial details of the land Dylan had optioned. No one at the Don was terribly interested, though.

"I also told them that I was donating my commission to the refuge." Rebecca hesitated, as if she expected a round of applause. All she got was a polite nod from Harry Hughes.

"I'll make the official announcement at the sand-crafting contest," Rebecca stated. "But Dylan thought it was very important that the committee members know of my role as a supporter of the expansion—as a representative of the business community."

Claire had simply kept her smile in place and subtly rolled her eyes at Pete. "I think I'd better get back to business myself." She excused herself from the discussion. "Let's take a run through the songs so we'll be ready for Friday."

Wes stayed behind a little past the others, talking animatedly with Rebecca and Harry Hughes. When he finally joined Claire on the stage, his dark eyes kept avoiding contact with hers.

"It's all right, Wes." Claire stepped close to him and kept her voice hushed. "Tomorrow I'll sing a couple of numbers with you. And you can have all you want of the Saturday show. You can butter up the Dragon Lady until both of you slide right out of my life. I'm not going to take away your shot at this," she declared. "After this, we won't be doing anything together unless it's strictly business and I set the terms."

He finally looked at her with a sheepish grin that registered his relief.

"But when I get ready to do my songs, stay out of my way," Claire directed him. To an observer, the conversation between them would have appeared amiable enough. Claire smiled and Wes's half grin wavered just a bit. But he got the point. He stepped back a few inches. When Claire handed him his microphone, he thanked her with a slight bow of deference.

After the rehearsal, the routine Claire had set up went like clockwork. During the breaks between sets that night, Claire stayed close to Pete. After the show, Pete drove her toward town, swinging off onto a side street, where she made a quick switch to Frazer's car, heading off in the opposite direction.

Each night the switch was made in a different location, but whenever Frazer entered the narrow road leading to Dylan's beach house, an unmarked police car waited there to double-check that they had not been followed. She and Frazer parked two houses down from the beach house, then walked back along the beach to the house, locking the heavy door behind them. The princess was in her tower for the night.

Just after midnight the telephone rang. Claire lifted the receiver but said nothing.

Then a familiar voice spoke her name. "Claire?"

"Yes," she answered.

"How did it go tonight?" Dylan asked in his low, mellow voice. "No sign of the guy?"

"Very uneventful," Claire assured him. "No trouble. How about your day with the powerful and the policymakers?" She meant to sound unruffled and casual, but all she wanted to know was when he would be back. Then she'd ask him face to face about the business maneuverings of Rebecca Stroud.

"A little slow. I'm going to be tied up here longer than I thought," he said grimly. "It may be Saturday before I get back, unless I can get a flight out sometime Friday night."

"Does that mean the funding discussions are going badly or that they're going well?" If Dylan was willing to overlook Rebecca's involvement in the corporate-owned land, it was undoubtedly because he needed her on his side. She wondered just what effect Rebecca's appearance had on the deliberations.

"I have a few more committee members to meet with," Dylan explained. "Things look very promising. I'll tell you all about it when I get back. I got sidetracked with some other business. That's what put me behind schedule. I just wanted to hear your voice and know you were safe."

"I'm safe," she assured him.

"I hear the sand-crafting contest is mushrooming." Undoubtedly the indispensable Rebecca was keeping him posted about the increasing excitement the event was generating—and she would very clearly add that the credit for its success was primarily hers.

"'Things look very promising,'" Claire teased.

"Good." He paused for a few seconds. "I want to see one of your castles out there on the beach. I'll even pitch in and help if you're in the market for an assistant."

"It worked out pretty well the last time," Claire recalled.

"It certainly did," Dylan replied, and he wasn't talking about castles of sand. "You've got a deal," he affirmed. "Saturday we build a castle." However, nowhere in the conversation had he asked about the concert. "Take care of yourself."

Afterward, Claire lingered by the wide glass doors, pulling them closed as the damp night air carried misty droplets in from the Gulf. A storm was coming. There was no moon. Far out over the water, dark clouds were edged in white as thunder rumbled and lightning charged the air. Claire heard the distant whisper of the rain slowly moving toward land. If it rained, the sand would be dense and moist for Saturday. Everything would be washed clean again.

And Dylan would be back.

CHAPTER FIFTEEN

BEFORE THE PERFORMANCE in the lounge actually began Friday night, Pete stepped out to the microphone and told the Don CeSar audience they were in for something very special. "Not that we want to put any pressure on you folks to clap a little louder or hit the dance floor with some fancy footwork," he teased. "But we are doing some sound tapes, and a couple of the numbers will be videotaped, as well. I just wouldn't want you immortalized without a little advance warning. So let's go."

Claire led off with several of the standard numbers while the sound crew and video cameramen adjusted and readjusted their equipment. Then Wes sang harmony, raspy and crackling with energy, and Claire did lead on "You Know It When You Got It." And the electricity between them still sent goose bumps down Pete's spine. Then Claire stepped into the background, with Wes stepping into the spotlight— like old times. Claire's smooth, soft backup was a perfect complement as Wes grated out his old songs in a gravelly voice that tugged at the heart. He was the old Wes, turning on the charm, only this time he directed the magic at the camera.

When the next set began, only Jess and his electric

violin joined Claire onstage. For this number, she would play her own keyboard. Her pale-gold hair fell forward in soft curls over her cheeks as she stood, head bent in concentration, waiting, while Jess began. Haunting and pure, the violin music drifted on air. Then, in the stillness of the room, her voice permeated the atmosphere like the scent of night jasmine, rich and sweet and touched with passion. She sang "Sara's Song" with a tremor that made Harry Hughes grin from ear to ear. When she did "Seabird," he barely moved.

> Seabird
> If I hold you softly in my hand
> Seabird
> I feel your pulsing heart, free and wild
>> You touch the earth, but free you fly
>> A fragile creature of the sky
>> Racing clouds, above all time
> Seabird in you I see the part of me that's nature's child.

"I have some folks who have got to see you," Hughes insisted the minute he had Claire seated at his table. "We've got to get you to Los Angeles and let my team take a look at what we've got. I had a feeling about you...." He rocked back in his chair, narrowed his eyes and bobbed his head up and down. "I wasn't so hot for the rock numbers. We can always get loud ones. But I thought I saw something in that tape, up close. And I did. On a ballad, honey, you are spun gold. And I'm talkin' records." He studied her with knowing eyes. "You want to talk contract now, or do you want me to contact your manager... your agent?" His attitude was crisp and professional—and very flattering.

"Let me talk to Pete first," Claire said, attempting to slow things down. "I'm just very glad you were impressed."

"I'm very impressed," Hughes acknowledged. "With your singing and your songwriting. You're good. You're really good."

"It's nice to have someone of your caliber say so," Claire said graciously.

" 'Someone of my caliber' would be crazy to let you or Wes get away," Hughes insisted. "I'll have to tell Doug Stroud that his little girl did me quite a favor. With a new song, just the right song, you and Wes could top the charts. Yeah, you two are something!"

"Together?" Claire frowned slightly.

"Sure. You and Wes. Great duo." Hughes grinned.

Claire looked from Hughes to the stage. Wes was laughing and talking with Bizzy and lapping up the appreciative comments from the ladies at the nearby tables. It was a scene she had witnessed too many times in too many places.

"That's out of the question," she stated flatly.

Hughes blinked as his smile slowly collapsed. "I beg your pardon?"

"I won't be locked into a duo with Wes Raines or anyone else under any circumstances. Working with Wes was a very temporary arrangement," Claire said firmly.

Hughes's dark eyes cut quickly to the approaching red-haired woman. "Rebecca, you sure know how to pick them." He greeted her with a broad smile that was more forced than a moment before.

"I gather Harry was quite taken with you and Wes," Rebecca Stroud commented as she glided into a chair and joined them. "I was sure there had to be something he could do." In spite of the pleasantries Rebecca offered, there was a rehearsed quality, as if this conversation were a postscript, a formality before a departure. A send-off.

Claire knew at once that was precisely what Rebecca wanted—to get her conveniently out of the way. Los Angeles would do nicely. And Wes Raines would be a perfect diversion, onstage and off. What troubled Claire was that Harry Hughes wasn't making the contract offer as a favor to anyone, not even Rebecca. He was impressed with Claire's work on her own and with Wes. The recording and concert career she had once dreamed of was being handed to her, but the package was tied with a ribbon of bad dreams.

"Wes and you are magical on that stage," Rebecca said sweetly. "I'm so glad I could be of help."

"Yes." Hughes nodded. "But apparently the magic is highly individual and separate. Wes has his own style and it suits him fine. Claire has her own." He hadn't emphasized the word "separate," but his meaning was clear. He was accepting Claire's terms.

Rebecca's smile wavered for a second. Then, as her mental gears readjusted to this new twist to the situation, she offered Claire her hand. "Congratulations.

Harry has just got himself a new recording star.''

"Two of them.'' Hughes corrected her.

"I'll have to congratulate Wes, as well,'' Rebecca added.

"I've got to get back to work,'' Claire said as she gave Rebecca's manicured hand a too-firm shake. "We have a lot to talk over.''

"Right!'' Hughes stood when Claire did. "I'll call some people on the West Coast in the morning. Then we can get together on this. We'll get all the details ironed out.''

With a polite nod to both Hughes and Rebecca, Claire went to find her brothers.

"If I were you, I'd go for it,'' Pete said simply.

"But you aren't me,'' Claire reminded him. "Signing up may mean skipping from one coast to the other and spending months away from here.''

"You can always come back,'' Pete replied. "You can't always make a contact like Hughes. IMPAC is big business, heavy into videos. Just keep an open mind, hear what he has to say, and then think it over real carefully.''

"Then grab it.'' Robby laughed and hugged his sister. "Someone around here should be famous.''

"While you're considering offers,'' Claire insisted, "I want to know what you can work out with the Don. Let's hear what kind of ongoing arrangement we can make with them. There is something about this place that I love.''

"Me, too,'' Pete agreed. "But Claire, this is not the big, big time. This isn't gold records and sold-out tours. Just don't underestimate yourself,'' he warned her. "You can tackle whatever you want. For your next move, your choices are wide open."

"They certainly are," Claire agreed. There was a very important area where her choices weren't quite clear, but careerwise, Claire was free. Like Sara, she had no cages, no fences. "It's open skies for you," Claire had told the white-feathered egret. "Just be careful this time."

Across the almost-empty room, Wes was writing down his phone number for a very attractive girl. Harry Hughes was nowhere in sight. He'd left, searching for a telephone. Rebecca Stroud had moved to a nearby table, where she sat with the dark-haired public-relations director from the Don, going over the last-minute paperwork and paraphernalia for the sand-crafting event the next day—entry forms, boxes of T-shirts, cases of sun visors, lists of sponsors and prizes.

"I have to get going," Claire said finally, glancing at her watch. It was one in the morning. "I've got to be back here early to stake off my place on the beach for building my castle."

"Then let's get you out safely," Pete said, and stood to walk her to her car.

"Could I see a registration slip?" Claire asked the PR director as they left.

"Sure." The woman smiled and pulled one entry form from the stack.

"You aren't planning to enter the contest," Rebecca asked as Claire and Pete looked over the form. "I thought I told you that the security problems are too complicated for that."

"You said that about my performing onstage. We weren't discussing my castle building. I'll be safe," she assured the green-eyed woman. "Dylan will be working with me. He's an excellent bodyguard."

"He's supposed to be helping me at the officials' table," Rebecca informed her. "I doubt he'll have time to play in the sand."

"But I have the time." Claire grinned at her. "I love a good contest. There's nothing I like better than a little competition. You never know what techniques you can pick up by studying the opposition. Things like cutting and scooping and slicing the ground out from under structures at strategic times. But I'm sure that's nothing new to you—since you're so deeply involved in land development." Without losing a beat, Claire tucked the entry blank in her pocket and picked up her conversation with Pete, hooking her arm in his as he escorted her out to his car.

"Rebecca...are you all right?" the public-relations woman asked her companion. Rebecca's jaw had suddenly become very rigid.

Quickly she regained her composure. "I'm fine," she said without much conviction. "It's just been a long day."

HE WAS AFTER the other one. He watched the one with the red hair and the note pad. She was running the show. Talking to everyone. Getting ready for the stupid contest. He could tell by the way she kept jotting things down. Page after page. She was the one. She could put her finger on anything—including an address. Or he'd cut off the finger. Just like that.

He wanted the whole thing to end. He wasn't having fun anymore. He liked being able to do his thing and read about it and then keep the clippings in his wallet so he could laugh at them. Even at night in bed all alone he had the clippings. He wasn't a nobody. He could make the papers anytime he wanted. He'd just gone a little too far this time. The blonde had gone on television and called him names. And she'd seen him. She made him feel like a freak, like he'd felt all his life. Now it had to end.

They'd been after him. He'd started a beard, let his hair hang over his ears. He'd even put on a few pounds. Just to throw them off. But with the limp he had to be real careful. The lift in the shoe helped, but it cost him twenty bucks. She'd have to pay for it. He was ready to collect.

He waited till the blonde left with the guy from the band. He knew the routine outside would be the same. People watching, cars going in one direction, then another. They wouldn't suck him into something stupid. He'd think of something else.

No witnesses.

No more name calling. They could play their funny little games with the blonde, but he'd fool them. No one would be watching the redhead.

Except him.

DYLAN STRODE THROUGH the corridor of the airport, trying to avoid colliding with the other passengers exiting Washington for the weekend. For most of them, connected in some way with the government, it was just routine commuting. But for him, his work in the city was finished; he was going home—to stay. He'd had his fill of forms and explanations, duplicates and triplicates, inquiries and interviews. And he'd done well for the refuge.

The federal government would give him the additional funding for the expansion. With one committee vote in a somber Senate chamber, the Gulf Coast Seabird Refuge moved from the red into the black.

And now there was time to think of himself. Glancing at his watch, he stopped abruptly in front of a row of telephones, but moved on. No time to call Claire. She'd already be on her way to the Don. His flight was loading. He'd be home soon enough.

Dylan settled back into the seat with a long, heartfelt sigh of relief. The scant leg room made him uncomfortable and the too-narrow armrests were restrictive, but he couldn't help smiling. In a few hours he'd be back on the beach, shoeless, shirtless and stretched out in the cool night air, talking of dreams coming true with Claire. And he'd tell her how the just-loved flush on her cheeks was the only sunrise he needed and the shadowy softness of her eyes the only night. And he'd get all the unsaid things out in the open—point-blank.

I love you. That should have been said a long time ago, but he'd held back. He'd been pursuing a dream; she'd been escaping a nightmare. She'd been loved before and that love had become twisted and destructive. She tried loving someone, and she thought that because the relationship had failed, she'd failed. But now the tide had turned. She was riding her own wave of success, and before it swept her far away, he had to ask her to hold on to him. He wanted to prove to her that loving him, being loved in return, could be different.

Will you stay? Marry me. . . I won't let you down. And I can't let you go. Let me be the one you come home to—always. While he was away the deep aching, that emptiness of soul, had never left him. There were two sides of the story—as much as he longed to be her sanctuary, her place of peace, he wanted her to be his. Coming home to a place wasn't enough. He wanted that special person there.

From the beginning there had been a rightness about her, a sense of completeness of spirit when they were together that the contrary aspects of their outside lives couldn't diminish. The castle at the beach the day they'd met brought together all the things he valued—creation, nature, humor, beauty and a sense of wonder. And Claire. Everything came together in her. With her. In spite of everything, he believed she really loved him. Even if she couldn't say so, to him or to herself, he could read it in her eyes, hear it in her heartbeat, feel it in her kiss. One day he'd hear it in her music. But for now he was sure enough for both of them. And that wouldn't change. They could hold on to each other without holding either of them down. They could fill each today with love and courage and trust. She didn't have to promise she would never leave, only that she would always come back.

Leaning back in the seat, Dylan sat framed in the bright shaft of the overhead reading light, looking out into the pitch-black sky.

Night flier. The wings that carried him were made of metal; the sound was a dull unnatural drone, the navigation by dials and charts, not instinct. But he was flying on course, homeward bound, nevertheless.

THE BIZARRE RITUAL of returning Claire to Dylan's beach house was repeated smoothly again—doubling back, changing cars and walking up the beach the last couple of blocks. Within twenty minutes she had waved Frazer off to sleep in the back room, checked the doors and windows again and was about to undress for bed, when she heard footsteps on the stairs.

"Robinson?" she asked quietly.

No answer.

Peering through the window in the door, Claire could see Rebecca's face, tense and white.

"Claire, I need to talk to you," Rebecca insisted in a voice that sounded strained and mechanical.

"Here it comes..." Claire muttered. The battle that had been contained for so long was about to erupt. "Just a minute." She hurried to the bedroom on the north side, where Frazer was sleeping. Very quietly she pulled closed his door.

"All right, Rebecca. Come on in." Claire opened the heavy wooden door. The expression on Rebecca's face was more strained than Claire expected, and the Dragon Lady was not alone.

The man behind her gave Rebecca a push forward. "I couldn't help it. He was in the parking lot. He said he'd kill me if I didn't bring him here," Rebecca

whined. The dim lamplight from the side table glint-
ed off something shiny in his left hand.

"He has a knife," Rebecca moaned.

The man held the long blade to her throat, then
shoved her forward, stepping into the kitchen and
ominously pushed the door closed behind him. The
irregular stubble of a beard made his jaw seem wider.
He'd switched from jogging shoes to leather shoes,
but he was the same man. Only now he didn't have
the hammer.

"It took a while...." He grinned at Claire
malevolently. "But I knew if I waited, I'd get you."

Claire stared at him. He still had a grip on Rebecca's arm and the knuckles of his hand were growing
white around the knife handle.

"But look at this," he said, smirking at Rebecca.
"I get to work on two high-class broads."

"You said you'd let me go..." Rebecca whim-
pered.

"You gotta be crazy," he sniffed. "I'm gonna
teach both of you a lesson." He thrust the knife
under Rebecca's chin, forcing her back into the corner. "You take this rope." He pulled a roll of heavy
twine from his jacket pocket. "You are going to tie
up Red here," he ordered Claire. "She's gonna
watch while I take care of you. Get the damn rope."
He tossed it at her. "Tie her up."

"No." Claire backed off a step, letting the spool
bounce to the floor.

"Pick it up or I'll lay her face open," he growled,
pushing the knife threateningly closer to Rebecca's
cheek.

"I couldn't care less," Claire said coolly, inching backward more. She kept her expression emotionless, refusing to play his game.

Rebecca's eyes widened in horror. All that escaped from her mouth was a desolate moan.

"Rebecca, were you stupid enough to think he'd let you go? You'd be able to testify against him for whatever he's planning to do to me. He can't afford to let you go. And we can't afford to let him tie either one of us up. Right now it's two against one. Even with the knife, one of us has a chance," Claire said with cool logic, moving back steadily.

"Make that three against one." Frazer came out of the bedroom carrying his four-foot metal-handled landing net and an umbrella—the only things he could grab in the dark other than his pants.

The intruder froze, his eyes wide and disconcerted. He'd planned everything, but this wasn't going as he expected.

Frazer passed the landing net to Claire as he stepped near her. "You go for his head." Frazer hunched over, his small form tight like a piston ready to fire. "I'll go for his soft spots," he growled, pointing the umbrella below the man's beltline.

"No, you don't." The man wheeled Rebecca around in front of him, using her as a shield, while he backed toward the door.

"There's nowhere to go, creep," Frazer said. "Drop the knife."

With a low animal cry the man shoved Rebecca forward. She crashed onto her knees in a heap in front of them. Then he leapt for the door.

"Don't go after him," Claire screamed, reaching out to stop the wiry old man from playing hero.

"I'm not that crazy. Call the police!" Frazer ordered Claire, slamming the door and locking it.

But when Claire picked up the receiver, the dial tone stopped abruptly. "I think he's cut the lines."

"Then go and check that all the windows are locked. I'll find something else to use on him." Frazer began scouring the beach house in search of a more formidable weapon than the umbrella.

"You aren't going out after him?" Claire asked. "I won't let you."

"I'm just lining up our defenses, wondering what this nut may try next," Frazer assured her.

Rebecca Stroud still hadn't moved. She knelt on the floor, wide-eyed and gasping. Claire reached down and gently helped her to a chair, all the while speaking softly to her, assuring her the danger was past.

They walked from room to room for several minutes, peeking outside and pausing to listen for any sound that would indicate where he was. The smell of gasoline made Claire stop. It was filtering up from below.

"I smell it, too," Frazer frowned as he entered the room carrying a hatchet he had found in Dylan's closet.

Before Claire could speak there came a muffled swooshing sound as the gasoline ignited. Suddenly the dark night was gone; the house was surrounded by a ring of fire.

"Scum...." Frazer spat out the word. Like a

heathen funeral pyre ignited to carry its sacrifices to an ancient god, the support pilings of the beach house were in flames. The blaze sizzled and hissed, while tongues of fire licked at the single set of stairs.

"Get in the bathroom!" Claire grabbed Rebecca's arms and dragged her out of the kitchen. The rooms were rapidly filling with smoke, and Frazer raced from window to window, looking for a way for them to get out.

"He's still out there. He's standing in the sand, staring up at the balcony, just watching," Frazer yelled.

"Come on, get in the bathroom," Claire came to get him. "Remember—the trapdoor! The bird elevator..." she shouted above the crackling flames. "We can run the shower and soak ourselves...wrap up in wet towels, then drop down through the trapdoor. If we get under the house, we can make a run for it."

"But he's out there," Rebecca wailed.

"He won't be for long. Someone will see the fire and send for help. If you stay here, you'll fry," Claire shot back impatiently. "Now shut up and get wet." She shoved Rebecca into the shower and turned on the water. Frazer dropped open the door portion of the bathroom floor, slowly letting down the cables that were designed to pull in a bird recovery cage. He knelt down to look for any sign of the maniac. What he heard was music to his ears.

Over the snapping noises of the flames came the distant wail of sirens. Then the anxious voices of neighbors shouting to them cut through the other sound.

"Anyone in there?"

"Wake up! Get out of there!"

A rock smashed through a window.

Claire soaked several large beach towels, then got in the shower herself. Drenched and dripping, she waited while Frazer stepped in.

"You go first," Claire yelled to Frazer. "Take the hatchet. I'll help Rebecca down from here."

He started to protest, then took a second look at the determined set of Claire's jaw, tucked the hatchet into his waistband and slid through the trapdoor, dropping out of sight.

The opening was becoming a chimney filled with dark, acrid smoke. Claire instructed Rebecca to take a deep breath and pressed a wet towel hard over Rebecca's mouth to filter some of the smoke. Then Claire pushed the panic-stricken woman to the floor, placed one of the cables in her hands and told her to slide down. When Rebecca hesitated, Claire gave her a very solid kick in the behind.

"I've got her!" Frazer shouted from below. "Now you get the heck out of there!"

By this time the heat in the room was ovenlike and the smoke so thick Claire could not see anything. Breathing through the wet towel, she finally located the opening in the floor, found the cable and swung herself into space.

The smoke and heat under the house were hellish. Claire held tightly to the cables until her feet touched the ground. "Frazer! Where are you!" she called through the choking smoke.

"Here!" Frazer yelled. "We're here." A hand

caught Claire's in the blinding inferno. "Let's make a run for it!"

Instinctively the three of them turned away from the hottest, brightest part of the circle of fire that surrounded them, then bolted forward. Five seconds later they were coughing and gasping, kneeling in the cool sand of the beach. Claire's face was blackened with smoke and one sleeve of her shirt was singed; otherwise she was fine. Rebecca and Frazer had likewise escaped without injury.

Then someone yelled, "Stop him! The guy in the car—stop him!"

Converging on the site, the emergency vehicles blocked the single roadway leading out to the main beach road. The lone car attempting to go against the influx veered off the road, cutting back toward the beach house. Then the car swung out of control, jostling over a fence of low pilings and jerking to an abrupt halt against an old Studebaker.

"He got my car..." Frazer wailed, charging toward the collision scene. "The scum hit my car!"

Two uniformed officers leapt from their patrol car, intercepted the hatchet-wielding Frazer and brought down the fleeing man. A flying tackle stopped him with a thud. Within a few seconds he'd been read his rights, cuffed and led to a police car.

"Look at that." Frazer shook his head as he walked back from his mangled Studebaker. "Docile as a lamb. The lowlife mutilates birds, damn near murders us, wrecks my car, then meekly goes off to jail."

"That's what counts," Claire said between breaths

of clear, ocean air. "He will be in jail. It's over."

DYLAN ARRIVED before the last flames were totally extinguished. White-faced and anxious, he leapt out of the truck and bolted across the beach calling out her name. "Claire...!"

The desperation in his voice produced an immediate response from one of the firefighters. "She's safe. Out in back." Now Dylan raced over hoses and debris, rounding the corner of the house at full speed.

Bleary-eyed and covered in soot, Claire and Frazer sat on a rise of sand, staring back at the charred walls of the beach house. The sight of Dylan charging toward them out of the smoke like a banshee out of hell, his coat flapping, collar and tie opened, brought them both to their feet.

Dylan grabbed Claire, then scooped Frazer up into his arms with a ferocity that was both frightening and exhilarating. "I'm glad you're safe." That was all he said. He held them both against him, gasping in ragged breaths, feeling as if his chest would burst.

"Welcome home, boss," Frazer said as he disengaged himself, leaving Dylan's other arm free to close around Claire. "Sorry about your place. We were roasting marshmallows...." He tried to make a joke out of the dismal scene, but Dylan wasn't listening. He was just holding on as tight as he could and trying not to cry.

Later Dylan spoke to the police briefly and to the newspaper photographer who'd come out to the scene. Then the last few firefighters picked up their equipment, loading it onto the truck. Badly scarred and blackened but still recognizable, the beach house stood like a long-legged spider, silhouetted in the faint moonlight.

"I guess we'd better find some place to sleep," Dylan said at last. "I think the Don CeSar could find a couple of rooms for us. Even on this late notice. Surely a couple of castlebuilders and their associate deserve a little special attention on the eve of a sand-crafting event."

"The contest..." Claire moaned. "It's almost morning. I can't sleep or I'll miss it."

"You'll sleep," Dylan said succinctly, steering her to his truck. "I'll take care of the rest."

"What about Rebecca?" Claire asked him. She'd been rushed off in an emergency vehicle for treatment for smoke inhalation. "She was running everything."

"She certainly was..." Dylan said tersely. "That's part of the reason I got her out of town for a couple of days. While she was helping me with my funding hearings, my attorney and an investigator were looking into a few of her business dealings. They uncovered some very damaging evidence."

"Such as her connection with Bay Trust?" Claire remarked.

"So you knew about Rebecca's corporate connection with the land deal," Dylan said, his brow cocked in surprise. "I should have guessed that Robinson wasn't the only one who was getting suspicious. But Bay Trust was only the beginning of her schemes. There's a lot more involved than her owning a piece of the land we're purchasing. She also used the momentum created by the refuge publicity to slip in some additional acreage of her own in the rezoning. She'd taken out an option on some real estate adjacent to the expansion property. Since the federal funding has come through, we'll be able to move ahead with our development. That means the neighboring land goes up in value.

"No telling what she had in mind for developing the adjoining land, but once she knew the funding was granted, she was in a real hurry to get back here, exercise her option and buy that land before the official word got out. Unfortunately, to set it all up, she used some shady tactics with everyone from the bankers to the zoning commission. And she probably would have pulled it off—no one would have made the connection—if Robinson hadn't said something."

Claire nodded thoughtfully, silently thanking Burt Crawford for the tip he'd offered along with his ten-thousand-dollar donation.

"Once my attorney started digging," Dylan continued, "it was like the domino effect. Pieces fell into place and the pattern became clear. Smoke inhalation is going to be the least of Rebecca's problems. When she wakes up tomorrow she's going to realize she's in trouble up to her eyebrows. All her records are being subpoenaed. Part of her testimony in Washington seems to have been perjured. I'm sure the Florida Board of Realtors will be conducting its own investigation." He paused and shrugged. "I guess we'll have to get along without her."

Claire looked at him intently. "I'd rather hoped we could."

He wanted to tell her then, to make the speech he'd been rehearsing on the plane. But he studied the oval face streaked with soot and the shoulders that drooped with exhaustion. This wasn't the time. "First you're getting some sleep," Dylan insisted, opening the door of the truck and helping her inside. Frazer climbed in next to her.

As they drove down the beach strip toward the hotel, Claire leaned against Dylan's shoulder while Frazer gave a blow-by-blow description of the encounter with the bird butcher.

"You should have seen Claire," Frazer boasted. "She just stood there telling that creep he could go ahead and have a go at Rebecca. She wasn't going to tie anyone up and give him any hold on her."

"Of course you were only acting," Dylan said, giving her a slight nudge.

"I'm not so sure that I was." Claire bit her lower lip thoughtfully. "I do think," she added almost as an afterthought, "that a bit of Rebecca's cold-blooded objectivity must have rubbed off on me."

"A shower will help," Dylan teased.

By now the morning sun was beginning to lighten the sky just above the horizon—a faint promise of the day to come. In a few hours its golden warmth would be chasing away the chill of night. The seabirds would take to the sky, plunging into the Gulf waters for their morning feast.

"Nice day to build a castle," Claire said wearily as they pulled into the parking area next to the Don.

They could see the beach—still, bare and beautiful, becoming more luminous with the approaching dawn. "Maybe we should go out there now and stake out our place," Claire suggested. Then she pressed both hands over her eyes, still burning from the smoke and sheer fatigue.

"I'll make you a deal," Dylan said. He held her close to him as they walked into the hotel with Frazer trudging along silently behind them. "I'll stake out the location once I get you two tucked away, and I'll get the mound built and wake you in time to do the sculpting."

"You promise?" Claire asked the man whose blue eyes radiated a calm and confident light.

"I promise." He smiled to himself. He had more promises for her, but they could wait. What he wanted most was her promise in return. A commitment for something far beyond a morning call.

CHAPTER SIXTEEN

Nature did an excellent job without our assistance—respect her creations and appreciate the surroundings. No littering.

THE BILLBOARD over the registration table at the Don CeSar set the tone for the entire sand-crafting event.

No radios without headsets.

The first restriction on the posted contest rules guaranteed that the competitors and the onlookers would enjoy the natural tranquillity—water sounds and bird cries—no man-made noises in stereo.

No paint, dye or foreign matter can be used to discolor the sand or alter its consistency. All decoration or detail work must be constructed from natural materials indigenous to the beach—shells, seaweed, etc. Caution: do not pull up the sea oats or any growing plants.

This carefully worded section was aimed at deepening the awareness of what was available in the natural surroundings. It also ensured that after the

concert, the beach would return to its original state—
with nothing left behind that did not belong there.

Entries can have no internal supports or external
superstructure. They must be constructed of
sand throughout.

Maximum of three participants working on each
entry.

No alcoholic beverages allowed on the beach.

Please do not feed the birds.

Dylan wiped the back of his hand across his brow,
then up each temple, brushing away the perspiration
as he took several long deep breaths. Glancing at his
watch, he hastily calculated the time until the judging
would take place. Then he lifted the shovel and thrust
a few more loads onto the pile he'd been making.
With each lift and toss, his upper-arm muscles ached
and his hard shoulders strained against the dampened
fabric of his shirt. He pounded the last scoop down,
then stomped the lower edges once more. Towering
six feet tall and flaring out into a base almost
as wide, this sand mountain was to be the raw
material for a masterpiece. It was time to wake the
architect.

"OKAY, SLEEPING BEAUTY," Dylan whispered in the
hushed stillness of the room. He looked down at her,
arms outstretched, pale hair tumbled over the pillow,

ensconced like a princess in the huge canopied bed. Still damp with sweat, he leaned over Claire, touching her shoulder gently, summoning her from deep, dreamless sleep. "You have exactly four hours to build your castle."

"Four...?" Leaning up on one elbow, Claire blinked drowsily, trying to focus on the face that went with the voice.

"I've already got a head start," he assured her, crossing the room to draw open the heavy drapes and let the bright sunshine flood the hotel room. "There are two of us to work on it. I've studied under an expert and I've got a little more experience than I had the last time. I'm getting better. We'll be finished by the time the judges make their rounds."

"The judging doesn't concern me...." Claire flopped back onto the pillow, stretching beneath the cool sheets, bracing herself for the labor ahead. "This castle has to be extraordinary. I just want today to be special."

"Oh, it will be," Dylan answered confidently.

Claire turned her head sideways to glance at him, noting the enigmatic smile accompanying his comment. All the desperation and concern his face had shown the night before was gone. In its place was a quiet assurance and a candidly seductive look in his sea-blue eyes.

"Now what's that look supposed to mean?"

"It means either you get out there, or I'm coming into that bed with you and the castle building will have to wait." The pure pleasure in his voice accentuated the sensuality of Dylan's words.

Claire couldn't suppress the slow, satisfied smile that tilted the corners of her lips. "You wouldn't dare...."

The unintentional challenge brought an immediate response. "Wouldn't I?"

His expression of eagerness mingled with a tenderness that sent a delightful tremor of excitement through her. He dared. Peeling off his sweat-dampened shirt, Dylan grinned at her, his eyes flashing an azure fire.

"Dylan!" Claire sat up abruptly. "You have to be out there running the contest."

"The contest is being handled quite efficiently by the staff at the Don. All I need is to be with you," he stated simply. "Nothing is more important or more essential. Just you." Then the khaki shorts were tossed away.

The sight of his golden body, unclad and graceful, made her heartbeat accelerate. This was what she wanted—this man, this moment, this bond—and that unqualified awareness made words and time irrelevant.

Claire smiled up at him, raising her arms so Dylan could lift off the T-shirt she'd worn to bed. Then she moved over, pulling back the top sheet to welcome him. In an instant he was holding her. When bare chest pressed against bare breast, the pleasure of the first brush of his skin against hers was pure and explosive.

Exalting in the sheer ecstasy of the moment, she became a part of him, arms and legs intertwined, lips warm and moist in a possessive kiss, intense and tantalizing. Then, hearts thundering and breaths uneven, their eyes locked on to each other, each silently awed by the sense of appropriateness—they should be together. Suddenly everything made sense. At first they touched tenderly, breathing in unison with each caress and kiss, arousing and giving pleasure. Then all the self-control that had kept them intact while they'd been apart yielded to the force of their passion more than either had imagined. They had survived an ordeal, and it was over.

"Love me now," Claire whispered, wanting mind and body liberated completely.

"Claire, I do love you," he said again and again as he drew her to him and found his own liberation in the warmth of her.

With bodies moving in exquisite harmony, they held each other, smiling in breathless anticipation as the tempo altered, drawing all their senses toward a primal destination—a celebration of love. Locked in each other's embrace, they gasped as the turbulence of their passion broke in waves of shuddering ecstasy. For a fragment of time they were suspended in a mythical world of their own. Then slowly and gently the waves subsided into quiet ripples and whispers of shared contentment—and this world claimed them once again.

But not totally.

In a room bathed in golden sunlight, they lay together, a sense of peace settling over them at last. "You did say you were getting better," Claire told him with a sigh of pleasure. "I thought you were talking about castle building."

There was a flicker of amusement under Dylan's half-lowered lashes. "I *was* talking about castle building," he answered with a low chuckle. "If you're interested, I have a partly demolished castle of my own that could use some reconstruction. It's a big undertaking, something I haven't the heart to start over with on my own." He let the underlying meaning of his offer drift into her thoughts. "I'm talking about a demanding job. Full-time commitment."

Claire leaned back against his shoulder and gazed into his eyes. His expression remained unchanged as he waited.

"Any fringe benefits?" Claire asked.

"Me, for one." Dylan gently kissed the tip of her nose. "Complete with a lifetime contract. I want to make this official. I love you, Claire. I know you love me. Marry me, castlebuilder."

Claire tugged herself into a sitting position, then leaned over, looking down at him, her eyes brimming with tears. "I don't want you to get carried away in the heat of passion," she said softly. "I have another offer to consider. I'm negotiating a recording contract. It may mean I'll be traveling back and forth occasionally, which could put a lot of strain on a relationship."

Before Dylan could protest, Claire rested one finger on his lips to silence him. "Think it over. Then if you still feel this way after the concert, ask me again." Claire still had one thing she wanted to do. She had a song to sing and a blue-eyed audience of one to sing it to. Grasping his wrist, she looked at his watch. "We have a three-hour-and-fifteen-minute castle to build, partner. Let's get going." She slid out of the bed and padded off toward the bathroom.

Dylan shook his head indulgently, then swung his long legs onto the floor. "I kind of like the heat of passion," he muttered just loud enough so she could hear.

"Enough passion. We have a castle to build," Claire shot back at him.

Dylan's grin widened as he moved about the room, collecting his scattered clothing. Standing near the window, he could see the beach below, covered with innumerable indistinct mounds of sand. Clusters of engrossed sand crafters all in bright-yellow refuge T-shirts were industriously cutting and scooping, bringing their creations into existence. This was a world she had brought to him. A world of gentle beauty where energy and imagination flowed freely—in an affirmation of something very personal and very fragile.

He breathed out a long sigh of contentment. It was going to be a fine day for castlebuilders.

DARK-EYED AND SPORTING a pelican T-shirt, the public-relations director from the Don CeSar stood center stage beneath the angular-peaked canopy that protected the platform. It spread across the rear deck of the Don CeSar like a giant kite—striped green-and-white—that had conveniently settled there between takeoffs. The performers were enclosed within the curve of the canopy's wings, the wind couldn't play havoc with the multitude of microphones placed around the stage, and the sand and salt air would not affect the instruments. On either side of the stage, massive speakers were mounted on scaffolding, aiming the sound waves out over a sea of suntanned faces.

Already the sun had slipped down over the water, sending a carpet of amber across the surface, right up to the shoreline of the Don. The "pink lady" was bathed in golden light. Flanked by a table laden with plaques and with an assistant holding the box of gift certificates, the PR lady summoned the crowd to attention.

"We have the results of the sand-crafting contest," the petite woman announced. "In each category there will be a gift of tickets or merchandise. In addition, the first-place winner will receive one of these plaques." She held aloft the striking wall plaque—a rectangle of rich gleaming wood bearing a pink shell, the Don's logo. Beneath the exquisite shell was an engraved panel stating the division by categories and "first prize."

"In the category of Beasties, the first prize, two tickets for deep-sea fishing on the *Miss Tarpon*, go to entry 27, for their fantastic dragon." One couple in the audience bounded to their feet, hooting in exhilaration over their victory.

"In the category of People—" the woman continued with the first-place awards "—the winner is number 8, for the seven-foot sculpture of Elvis." A loud round of applause greeted the three builders, a gray-haired grandmother and her two teenage grandsons. A retired schoolteacher, the portly woman had stood on a stepladder half the morning, crafting the face alone. She and her grandsons, all in T-shirts stamped Gulf Coast Seabird Refuge, had attracted quite a crowd throughout the day, and their fans cheered wildly as they took the stage.

In the children's category there were subdivisions by age, instead of by the type of entry. With every award the firm donating the prize was announced and thanked, and the audience responded with an appreciative cheer.

When it came to the Castle competition, Claire reached over and squeezed Dylan's hand. Complete with minarets and prayer towers, they had completed an extravaganza right out of the *Arabian Nights*. "It's a beauty." Dylan had stood next to Claire, his arm resting comfortably around her waist, his thigh brushing lightly against hers. With a sigh of relief, they'd surveyed their masterpiece, completed four minutes before the team of judges reached their division to inspect the entries. Covered in sand and both reddened by the sun, they had worked feverishly in near silence, looking up only occasionally to exchange a quick, secret smile or comment on the design. Now, sitting cross-legged in the sand, they waited.

"In the Castle division, the first prize goes to number 2." Claire flung up her arms in a wild gesture of triumph. "Yahooo...." she squealed, bounding into the air, grabbing Dylan by the hand and dragging him through the crowd. "A weekend holiday for two at the Don," the PR woman said, announcing the gift that went with the plaque. "Congratulations."

"A whole weekend...." Dylan tightened his grip on Claire's hand. "I hear the honeymoon suite is really beautiful," he murmured in her ear as they reached the stage. "I mean, as long as we happen to be in the neighborhood...and the castle doesn't have indoor plumbing...."

Claire didn't even reply. Glowing with a childlike radiance, she hurried forward. Clasping the plaque, she bounced up and down, unsuppressed joy bubbling in her words and shining in her eyes. "I've never won anything before—not in my whole life!"

"I've heard that making love to an environmentalist will change your luck," Dylan muttered quietly, keeping a perfectly straight face for the benefit of the PR lady, who couldn't hear what he said. "See. It's working already." He laughed softly, reaching past Claire to accept the envelope.

"You can make the reservation anytime." The dark-haired woman was obviously delighted they had won.

"I'm working on it," Dylan assured her. "Believe me, I'm working on it."

Lost in a cloud of euphoria, Claire was barely conscious of the pressure of Dylan's firm grasp on her arm as he guided her offstage, then over toward the press area. The photographers would be waiting, and for once the news would be good. While the PR representative handed out other envelopes, containing hotel accommodations, tickets for dinners and boat trips, gift certificates and whatever else had been donated, Claire and Dylan posed with their awards.

"How about one by the castle?" With an accommodating nod, they moved.

Framed by the setting sun, they stood together, birdman and castlebuilder, with the castle they had created.

Pete Parnell squeezed through the crush of people around his sister and her co-worker. "As soon as you can get away, you'll have to shower off and get ready for the show," he reminded her. "And someone up front needs to talk to you about the money that's been collected for the refuge." He aimed that information at Dylan. "Nice job, you two..." Pete congratulated them, eyeing the structure appreciatively. "But let's hustle. It's almost time for the music to start."

WHEN CLAIRE STEPPED OUT on the stage, hair still damp and skin tingling against her gauze dress, the breeze from the Gulf came cool and soothing off the water. Little groups of sandpipers now scampered along the water's edge, and offshore a few pelicans bobbed in the water like corks, watching the peculiar goings-on.

The glorious sunset that ended the day was leaving a tinge of rose on the fringe of low dark clouds. Gradually even that disappeared, and the entire beach became a magic kingdom, twinkling with the candlelight from hundreds of miniature hurricane lamps that the Don had donated as souvenirs. Lounging on blankets and in beach chairs, the crowd spread out amid the sculptures—the prize-winning ones had been roped off and were sporting ribbons.

Picnic lunches had replaced shovels and buckets, shirts and jackets covered sunburned skin and the mood had mellowed.

Claire had missed the beginning of the show when Dylan had given the official welcome, speaking briefly to the assemblage, thanking them for their efforts to support the refuge and commending the sand crafters for their artistry. Claire had recognized his voice coming over the sound system as she padded about the hotel room, half-naked, trying to put on her makeup, while Pete carried in the clothes he'd brought up. All the ones from the beach house reeked with smoke from the fire, and Pete had packed up several outfits from his place. Finally finding one that floated in cloud-soft layers over her sunburned skin, she listened to the first group of performers begin the show while she dressed. Later Wes would sing and play with Pete's band. Then she'd join him for one number. After that she was on her own.

For Dylan she would finally sing "Sara's Song." And for the winged creatures nestled on pilings or in twiggy nests or sweeping low over the water, night feeding, she would do "Seabird." When her part of the show was over, Dylan wouldn't really need to ask her again. When they looked at each other, they'd both know the answer.

When she began, Dylan was standing by the side of the stage, out of the direct line of the speakers. Just as scheduled, Claire first spoke into the microphone, telling the onlookers about becoming a volunteer at the refuge. Briefly she told them the story of Sara and how they had helped each other. And even now her voice wavered as she remembered that last farewell on the sandy island. Standing in the night, with wind rippling her hair and her tanned face glowing in the overhead lights, Claire sang "Sara's Song," her pensive anthem about loving and caring.

At first she couldn't see Dylan at all, and for a fleeting instant she worried that he wouldn't realize that this time the song was meant just for him. But then she caught a glimpse of him moving through the crowd, staying just beyond the glare of the footlights. As if mesmerized by the lady in a dress fluttering like feathers in the breeze, he stood directly in front of her, inadvertently blocking the view of those seated behind him. Arms crossed casually over his chest and eyes meeting hers, he knew she was keeping her promise; this song was just for him. And no one minded at all.

Don't really know how to tell you.
Words don't come easy to me.
But I know how I feel and the feeling is real.
My love's just a melody.

Talkin' in dreams comes so easy for me
I can say how I feel in the night.
But day comes my way and the words slip away,
Still the feelin' inside's so right.

Music is the language of love
When your body's movin' close to me.
Music—is a symphony—with you.

Dylan's lopsided grin flashed briefly. Then his expression softened as he watched her with eyes gentle, understanding and glowing with pride.

To say it out loud may not sound right,
I know you've been waiting so long.
Before words slip away, how I want you to stay,
So I'll say how I feel in this song.

Dylan slowly eased down onto the sand, cradling his knees in his arms. Claire sang the bridge once more, her eyes brimming with tears as her music filled the night. A part of her still hoped that somewhere in the darkness, the wind would carry the song to Sara. She would always remember soft and lovely Sara.

If "Sara's Song" carried the message about holding on, "Seabird" was the counterpoint. Haunting and lyrical, it was about letting go—of old sorrows, old fears. Of needing freedom. Of sharing strengths and reaching new heights.

Of trying again.

Seabird
Come settle with me here in the sand
Seabird
Come and sit here with me facing in the wind.

In her mind the images kept overlapping—sandpipers and sea gulls, castles and stilt houses, Tammy and Ariel, Frazer and the pelicans, Sara—and always Dylan. He was her solid connection to the earth. She could be the free flyer. But they belonged to each other. Side by side.

> Seabird, let's go skyward
> Like you I am a free bird
> Rising again together me and you
> Seabird. . . .

Without lifting her eyes from his, Claire finished the song, knowing that as soon as she did, the powerful arms that were now locked over his knees would reach for her and she would be home at last.

> I'll fly like you
> For your wings have taught me
> To fly like you. . . .

Claire sang the last lines again, her velvet-edged voice, strong and pure, gliding through the air on wings of love.

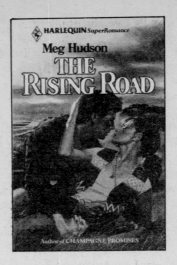

HARLEQUIN *SuperRomance*

Meg Hudson

THE RISING ROAD

Author of CHAMPAGNE PROMISES

September's other absorbing
HARLEQUIN *SuperRomance* novel

THE RISING ROAD by Meg Hudson

When Timothy Flanagan came to her rescue in a
pub in south Boston, Anne Clarendon couldn't
believe her luck. She was even more surprised when
she discovered this man with the twinkling green
eyes and coppery hair was the lawyer handling her
father's estate.

By the time she sorted out her impressions she had
fallen in love with the charming Irishman. But
Timothy felt he couldn't return that love—not until
he found out about his family, and his past. . . .

A contemporary love story for the woman of today

These two absorbing titles
will be published in October
by
HARLEQUIN
SuperRomance

SILVER HORIZONS by Deborah Joyce

Minta Cordero, FBI undercover agent, had been
ordered to take a vacation and stay out of trouble.

She chose the Cayman Islands in the Caribbean. So
did Brad McMillan who was conducting top-secret
tests on his underwater robot. From the moment
they met, and even after they fell in love, Minta
suspected Brad was involved in something dangerous.

When she learned the devastating truth about him,
Minta was forced to make a choice. Either turn in
the man she loved, or turn her back on justice.

THROUGH NIGHT AND DAY by Irma Walker

There was a saying that the Pelente men loved only
once, and when Mayi Jenner married Laurens
Pelente, she knew it would be forever.

They would spend their lives in a fairy-tale village in
the high Pyrenees, the Basque country Mayi readily
adopted as her own. When the letter came, she saw
her dreams shatter.

Laurens didn't want to believe the startling revelation about his wife, but as head of the Pelente
household he could not ignore it. So Mayi set out to
win back the love—and trust—of her proud husband.

HARLEQUIN *Love Affair*

Look out this month for

MIX AND MATCH   *Beverly Sommers*

Scott Campbell may have looked like a surfer, Ariel thought, but he could never have been a good one. Scott seemed to be as blind as a bat. Why else would he bypass the bikinied denizens of Seal Beach, California, to make a play for a woman who was almost middle-aged? A woman whose teenage daughter cast disapproving glares at him and whose younger daughter skulked around him menacingly, distressingly attired in combat fatigues.

True, Ariel respected Scott's advice—he had improved both her painting and her business. But anything more than a friendly relationship was unseemly. Preposterous. And so appealing. . . .

THE DREAM NEVER DIES   *Jacqueline Diamond*

Consultant Jill Brandon walked into the offices of the Buena Park newspaper and received two rude shocks. One was Kent Lawrence, the paper's managing editor. As Jill tried to revamp the daily, Kent dogged her footsteps, hurling the same bitter accusations she had heard from him years before. Kent Lawrence had not forgotten her one rash act as a young reporter, an act that had launched her career and ruined their relationship. Nor had he forgiven her for it.

That was the first shock—that Kent still despised her. But the second shock was much worse. After all the years, Jill still loved him.

MISPLACED DESTINY   *Sharon McCaffree*

Carla didn't recognise him at first—after fifteen years, Brigg Carlyle had changed. But the atmosphere at the Shelbyville reunion catapulted Carla into the past, and she found herself responding to Brigg as though he were still her best friend's obnoxious older brother.

Brigg didn't like that. And after the reunion, in Chicago, Brigg made Carla realize that the fireworks that still erupted between them were now the result of adult emotions, not youthful high spirits. Brigg loved her. He had always loved her. But Brigg was no longer the familiar boy of Carla's past—he was a man, and a stranger.